# ROAR OF THE BROKEN BEAR

---

## LEGEND OF THE DRAGON LORD
### BOOK 3

## PETER WACHT

Roar of the Broken Bear
By Peter Wacht

Book 3 of The Legend of the Dragon Lord

This book is a work of fiction. Names, characters, places, and incidents are the product of the author's imagination or are used fictitiously. Any resemblance to actual events, locales, or persons, living or dead, is coincidental.



Cover design by Ebooklaunch.com



Published in the United States by Kestrel Media Group LLC.

ISBN: 978-1-950236-67-1

eBook ISBN: 978-1-950236-68-8

Library of Congress Control Number: 2025906494

 Formatted with Vellum

# ALSO BY PETER WACHT

## THE REALMS OF THE TALENT AND THE CURSE

### LEGEND OF THE DRAGON LORD

*A Painful Truth* (short story)*

*Stealing the Light*

*Sacrificing the Queen*

*Roar of the Broken Bear*

*Rise of the Dragon Lord* (Forthcoming 2026)

### THE TALES OF CALEDONIA

(Complete 7-Book Series)

*Blood on the White Sand* (short story)*

*The Diamond Thief* (short story)*

*The Protector*

*The Protector's Quest*

*The Protector's Vengeance*

*The Protector's Sacrifice*

*The Protector's Reckoning*

*The Protector's Resolve*

*The Protector's Victory*

### THE TALES OF THE TERRITORIES

(Complete 8-Book Series)

*Stalking the Blood Ruby* (short story)*

*A Fate Worse Than Death* (short story)*

*Death on the Burnt Ocean*

*Monsters in the Mist*

*The Dance of the Daggers*

*Bloody Hunt for Freedom*

*A Spark of Rebellion*

*Shadows Made Real*

*Shadow's Reach*

*Storm in the Darkness*

THE SYLVAN CHRONICLES

(Complete 9-Book Series)

*The Legend of the Kestrel*

*The Call of the Sylvana*

*The Raptor of the Highlands*

*The Makings of a Warrior*

*The Lord of the Highlands*

*The Lost Kestrel Found*

*The Claiming of the Highlands*

*The Fight Against the Dark*

*The Defender of the Light*

THE RISE OF THE SYLVAN WARRIORS

*Through the Knife's Edge (short story)**

THE FALLEN KNIGHT SERIES

*The Death of the Dragon (short story)**

*The Dragon Awakens*

*Duel With a Dragon*

*Beware the Dragon*

*The Dragon Returns*


* Free stories can be downloaded from my author website at PeterWachtBooks.com. My books are also available on Amazon and other online retailers.

# YOUR FREE STORY IS WAITING…

This eBook is a prelude to the events in my epic fantasy series *The Tales of Caledonia* and is free to readers who receive my newsletter.

Join Peter's newsletter and get your FREE eBook.
PeterWachtBooks.com

1

# TAKING A CUT

"Everything in place?" Mikel asked. Every other step he glanced toward the roar of the water flowing below him.

"Yes, we're ready to go. Just in time too."

Teddy and Mikel walked along the southern shore of the Eastern River, one of the four rivers that ran fast and often rough until it struck the Crux and joined the maelstrom that was the Churn that surrounded the island.

With the darkness complete except for when the moon intermittently broke through the heavy clouds, they were careful with their steps along the rough ground. Neither willing to reveal themselves with lanterns despite the certainty that a fall meant a horrendous death.

They had selected this location not only because it was one of the narrowest points on the river -- no more than a few hundred yards separated them from the northern bank -- but also because they stood on a crag that rose more than one hundred feet above the rapids.

"Our target's approaching?"

Teddy nodded. "Samuel's crew has been tracking it. It'll be visible in a few minutes."

"Good to hear." Mikel placed a hand to his right, pushing off the boulder to climb between the two large rocks that blocked the rugged path, the call of the fast-flowing river just a clumsy slip away from claiming him. "I'm looking forward to this. It should be fun."

"You have a strange definition of fun," Teddy grumbled even as the giant of a man clapped Mikel on the back in friendship, although not so hard as to dislodge him as he climbed through the gap.

"You already knew that."

"I did, yet still I wonder."

"Wonder what?" Mikel stopped when they reached the highest point on the crag that jutted out into the river. Their current position reduced the distance to the far shore by fifty yards. Three towers stood tall among the rocks, each one ten yards away from the other. All of them invisible in the gloom of the night.

"Whether your definition of fun comes back and bites you in the ass more often than not."

"As long as it's not the knee." Mikel rubbed his aching joint, boot propped up on a rock. Scaling the boulders that made up the path aggravated his old injury, which was a constant source of pain. It was just a matter of how much pain.

Mikel gazed out into the darkness, tracking the steel cables bolted to the top of each stone tower before he lost them in the gloom. Perhaps Teddy was right. What they were about to attempt wasn't fun. However, he did believe that it was necessary. And he hoped that it would work. Not wanting to think any more than he already had about the consequences of failure.

"That I can understand," Teddy said as he took his place next to Mikel, sitting down on the rock and leaning his back against the base of the stand.

Sensing several more presences coming up behind him, Mikel turned then smiled.

He nodded to Samuel as the lanky fellow dressed all in black, just as he and Teddy were, walked past. Mikel appreciated Samuel's thoroughness. He counted a dozen daggers strapped to his body, and he was sure that the thief carried several more than just those hidden within his clothes and boots.

"Five minutes, no more," Samuel reported as he took up his assigned position by a tower.

Mikel stood straight again. He offered handshakes and pats on the back along with a few words of thanks and encouragement as well as questions about family to each of the men and women who walked past and joined him on what he hoped didn't prove to be a foolhardy expedition. Grateful for their courage and their trust in him.

Once they reached their assigned towers, Mikel's crew began to strap on the gear waiting for them. Silent. Focused. Determined. Running through their minds what would be required of them.

Mikel hoped that his outward calm helped to settle whatever nerves they might be experiencing. They had one chance to make the attempt. If any of his crew missed their mark, the difference between success and failure no more than a heartbeat, then they would die.

Even so, when Mikel asked them to assume that risk, none had hesitated. None had said no. All had faith that they could do the job. All had faith in him.

A heartwarming and frightening trust, and Mikel felt that great weight on his shoulders. He had no time to dwell on it, however.

Teddy, sensing the change in Mikel and seeing how his expression shifted toward contemplation, decided to lighten the mood atop the crag by using his friend as his dartboard.

"So how is the Queen of the Crux?" Teddy's tone was light though sharp.

"Seriously? You're asking me that now?" Mikel sat down next to his friend, not missing how his crew continued to prepare themselves while their quiet conversations came to an end. All of them curious. That didn't surprise him. He couldn't say that it pleased him, however.

"We have a few minutes," Teddy replied with a shrug. "It's a worthwhile topic, don't you think? You have been spending a good bit of time with our beneficent Queen."

"Only because I have to," Mikel replied quietly. Shaking his head in annoyance, he really didn't want to have this discussion, but he saw no good way to avoid it. Not with so many eyes on him. Besides, he understood what Teddy was trying to do.

"Right." Based on Teddy's skeptical tone, clearly he didn't believe Mikel's claim. "Quite a lot of discussing going on in her private quarters at all hours of the night."

"It's the only place we can meet without being discovered, and it's the only time that either of us have." Mikel hoped that his argument didn't sound defensive. He couldn't tell. Although the smiles that he was receiving from Samuel and several others suggested that he had fallen short. So be it. Any embarrassment was worth the price if it helped with this job.

"And that's exactly my point." Teddy's broad grin threatened to break through the darkness and reveal their position. "When else are illicit rendezvouses supposed to occur?"

"It's not like that," Mikel growled. He refused to look at Teddy. Instead he focused his attention to the east, looking for any hint of the dark shadow that was coming their way and would close this conversation. Unfortunately, he doubted that the target would arrive soon enough and dreaded that he would need to suffer through a few more minutes of Teddy's questioning.

"Not like what?" Teddy asked innocently.

"It's just business, Teddy. No more than that."

"Of course it is," Teddy confirmed with a sharp nod, the doubt in his voice impossible to miss.

Mikel shifted his gaze from the river to his friend, not appreciating the smug grin that greeted him. "Do you honestly believe that Celindria Dengannon would be interested in me in the way that you're suggesting?"

"It does sound quite ridiculous when you say it that way."

"Exactly."

"Nevertheless, stranger things have been known to happen."

Mikel took a deep breath, once again scanning the gloom for the shadow that would rescue him from this interrogation. "Teddy, you need to leave off. It's just business. Nothing more."

"So that's what they're calling it these days. Business?"

"Teddy ..." Mikel's voice was quieter, harder, his patience for his friend's teasing waning.

Teddy heard the change. He chose to ignore it, the grins of the men and women waiting by the towers egging him on. "The heart wants what the heart wants, my friend. You know that just as well as I do."

"That may be, but ..."

"I'm not suggesting anything ..."

"You are suggesting something," Mikel corrected.

Teddy ignored him again. "But you must know how it looks. You closeted with the Queen of the Crux almost every night. Privately. And you rarely return before first light. It suggests more than a business relationship."

"As I said, it is the only time we can talk privately." Mikel shook his head. He would almost be amused by Teddy's prodding if he wasn't the target. He could have ended the game. He chose not to, however, seeing how their conversation had captured the attention of his crew. Better that they were thinking about Mikel's difficulties rather than allowing their minds to concentrate on the risk they were about to assume.

"So now it's not business. It's *talking*."

Mikel didn't appreciate the emphasis Teddy placed on the last word. "Teddy, you're pushing your luck."

"I'm just explaining how it appears, Mikel. I'm by no means criticizing. I'm just trying to get a better sense of what's going on." He leaned in toward his friend conspiratorially, though he spoke loud enough for all to hear. "You know it just as well as I do. Often appearances are more important than reality. Truth is a fungible concept."

"That may be, but again, why would anyone even think that Celindria Dengannon would be interested in me?" Mikel's tone was less defensive this time, a hint of truth contained within his query. "You know the saying a face that only a mother could love?"

"You are the King of the Underworld, Mikel. I can see how that might attract her notice."

"You're reaching, Teddy."

"Perhaps, though as I said, stranger things and all that. You do raise a good point, however. You're not much to look at."

"On that we agree." Mikel laughed softly, as did the men and women waiting with him. He couldn't argue that point. His hulking presence tended to put people off though it was quite deceptive. Mikel was extraordinarily fast, particularly with a blade in hand, for someone with a bad knee. "I blame my uncommon looks on my many broken noses."

Teddy reached over and patted Mikel on the shoulder, shaking his head sadly. "I'm sorry to say it, Mikel, but someone must. All the broken noses actually are an improvement."

A louder round of laughter broke out on the crag, the sound smothered by the rush of whitewater far below them.

"Thank you for your honesty," Mikel snorted. "Although I would expect nothing less from you."

"Of course," Teddy replied, offering Mikel a nod. "I'm always happy to put you in your place."

"You do enjoy it," Mikel agreed.

"And I must admit as well that I have heard that some women are attracted to bruisers like you."

"You know, you would fit the parameters of a bruiser as well."

"That may be," Teddy nodded, understanding what Mikel was attempting to do, "but we're not talking about me. I'm not the one spending almost every night with the Queen of the Crux."

"I am not spending every night with the Queen of the Crux," Mikel sighed in exasperation.

"I didn't say every night," Teddy clarified, holding up a hand to halt the additional argument Mikel was about to offer. "I said *almost* every night."

"Thank you for that clarification," Mikel groused.

"My pleasure," Teddy replied, his broad smile somehow getting bigger. Obviously, he was pleased that he could poke at his friend at least for a little while longer. Of course, Mikel was making it a bit too easy for him, and he appreciated why. "You could be right, of course."

"I'm afraid to ask." Mikel shook his head, continuing to give his friend free rein and waiting to see what dart Teddy was going to throw at him next, because he could see how the banter between them continued to ease the strain his crew was feeling. They were about to attempt a maneuver that had never been attempted before, and Mikel preferred that they not think about their chances of success.

"No need, I'm happy to tell you." Teddy's comment gained a few soft chuckles from Samuel and the others. "She might not be attracted to you because you're a bruiser. Even though we can all agree that you are a bruiser. Isn't that right, Samuel?"

"It is indeed," Samuel replied, "but he could be called much worse. Terrible reputation that he has in certain circles."

"Very true, Samuel, a fact that can't be ignored," Teddy agreed. "Be that as it may, perhaps her interest in you isn't because you're a bruiser. Rather, perhaps she's interested in you because she perceives you as her knight in shining armor."

"An unfair description," Mikel challenged. "I've never worn shining armor in my life." That comment earned another round of laughter from his crew.

"Perhaps you should," Teddy suggested, "and a helmet to hide that many-times-broken nose of yours." The laughter around them only got louder. "During one of your late-night assignations. The Queen of the Crux might enjoy a little role …"

"Teddy …"

"Right, sorry," Teddy replied, raising his hands as a way of apologizing. He had noticed the spark in the back of Mikel's eyes and realized that he had been about to push a bit too far. "The image that I've conjured is quite unlikely and a bit disconcerting as well."

"More than disconcerting," Samuel offered in a chuckle. "Downright frightening."

"I couldn't agree more," Teddy said. "I'm simply suggesting that perhaps the Queen of the Crux keeps agreeing to your late-night assignations because you are, indeed, her knight in shining armor. You've saved her Kingdom what, twice now? And her life how many times?"

"You give me too much credit, Teddy. Right place, right time. No more than that."

"Perhaps, but right place, right time is a poor argument. You made a conscious decision. You know that just as she does. I simply throw out for your consideration the possibility that she views your decisions as more than just business decisions."

"You're seeing more than is actually there, Teddy." Even so,

Mikel detected a kernel of truth in Teddy's words. A truth that he really hadn't wanted to consider.

"Perhaps." Teddy shrugged, his expression becoming more thoughtful. "Perhaps not. Even so, it's worth it just to have a little fun with you."

"I'm glad that I could offer you and the rest of the crew a few minutes of entertainment."

"We do appreciate it," Samuel said with a gap-toothed smile. "A good way to pass the time. Best not to think too hard on what we're about to do."

"As I said, happy to help," Mikel growled.

"Although I should offer a word of warning."

"Once again, Teddy, I'm afraid to ask."

"No need to ask. I'll just tell you."

"That's very kind of you."

Teddy ignored the heavy dose of sarcasm that laced Mikel's words. "Liria isn't going to like this."

"Like what?"

"Like this," Teddy repeated. "You having ... business relations ... with the Queen of the Crux."

"There are no relations between us," Mikel stated, a touch of defeat in his voice. Though Teddy was right.

Despite their history, despite the fact that he had every right to kill her, Liria still seemed to be interested in him. They were connected in some way that he didn't quite understand and that he had little desire to explore. Although, thinking about that some more, placing his former partner against Celindria Dengannon, upon initial review, he would give the edge to Liria. She was a dangerous woman. Yet there was a steel to the Queen of the Crux that ...

Mikel shook his head, seeking to clear it. He didn't have the time for his thoughts to follow that track, knowing exactly where it led. "It's just business ..."

"Exactly my point," Teddy cut in, offering Mikel a suggestive nod and wink. "Just business."

Mikel sighed, surrendering the fight. "You really are a pain in the ass. You know that?"

"You regret saving my life?"

"Every day," Mikel confirmed in a tired voice.

For a moment there was a silence between the two friends before they both broke out into a long laugh.

"What's so funny?" asked a new voice joining the conversation.

"We're just discussing the women in Mikel's life," Teddy explained. "He is struggling to navigate the challenges they bring with them, Leonardo."

"I can't help you with that. I've got enough challenges as it is, and I don't need to complicate my life any further." The young inventor sat down next to Mikel.

He was nervous. He always was right before he tested one of his new creations. Although this one was fairly straightforward, based almost entirely on physics. It was just a matter of getting the math right, and he believed that he had. He had checked his work several times. Of course, he wouldn't know for sure until the test in real-world conditions was complete.

"Can you help us with what we're about to do?" Mikel asked. "That's all that matters now."

"I can. Have no fear of that. All of my calculations are correct. It's just a matter ..."

"Of putting theory into practice," Teddy finished for him, having heard much the same before from Leonardo.

"Exactly," Leonardo confirmed with a nod.

"I never did," Mikel replied, seeking to settle the young inventor's nerves. "All well at the Splintered Bridge?"

Leonardo's expression brightened at the compliment. He was grateful that Mikel had plucked him out of obscurity and given him the opportunity to make full use of his talents. And he relished the work that he was doing at the causeway that spanned the Trench and connected the Kingdom of the Crux to the Kingdom of the Tor.

At first, he had been reluctant to accept Mikel's commission because he had so many projects underway. Mikel hadn't pushed him, however. He had simply asked that Leonardo explore the possibility. Spend a few days there and see what he thought.

That gentle request from the King of the Underworld was exactly what Leonardo needed. He discovered quickly that aiding the Battle Lord and the soldiers of the Crux was the best possible testing ground for many of the ideas that swirled around in his head. At the moment, his thoughts on how to reconfigure for use against the soldiers of the Tor the invention he was about to test. Assuming, of course, that the test worked. Because if he lost his primary benefactor ...

"As well as can be," Leonardo replied, swiping at his long, curly hair to keep it out of his eyes. "General Booruz has his Tor soldiers attack with a frightening regularity. He doesn't seem to care about losses."

"It might not be Booruz," Mikel suggested. "It could be Dragoran. Probably is. Booruz has led the King of the Tor's army long enough to know that to keep leading it he needs to do as Dragoran wants. Regardless of the price paid."

"A fair assessment," Leonardo admitted. "So far we've held them. And I think we'll continue to do so. Only so many Tor soldiers can attack across the Splintered Bridge at one time, and we've got the tools now to make that exceedingly difficult for them."

"But ..." Mikel prodded. He caught Leonardo's worried expression, the young man holding something back.

"But that lasts only so long as the game remains the same."

"A good point," Teddy muttered. "Dragoran will not accept failure. Has he tried anything out of the ordinary? Any new strategy?"

"Not yet," Leonardo said. "Even so, the Battle Lord is worried."

"He's right to be worried," Mikel said. "Dragoran is many things, but he's not a fool. He won't allow the stalemate to continue forever."

"Which is why I'm here now. If what you two are about to do works, I might be able to use it on the Splintered Bridge."

"So that's why the Battle Lord gave you leave to join us. Research." Mikel couldn't fault Henri Dengannon for that. If Mikel was in his shoes, he would do much the same.

"Exactly so," Leonardo said with a smile. "When I told him why and who we were focusing our efforts on, he was more than happy to give me a few days."

"Yes, the Battle Lord does have a strong dislike for our current target," Teddy murmured.

"Deservedly so." Mikel pushed himself up, the shadow he was searching for finally appearing in the darkness. Faint, though growing steadily larger as it raced down the river. "We ready?"

Leonardo nodded and then got to his feet. "Yes, let me show you what I have for you. The ship will be here in just a few minutes."

~

"Why are you so nervous?"

"I'm not nervous." Even so, Marak couldn't help himself. An edginess deep in his bones forced him to stalk around the helm. Constantly glancing toward the far shores shrouded in darkness, he glimpsed nothing that caused him any concern beyond the lanterns lining the rail of the riverboat. He heard nothing but the rush of water beneath them, yet still he felt as if some unknown peril was about to strike.

"You are nervous. You're making me nervous." Junius stood at the helm of the riverboat, eyes passing over the large hooks situated at the bow and the stern that were designed to latch onto the steel cables that would pull them across the Churn.

He had captained for House Hanover for eight years, and he had known Marak for twice as long, serving with him in the Hanover Guard before he returned to his true love. The four rivers that became one at the Crux.

"You're right," Marak growled, stopping himself an almost physical effort. "I don't know." He lifted his hands to the star-filled sky as if he might receive an answer then began his prowl once more when no reply came.

"Another of your premonitions?" Junius asked. He wasn't making fun of Marak, his question serious. His friend became the leader of the five hundred soldiers sworn to serve the current Lord of House Hanover because of his grit and instincts.

Marak didn't stop his pacing, now squeezing the fingers of one hand with the fingers of the other. "Yes. I know we have little to fear, but ..."

"Still you fear." Junius nodded in understanding. His friend's anxiety didn't surprise him. Not when so much depended upon their mission.

"The curse of leadership, my friend." Marak clasped his hands behind his back, trying to exercise some control over the brittle energy pricking at him. "How far?"

"Ten leagues at most," Junius stated with the confidence of a man who had made this run dozens of times before and knew the river like the back of his hand.

Needing a break from his friend's infectious anxiety, Junius shifted his attention to the crew working the deck. There were only a handful at this hour of the morning, the sun not rising until they were closer to the Crux. Even so, his sailors went about their tasks with an efficiency that calmed him. They were masters of their jobs just as he was the master of his.

"Take heart, my friend," Junius prodded, turning the wheel ever so slightly to the starboard to account for the bend in the river they had entered. "No one knows that we are here. No one knows what we carry. And if anyone did, there is nothing they could do about it. Out here, we are safe."

Marak snorted out a laugh that really wasn't a laugh. "How can you be so certain of that? Lord Hanover has poked the King of the Underworld, and the King of the Underworld has punched back. He seems to know all that goes on in the shadows and he's never been shy about taking risks."

"In most shadows, yes, he probably does," Junius agreed. "But not these shadows." He motioned toward the surrounding gloom. "Even if he knows that we are here, he has no way to touch us." He reached out a hand and grasped his friend's shoulder, offering Marak some of his confidence if he was willing to accept it. "We are safe. The King of the Underworld could be watching us now. If he is, it doesn't matter. He couldn't get to us even if he wanted to. You have my word on that."

Marak sighed then nodded. Junius spoke the truth. He knew it. They were in the middle of the fast-flowing Eastern River. The only dangers they faced were the rough current and the rocks hidden just beneath the surface, both of which Junius had defeated time and time again.

He snorted out a real laugh this time. He wasn't nervous so much because of the King of the Underworld. He was more nervous because the cargo they carried was so essential to the success of the House. Lucius Hanover had made that abundantly clear to him.

"You're right, my friend." Marak gripped Junius' arm in thanks then leaned back against the railing, crossing his arms over his chest. "All is as it should be at the dock?"

Junius nodded. "Half of the Guard will meet us there. They will remove the cargo and take it to House Hanover. Then your job will be done. Truly, you have nothing to fear."

"I fear everything, Junius. The future of House Hanover hinges on what we carry."

Marak still hadn't decided if his Lord had made the right decision. He had been thinking about the deal agreed to ever since he stepped aboard the riverboat on the eastern side of the Trench. In retrospect, it seemed like the only decision that Lucius Hanover could have reached after making a series of other decisions that narrowed his options until he had none remaining.

Lucius Hanover had spent so much of the House treasury on the bribes and other schemes he put in place to gain the throne of the Crux that there was scarcely anything left. Yet still desperate for the throne, he had bound himself and the fortunes of his House, as well as the fortunes of those serving House Hanover, that much more tightly to Malor Dragoran.

The King of the Tor allowed Lucius to borrow thousands of golds all with the goal of unseating Celindria Dengannon. A risky play to begin with. And not just because Lucius Hanover had tied himself in a knot from which he would likely never be able to extricate himself.

Since assuming the throne, the Queen of the Crux had worked hard to solidify her hold on what had been her father's seat. The First Families acknowledged her rule, many supporting it, those against it or undecided about having a young woman guiding the future of the Crux keeping their mouths closed, in large part because of her ally who preferred to do his work from behind the curtain. An ally, some said, who was stronger than all the First Families combined.

"You have nothing to fear, Marak, I promise you that. As I said, no one can bother us out here. And once we dock, we'll be fine. It shouldn't take more than a few hours to unload the cargo. And with so many of the House Guard there, no one would be foolish enough to make a play for it."

"You seem to think that the King of the Underworld won't be watching for us when we reach the Hanover dock," Marak warned. Despite Junius' assurances, he was having a difficult time letting go of his concern.

"Why would he?" Junius scoffed. "We're nothing to him. Just one of dozens of riverboats making their way to the Crux. And again, he has no way to reach us, whether on the water or on land."

Marak frowned, not pleased by the captain's lack of perspective. Yet he had no good argument to broaden it. "As you know, Junius, the King of the Underworld has taken an interest in the Crown's fortunes."

"He'll lose interest once we bring this fortune across the Churn and our Lord Hanover works his golden magic. Have no worries about that. The King of the Underworld is first and foremost a businessman. He makes decisions with his brain, not his heart."

"You sure about this?" Mikel wasn't concerned so much as he disliked being one of the inventor's test subjects.

"Yes, completely," Leonardo stated with complete confidence. "It will work. I tried it myself."

"You tried it yourself?" Mikel's tone was dubious.

"On a smaller scale," Leonardo admitted as he nodded toward his invention. "And not here for obvious reasons. But yes, I tested it. It will do what's required so long as you do what's required."

Mikel and Leonardo stood atop one of four platforms built around a pyramidal tower constructed of wood and stone, essentially four ladders thick at the base that narrowed to a point where they were bound and bolted together with a steel cap set at the top. A long cable extended from the cap of each tower. Each cable was bolted to stone blocks on the far side of the river that ensured a downward angle for the four lines that were lost in the darkness.

Leonardo selected this section of the river not only because it was the narrowest, but also because their target would need to slow in order to navigate the turn safely.

"And if we do what's required of us, how do we know it will work? How do you know the cables won't snap?"

"They won't. I promise you that. The math is right. The greatest potential for error lies with you." Leonardo lifted his hands when he saw how his friend's expression stiffened. "No criticism intended. It is simply the truth. The timing must be perfect. Off by just a split-second when you and the others release ..." He shrugged his shoulders. Not to suggest that he didn't care. Rather to remind Mikel that it was out of his hands and in theirs. "The equipment will do what's demanded of it. Success will come down to your crew. Do you trust the men and women you selected?"

Mikel nodded without hesitation. "With my life."

"Then trust me as well. This is basic math and science. Nothing more. Physics. Force, acceleration, and momentum. You need only worry about staying on the cable until you no longer should be on the cable. If your crew remembers what we discussed, how to judge the release point, they'll be fine. And if they don't ..."

Mikel didn't need Leonardo to finish. Anyone off in their timing would end up in the river. A death sentence.

"I see it," Teddy called. He stood first in line on the platform just a few yards to the right of Mikel. The shadow they were waiting for was finally breaking free from the darkness.

"Let's get to it." About to put his latest creation to the test, Leonardo was all business. He was also now in command.

Three raiders, one lined up right after the other, stood on each platform, the pyramid at their backs. Grasping tightly to the steel bars with the leather grips Leonardo had crafted specifically for this assignment, they stared out into the darkness, tracking the large shadow as it approached from below.

Leonardo knelt at the very edge of the crag. He doubted that he could be seen with the darkness, but he didn't want to take the risk. Not after all the work that had gone into preparing for this moment.

He would be the one to release Mikel and his raiders at the desired intervals. It was on his shoulders to ensure all had a chance to reach their target, yet not at the risk of knocking one another from their line.

"On my count," Leonardo said, never taking his eyes from the shadow drifting along the river, reviewing his calculations in his mind, knowing that what he was about to do was more art than science now. The lives of the people about to soar off into the black in his hands. "First in line. Go!"

Mikel, Teddy, Samuel, and Ritzi pushed off the platform, picking up speed swiftly as they zipped down the line, knees tucked to their chests to reduce the drag. Eyes focused on the riverboat that was growing larger and curling toward them. Counting down in their heads when it was time to let go.

Tired of speaking with Junius, his friend's continuing assurances beginning to grate, Marak climbed down to the main deck so that he would have more space to continue with his pacing. Everything Junius said was correct. They had little to fear in the middle of the Eastern River. They had little to fear when they reached the Hanover dock. Yet he couldn't shake the premonition that plagued him.

Having reached the bow, crates of various sizes stacked in

the middle of the deck to keep the rails free, Marak turned so that he could make for the stern. As soon as he did, he jumped back a few inches. Startled. One of the biggest men he had ever seen stood before him.

"I know that I should have made a reservation, but are any cabins still available?" Before Marak could respond, not quite sure what was happening, he collapsed to the deck.

"Just as efficient as always," Mikel murmured quietly as he stepped up next to his friend and looked down at his work. Teddy knocked out the soldier with a single blow of his cudgel across the side of his head.

"I aim to please," Teddy replied softly, smiling at what he viewed as a clever pun. "Did everyone make it on board?"

"They did," Mikel confirmed with a pleased smile, ignoring his friend's attempt at humor. "Let's get to it. I've always wanted to be a pirate."

"THAT'S THE LAST OF IT," Samuel reported.

Once he and Mikel's other raiders gained control of the riverboat, Junius had been more than willing to steer to the far southern shore, recognizing that he had little choice. Especially when Mikel promised him that no one would come to harm unless they brought it upon themselves.

The riverboat captain had never met the King of the Underworld, but he knew one truth about him. His word was good, and that was all that mattered.

Junius served House Hanover. Still, he had no desire to throw away his life. The rest of his crew adopted the same perspective given the choice of behaving themselves or attempting to swim the rapids with heavy chains wrapped around their wrists and ankles. Marak and his soldiers didn't get a say. They were bound and gagged.

"Well done, my friend. You and your crew are to be commended." Four wagons were required to cart off the gold Malor Dragoran lent to Lucius Hanover to fund his multitude of efforts to destabilize the Crux.

"All in a day's work," Samuel replied. His broad smile revealed his pleasure. Not only that they had made such a score, but also that all of the men and women he led made it through the attack with barely a scratch. Only Hedley was hurt, spraining his ankle because he landed awkwardly when he let go of the steel bar. "Should I take all this to the usual place?"

"Yes, Nat will be waiting for you."

Samuel nodded. Before he walked away, he had a question that begged asking. "What do you have in mind for all that gold?"

"You mean after you and your crew receive your cuts as well as bonuses?"

Samuel's smile broadened all the more. Thieving had not paid so well as it did until he linked his fortunes to those of the Broken Bear. "Yes, and thank you for the additional consideration. My crew will appreciate your generosity."

"It's deserved. Everyone performed brilliantly." Mikel nodded toward the wagons that were already on the move, heading away from the river before turning west. "And to answer your question, I have several worthy causes that require funding. Now that Malor Dragoran has graciously agreed to support these endeavors, work can begin."

"He's going to love that," Samuel said as he strode toward the last wagon. "Once he finds out what happened, he's going to come after you."

"I certainly hope so," Mikel replied, his visage turning to ice. Dangerous, threatening, if only for a few seconds as his mind shifted toward the last piece of business to be concluded before the sun broke the horizon. "The boat empty?"

Teddy nodded as he strode up the embankment from the shore. "Burn it?"

Marak and the soldiers sat farther up the bank beneath the few trees fighting to subsist among the rocks. Junius had permission to cut them loose once Mikel was gone and an hour had passed, Mikel having no doubt that the riverboat captain would keep his word despite whatever the Captain of the House Hanover Guard might demand of him.

Mikel shook his head in answer to Teddy's question.

"Cut it free?"

Mikel shook his head again.

"I can see the wheels turning. Tell me."

"No grand plan," Mikel shrugged. "I just have a feeling that we might need to make use of the riverboat captain's services at some point in the future, and he won't be of use to me if he doesn't have a riverboat."

Teddy chuckled softly. "Always scheming."

"I prefer to describe it as planning. It's like a game within a game within a game. Managing various pieces as you seek to create the outcome that you want."

"Scheming. Planning. Manipulating. What does it matter what we call it?"

"It doesn't. All that matters is perspective. That we see what is truly before us. Not what we want to see. That's the trick for winning the game, whatever that game might be."

"And what do you see?"

"An opportunity," Mikel replied, his smile becoming almost dastardly.

"I'm afraid to ask."

"You don't need to. You already know."

Teddy put his hands on his hips, studying Mikel. He had known him for more than a decade. Each one saving the other's life. Each one trusting the other with their lives. "Lucius Hanover is a small fish."

"That he is," Mikel agreed.

"You want to go after a bigger fish."

"That I do."

"And you have a plan in place already?"

"More like a scheme," Mikel replied, earning a laugh from his friend as they strode off after the wagons.

## 2

# TRAINING SESSION

"Where did you learn to do that?" Nat sat on a bench placed along the back of The Fox's Lair's inner court-yard. A book open on her lap. Several more were placed in a neat pile by her feet. Her eyes tracked Mikel as he danced around the practice ring he had drawn in chalk on the stone tiles.

"Kaduna." His leg was bothering him as he spun and whirled, cut and lunged, slashed and stabbed at imaginary opponents. That didn't stop him, however. It motivated him, keeping at the top of his mind what could happen if he made a mistake during an actual combat. So he ignored the ache that he was certain would soon escalate into a sharp pain right behind his kneecap.

Aggravating to know what was coming and that there was nothing he could do about it, yet it was strangely comforting as well. It was as if the pain had become a familiar friend to him. A reminder that he was alive. And lucky to be so. Because Mikel believed that he had no right to survive the encounter that had led to his injury.

The experience granted him a humility he might not have

gained otherwise. It offered him an additional obstacle to over-come as well by challenging him to segregate the pain from his consciousness and maintain his concentration. A skill that he had mastered, though it remained a continuing test that had served him well in the past and would do so again in the future.

"Kaduna?" Nat asked distractedly. Her thoughts were still on the text that she had been reading.

Mikel had given her the biography of a famous warlord, explaining that it was less about business and more about leadership and strategy. He promised that she would see the value and connection between the two the more they dug into the great successes and even greater failures of the Kaisari. A man from ancient times who brought together the Twelve Tribes into a single whole and ruled all the Realms. A man murdered by those he believed that he could trust.

"The woman who raised me."

"Your mother?"

"She wasn't my mother. She was like my mother." Drenched in sweat as he spun and glided around the practice ring with the Blade of Light, the glowing steel leaving a trail of white as he cut through the air, he relished the constant movement. The freedom it gave him. The memories as well, sparked by Nat's question.

"Like your mother," Nat nodded, closing the book, though leaving a marker so that she'd be able to return to where she was reading without needing to flip pages. "I remember you telling me about her. She raised you."

"She did."

"Like you're raising me." That thought brightened Nat's usually pensive and guarded features. She'd had a hard life until Mikel took her in as his ward. The level of difficulty had only increased under Mikel's tutelage. Nevertheless, she savored every moment. Every test he placed in her way. Every opportunity he gave her.

"Trying to," Mikel grunted as he slashed then rolled on his right shoulder. Popping back to his feet with a remarkable dexterity for such a large man, he continued his motion to the right. He cut then stabbed before pivoting and slashing backward. Always moving. Always thinking. Mind and body one.

"Trying to?" The instant Nat asked her question she realized that she had fallen into Mikel's trap.

"You make it difficult at times." Mikel offered Nat a wink as he stopped right in front of her. Sword leveled. The sharp tip just a knuckle away from her throat.

"Funny," Nat grumbled.

"I thought so," Mikel replied with a pleased grin. He could have continued his training session, but there was no point.

He already had been working on his own for more than an hour, seeking to keep his skills sharp. Besides, he had learned that there was no reason to push himself when it felt like shards of glass were crunching against one another in his knee. The quality of his training inevitably declined when he reached this point. It was better to rest for a few minutes before moving on to what he had planned next for that morning.

Several barbed responses waited on the tip of Nat's tongue. She didn't fall for the bait, however, having learned that Mikel didn't like to speak about certain matters and that he was attempting to deflect her interest. His past one of them. Though she also had learned how with a little bit of patience she could dig out a few pieces. "From what I recall Kaduna taught you a lot."

"She did."

"She taught you how to fight? You hadn't mentioned that before."

"She did. She set aside time every day. Until she died." The sadness in Mikel's voice confirmed that the memory was still fresh.

"She was a good fighter?"

"She was," Mikel confirmed with a nod. Resting the glowing blade on his shoulder, he lifted his bad knee to the bench and began to knead it, seeking to relieve some of the discomfort, understanding and accepting that he would always feel some pain because of the damaged leg and joint.

"Why did she teach you the blade? I thought she was a Magus."

"She was. But there are certain situations when you can't or shouldn't employ the Talent. In those situations, she stated time and time again that your best weapon was your intellect. Finding the solution even when there wasn't one to be found. And never hesitating when the only solution proved to be steel, though Kaduna argued that should be a last resort."

"Unless you're seeking to make a point," Nat countered with a slightly feral grin.

"Funny," Mikel chuckled, appreciating her humor, "and true. Though I've learned that in most situations, if you've set the stage as you should have, you can play out the scene without need for Talent or blade."

"You just couldn't help yourself, could you?"

"What do you mean?" Mikel asked, his tone and expression the picture of innocence.

"Another lesson. It seems that you can't go more than a few minutes without offering me a lesson."

Mikel chuckled softly. "Sorry, but it's a hard mold to break."

"Kaduna did it to you as well?"

"She did. It seemed like every waking moment was packed with a lesson and another lesson and then one more, one right after the other." Mikel pulled back from the bench, standing straight. He leaned down, catching Nat's eyes. He wanted to make sure that she was listening. Also because he needed to stretch his back, which was tightening up again. He wasn't very old, but living hard and pushing himself for so long had consequences that he couldn't ignore. His injured knee and leg only the most obvious example. "But she believed that it was necessary, and it was."

"Why?" Nat was intensely curious, Mikel touching on a matter that he had only cut around the edges the few other times she had raised it with him.

"Because the world is a hard place for most of us. Only a lucky few get to live on the Royal Ring, and I would argue that isn't always so lucky." His eyes sharpened, almost as keen as his blade. His expression hardened as well. He wanted Nat to remember what he said next if nothing else from this conversation. "We make our way in the world with our wits and our natural abilities and even then …"

"There are no guarantees," Nat replied with a shake of her head and a deeper voice meant to mimic Mikel's.

"I'm glad that you were listening." Mikel kept the chuckle that threatened to break free to himself. He refused to give her the reaction she desired.

"To that, yes. But not to everything you say."

Mikel smiled, biting back the chuckle that was now closer to a laugh. "I'll take what I can get."

Nat appeared thoughtful for a few seconds, her humor just one of the ways that she protected herself. "I understand that not every situation requires the Talent or the blade. Yet why did Kaduna have cause to master steel herself?"

"She liked to be prepared. For everything. She believed that it was the only way to keep me safe." Mikel sighed, several memories that he thought long lost popped unbidden into his head. "When we left the Bitter Heights it was not a good leaving."

"Meaning?"

"Most of the Caledonii were happy to see us go. A few firmer in their beliefs about what to do to a Caledonii without skill in the Talent were not."

"They tried to stop you?"

"They tried to kill me."

"Just because you couldn't use the Talent?"

Mikel smiled sadly. He had never spoken with anyone about this before, yet he felt the need to do so with Nat. He needed her to understand.

Not so much about what happened to him. Rather regarding the innate unfairness of the world. That she would need to make her own way while evading or battling misguided, hateful, and archaic perspectives and prejudices that would seek to hold her back.

"It was a strange almost surreal situation to be in. All Caledonii can use the Talent to a greater or lesser degree. I am the only Caledonii who can't. Most of my people wanted me gone, not viewing me as a true Caledonii and washing their hands of me. Some of the Caledonii tied to the older ways believed that I should be put to death. That I should have been put to death as soon as it was confirmed that I could not use the Talent."

"That's terrible."

"But not uncommon. Old beliefs die hard. Some never do. So another lesson learned."

Nat didn't take issue with Mikel this time, thinking about and grateful for what he shared with her. "Forced from your home because you are different, yet here you face the same challenge because you are different. Here on the Crux you are looked down upon by those who view the Caledonii with scorn if not with open hatred."

"Thankfully only a few rather than many," Mikel admitted. "You've likely noticed during the time you've been with me. The people who work with us, work for us, do so because we are fair and they can trust us. That's what they want. And that's all we can hope for in return. Trust and fairness. Rarely given easily, but once earned to be held onto tenaciously, because once lost it can rarely be gained again."

"And yet another lesson," Nat snorted, feeling the need to inject a little humor into what was a difficult topic.

"I make no apology for it, and I wouldn't waste time or breath if I didn't believe that such knowledge was necessary."

Nat nodded, acknowledging the truth in Mikel's words. "Still, it is a difficult position to be in. How can you make your place in the world when the world seems to have no place for you?"

"A difficult position, yes, but not an impossible position once you understand what the world is and what it can be."

Nat nodded again, this time lips scrunched together, lost in thought. "The Kaisari said much the same."

Mikel smiled. "He did." He motioned toward the book in Nat's lap. "Kaduna made me read that when I was about your age."

"What will be will be, unless you be who you want to be."

Mikel's smile deepened. Then he nodded. The quote Nat offered from the Kaisari himself right on target to the matter they were discussing. "You must be willing to put in the work to create the world you want. To fight for the world that you want. You must do what you must do, otherwise the world will do what it believes it must."

"Don't allow others to define you," Nat murmured very quietly, nodding her head slowly. "Define yourself."

"Exactly," Mikel agreed. "In the end, success or failure won't be defined by how many golds you have in your safe or military victories you've won. Only you can define your success and failure. Only you can say whether you've created the world you wanted. Only you can say whether you've lived in that world as you believe you should have."

"It seems that your Blade agrees with you," Nat said, changing the subject. The dim glow of the steel was brighter, defeating the lamps surrounding the courtyard.

"That it does," Mikel agreed. He knew the cause as well, but he preferred to have that conversation in private. He shifted his focus back to Nat. "You should be in bed."

"I'd rather be here," she countered.

"Watching me make a fool of myself?" Mikel asked with a raised eyebrow as he nodded toward the Blade. He was done with the forms Kaduna had taught him. However, he was not yet done practicing all that the Blade of Light offered him.

The energy surging within the ancient artifact made the hair on his arms and neck stand on end, calling to the power surging within him. The connection between the two seamless. Undeniable.

Mikel understood now how the Light of the Blade worked with the Light that resided within him, his very spirit, to form a stronger whole. Understanding as well that he had a great deal more to learn if he was to wield the Blade of Light as he knew would be demanded of him. A responsibility that he didn't relish, yet one that he also didn't believe that he could avoid.

"Something like that," Nat admitted. She couldn't touch the power she sensed flowing within Mikel. She couldn't understand it. Yet she didn't need to in order to comprehend just how vast and potent the energy at his fingertips truly was. Assuming he could master it, of course, before it mastered him.

"Care to have a go?" Nat did need to go to bed, but Mikel glimpsed the anticipation in the back of her eyes. And he had little desire to engage in a battle of wills with her, knowing how that would likely end.

Besides, his connection to the Blade felt right. As if he and the Blade of Light were in balance. Just as it should be between them.

It hadn't been like that at the beginning. At first, it had felt like an intrusion. No more, however.

Now he sensed the connection that was developing between him and the magic contained within the Blade of

Light. A magic similar to the Talent yet not quite the same. Older. More primal. More potent.

Even more so he sensed the connection between him and the many other essences teasing at the very edge of his consciousness.

"Definitely." Nat pushed herself up, placing the book about the Kaisari on top of her pile. Carefully. Making sure that the edges were straight. She had exercised little control over her life before Mikel came into it. Now, she valued the ability to do that. As she and Mikel had been discussing, to be who she wanted to be. To define herself.

"You'll go to bed afterward?" Mikel sheathed the Blade of Light in the scabbard across his back. He did not need to touch the weapon for the contest about to begin. His skill was improving thanks to the knowledge and wisdom shared by those who had served as Bearers of the Blade before him.

"Yes, I promise." Nat's excitement was almost a physical thing. She understood that this was another of Mikel's lessons. Or at least that's how he looked at it. Even so, she viewed the encounter to come as fun.

Mikel nodded. "Try not to hurt me."

"I'll do my best."

"Very kind of you." Mikel glided slowly to his right. Nat did the same. Both followed the border of the training circle and kept the distance between them.

Finn had told him that Nat was becoming much more proficient as a Magus. Her natural affinity for magic aiding her development.

Mikel wanted to get a better sense of how far she had progressed, already impressed based on what she had done for him when he and Drin were making their escape from the Tor.

That clash confirmed for Mikel that Nat preferred to attack. So he wasn't surprised when a ball of flame shot toward him.

Rather than relying on his unique ability that negated the

Talent and the Curse, he called upon the power that was making his blood boil. The Light scalding. Cleansing. Welcoming.

A shield formed on his forearm the instant before the Talent struck, Mikel deflecting the energy up into the sky. "A bit dramatic, don't you think?"

Realizing that it would be best to keep their combat quiet, Mikel used the Light to craft a shimmering dome of white that circled the practice ring. This allowed them to conduct their session without being interrupted and without having to worry that a stray bolt of energy might cause unnecessary damage or harm.

"Not dramatic," Nat argued as she began to circle once more, Mikel moving with her. "Decisive. One of the first things you taught me was that in any combat, strike the first blow ..."

"If there's a good chance it can be the only blow," Mikel finished for Nat. He smiled. Pleased that she had listened to him about this as well. Pleased, in fact, that she seemed to be listening to him more often than she wasn't.

Nat gave Mikel a quick lift of her eyebrows. "But there's a piece missing from that advice."

"And what would that be?" Mikel anticipated what was coming next. However, he chose to give Nat the moment that she desired.

"The first blow doesn't have to be the only blow." Nat followed her argument with a cascading attack, sending small pellets of energy streaking toward Mikel. Then bursts of the Talent. Shards. Spears. Increasing the intensity of her assault with each creation, she strove to break through his defenses. And, failing that, prevent him from attacking her.

Mikel withstood Nat's attack with a teasing grin. Proud of her efforts. Finn was right. Her skill in the Talent had grown by leaps and bounds in just a few short weeks.

He was proud of himself as well. He was using the Light to

defend himself, ensuring that none of Nat's attacks struck home.

Although he was most comfortable in the use of the magical shield fixed to his forearm, Mikel realized that he needed to expand his repertoire of tools and test himself with other applications of the Light.

Releasing the shield, he crafted circles of blindingly bright natural magic that hovered all around him. A unique defense, the shields seemingly had minds of their own as he protected against Nat's onslaught.

In this way, Mikel allowed Nat to become comfortable with her strategy. He wanted to see how well she would do when the tenor of the combat shifted unexpectedly.

Hearing Nat growl a curse thanks to her lack of success, Mikel defended against a stream of power that she shot toward him with one hand.

Before Nat could bring her next weapon to bear, folds of energy spinning in front of her, Mikel seized his chance. Calling upon the Light, he flicked his left hand.

A cloud of white sparks blasted out from his palm.

Eyes widening in surprise at the suddenness of Mikel's assault, Nat abandoned any thought of continuing her attack. Instead she formed a barrier of energy right in front of her, grunting from the effort required to hold back Mikel's magic.

But Nat wasn't done. Gliding around the practice ring, seeking to turn the tide, she grunted in anger. Mikel had seized the upper hand and had no desire to let it go. He moved her this way and that by sending one blast of energy after another in her direction.

The speed and intensity of his assault worried her, making Nat question her own tactics and wonder if perhaps she should have been more cautious at the beginning of the combat rather than revealing much of what she could do with the Talent, thereby allowing Mikel to adjust and then adapt.

Nat expelled another curse when she ducked down, shield in place, avoiding most of the blast of Light Mikel shot toward her. What she couldn't pushed her back toward the dome, only the shimmering energy behind her keeping her on her feet.

This was not what she had anticipated when she accepted Mikel's challenge. She had assumed that she would have little difficulty against him since he was a novice when it came to the potency that had become his just a short time before.

She had misjudged, however. Mikel had a natural acuity for the Light just as she did with the Talent, and he was learning just as fast if not faster than she was.

Another lesson learned thanks to Mikel.

Never underestimate your opponent.

And always be ready to take your chance. Because you might only get one.

Nat didn't need to think when Mikel overextended himself. Just slightly. Barely. Still, enough for her to act.

With a quick flick of her wrist, she sent a bolt of energy no larger than a needle curling around her shield and along the edge of the dome, the needle cutting back in toward Mikel once it was past his own shields.

"Blast it!" Mikel was unaware that it was even there.

Mikel released his hold on the Light when he felt the touch of the Talent against his side. Against anyone else, a deadly blow. Against him, no more than a tickle. Even so, enough to confirm what he saw on Nat's face.

Victory.

"Well done ..."

Mikel didn't have the chance to finish congratulating Nat, opening his arms as she hugged him. The joy of her success contagious, his scowl swiftly became a smile. Savoring the moment, he allowed the dome to fade away, the natural light of the lamps once again gaining dominance in the courtyard.

"I never thought that I could beat you."

"Neither did I," Mikel grumbled, trying to be annoyed and failing miserably. Instead pleased by her success. "Now off to bed."

"But I can't be expected ..." Nat pulled back from him, preparing to argue her case.

"And take your books with you. You have your lessons tomorrow morning and you need to sleep. It's not like Teddy will give you a break just because you beat me."

She was about to ask Mikel for another round, then decided against it, her smile broadening. Nat decided to relish her victory rather than seek another one, discovering that she was exhausted, the adrenaline of her triumph draining from her quickly.

Without another word, Nat did as Mikel instructed. Picking up her books and leaving the courtyard for her apartment, though not before giving him one more hug.

The quiet that followed didn't last for long, just as Mikel assumed that it wouldn't.

"You're just a big softie, aren't you?"

Mikel turned at the rumble of the voice, then smiled. "I've been called worse."

~

"Was that a mistake? Or did you do that on purpose?"

"Do what on purpose?"

"Show your hand to the young Magus?"

"You know how it is in a combat," Mikel replied with a shrug. An answer that wasn't really an answer.

"I do. That's why I'm asking you." Knute, the King of the Giants of the Rime two generations before Cadmus, along with Maria Roucheau, Savior of the Bloody Steppe, took shape when Nat left. Both half again as tall as Mikel, and Mikel was taller than most men. They looked exactly as they did when they were alive except for the shimmering light wrapped around their figures. Their presence in the Natural World permitted because of the power contained within the Blade of Light.

"Leave him alone, Knute. You know he did what any good father would have done," Maria chided.

"He's not her ..." Knute stopped talking, Maria's short sword at his throat. He chuckled. He had reacted as if he were still alive. There was nothing that she could do to him now that they were both dead. Except perhaps drive him insane with her incessant questions.

"Be careful, Frost Lord," Maria warned. "Blood does not make a man a good father. I can tell you that from experience."

"Of that I'm well aware," Knute grumbled. "I'm simply trying to explain that allowing the young Magus to gain a victory she didn't earn doesn't necessarily help with her development. She must experience both success and failure, love and loss."

"She has experienced all of that and more, Frost Lord. You can see it in her eyes. And I take the opposite perspective," Maria argued. "I say that it does. I say that her victory over the Steelheart builds her confidence and helps her acquire the skills she needs at a faster pace."

"Just because you feel the need to coddle ..."

"Has this been going on long?" interrupted Mikel. He stood there, arms crossed, a grin on his face that was in small part amusement and in large part annoyance, having little patience for the bickering.

"What are you talking about?" Knute demanded, not liking how the Steelheart cut him off.

"This constant arguing. The centuries must be taking their toll."

"You have no idea, Steelheart." Maria snorted out a sharp laugh as she pulled her glowing blade away from the Frost

Lord. "Some of us have been tied to the Blade of Light for thousands of years. It is only natural. We know each other too well."

"Much like being married to someone for ..."

"We are not married," Maria clarified swiftly, blade moving back toward Knute's throat before she caught herself and realized what she was doing.

"I was not saying that we were," Knute explained, giving Mikel a wink. He understood after being tied to the master swordswoman for so long just how testy she could be. And clearly he was pleased at how easily he irritated Maria. Another skill he had mastered over the centuries. "Have no fear of that."

"Because I'm not pretty enough for you?" she demanded.

"Of course not," Knute replied. "You are quite beautiful." And she was in his opinion, the long scar running across her face appealing to him in a way that few could understand. More appealing was the fact that they had both led the Giants of the Rime during dark days and emerged victorious. "I was simply trying to explain."

"Good," Maria grunted. Once she was certain that the Frost Lord had nothing else to say, she turned her focus toward Mikel. "You are doing well with the Blade, Steelheart. As you asked the young Magus, would you care to have a go?"

"You'll be gentle with me?" Mikel offered Maria a wink that earned another sharp bark of laughter.

"No promises, Steelheart."

"Good enough for me." Pulling the scimitar from his scabbard, he used the Light to recreate the dome of energy, enclosing the practice space so that they could engage in their session without fear of interruption.

"Why don't I get to have a go?" demanded Knute, the Giant of the Rime gliding out of the ring and leaning against the magical barrier.

"You need to be faster, Frost Lord. Otherwise you'll miss your chance."

Knute wasn't quite certain as to what Maria was referring. He couldn't ask her for clarification, however.

Because she was already moving. No more than a blur, she surged toward Mikel, blade raised above her head. Her target where his neck met his shoulder.

Mikel didn't bother to move. He couldn't escape her. Maria was too fast.

Instead, understanding that raising his sword to block the strike would take too much time, he chose the only option that he believed would allow him to stay in the fight that had only just begun.

To defend himself he called on the Light. A shimmering bar formed just in front of him. The bar functioned like a sword. Obeying Mikel's will and moving as Maria adjusted her angle of approach, her magical blade struck Mikel's bar rather than him.

He didn't stand still to exult in his success. Pleased by the brief look of surprise that flitted in the back of Maria's eyes, he moved. The Blade of Light held to his front, the Light itself roared through him, his consciousness and that of the ancient weapon in his hands functioning as a single entity.

Always moving.

The Blade slashing and cutting as Mikel dodged this way and that.

Willing to take what his opponent offered him as she pressed for an advantage.

Maria refused to allow more than a few feet of space between them, believing that the constant pressure she applied would prove to be Mikel's undoing.

As they glided around the practice ring, her sword and his flashed brightly, streaks of light denoting their passage, sparks flying when the blades struck. Mikel didn't comprehend how the weapon of a spirit could have substance in the Natural World but he wasn't in a position to ask that question. Not with the intensity of Maria's attack.

To lose concentration if only for a heartbeat ensured his defeat.

Therefore, he had eyes only for his opponent as she put him to the test.

The next few minutes demonstrated to Mikel why Maria Roucheau was declared the Savior of the Bloody Steppe. She was the Bearer of the Blade when she led the Giants of the Rime in support of Frisia and the other Kingdoms of the Bloody Steppe against the Dread before that font of evil finally proved victorious through deception and murder, the Murk falling upon the land now called the Wyld.

"You do well, Steelheart." Maria offered Mikel a nod of respect, delighted that he was holding his own.

"I seek only to learn," he replied humbly and truthfully.

"As you should," Maria acknowledged, "but you should also try to win."

Mikel's expression tightened. She wasn't trying to goad him, but she was calling him out. And he understood why. He was only using the Blade of Light in its most traditional sense. He wasn't making use of all that the Blade offered him.

"Do what you must, Steelheart," Knute called out from the other side of the ring. "Be who you must be."

"You cannot escape what the future holds," Maria warned, her blade sweeping down toward his shoulder. "Listen to the Frost Lord. Listen to yourself."

And he did. Before Maria's blade could strike true, Mikel called upon the Light once again and blocked Maria's attack with a spinning shield of natural magic.

Forced to turn away, when Maria finally looked back, he was gone.

Pleased by that small success, Mikel allowed the Light that filled him to take more control over his actions and thoughts.

The result was energizing. Eye-opening. And frightening, a quiet murmur of warning, what Mikel took to be the combined voices of the other Bearers of the Blade, growing louder in the back of his mind.

But why the concern?

He had seized the momentum, gaining the upper hand on the Savior of the Bloody Steppe.

He was moving with greater speed.

He was making decisions with barely any thought.

He was using the Light that only he could command, not just his steel.

He was forcing the former Bearer to dance to his tune, herding her where he wanted her to go, Maria unable to stand against the magic he employed.

Shards of the Light required her to dive out of the way and roll and then roll again. Long sheets of energy threatened to wrap themselves around her, Maria only breaking free with a few deft cuts of her blade.

The Savior of the Bloody Steppe was always on the move, and in a direction not of her choosing.

As a result, the tempo of the combat was different now.

Mikel had taken charge.

Knute nodded with pleasure as he observed the duel and then the transition. He always enjoyed the skill that Maria displayed. Yet even more so, he savored the Steelheart's prowess.

Steel and Light working together.

A devastating combination against which only a former Bearer of the Blade could stand. Though not for long as he saw and sensed how Maria was beginning to struggle.

Knute realized that in this combat the Steelheart was

becoming more than what he had been. He was becoming more of what he needed to be. He was becoming the …

"You must find a balance, Lightcrafter," Knute urged, a note of concern tinging his deep voice.

The combat had halted with a breath-taking swiftness. The result not inevitable though not surprising. Mikel held the Blade of Light up against Maria's throat. Pulses of the Light flashed all around the pair. Evidence of the power at Mikel's beck and call.

The Lightcrafter had given himself to the Light. Just as he needed to do if he was to live up to his true potential.

But had he given too much of himself?

That was Knute's concern.

"I don't know if I can," Mikel growled. He understood what Knute was requiring of him. He just didn't know how to attain it. And he feared that the strain of that challenge would be too much for him.

With the incredible power surging through him, he felt as if he were being torn apart. His spirit being ripped from his body. The demands of the Blade conflicting with the innate weaknesses of his body. Even more, his lack of knowledge.

Never having experienced this before.

Never having the chance to prepare for this battle within him.

Because he never received the training required to navigate his current struggle. A struggle that could leave him less than what he was. A shell of his former self.

He silently cursed Kaduna. Something he never anticipated that he would do.

All Caledonii could touch the Talent. But he couldn't.

Instead, he could do something much more distinctive.

He could touch the Light.

Yet rather than tell him this, rather than teach him what

was required so that he could manage this unique skill safely and well, she had locked away his ability, hiding it even from him.

Arguably to keep him safe.

Yet now, her error could cost him a great deal more than just his life.

His stealing the Blade of Light and the Blade choosing him allowed him to break through the block she had set within him. He could now exercise a power that was indescribable. Yet at the same time that power threatened to destroy him.

He needed to exercise control.

He needed to do it now.

And he needed to do it on his own, because neither Knute nor Maria could aid him in the endeavor.

He either succeeded or failed.

And if he failed, death was the least of his worries.

"Be who you need to be, Lightcrafter," Maria urged.

She offered Mikel a smile despite the fear in her eyes. She was a spirit. Tied to the Blade. But Mikel exercised the power now to destroy her utterly and completely. A single slice of his steel across her throat would condemn her to the darkest depths of the Spirit World.

And though she may complain from time to time about being linked to Knute and the other previous Bearers of the Blade and how tiresome it could be, she was not yet ready to let go of what she viewed as a critical responsibility. A truth that was playing out right before her eyes.

*"Get what needs to be gotten, then get gone."*

One of Kaduna's favorite sayings ran through Mikel's mind as he fought to maintain his grasp on the potent magic racing through him. The Light demanded to be released. It roared in his ears, forcing him to do its will rather than the other way around.

Yet despite the intense strain that only increased with each passing second, he couldn't get that saying out of his head. And he couldn't understand why that saying in particular, because Kaduna never lacked in sayings.

He had always assumed that specific maxim applied solely to his work as a thief.

But perhaps that wasn't the case.

Perhaps Kaduna was attempting to instruct him in more ways than one.

Mikel faltered, a burst of fear shooting through him and threatening his tenuous hold on the Light.

He realized that he wasn't controlling the Light so much as the Light was controlling him.

Knute was correct. He needed to find the balance required to wield the Blade of Light. The balance that ensured he could be who he needed to be. Not who the Light demanded he be. But how?

*"Get what needs to be gotten then get gone."*

Kaduna's words floated through his mind once more.

That's when an idea struck him.

The power that he could exercise with the Blade of Light was almost incomprehensible. But he didn't require all that power to do what he needed to do. He required only a small portion of it. And he needed to be the one to decide how much of the Light he called upon.

His instincts and reason needed to take precedence.

He was connected to the Light through his very essence. Just like the other Bearers. And he made use of the Light with his thoughts.

Perhaps that was the key.

Refine his thoughts and he could refine his control.

He remembered his lessons with Kaduna, how she made him sit in the darkness staring at a candle flame. She charged him with letting the disparate thoughts in his mind go and demanded that he see only the flame of the candle. That he be one with the flame of the candle.

A challenging requirement.

One that took him years to master.

Until he could block out everything around him. Until he could see nothing except for the flame. Until he could view the world through a vacuum.

He did that now, imagining the Light within him, the power at his command that sought to command him, as the candle flame.

And then it was done.

In that instant, Mikel achieved the balance required.

The balance Knute demanded of him.

The balance that ensured he remained who he was and was given the chance to be who he not only needed to be, but also wanted to be.

His free will still his own.

Because he was in control.

Mikel stepped back then, the blazing light of the Blade in his hands returning to a dim glow.

Sheathing the weapon he offered a nod of respect to Maria and then one of thanks to Knute.

He was by no means an expert in the use of the Blade and the Light, but at least now he understood how to ensure that he never lost control of the magic available to him. The magic that could do just as much if not more damage than good.

"Well done, Lightcrafter," Maria sighed, grateful for Mikel's strength of body and will.

"Well done, indeed," Knute agreed. "Even so, you need to improve your skill. We can help, but only so much."

"Then what would you suggest?" Mikel was pleased that he had achieved the necessary balance with the Light, but he feared that maintaining that balance would be a continuing challenge.

"You need to speak with Cadmus, Lightcrafter," Knute explained. "He can teach you what we cannot."

Mikel nodded, hearing the truth in Knute's words. However, the meeting with Cadmus would have to wait. He needed to speak with Drin first.

3

## A DANGEROUS PLAY

"Why are we here, Malor?" Assindra leaned back against the stone balustrade. The sunlight glinting off the Barbed Path visible over her shoulder, she ignored the panorama that spread out behind her. Having eyes only for the King of the Tor, her thoughts were on what she needed to do. On acquiring what she deserved. She had little patience for her ally right then, believing that he was wasting her time.

Malor ignored the pique in her voice. Amused by it, though he kept that to himself. She would learn soon enough. He stood on the far side of the tower staring down at Graz, the city extending to the very edge of the Tor in all directions.

His city.

His Kingdom.

He had made it so.

He had fought to keep it his.

However, for the first time since seizing control those many centuries before, he felt the reins of power slipping from his fingers.

Thanks to that spreading weakness he seethed on the inside, believing the fault wasn't his. Rather it rested with the

Dark Magus standing before him who was supposed to have completed a simple task.

Once she retrieved and gave that ancient artifact to him, there would be few if any who could challenge him.

Yet she had failed to do so. Time after time in fact.

So many opportunities. All failures.

Worse, Assindra offered him excuses rather than the desired item. The essential item.

Malor shook his head, a mixture of anger and resignation. He realized that now was the time. He needed to step out from behind the mask that had shielded him for so long. He needed to be who he truly was.

Not an unexpected development. Just sooner than he had anticipated. Sooner than he would have preferred.

Orchestrating from the shadows had allowed him to work faster. But no longer.

All had been moving forward as it should.

All had been shifting in his favor.

The scales tilting as he applied the required pressure with a delicate touch.

Until they no longer were.

Until those scales were shifting away from him despite his best efforts.

Thanks to the King of the Underworld.

More galling, that thief was now the Bearer of the Blade.

The Blade that belonged to him.

He still couldn't understand how that happened.

Why would the Blade of Light select a thief? A man of no consequence. Of no real power. Of no real ability.

It made no sense.

In one form or another, Malor had ruled the Tor for centuries. Hiding who he truly was. Taking new identities as time passed. Yet always presenting himself as a Dragoran. A long, unbroken line of succession based solely on him.

Building his power.

Waiting patiently.

Until the time was right.

Until he could emerge once again.

Until he could reclaim all that rightfully belonged to him.

All of that was now in jeopardy.

All because of one unanticipated obstacle.

An obstacle that was proving to be more of a challenge than Malor imagined possible.

Locking away his simmering anger, he turned his mind to what he needed to do next. The steps required to ensure his plans remained on track.

The first question was the most obvious.

What was he to do about the thief?

To Malor the answer to that dilemma was crystal clear.

Removing the thief would remove many of the complications that currently delayed his plans. Yet not all of them.

And what was he to do about the recalcitrant Queen of the Crux?

Because it was becoming more and more obvious that the fortunes of Celindria Dengannon and the King of the Underworld were tied together. Those fortunes now linked inextricably to his much like an anchor tied around his neck.

Malor needed the Crux. Bringing the Crux and the Tor back together, reforming what had been known for centuries as the Splintered Empire, would give him the base of power he required to expand his rule to other Realms.

He could seize again what once had belonged to him. He could become once more the power he had been.

In fact, he could become more than that. He could become whatever he wanted to be. With the Splintered Empire in one hand and the Blade of Light in the other, he would be invincible.

Even those who had betrayed him so long ago wouldn't be able to stand against him.

A complicated dilemma that he faced. That was the truth.

Yet not so complicated that he couldn't find a way through it. A path that would allow him to create the future that he deserved. A future where he stepped out of the shadows, making the myth real once more.

"Come with me," Malor ordered.

He didn't bother to look at Assindra, certain that she would do as he commanded. She had no choice. She had bet on the wrong horse. Herself. And now there was a debt to be paid that resulted from her arrogance and poor decisions.

With a flick of his wrist, wispy strands of black surged out from his fingertips. Those strands connected, becoming a greater whole. Spinning faster and faster, the circle of black expanded swiftly. Until the portal crafted from the Curse revealed a cavern lighted by only a few torches, those burning feebly and struggling to hold back the gloom.

Assindra followed right behind Malor after he strode through. As she did, she castigated herself for failing to recognize the signs. For failing to realize that the power Malor controlled was more than just political. That Malor was much like her.

A Magus with an insatiable curiosity who had chosen to take a forbidden path. Yet different from her as well. Because he had the unique skill of masking the magic that he controlled. Preventing her from sensing it. Until that very moment.

Worse, and more frightening, she realized too late that when it came to the Curse she was no more than a candle to his flame.

"Where are we?"

Assindra stood in a large cavern, water trickling down the wall behind her. She sought to penetrate the darkness and failed to do so. The air was dank. Musty.

The shadows ruled here. The torches sickly sentinels and too weak to breach the blackness for more than just a few feet around.

"One of my kennels," Malor replied with a bark of a laugh. He had sensed the change in her when they stepped through. Assindra was beginning to understand the severe gravity of her many mistakes, and he was looking forward to when her new reality fell completely on her shoulders. He was curious as to whether it would crush her. Though he guessed it probably wouldn't. The Dark Magus was too much of a survivor. Once she found her feet the game between them would begin again, though this time the dynamics between them would be different. Painfully so for Assindra.

"Kennel?" She didn't understand. Until she saw the eyes, gleaming brightly in the darkness, all a golden yellow.

Only a few pair at first. Then a dozen. And a dozen after that. Then even more were streaming forward from the depths of the cavern. Assindra lost track of her count when she realized that hundreds of pairs of eyes stared at her from the darkness.

"How fare you, Janus?"

"As well as can be expected, my Lord." A hulking figure stepped out of the gloom, his golden eyes shining brightly in the torchlight. Appearing to be more bear than man, he offered Malor a respectful bow. He didn't bother to acknowledge Assindra, who couldn't take her eyes off this new player in the game that she sensed she was losing if she had not already lost.

What was it about this man that made her so viscerally uncomfortable, the hair on her arms and the back of her neck prickling?

He was a towering and domineering figure, that was undeniable, and clearly he was a skilled soldier. The scars on his face and crisscrossing his arms confirmed that. But there was more to it than just that.

Perhaps it was how he held himself. And those eyes. They suggested a savageness and bestiality that she had never come into contact with before.

With scarcely a glance from Janus, she experienced a fear she had never known before. A primal fear. As if she were being hunted.

She would have scoffed at the notion. She the prey and this soldier the hunter. If not for those eyes. Not just golden she realized. Sparks of black in the back as well.

Janus had been touched by the Curse. No, she decided upon extending her senses to get a better feel for what she truly faced. Crafted with the Curse. Janus had been made into something different with the Curse. He had been rebuilt in an unnatural way.

She took a step back from the soldier, her eyes widening when it struck her. Discovering that Malor was stronger than she was in the Curse was shock enough.

But this?

This couldn't be.

Yet it was.

"You look surprised, Magus," Malor said in a pleased tone.

She lifted her head, catching Janus' eyes. The soldier stared down at her with a feral grin. Teeth changing before her very eyes, his incisors lengthened, growing sharper. "This cannot be." Assindra almost couldn't get the words out, struggling to come to grips with this new earth-shaking reality.

"It can and it is, Assindra." Malor's deep voice echoed in the chamber. The power within, carrying a hint of compulsion, forced Assindra to wrap her mind around the new world that was taking shape before her eyes. Satisfied that the Magus now understood the truth that had struck her such a savage blow, Malor turned his attention back to Janus. "How many are here with you?"

"Five hundred, my Lord."

Malor studied his captain. His eyes tightened as he considered the decisions that he needed to make, the likely repercussions of each, and then the resulting possibilities with which he would have to grapple. Many of those decisions filled with uncertainty. Yet there was no uncertainty attached to the man who stood calmly before him.

Janus Domitian had proven his loyalty to Malor many times over during the centuries. In fact, after Malor fell in battle Janus led the escape of the Ten Thousand from Stronghold and back through Frisia. Fighting their way past the Wraiths, their former brothers in arms, they gained the safety that lay beyond the Murk after more than a week of bloody and savage clashes. Their numbers were reduced greatly. Nevertheless, Janus ensured that Malor survived despite the Wraiths' fervor to kill him.

Because of all that and what had come after, Malor had little doubt that Janus would complete with his usual harsh alacrity the task he was going to give him.

"The Crux and the Tor have remained distinct Kingdoms for too long. I require your assistance to change that."

"The Splintered Bridge, my Lord?" Janus asked. His eyes flashed in delight at the thought of what would be required to make his master's desire material. Of the blood that he would spill.

Malor nodded. "Do you need more soldiers of the Ten Thousand than you have here?"

Janus didn't even need to think about his response. "No, my Lord. We will claim the Splintered Bridge. Have no fear of that." Growls of agreement from the soldiers standing behind Janus in the darkness rumbled off the surrounding stone.

"Then get to it, Captain Domitian. Time is short."

After a sharp nod and deep bow of respect, Janus turned and faded into the gloom along with half a thousand fighters.

"He was truly of the Ten Thousand?" Assindra murmured

softly, fearing that Captain Domitian might still be close enough to hear.

"He and all the rest, yes." Malor's grin broadened. He had always enjoyed surprising people. Even more so, frightening them. And that was the look he saw and relished in Assindra's eyes right then. A deserved terror.

"He's a ..." She was having a hard time completing her thought and not understanding why. She was a Magus. One of the most powerful in all the Realms. Beyond that, a Magus unafraid to touch the Curse. Yet to learn that she was no more than a child compared to Malor when it came to that tainted power and then to come face to face with an abomination?

It was almost too much for her. For it led to only one shattering conclusion.

"If he and all the others are of the Ten Thousand, then you are ..."

Malor's wicked smile broadened as he nodded slowly. "Yes, my dear, I am what you believe me to be."

Assindra had been a fool. She had seen what she wanted to see in Malor. A tool to be used, nothing more, and a tool to be discarded when she was done with him.

She had failed to see not what was truly there. Not who Malor truly was. In part because of her own weakness, even more because of Malor's strength. The glamour wrapped around him impregnable.

"This can't be possible," Assindra said ever so quietly, trying to reconcile herself to the likely lethal consequences of her error. "You can't be possible."

"More than possible, my dear," Malor replied in a silky-smooth voice. Reaching out, he ran a rough hand along her cheek. Assindra flinched, though she held her ground. He chuckled softly at her attempt to demonstrate her spine in such a small, inconsequential way, then shook his head sadly. "You believed that you were the real power in our relationship, and that's how I wanted it." He pulled back his hand. His voice took on a steely edge. Colder. Ancient. "Until now."

"But you couldn't have survived. The King of Frisia. In your combat with him, he …"

"I more than survived, my dear," Malor cut in. "Julius Rache put up a good fight. Just as I expected he would, the lives of his family depending on his efforts. Even so, he could not destroy me. He could only wound me. And I give him credit for that."

"And since then …"

"I have hidden in plain sight. I have healed. I have rebuilt my strength. I have become whole once more."

"But the Wraiths …"

"Do not speak of the Wraiths," he roared, spittle flying from his lips. He growled, a sound similar to that made by Janus and the soldiers before they slipped away in the darkness. "The Wraiths were my greatest mistake and my greatest betrayers." He knelt down toward her then, dark eyes flashing with a burning hatred. "They will pay for their treachery when the time is right. And you will help me with that."

"All this time you have …" Assindra understood what had happened. What Malor had done. Yet she still couldn't quite accept it. A weakness she needed to get past. Quickly.

"I have been here on the Tor," Malor replied with a pleased grin. "Always the same. Yet always different."

Assindra closed her eyes, seeking the calm that would not come. She was impressed by his perseverance. Terrified as well.

Malor had made his way to the Splintered Empire at the perfect time. Right after confirmation of the schism, an uneasy peace settled between the two Kingdoms, the Crux and the Tor both turning inward for a time. Both needed to rebuild their strength. Both sought to protect themselves from the other. Both having little doubt that the enmity between them would gain precedence once more.

Malor arrived at a time of chaos. Several hundred years in

the past. Always there, yet always different just as he said. Ruling the Tor all the while by adopting distinct yet connected personas.

"Why did you deceive me?" Assindra asked when she opened her eyes, hoping that the expression of calm confidence she offered her exceedingly dangerous partner now turned master hid the fear roiling through her.

"I never deceived you, Assindra. You deceived yourself. If you were as great a Dark Magus as you believe yourself to be, you would have seen me for what I am long ago. Instead, you saw what you wanted to see. No more. No less."

Assindra wanted to argue against Malor's claim, but she couldn't. Because he was right. The anger rising within her that burned away her fear directed at herself. Not at Malor. Or rather at who Malor truly was. Yet with that anger came an unsettling truth.

She was trapped.

All the while she believed that she was using the King of the Tor for her own purposes, but she hadn't been. Malor Dragoran had been using her. And he would continue to do so. Because she couldn't fight him.

Malor was too strong. He had always been too strong. He had simply allowed her to believe otherwise.

"You see it now, don't you?"

Assindra had a great deal more to say. None of it beneficial to her current circumstance. So she kept herself in check. She nodded pleasantly. "You have done well, Malor, if I may continue to call you that. I must give credit where credit is due."

"I am glad that you're handling this so well, Assindra. I feared that I would need to give you a harsh lesson if not dispose of you before time."

"Is that a warning?" Assindra refused to allow her mask to crack. She would not surrender to her fear once again. She needed to be strong. She needed to think clearly. She needed to find some way to get out from beneath Malor's thumb ... assuming that was even possible.

"I don't give warnings, Assindra," Malor replied with a devilish glint in his eyes. "I offer you only the truth."

Assindra nodded, finally having come to terms with where matters now stood between them. Her thoughts already turned toward seeking some way to adjust those terms more in her favor. "And, in truth, will sending out your beasts be enough for you to gain the victory you desire?"

Malor didn't reply right away. He stared at Assindra, almost as if he could read her mind. Then he nodded, his smile more a sneer. "No, there is more for me to do. And you as well." The malicious glint in his eye promised a terrible fate if she failed.

"The Blade of Light."

Malor nodded. "This is your last chance, Assindra. Bring me that ancient weapon."

"Not an easy task as you've seen."

"I have faith that you will succeed. Perhaps you simply need to use your maternal connection to your advantage."

Assindra's eyes narrowed. Her only sign of pique at Malor's barb. "And what will you be doing while I risk my life for you?"

"Come now, my dear. There is no cause for such bitterness. So long as you prove useful to me, you will have a place at my side. And when you do not ..." Malor shrugged, his lack of concern a knife in Assindra's gut. "Well, there is no need to speak of that. I can see in your eyes that you understand. Now go do as you have failed to do. Bring me the Blade of Light."

"And where will you be?"

"I have an engagement with some allies of old," Malor replied with an evil grin, wisps of black forming at his back. Spinning. Faster and faster. Another portal forming. "I believe it's time for them to walk in this world once more."

4

# TREACHEROUS DANCE

"You asked to see me, my Queen."

Celindria Dengannon jumped slightly where she sat at her desk, several of the papers she had been reading floating to the floor. The soft voice at her back startled her, and she was less than pleased. Looking up, a disapproving frown gracing her features, she glared over her shoulder.

"You need to stop doing this," she chided in her best regal tone. Drin frowned, shaking her head slightly as she might at an unruly child, understanding that it would have little impact on her unannounced guest who took a particular pleasure in keeping her on her toes.

Mikel had slipped into her private study through one of the many secret passageways cut into the Citadel. That fact wasn't as bothersome as the fact that it was a passageway that she wasn't aware of.

She would remedy that lack of knowledge when it was time for him to go. Now that he was finally here, however, they had business to attend to. She nodded toward the seat on the other side of her desk.

"Doing what, Queen Dengannon?" Mikel asked as he sat

down, clasping his hands in front of him, his expression one of wide-eyed innocence.

"You know quite well of what I'm speaking."

"I was simply responding to your request that we meet," Mikel explained with half a shrug. "I assumed that whatever you wanted to discuss was urgent. So I came as soon as I could."

"You're welcome to enter via the main gates, Mikel. In fact, I would prefer it." She filled her tone with dissatisfaction, even though she knew as she did so that it was wasted effort. Mikel didn't function like anyone else she worked with. He rarely demonstrated respect for her authority unless the situation demanded it. Not if she demanded it. "We've talked about this. More than once."

"It's a hard habit to break," he replied. "Besides, meeting with you privately at this hour makes it easier for me to conduct the business we have between us. You as well, I imagine. There are enough rumors floating about the Citadel and throughout the Crux as it is."

"That may be so, but you said you came here because you believed it was urgent." Drin leaned back into her chair. Trying to imbue a gravitas beyond her years into her posture, expression, and voice, she saw by the glint in Mikel's eye that either he missed her effort entirely or didn't care. Likely the latter based on his small smile. So infuriating. Yet so ...

"I did. I came as quickly as I could."

His comment pulled her from the road her mind had begun to travel upon. "I sent my summons to you first thing this morning." Drin leaned forward, feeling edgy, wanting to move, yet trying not to give in to that urge. She placed her forearms on the desk, seeking to apply some pressure with her hard gaze and only earning a broader, curious smile in return.

"Yes, Queen Dengannon. Unfortunately, our business isn't the only business that I needed to attend to today."

Mikel offered no further explanation. Drin's hard gaze

shifted from a frown to the beginnings of a scowl. What business could Mikel have that was more important than the business with her? She restrained herself from asking that question, doubting that he would answer and not wanting to appear petulant.

"Most any other loyal resident of the Crux would respond to their Queen's summons in an instant. Without thought. Without hesitation. They would push everything else to the side."

"Of course they would, Queen Dengannon." Mikel leaned forward in his chair, placing his arms on his thighs, his right hand rubbing gently at his aching knee. "But I am not like most any other resident of the Crux."

"No, you're not, are you?" Drin admitted, eyes narrowing. The man who had become her closest ally was still a mystery to her in many ways. And she couldn't help but notice how he failed to remind her of his loyalty. Definitely not an oversight on his part. She was sure of that. Because whatever Mikel did or said, or in this case didn't say, was done for a reason. Always. His mind more calculating than most.

"If I was, I doubt that I would be of much use to you."

"In that you're probably right," Drin admitted reluctantly, sighing her displeasure.

Mikel smiled then. A real smile. A warm smile. Despite the table between them, thanks to his great size his nose was only a few knuckles away from hers. Memories of their time after crossing the Trench invaded her thoughts.

Drin pushed those thoughts out of her mind as swiftly as they came to her, not wanting them to stick. Not then. "Since you prefer to visit me in the dark of night, and since we are alone, do you not remember that you may call me as you did before I assumed the throne?"

"I do recall that, Queen Dengannon."

"And yet you persist with the formality."

"I do."

"Why is that?" Drin shouldn't be enjoying the dialogue between them. She should have been irritated with the King of the Underworld. More than irritated. But she wasn't. Although she would never reveal that to him.

"Because as you've said many times before, I have a difficult nature. A friend even describes it as obstreperous."

Drin laughed. Pulling back as she did so, she breathed a little easier now that there was some more distance between her and Mikel. The warmth that had been rising within her bringing a flush to her cheeks that she hoped he couldn't see in the lamplight.

"You're incorrigible."

"I am, Queen Dengannon. Thank you for noticing."

Drin bit her lip, refusing to laugh again.

Maybe this was what had caught her from the very beginning. This streak within him.

An insolence, though she didn't believe that was the right term. Obstinance, perhaps?

Clearly it had served him well. He could not have achieved his standing on the Crux and on the Tor without it.

Moreover, this aspect of his personality demonstrated a playfulness that no one would expect from a man who ruled the shadows of two Kingdoms with an iron hand. A man who had proven time and time again that he would do whatever was required to protect his interests and the people he was interested in. People like her.

So there was little point in trying to change him. And she really didn't want to.

He was too used to working in the shadows. And there was really no reason to take him to task since it was his skill at navigating the darker side of the world with a deft and steely grace that she relied on the most.

Yet what was it that she really wanted from him? Beyond the obvious, of course.

Yes, he had proven to be her staunchest ally when he didn't have to be. He could have allowed her fate to play out without involving himself. The risk associated with helping her was immense.

But he had involved himself. Several times. Whenever required. Putting what he had built at peril because of her. For her.

That suggested a possibility that teased the very edge of her thoughts. In part because of their engagement during her escape from the Tor. What at the time she had put down to the stress of returning to the Crux safely. Yet since then she had wondered if there was more to it than just that.

Thoughts that at that very moment offered little value to the conversation they needed to have.

"You're lucky that you're of use to me."

"Indeed I am lucky, Queen Dengannon."

"Enough, Mikel," Drin ordered. They needed to have a serious conversation. They couldn't do that when they were dancing around one another with words ... and in other ways. "There is business to discuss."

"When is there not, Queen Dengannon?" Mikel offered her an amiable smile, using that to hide what was churning within him. Thoughts and prospects that both appealed to and frightened him.

She was right. There was business to discuss. Yet there was a part of him that wanted to discuss another matter. Because even with all that was in play, Mikel was spending more time than he believed healthy thinking about Celindria Dengannon.

Not as the Queen of the Crux. Rather as something more. Or less. He wasn't entirely sure how to put it, even only to himself.

Though he could say with complete honesty that the

Queen of the Crux confused him, which he found more than just a little unsettling. Usually he could read a person and their intentions in a single glance. When it came to the Queen, however, he couldn't see all that he should be able to see. Perhaps it was because when he looked upon her now he felt a stirring within him that he thought had died long ago.

"I heard there was a problem with one of Hanover's riverboats."

"Yes, quite unfortunate." Mikel leaned back into his chair, turning his thoughts to what he assumed was the reason she had summoned him. "Attacked along the river only a few leagues before the Churn. Shocking."

"Very bold," Drin said, her eyes never leaving Mikel's. She searched for any hint, any break in his countenance, that would reveal what she wanted to know. But nothing. His expression dispassionate and discreet just as usual.

"How many lives were lost?" she asked.

"None that I'm aware of," Mikel shrugged, as if he had little interest in the incident that was the talk of the Crux. "Once the cargo was taken, the boat, its crew, and Hanover's soldiers were released without a drop of blood spilled."

"Do you have any idea who could have conducted such an outrageous hijacking? From what little I've heard, the raiders flew out of the dark."

"I do, Queen Dengannon."

Drin waited. Then waited some more. Still seeking that break in his armor Drin studied Mikel, who offered her nothing more than that smile of his that could be interpreted in a multitude of ways. "You won't share who that might be?"

Mikel shook his head. "No, Queen Dengannon."

She could have made him answer. At least she thought she could. She hoped she could. Though she chose not to test that hope. Not really needing an answer to her question, because she already knew the answer. Or so she believed.

"Very unfortunate," Drin mused, not missing the spark in Mikel's eye.

"Very unfortunate indeed," he agreed.

"Any idea what was on the riverboat?" She leaned forward again, tilting her head as she did when she believed that she was close to gaining the truth. Wondering if the look she gave him now, a mix of curiosity and another emotion, might cause him to slip up. "And why that boat out of all the boats traveling the river?" She knew the answer to her question, at least in part. She wanted to see just how much Mikel was willing to give her.

It turned out to be very little, Mikel shaking his head while he replied. "I was told that whatever was on the ship will never be seen again. At least in its current form."

"Is that so?"

"It is."

Drin believed him in that respect. Not entirely, of course. He was holding back a good chunk of information. She had little desire to parse his words, however, understanding that it would only lead down a rabbit hole. She also had little desire to press. At least too hard. "You're not keeping anything from me, are you, Mikel?"

"Nothing of consequence," he offered with a shrug, his expression one of cool disinterest.

"You're really not going to tell me?"

"We discussed this before, Queen Dengannon. You said that it was better if you didn't know all that was going on."

"Of all the things that I've said, that's what you decided to listen to?" Drin shook her head in mild disbelief, her voice rising.

"It was, Queen Dengannon."

"Would you stop with the Queen Dengannon?" she growled. "We've been over this before. When we're alone you can call me Drin."

"Yes, Queen Dengannon."

"Mikel …"

"Sorry, couldn't resist." Mikel raised his hands as way of an apology. It had been a long few days, and he had just returned to the Crux early that morning after his late-night adventure along the river. He leaned forward then, done having his fun. Thoughts of his bed beginning to dominate, they forced him to concentrate all the more, because he was beginning to imagine being in bed with … He shook his head to clear it. "On what foundation are the First Families built?"

Drin's initial response that came to mind was history. She didn't offer it, however, remembering Mikel's perspective on the value of history for maintaining a great house's claim for power and legitimacy. To his way of thinking, the variables were simpler and much more tangible. And, in all honesty, she couldn't disagree with him. "Blades and gold."

Mikel nodded approvingly. "Exactly. I can't do anything about the blades right now."

"So you're going after his money." It was Drin's turn to nod approvingly.

"He doesn't have any money," Mikel corrected.

"What do you mean?"

"Lucius Hanover desperately wants your throne. So much so that he spent most of his family's fortune to claim the Crux for his own. Yet, despite his recent failures and his swiftly dwindling coffers, still he persists."

Drin nodded, understanding coming to her. She wasn't the least bit surprised, well aware of Lucius' desire to sit where she did now. "Promises for loans."

"Exactly so. In fact, not surprisingly, so many loans that he's mortgaging the future of his House on a dream."

"Others have done the same."

"They have," Mikel agreed, "and few of those Houses remain."

Drin scrunched up her lips then offered Mikel a raised

eyebrow. "You're trying to ensure that happens to House Hanover."

"And why not? House Hanover is the cause of most of your problems on the Crux. I can't think of a nicer fellow than Lucius Hanover who deserves such a fate."

"I have no cause to argue with you, Mikel."

"That's very kind of you." Mikel offered her a grin that gained a snort of laughter.

"What have you done, Mikel?" She could tell by the spark in his eye that he was quite pleased with some of his recent actions.

"Taken advantage of some unique opportunities. That's all."

"Mikel ..." Drin prodded.

Despite the flintiness of her voice, he couldn't be moved from his reticence. "Hanover is in a great deal of debt."

"You're buying up that debt."

Mikel smiled, fully expecting her to figure it out. "For a steal."

"Yet as you say still Hanover persists. He still has his family Guard. I'm assuming he's paying his soldiers somehow."

Mikel nodded. "Some of the First Families were helping him."

"Were?"

"They thought better of their support," Mikel explained with a shrug. "They've since broken ties."

Drin leaned forward. More than curious. Slightly concerned as well. Having first-hand experience in just how ruthless Mikel could be when the situation demanded such ruthlessness. "What did you do?"

"This and that."

"This and that?" Drin lifted an eyebrow, her way of pressing for more detail.

"This and that," Mikel confirmed.

"Mikel, you are really testing my ..."

"I did what was necessary to cut off those options for your betrothed. In truth, it wasn't all that difficult."

"Lucius Hanover is not my betrothed." Drin's voice was hard and cold, insulted by the claim despite it not being too far from the truth. Or rather what could have been the truth if Mikel hadn't intervened.

"Former betrothed," Mikel corrected. "Regardless, it didn't take much. The First Families may not support you entirely. Some may never support you. Not all of them. But I can guarantee that they will not support Hanover. Never again."

"That's quite a statement." Drin couldn't prevent the small smile of pleasure from curling her lips, so she didn't bother to try.

"Not a statement. A promise." Mikel leaned forward, right hand massaging his injured knee and leg. "The First Families will not participate in a fight for the Crown so long as you sit upon it."

"So I remain a target," Drin groused.

"You will always be a target. You knew that as soon as your father declared you his heir." Mikel didn't have time for Drin to feel sorry for herself.

Nodding in acknowledgement of Mikel's gentle reprimand, she picked up the thread that had been twisting free from all the rest. "If the First Families have cut off their support, then where is Hanover getting his funds?"

"You already know the answer to that." Mikel waited, anticipating that it wouldn't take long.

Drin nodded. She did know. "Hanover still trusts Dragoran to give him the throne? If he does, he's a fool. Dragoran wants the throne for himself. Whether I'm still a part of the package after what happened is of little concern to him."

"Desperation can make fools of the wisest of people. And I can tell you straight out that Lucius Hanover is not wise and never will be."

"On that we agree." Drin leaned in toward Mikel again. Their faces were no more than the span of a hand away from the other, Drin catching the spark in the back of his eyes. "You're doing more than cutting off Lucius' money."

"What are you accusing me of now?" Mikel's grin broadened, clearly enjoying the give and take between them. The close proximity as well.

"You're sending a message."

"Of a sort," Mikel admitted.

"You risk a great deal."

"We both do. Nevertheless, I believe that the risk is worth it."

"And you have nothing to fear because Dragoran already has his eyes on you."

Mikel nodded. "Just as he has his eyes on you."

"You're going all in," Drin nodded, appreciating his moxie.

"I've been all in since I found you in the Frozen Waste." Mikel pulled back slightly, not planning on saying out loud what he was thinking. A flush of heat rushed through him when he did. Unfortunately, he couldn't move back any farther even though he wanted to, Drin's eyes holding him in place.

When he felt the soft touch of her fingers on his face, Mikel was lost, though he didn't mind in the least. Leaning farther forward, he saw nothing except for Drin's eyes.

Drin allowed the heat that had been smoldering within her to intensify. To push her down the path that she had been trying to avoid.

Mikel was the wrong choice for her. She was the queen. Since she was a young child she had in her mind a vision of what her love would look like. And it was more Lucius Hanover – handsome, charming – than the hulking King of the Underworld.

Yet she couldn't deny her attraction despite Mikel being

who he was. Doing what he did. Despite him being many things that never appealed to her until …

None of that mattered. Drin pulled Mikel toward her. Her lips touched his and a spark shot between them. Both chose to lose themselves in the moment rather than to think or question.

How long they remained that way, Drin couldn't recall.

"We should get back to business," Drin urged, though she couldn't seem to wipe the smile from her face and didn't bother to try.

Mikel didn't reply right away. His thoughts elsewhere. Never believing that …

He shook his head. It didn't matter what he believed or what he thought or what he wanted. All that mattered was what was. Best to focus on that. "Hanover will be back on the Crux soon."

"You're certain?"

"I am," Mikel confirmed with a sharp nod. "And he'll be even more desperate and reckless now that we've cut off his access to the gold he requires."

"That only makes sense," Drin agreed. "He'll feel the pressure of Dragoran on his back. He'll continue with his plans, it will simply be more of a struggle for him."

"He won't stop. You're right. And you understand that he will do anything to take the throne from you? Even if he's only keeping it warm for Dragoran."

"I do."

"You don't seem all that concerned about it."

"Need I be?" Drin asked, not giving Mikel the chance to answer her question. She had faith in her Broken Bear. "Do you have something in mind for when Hanover makes his play?"

"I do," Mikel confirmed.

"Do I need to know about it?"

Mikel leaned back into his chair, his smile growing wider. "Not yet."

## 5

## TOO PRETTY

"Couldn't you just create one of these in the Citadel?" Lucius Hanover grouched. "It would make what I need to do a great deal easier."

Assindra released her hold on the Talent. The streams of energy, what had once been a pure white when she was younger yet were now an oily black, faded then disappeared entirely.

He was right. Traveling by portal certainly was easier. In this instance allowing them to avoid the Trench and the Splintered Bridge, which had become a battleground.

"I could, but it's not a question of what I can do," Assindra stated with a cool disinterest. "It's a question of what I should do."

She ignored the look of confusion Lucius gave her, forcing him to follow her as she strode out onto the balcony on the highest level of the mansion she had acquired just below the Royal Ring in Innsbruck. Placing her hands on the rail, she gazed out upon the city.

It appeared to be just like any other day. The sun was beginning to rise. The mouthwatering smells from the bakeries drifted on the gentle breeze. The Churn along the rim of the island roared in the background.

Yet the day was anything but ordinary. A new beginning of a sort. An ending as well. Of that she was certain. So long as all went to plan.

"Speak plainly," Lucius demanded. The thought of slipping through a magical portal and then slipping a knife into the Queen's back held a certain appeal to him. The irony too rich to ignore and the easiest way for him to gain what he most desired.

Assindra decided to respond, though her eyes darkened as she did so. Her temper was beginning to bubble. She didn't have time for this pup playing at lord. There was work to be done. "As you know, Celindria Dengannon is a Magus. She would sense the portal in the Citadel. The instant we stepped through, soldiers would be waiting."

"What does that matter?" Lucius scoffed. "Couldn't you defeat Celindria with the power you control?"

"Of course I could," Assindra stated in a voice as hard as iron, insulted by any thought to the contrary. "I doubt it would be a quick victory, however. She is inexperienced but she is strong. And even though the outcome of that duel is predetermined, steel can kill me just as well as it can kill you. Therefore, best to avoid that risk since it's a risk we do not have to take."

She turned her simmering eyes toward the Lord of House Hanover. A House that had fallen on hard times under Lucius' stewardship. His blind ambition and poor decision-making the cause, though he certainly wouldn't acknowledge that truth.

Yet still there was a role for him to play. The question was, could he do what was required of him? Could he be trusted?

Regarding the latter, Assindra was certain the answer was no. Trusting a man who allowed his ego to rule him could lead only to disaster. In terms of the former, whether he could do as was required of him, that was still up for debate. And there was but one way to discover the answer.

Assindra caught his eyes with her own. Giving him a questioning look, she measured him. Not entirely convinced by what she weighed within him. She wondered why the creature who played at being Malor Dragoran still found this greedy pup useful.

Nevertheless, there was nothing for it. She was no longer a partner to Malor Dragoran. She was a servant. And despite how much her new circumstances chafed, she had no desire to challenge him. Not with the outcome of any conflict between them foreordained.

Therefore, she refused to allow her misgivings to become more than just that, understanding the cost of doing so.

"I admit I don't know you very well, Assindra," Lucius chuckled, shaking his head in amusement, "though I thought you had more of a backbone than you ..."

Lucius' chuckle died in his throat, which was closing. Gasping for breath, body frozen, his eyes bulged and his face slowly turned red. The Lord of House Hanover desperately wanted to take a deep breath.

He couldn't.

He couldn't do anything more than wheeze and whimper.

He could see little else except for Assindra's eyes and the thin threads of black swirling around him, every so often caressing his cheeks and poking at his face. More than a warning there. A promise. And a dire one at that.

"You misunderstand your position in our arrangement, Lucius." Assindra's eyes were beyond cold. More inhuman. Completely black, irises and scleras. Churning. Her harsh gaze promised a path to the other side. "You are here to serve, and that you will do."

Lucius was desperate to defend himself. But he couldn't.

He couldn't move.

He couldn't breathe.

He could barely think.

His terror threatened to send him over the edge. His terror competing with his hate at being made to look so weak. Even more, detesting that he was so vulnerable.

"You will deal with the Queen of the Crux as you have been ordered to do. Kill her. Claim her. I care not. All that matters is that she no longer exercises the power of the throne. If that means you supplant her, so be it. Just know that if you succeed, you do not rule here. You rule for Malor Dragoran until he chooses otherwise. Is that clear?"

Lucius would have nodded his head if he could. He would have done anything to acknowledge his loyalty to the King of the Tor. More than willing to admit his weakness.

But he couldn't. He couldn't do anything other than acknowledge that partnering with Malor and his Dark Magus was a very bad yet now inescapable decision.

The threads of black played across his face now with greater frequency. And along with those threads black specks appeared at the edge of his vision, his lungs demanding the air that wouldn't come.

And then it did.

Lucius reached out a hand and caught himself before he collapsed to the floor. Gasping for breath, he savored the feel of his lungs expanding. His color returned, his mind functioning once more.

His ego damaged, and his rage at being used as a tool stronger than ever, yet smartly under control. For now.

"I will do what's required of me. Do not fear. But I warn you."

"You warn me?" Assindra's expression tightened. What little of her patience remained was balanced on a knife's edge. "You require another demonstration?"

"No, I don't," Lucius responded swiftly, "and in terms of a

warning, I don't mean it in the way that you're interpreting it." He pushed himself up so that he was standing straight again, at the same time recognizing just how precarious his position was. How badly he had misjudged the Magus. She had released her hold on him, yet still sparks of black flashed and spun around her palms, her anger and eagerness to be rid of him plain.

"Explain," she ordered.

"I will do as Malor requires. One way or another Celindria will no longer be a threat to us. However, my ability to complete this task is doomed to fail if the King of the Underworld keeps cutting into me."

Assindra did not respond right away, allowing her thoughts to return to that first meeting with the thief she had hired to claim the Blade of Light. The thief who had stolen the artifact yet kept it for himself, failing to meet the requirements of their bargain. The thief who was so much more than a thief. The thief who dredged up memories that she preferred would remain buried.

"Leave the King of the Underworld to me," Assindra instructed ever so quietly. The feeling of loss and defeat that had settled in her stomach during her encounter with Malor soon was replaced by a new purpose. A hope that she had never expected to feel again. "I will deal with him."

"How do I know that you will do as you say?"

All emotion drained from Assindra's countenance at the foolish challenge. Her anger blazed brightly once again. The fear and rage she had experienced while in the presence of Malor Dragoran ready to be released on the sap standing before her. The only reason he remained alive was the fact that she exercised an iron grip on the potent magic within her that begged to be liberated.

"You presume too much, Lucius Hanover. You believe you are the head of a great House."

"I am the head of a great House," he stated in a voice that cracked at the very end, finally picking up on the Magus' mood and state of mind. He realized that now was not the time to push and that perhaps he had reached this conclusion much too late.

"You were the head of a great House. A House that is crumbling. Because of you." She stepped close to him, clearly unconcerned that his right hand rested on the hilt of his dagger. "Do as you are required to do, and I will do as I am required. Have no doubt of that."

"You can say what you ..."

Assindra was just a breath away from making use of the Curse again. The sparks of black were dancing across her palms with a greater violence, mimicking her mood. "What I say is what will be. Now go before I decide to deal with you as you deserve to be treated for your insults."

Lucius reached up with his free hand, running his fingers across his neck. Feeling his throat begin to tighten again, strands of black slid across his upper body.

A reminder.

And a guarantee. That knowledge made him want to be anywhere else but there, so he stomped away as swiftly as he could while still maintaining what little dignity remained to him.

"Do you trust him?" Assindra asked the darkness after Lucius was gone.

"I don't trust anyone as pretty as he is," Liria said, stepping out of the shadows that draped the corner of the balcony.

"A good decision on your part." Assindra studied Liria for a time, curious to see if she would wilt like so many others, including Lucius Hanover, had under her gaze. She didn't. A good sign. Though not a sure sign. "Can I trust you?"

Liria shrugged, almost as if she expected the question. "You know the answer to that already."

Assindra nodded sagely. Then she smiled. "You heard what Hanover is supposed to do."

"I did."

"Your task is more of a challenge."

"Why am I not surprised?"

"You will kill the King of the Underworld for me."

"The same task as before?" Liria grunted.

"You are reluctant?" Assindra murmured quietly. Her primary assassin had failed to complete this task. Several times, in fact. She had assumed that Liria would welcome this chance to make amends. To wipe this stain of failure from her conscience. But perhaps she had misjudged. "You still care for him."

Liria shrugged. "He is not much to look at but he has other qualities that you might find attractive."

"Does he?"

"He does," Liria argued quietly but insistently. "Perhaps instead of killing him right from the start, I should try to turn him toward our cause. Would that not serve *your* purposes?"

Assindra's lips curled briefly, not missing what her assassin was really telling her. Then she laughed softly. Peculiar how the world worked. Liria's thoughts mirrored her own. Up to a point. "If you think you can turn him you're a fool. No better than a lovesick girl. The King of the Underworld is many things, but I doubt that he will turn."

"We'll never know if we don't try."

"He risked his life to save the Queen of the Crux. Whatever he was when he was with you, he's not that any longer. He has moved on, and to a queen no less. I suggest you move on as well. He is no longer yours. He belongs to someone else."

That possible truth didn't sit well with Liria. And she was about to argue further, then decided against that course of action. Not wanting to experience what Lucius Hanover had, she nodded, accepting her assignment, then headed for the exit.

"Although I might offer a slightly different way of looking at the task assigned to you," Assindra murmured softly.

Her words stopped Liria in an instant. "What way would that be?"

"You were dead though not really dead."

"Not by choice," Liria replied. "By necessity."

"Just so." Assindra's voice became more of a purr, her mind finally working again now that she was free of Malor Dragoran's hypnotic presence. "Perhaps the same can be done for the King of the Underworld. Perhaps he could be dead, though not dead."

Liria didn't reply. She didn't turn around. All she did was offer a slight nod before gliding off the balcony and into the shadows of the rooms beyond.

Assindra watched her go then turned back toward the Crux and stared off into space. Thinking for a time, she searched for any hint of the maternal instinct that Malor had referenced. Not surprisingly, she was unable to find the tiniest trace.

She believed that was a good thing, because it would only get in the way of what she needed to do.

However, that didn't mean she couldn't still try to use the connection she had with the King of the Underworld to her advantage.

Because he could indeed be the key.

He could be what she needed to free herself from the chains Malor Dragoran had wrapped around her.

**6**

## BEWARE THE FIRE

Henri Dengannon nodded to every soldier he passed, stopping to speak with as many as he could. Asking about their families. Asking about them.

He knew all of them, having learned that to earn the trust of the men and women who fought for him, they needed to trust him as well. That meant demonstrating that he cared about them and what they cared about.

An absolutely essential requirement as he made his way farther along the Splintered Bridge toward the center that marked the boundary between the Kingdom of the Crux and the Kingdom of the Tor. For without that trust, without that belief, none of them had any hope of surviving the onslaught the King of the Tor was about to unleash upon them.

The forces of Malor Dragoran continued to push, hunting for the weakness that would allow them to cross to the western side of the Trench and place Innsbruck under siege.

Henri and the soldiers with him were all that stood in their way. Despite being lesser in number, their defense held. Their success a combination of a stubborn determination, skilled leadership, and the tools gifted to them by a young man who viewed the fighting along the mile-long expanse that spanned the Trench as an opportunity to test his ideas and expand his knowledge.

"How is Ethyln, Magnus? Last I heard she was preparing for the birth of your third child."

"She is well, Battle Lord," Magnus beamed. The Sergeant, standing guard near the mobile wall that stretched across the bridge from north to south, was pleased that his commander recalled such a detail while having to juggle so many other demands.

"No complications, I hope."

"None, Battle Lord. She is due to give birth in a few weeks. The physick has prescribed bedrest until then."

"And how is that going with Ragnar and Rollo so full of energy?"

Magnus snorted out a laugh, chuckling as he thought about his children. Doubly pleased that the Battle Lord remembered so much about his family. "As well as can be expected. Those two younglings have more energy than they deserve. When I'm home, I can barely keep up with them."

"They must take after their father."

"In that you're correct, Battle Lord," Magnus nodded appreciatively. "I was much like them when I was a child."

"Then I truly feel for Ethyln. Please give her my best next time you see her."

"I will, Battle Lord," Magnus promised.

"And I take it that the unease you're feeling isn't coming from what's going on back home." Henri stepped in closer to Magnus, he leaned his hands against the low parapet that lined the southern side of the bridge. During the day, he would have seen the dozens of rocky spikes that rose from the floor of the Trench and peeked through the grey clouds that blanketed the canyon.

"You feel it as well, Battle Lord?" Crow's feet formed around Magnus' eyes, his voice quieter than before.

"I do," Henri replied with a sigh. "Any ideas as to the cause, Magnus?"

The soldier shook his head. "No, it's just as you said. It doesn't feel right. It's as if we're waiting for something to happen and whatever that is, it isn't going to be good. That's the only way I can describe it."

"Is that why you doubled the guard, Magnus?"

"I should have asked you, Battle Lord."

"You did the right thing, Magnus. I prefer that the soldiers fighting with me make their own decisions. Follow their own instincts."

The Sergeant nodded. "I might not be able to explain this feeling of mine, but I learned long ago to heed it."

"Good man," Henri confirmed. "Nothing from the scouts?"

Magnus shook his head, his frown deepening. "Nothing reported by those who have returned. One is missing."

"Missing?"

"She should have reported back a quarter hour ago."

"That's not very long of a delay."

"It's not. And usually I wouldn't be worried. But ..."

Henri nodded, understanding. "This feeling of yours that I feel as well."

He pondered the information Magnus provided. Scouts returned when they could or when they had to. They didn't adhere to a timetable.

Yet this scout's disappearance made the hair on the back of his neck stand straight. An alarming premonition.

Just like Magnus, he trusted feelings such as the one he was experiencing now. As it sharpened, a sense of dread settled in the pit of his stomach.

The last few weeks Tor soldiers had attacked or harassed his soldiers from a distance, enjoying little success thanks to the barriers constructed to thwart their efforts. The Zaroi, nasty creatures who nested beneath and often within the large holes of the crumbling Splintered Bridge, had been active as well. Slinking out as soon as darkness fell with the goal of claiming an easy meal.

But not tonight.

What was different about this night compared to all the others he had stood in this very same spot thinking about how to keep the Crux free from the grip of Malor Dragoran?

It was this question that added to Henri's already significant pile of worries.

Although the evening was much like any other, a breeze gusting across the bridge from north to south, the moon shining so brightly that there was little need for lanterns in order to pierce the dark, it didn't feel right. Just as Magnus said. Just as Henri's own instincts were telling him.

It was too quiet.

And there wasn't a hint of movement from the other side of the barrier that extended across the width of the bridge. The Tor soldiers had pulled back to their primary outpost at the eastern edge of the Trench.

More perplexing, the Zaroi kept to their lairs rather than trying to pluck an unsuspecting soldier for a meal.

Strange.

Concerning.

There was some stratagem in play. Henri was certain of that.

But what could it be that was ...

Henri tilted an ear over the side of the bridge.

Barely audible because of the gusting wind, yet still he could hear it.

A scraping sound.

Much like steel digging into stone.

Or claw.

His fears rising, that ball of dread growing, Henri looked warily over the side of the bridge, relying on the light of the moon as he didn't want to reveal his location by using a lantern.

He could see very little. The moonlight struggled against the shadows draping the southern side of the bridge in an impenetrable darkness.

Except for one anomaly.

A pair of golden eyes were moving toward him from below the span.

And then a few more.

And a few more after that.

Henri understood now why all was quiet. Why even the Zaroi had not made an appearance that night.

A deadlier predator had invaded the Zaroi's territory.

"Soldiers of the Crux, to your strongholds! We are under attack!"

"Magnus, at your back!"

Henri couldn't get to him in time. He had his own combat to fight. Slashing with his sword at the claws grasping for the top of the parapet, he missed one, the attacker pulling back just in time. Though the monster wasn't fast enough to avoid losing several digits from his other claw. The resulting howl was music to Henri's ears.

The golden-eyed assailant fell away from the parapet. His section of the tower clear for the moment, Henri turned, planning to go to the aid of his Sergeant.

He sighed with relief. Magnus had heard him. The soon-to-be-father fought with a wild ferocity as he swept that side of the stronghold clear with a long pike, the steel blade stained by the blood it had claimed gleaming a dark red in the moonlight.

Once again Henri offered silent thanks to the young

inventor who Mikel had sent his way. He had no doubt as to where he and his soldiers would be if not for Leonardo's unique way of addressing the challenges Henri threw at him. The circumstances atop the Splintered Bridge difficult but not dire. Not yet.

Recognizing the primary danger presented by the soldiers of the Tor -- their greater number, Henri sought to mitigate that advantage by making use of the limitations presented by the dimensions of the span that connected the Kingdom of the Tor to the Kingdom of the Crux.

Henri was quite familiar with the brochs the Highlanders had used hundreds of years before to defend against the Wraiths who descended upon them with the coming of the Murk. That was, of course, until Jakob Kestrel gave the Highlanders the ability to fight in the grasping grey and push the Wraiths back to the north.

Although the Wraiths no longer threatened the Highlands, which were situated far to the south of the Crux, when Henri was first named the Battle Lord of his homeland, he had traveled through the Highlands and other Realms in search of ideas that could prove useful to the daunting responsibility he had assumed at his brother's request.

The strongholds that dotted the Crux side of the Splintered Bridge were modeled after the Highlanders' brochs. Smaller in size, they were only thirty feet in height with no more than ten men able to fight from the battlements at one time. A steel trap door on the roof was the only means of entering.

Much like the Highlanders in their battle against the Wraiths, the soldiers of the Crux valued these smaller brochs. The strongholds granted Henri and his soldiers the chance to hold their ground and negated to a large extent the advantages enjoyed by their adversaries.

And these new enemies who emerged from the shadows beneath the Splintered Bridge were learning just how difficult it was to seize a stone tower. Although Henri believed that it was only a matter of time before that happened.

Because on this night the soldiers of the Tor remained on their side of the bridge. Not bothering to attack. Not needing to attack. Instead, they waited to claim the bridge when all was said and done as a more lethal and proficient enemy took their place.

The soldiers of the Ten Thousand.

Fighters of yore, what Henri had once believed were no more than remnants of history now come back to life.

Hard to believe. Yet he did.

Seeing those golden eyes he couldn't doubt what he and his soldiers fought against.

His belief was confirmed as he watched with a rising apprehension this new enemy climb along the outside of the Splintered Bridge from the eastern side of the Trench, swarming toward them, emerging in front, behind, and from both sides to fit Henri and his Crux soldiers neatly into a noose.

As they charged the brochs, the servants of the Dread shifted.

Their bodies broke apart and reformed, revealing them to be a mix of animal and man.

The merger gave these unnatural creations greater strength. Greater speed. Greater agility. Greater ferocity.

Weres.

The foot soldiers of the Dread.

Monsters from the past thought lost to history.

Reminders of what could occur when the conceit of one man was allowed to reign.

After they took their unnatural forms, the Weres still wore their leather armor. They still carried their preferred weapons, whether short sword, battle axe, or shortened spear.

Yet none looked like the men they had been just seconds before.

Some resembled wolves. Others appeared as leopards. A few tigers. Some panthers. Bears. Lions. Whatever their master had bred them with while applying his tainted magic.

The soldiers of the Ten Thousand fought with fang, claw, and blade, seeking to crush the resistance offered by the soldiers of the Crux with a fast and devastating blow.

If not for the strongholds, they would have succeeded.

Henri slashed with his long sword, scraping the steel across the stone of the parapet. The Were he was fighting slid back down the wall, avoiding the blade. But, claws dug into the stone, the monster was back up the parapet just as fast, swiping at Henri with a free claw.

Henri dodged backward, though not too far, refusing to give too much ground. If he did, the Were would gain the top of the tower, and once that happened, the battle atop the stronghold would be lost.

Despite his initial failure, the Were -- half man, half wolf -- howled in anticipation of his victory, the creature launching itself into the air, claw and battle axe cutting down toward Henri.

Having nowhere to go, the soldiers with him fighting their own desperate combats to prevent the Weres from claiming the stronghold, Henri did the only thing that he believed didn't ensure his death.

He rushed forward, swinging with his sword as if he was chopping wood. Though, in this case, instead of biting into a log, his sharp steel cut deep into the Were's groin.

The monster's howl changed mid-cry from one of certain victory to a devastating agony.

Henri forgotten, the Were crashed to the roof, a pool of blood forming around the beast. The rage of the battle still upon him, the soldier of the Ten Thousand tried to push himself back to his feet despite his grievous wound.

The Were was too slow, Henri already on him. The Battle

Lord plunged the tip of his sword through the back of the Were's neck.

Leaving the body in his wake, Henri returned to the parapet and surveyed the clash atop the stronghold once he confirmed that his position was momentarily clear.

Magnus and the other soldiers were performing with a practiced efficiency. Just as he knew that they would. Keeping the Werebeasts of the Ten Thousand back from the parapet, the Crux soldiers prevented their attackers from claiming a foothold. Only the beast Henri dispatched had fought his way past the battlements.

Yet despite their success, despite the fact that the Weres had yet to conquer a stronghold, Henri recognized that he and his soldiers swam in deep water that would soon rise and drown them.

It was only a matter of time before the Weres gained the upper hand. More of the beasts were climbing up onto the Splintered Bridge to join the fight. The compact size of the strongholds aided the defenders, as only so many Weres could attack at one time. Nevertheless, all it would take for the Weres to gain the opening they desired was a single break in the line. And it could be something as simple as a defender slipping in a pool of blood.

Before that happened, Henri needed to change the tenor of the battle.

Glancing back over his shoulder toward the Crux side of the bridge, an idea came to mind. The Weres swarming the span had not yet advanced toward the bulwark built across the bridge where it connected to the Trench on the western side. That was a tactical error that Henri hoped to play upon.

"Magnus, raise the red flag!"

Magnus hesitated for just a second, understanding what that meant. Still, he obeyed. Trusting his commander, he gained faith from the Battle Lord's hard but certain gaze.

Magnus lifted the red flag, waving it through the air a few times before locking it into place atop the tower. The flag unmistakable in the bright moonlight.

Henri didn't know if what he had in mind would work, but he believed that it was the only move they could make that offered them any chance of surviving this attack.

Assuming, of course, that Leonardo was paying attention.

"Just a little longer, lads and lasses! Just a little longer!"

Henri glided around the top of the tower, long sword a blur as he aided the soldiers fighting with him. The Weres were dangerously fast. Yet not so fast as to be able to avoid a steel blade coming at them from the blind side.

Even so, killing the beasts proved to be a challenge. Their hides resisted all but the truest of strikes. Thus, Henri's focus on keeping the Weres back. He didn't need to kill them. He just needed to keep them fighting a little while longer.

Or so he hoped.

The soldiers of the Crux understood the grim nature of their dilemma and battled with a ferocious energy, burying their fears as men bred with wolves, bears, leopards, and more predators sought to claim a clawhold atop the tower.

More of the Weres were scaling the side of his tower just as was happening to the other strongholds. Some of the beasts required only a single leap to bring them just a claw away from grasping the top of the parapet and hauling themselves over the lip.

Leonardo had to have seen the red flag. He had to. And he knew what to do when he did. He couldn't hesitate. He needed to act. Now. That's what he and Henri had discussed. An immediate response once the red flag was raised.

"Battle Lord!" Magnus pointed back toward the bulwark guarding the far side of the bridge.

Henri looked over his shoulder. Ten sparks of fire burned brightly along the length of the wall, growing larger as he observed them.

"Down into the broch!" Henri roared, pushing men and women in front of him. Magnus used his pike to sweep the parapet clean if only for a few seconds, the roars and howls from below the battlements confirming that the next attack was just moments away. Henri hoped that the soldiers atop the other strongholds acted as swiftly as he and his fighters did. While he jumped through the trapdoor, he issued his next order. "Close the hatch!"

Magnus didn't bother to untie the rope holding the trapdoor open. He cut it with the dagger he pulled from the sheath on his hip. And just in time.

A Were matched with a bear lunged for the opening, claws reaching for him, the heavy steel slamming shut before the beast could tear into his flesh. The keen edges of the plate cutting through the beast's front claw, five razor-sharp digits dropped into the tower with them.

When Henri heard the loud click signifying that the trap door was locked, the Weres unable to break through, he scrambled over to the slits carved into the stone. Usually, they were used by the archers when the Tor soldiers or Zaroi attacked during the night. Now, they offered him the perfect vantage point.

He didn't have long to wait.

Ten long streams of fire shot across the bridge, arcing down from atop the bulwark.

Caught by surprise, several dozen Weres who failed to escape over the sides of the bridge were burned alive as those streams of fire swept across the span, covering every inch from the movable wall that blocked access from the eastern side to the broch placed at the very center of the span. While several of those streams cleansed his stronghold, Henri closed the steel plate. The temperature within the broch rose swiftly to a stifling level, but it was nothing compared to what was happening on the outside. The shrieks of the Weres caught atop the tower could still be heard, although muffled by the stone and steel.

Another lethal success, Henri believed. This one leaving behind the sickening stench of burning pitch, leather, flesh, and hair.

Leonardo's latest invention played off the vats of boiling pitch that often were spilled from a castle's walls during an attack, the inventor creating a mechanism that shot the flammable liquid, set alight as it left the tubes, several hundred yards with good accuracy.

When the sound of the roaring flames subsided, Henri carefully opened the glowing steel plate with the glove designed solely for that purpose.

It was a gruesome sight. Charred bodies littered the bridge and the strongholds. He could only hope that none of those bodies belonged to his soldiers, all the while knowing that such a hope was unrealistic. He had seen several of his soldiers try and fail to disengage from the Weres before the streams of fire struck.

A success indeed. He couldn't deny it. Yet one with a great cost. The loss of just a single Crux soldier a dagger to his heart.

"It worked well but not well enough," Leonardo grouched. Surrounded by a troop of soldiers, he advanced out from the bulwark and joined the Battle Lord and Magnus on the scorched bridge, muttering beneath his breath the whole way.

"Not well enough?" Henri didn't understand the young

man's comment. From his perspective, this untested weapon had worked perfectly against a foe who threatened to overwhelm and slaughter the bridge's defenders. Thankfully not as many of his soldiers were caught in the cleansing as he feared.

"It needs to be more precise," Leonardo explained. "The stream was effective but didn't maintain its shape the farther we aimed up the span. I want to work on improving that. We must have pinpoint accuracy."

"I'll leave that you, my friend." Henri clapped Leonardo on the back in thanks, the inventor already heading toward the bulwark, still muttering to himself, clearly intent on addressing immediately the challenge he set for himself.

Henri watched him go. He understood Leonardo's drive for perfection, knowing as well how rarely perfection could be achieved and the potential cost when perfection was the goal.

For despite Leonardo's concern about the lack of desired precision, the dragons, as Leonardo called them, had worked. Better than anticipated in fact. So, in that respect, Henri was quite pleased.

But he was nervous as well.

The Weres added a new dimension to the battle for the Splintered Bridge.

The soldiers of the Ten Thousand, long thought lost to history, appearing now in service to the King of the Tor, chilled his blood. Because if he was right ...

"Magnus, return to the Crux and Ethyln. I don't want to see you back here until the birth of your child."

"But Battle Lord ..."

Henri cut him off. "However, before you visit with your family, find the King of the Underworld. Tell him I need him here with all possible speed."

**7**

# OFFERS AND THREATS

"How do you keep doing this, Millie?"

"Doing what?" The madame of The Silken Pleasure leaned over Mikel's shoulder as he studied the books for the last month. Her breath tickled the back of his neck. Every so often she rubbed her chest against his shoulder, hoping for a reaction yet receiving very little in return. She wasn't surprised. Nevertheless, she was undeterred. A game of sorts between them. And if it led to more she certainly wouldn't complain.

"Increasing revenue so swiftly and so consistently. You've done a remarkable job. And not just here, but the other houses as well."

Millie shrugged, then placed a hand on his other shoulder. "I've been implementing some of the ideas we discussed as well as a few of my own." She leaned closer to him, whispering into his ear while she restrained herself from taking a gentle bite. Not wanting to push too hard. "Besides, now that we're partners, I'm seeking to prove that you made the right decision."

"I know I made the right decision, Millie. I wouldn't have done the deal with you otherwise." He reached up and patted her hand on his shoulder, then pushed up from his chair, forcing her to step back. She frowned briefly, disappointed, thinking that finally she might have had a chance, then smiling again when Mikel turned to face her. "I'm impressed. I knew that you would do well. Just not so well so swiftly."

"I'm glad you're not disappointed."

"How could I be?"

"Because I'm disappointed."

"Why are you disappointed?" Mikel didn't understand. She had always run The Silken Pleasure with a valued efficiency. And upon Mikel granting her an ownership stake and an expanded responsibility within his business empire, she had made some of his most profitable businesses a great deal more profitable in a very short time.

"You know why, Mikel." Millie stepped forward, placing a hand on his chest and leaning in close so that he could see nothing else except for her eyes. "You've always known."

She anticipated how he would respond. Still, she couldn't help herself from trying. She liked Mikel. How could she not?

But there was a professional aspect to the effort she made now. How could he turn down the madame of his most profitable pleasure house? It just wasn't right.

"Millie, you know that I think you're ..."

"Beautiful, yes, I know," Millie sighed. "That I'm attractive. And that you appreciate my business acumen." She patted him on the chest, then smiled sadly, acknowledging her defeat. "I hope you understand that I had to try."

Before she stepped back, she stared into his eyes. Others described those dark orbs of his as cold and hard. With her, they typically were thoughtful, sad even. Yet now ...

This time there was more there for her to interpret. He was revealing aspects of himself that he never had before, likely doing so without even realizing it.

She glimpsed the shadows of grief still lurking in the back, and she believed that those shadows would never disappear entirely. There was something else there, however.

Millie's countenance brightened, the truth coming to her. "You've found someone."

"I'm sorry?" Mikel almost flinched at her statement.

"I can see it in your eyes. The darkness that had been there ever since I've known you has receded somewhat."

"I haven't found someone, Millie." He wasn't going to challenge her comment about the darkness within him. He couldn't argue with the truth. And he had no desire to discuss the other matter she had raised. "I haven't been looking."

Millie chuckled softly at that. "It doesn't matter whether you were looking, Mikel. It never does. It happens when it happens. It's often more fun when you find someone when you least expect it."

"Millie, I ..."

She placed her hands on his shoulders, then stood on her toes, giving him a soft kiss on the cheek. "I know that you will want to run, fearing it will only make you vulnerable, but don't do it, Mikel." Her words were sharp, as if she were scolding him because she knew him better than he knew himself. "You may not believe it, at least not yet, however I do. You are worthy of the one you have found, whomever that may be."

Mikel studied Millie, confused by her claim, even more surprised by the ardor of her conviction. How sure she was of what she said. Then he frowned. Uncomfortable. Her words brought to mind someone he was trying not to think about with everything else he was dealing with at that moment. "Why would you say such a thing?"

"Because I know you, Mikel. I've known you for a long time. You have helped me. You have helped so many others. You have created a community here on the Crux that would never have been possible without you."

"That may be, but I don't understand why that's important to what we're talking about now."

"You have done so much for so many others, and you do it because you want to and because you feel you need to. That is not a criticism, simply a fact," Millie explained when she saw how his expression changed, Mikel preparing to argue against her. "There is nothing wrong in doing something for yourself. There is nothing wrong in believing that the world might offer something more to you than it already has. Or someone. Who you lost cannot be regained, but that does not mean you don't deserve to have another chance."

Instead of disagreeing as was his first instinct, Mikel stared into Millie's eyes. Searching for any falsity. Seeing none, he nodded. What she was offering him came from her heart. "Thank you."

Millie nodded, then stepped back, giving him a final, gentle pat on the chest. "Now get out of here. I have a business to run and my partner can be quite demanding when our goals are not met."

Mikel laughed softly as he walked out of The Silken Pleasure, spending a few minutes speaking with Curtis and May, asking about their families and catching up before the establishment got busier later in the afternoon. The two very large, very intimidating men were stationed at the main door to ensure that only invited clientele were allowed to enter.

Mikel would have continued to talk with them if he had the time, but it was late morning and he still had several tasks to accomplish before returning to The Fox's Lair to meet Teddy.

Stepping into the street, he had gone no more than a hundred yards down the main boulevard when he changed his plans, cutting into an alley and then in among the warren of side streets that paralleled the road on both sides.

His other tasks would have to wait.

First, he needed to identify who was following him.

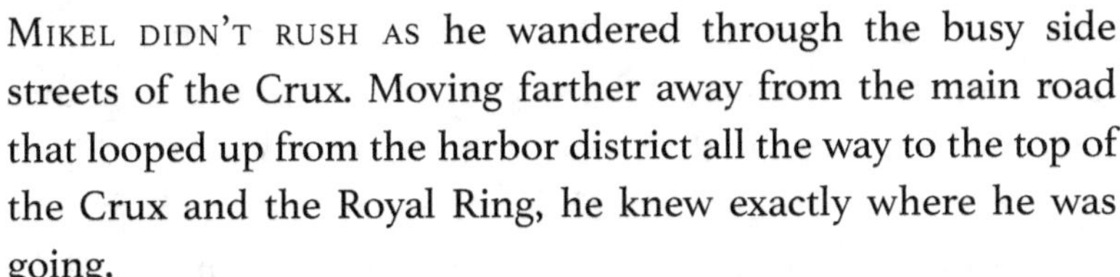

MIKEL DIDN'T RUSH AS he wandered through the busy side streets of the Crux. Moving farther away from the main road that looped up from the harbor district all the way to the top of the Crux and the Royal Ring, he knew exactly where he was going.

Never looking over his shoulder.

Never having to.

He sensed that his shadow was staying with him no matter what direction he turned.

And that didn't bother him in the least.

Turning to his right and then to his left, he chose alleys scarcely wide enough for two people to walk side by side. Mikel cut to his left again, placing his back up against the wall as he slid into the shadows of the small walled courtyard.

He didn't have long to wait.

A woman wearing a cloak that hid her face glided silently into the courtyard, coming to an abrupt stop when she felt his cold steel against her throat.

"You can't kill me, Mikel."

"Why not?" He sounded resigned more than anything else, his dagger never leaving her neck.

"You had your chance before." Careful of the blade, the woman pushed the hood of her cloak back onto her shoulders. "Several chances, in fact. Yet you've always held back."

"Mercy isn't a weakness, Liria."

If not for his blade she would have shook her head in disagreement. "It is, but it's not mercy that you're showing me."

"It isn't?" A touch of the coldness in Mikel's voice melted, a hint of curiosity taking its place.

"No, it's not." Liria's statement was strong and filled with conviction. "You still love me."

Mikel snorted and stepped away from her, needing some

space as he remembered the danger of being too close to the woman who had been more than a partner for almost five years. Too many emotions welled up within him when he could reach out and touch her. As he stepped back, he made sure that he blocked her path to the exit so that she couldn't slip by him.

"Why are you here, Liria?" Mikel believed that his former partner had died during their last job together. By his hand, in fact. That memory should have been filled with a deep sadness. Instead, it set his anger to a slow boil. It was on that job that Liria betrayed him. Yet somehow she had crawled out from beneath the Tor so that she could continue to torment him.

"The great King of the Underworld doesn't know?"

"I have a good sense of things, though I'd prefer to not waste my time asking questions that give you a chance to dissemble and deflect. Why, Liria?"

"You know why, Mikel." She offered him an impish grin, just like she had done so many times before when they were more than partners, hoping to pull him back toward those remembrances and draw a smile from him. Instead, she scowled, briefly, disappointed that his demanding expression never wavered.

"You're here to kill me." The flintiness of his voice suggested that concept didn't worry him.

"I am," she acknowledged with a nod and cocky grin, expecting just such a reaction from him. "I am here to kill you ... but not kill you."

"Not very helpful." The tightening around Mikel's eyes confirmed that he wasn't amused by her response. "Very mysterious of you and just as murky as always."

"Did you even know I was in the city?"

Mikel didn't smile, not fully, just a brief curl of his lower lip. That was all the confirmation that Liria needed. "Does it matter?"

"I was just curious," she shrugged. "I assumed as much."

"Apparently more than curious," Mikel prodded.

"Fine, more than curious," Liria scowled, though more in amusement than annoyance. "After our last encounter I thought there might be a chance to revive the spark between us."

"You thought wrong."

"Did I?" Liria stepped closer to Mikel, head tilted to the right as was her habit when she studied him. Not worried about the dagger he held against his thigh. If he truly wanted to kill her, he would have done so already. "I'm not so sure about that."

"You always saw what you wanted to see, Liria."

She didn't reply right away. Her expression became serious, which was rare for her. "Perhaps, but when it came to you I was rarely wrong. You've missed me. I can see it in you."

"After you betrayed me? You give yourself too much credit."

"Sometimes, yes, but not in this respect." She nodded as if she saw some part of Mikel that she hadn't seen before, and she wasn't quite sure what to make of it. "It was just business, Mikel. You should have known that. My intention was never to kill you. I just wanted to prevent you from coming after me." She motioned toward his knee where she had slashed across his previous injury with her dagger, then his side, her steel finding a home there as well. "We all make mistakes. I didn't have a choice. And I could have done much worse to you."

"You got greedy, Liria. That was always your greatest weakness."

"And yours, Mikel, was me. In fact, I'm quite certain that it still is."

Mikel chuckled softly at that. He wanted to deny it, but he couldn't. Because there was a truth there that he dared not ignore.

She had betrayed him, that was undeniable, and he hadn't seen it coming even though he believed that he should have.

Because of that, he still wasn't sure what bothered him the most. Liria's failure or his. "*Was* being the key word, Liria."

"Tell yourself what you must, Mikel, but I sensed the connection between us in your office when last we crossed blades. Time may have passed, yet the link between us remains strong. You can't deny that, so don't bother trying."

"And yet despite this connection you claim still exists between us, you're here to kill me. A bit of a contradiction, wouldn't you say?"

"As I said, Mikel, I'm here to kill you but not kill you."

"You'll have to explain that to me." His expression, still flinty, became more thoughtful. "There's more to it, though, isn't there?"

"There always is, Mikel, you should know that. Nothing was ever straightforward between us."

He didn't bother to ask because he didn't believe that he needed to. "You're holding Hanover's hand now that he's back on the Crux."

"More keeping an eye on him. Just in case." She shrugged, as if to say the matter was of little concern. "He's not the most trustworthy of allies, and you've been having a great deal of fun with him lately. So the thought was that perhaps I could help in that regard."

"I help you and I continue to draw breath." For Mikel, it was the most obvious calculation.

"Me and one other."

Mikel didn't need to ask who that was, his thoughts of the Dark Magus clouding the somber emotions that already swirled within him. "You trust her?"

"Assindra?" Liria pursed her lips as she considered how she wanted to reply. "I trust that she will do what is necessary to achieve what she wants. Just like most of us will. So in that regard it's quite easy to know where you stand with her."

"Not a glowing recommendation."

"No, but an accurate one," Liria stated. "Besides, she exercises a power against which few can stand. Why fight it when doing so can only lead to more grief?" She took another step toward Mikel. Now only a few feet between them. He didn't back away, which she viewed as a good sign. "She demonstrates an interest in you that is quite puzzling. Close to disturbing, in fact."

"Again, not a glowing recommendation."

"Perhaps not. Even so, I believe you should speak with her."

"Before you kill me?" Mikel asked.

"What better time than that?"

"I will think about your request."

"Good. Just don't take too long. Assindra is not patient." Liria shrugged. "And I would prefer not to kill you."

"That makes me feel so much better. Now what else do you want? I'm not so vain as to think I caught you without you wanting me to catch you." Mikel was certain of that. If Liria wanted to kill him that morning, he never would have seen her coming. Not until her blade was about to slide into his flesh.

Liria's smile, at first predatory, turned sultry. Seductive. "You used to enjoy ... catching me," she said with a raised eyebrow.

"Times change, Liria. Just as people change."

"And you've changed, Mikel?" She pursed her lips, head tilting to the right, studying him again. "It seems that you're doing much the same as you did when we were together."

"What would that be?"

"Looking out more for others than for yourself."

"That's a bad thing?"

"It's a selfish thing, Mikel."

"Selfish?" He snorted in disbelief. "You'll have to explain that to me."

"We were a team, Mikel. We were supposed to put ourselves first. You and me. Always."

"Even when that wasn't the right thing to do?"

"Even then," Liria confirmed with a sharp nod. "We define right and wrong subjectively. You never seemed to understand that. What was right and wrong for us needed to come first, not the concerns of others. You couldn't seem to remember that when it mattered most to me."

"Some would argue that there is little subjectivity when it comes to right or wrong."

"You would argue that, Mikel. Only you. Because you seek to move through the world according to some code that most wouldn't understand much less try to apply to themselves."

"Most do understand, Liria." He looked down at her with a deep sadness in his eyes. "You never did."

"So in that you have not changed. You remain bound by a perspective of the world that can do you more harm than good."

"That's how you describe it, Liria. How I view the world offers me a necessary clarity."

"And yet you say that you've changed since last we were together." Liria offered Mikel a raised eyebrow once more, her mercurial personality coming to the fore. The spark in her eye and the curl of her lower lip a reminder as to what it had been like between them before they went after the prize beneath the Tor.

"I haven't had much choice."

"I find that hard to believe for more reasons than one."

"It was always difficult to convince you of anything, Liria, so I have little desire to try."

"My skepticism has helped to keep me alive, Mikel. You know that just as well as I do."

"Your skepticism has done other things for you as well, not all of them positive."

Liria's expression tightened, not caring for Mikel's words. "You've been spending a good deal of time with the Queen of the Crux."

Mikel nodded, not bothering to deny her claim. Now certain that Liria had eyes and ears on the Crux. Just as he assumed would be the case. "I haven't had much choice with the trouble your employer is causing."

"That's the reason?" Liria snorted softly, her disbelief obvious.

"It is." Mikel shrugged, not caring if she thought he was telling her the truth.

"As I said just moments ago, I find that hard to believe."

"I don't care what you believe."

"You will, because what I believe will determine whether you live or die."

"I'm tired of dancing around what it is that you truly want to discuss. You are here to kill me but not kill me. And you dance around the possibility of a deal. Speak plainly, Liria."

She bit her lip, taking a few seconds to decide how to respond. She could continue to play with Mikel. It would bring her a small amount of pleasure. However, the pleasure she desired from him required that he shift his current position, and the only way to do that was to push him onto the path Liria wanted him to take. "Assindra is here on the Crux, though by the look in your eyes you already knew that. What I have been trying to say is that she is conflicted."

"How so? I assume she wants the throne for Malor Dragoran."

"That's only one of her desires, and from what I can tell not the one that pulls at her the most."

"Assindra does what she does for herself, which explains why you betrayed me for her."

"That is neither here nor there, Mikel. I will only say that her perspective on the world is less complex than yours. It better fits with my perspective."

"Liria, you are truly trying what little patience I have left."

"She wants you dead. That's why she sent me. In that regard, I speak the truth."

"Then why not just kill me? You tried the last time we met, and despite whatever attraction remains between us, you do what you must to get where you desire to be."

"So you feel the attraction as well?"

Her eyes sparked with a desire that Mikel was more than just a little familiar. A desire that used to excite him. Now, it worried him. Because it was affecting him just as it did before their falling out. "Liria."

"You used to be a lot more fun than this."

"As I said, times change. So do people."

"A truly unfortunate reality in some respects." She leaned in closer to Mikel. She was about to reach for his wrist to pull him close, but then thought better of it. The hints and signals she was giving him were not affecting him as they once had. Or if they were, he was doing a masterful job of hiding his emotions and desires from her. "Assindra sent me here to kill you. Yet she doesn't really want you dead. Not in the way that you might imagine."

Mikel's frown deepened. "I don't understand."

"*I* don't understand, but *you* do. I can see it in your eyes."

And he did understand. He knew why Assindra was interested in him. Their history brief but deep. Deeper than he would have preferred.

"If you're not here to kill me, at least not yet, then what do you want?"

"It's not what I want, Mikel. It's what you want."

Mikel leaned backward. He should have assumed this would happen. Liria was never good at getting straight to the point. She preferred to talk in circles and travel down various tangents so that she always had the space to wriggle free from whatever she said or promised. "And what do I want?"

"Other than me?" The desire with which Mikel was so

familiar, that he had once been helpless against, had returned once more to Liria's eyes, which flashed with dark promises and pleasures.

Mikel snorted, needing to break the spell she sought to cast upon him. "That was a long time ago, Liria."

"Not so long ago as you seem to imagine."

"I don't imagine it, Liria. Not anymore."

"I doubt that, particularly since your cheeks are coloring just as they used to when we were together." She laughed softly. She had not anticipated how much fun it would be to speak with Mikel again in this way, the risk she had taken to meet with him that morning well worth it. "But we can continue on this topic later when we have the guarantee of more privacy."

She crossed her arms, her expression shifting swiftly. Her teasing smile gone, now she was all business. "I was merely suggesting that instead of me killing you, you consider how we -- you, me, and Assindra -- might be able to work together. You should think about it, Mikel. Because I know that for you the world we live in comes down in its most basic form to transactions. This is a transaction that would benefit all of us if a deal can be struck."

"Assindra said as much?"

"She didn't. She couldn't. But it's what she was implying when we spoke."

"Why are you telling me this, Liria? Even with our history together, you are taking a risk that I would not expect from you."

"Because I want you to know," she replied simply, not feeling the need to expand on her decision.

"There's more to it than that."

"There is."

"What?"

Liria bit her lip. She should have assumed that he would ask her these questions. He was never one to accept what she told him blindly. He always needed to approach a decision from several different directions to determine if he could poke a hole in it. And she had learned that she could never get him where she wanted unless she revealed all that she knew or believed. "I don't trust her. You shouldn't either."

"Again, why are you telling me this?"

"Because though she pays me well, I still worry about you." Liria could have said more. She felt the urge to do so. Yet she clamped down on that urge swiftly, refusing to place herself in such a vulnerable position.

Mikel wanted to laugh, not believing her, yet her look of concern and contriteness told him that he should. "You didn't worry about me when you left me to die."

"I left you, I won't deny that," Liria replied, "but I didn't leave you to die. The giant was with you and your injuries were painful though not debilitating. I had no doubt that you two would survive the peril you faced."

Liria glided forward then, her movement as quick as a snake preparing to strike. Mikel raised his dagger, placing it at her throat. Even so, the cold steel didn't stop her.

Leaning up, she kissed him. Memories of the past flooded into Mikel's mind. Before those desperate hours beneath the Ring. Those memories bringing to mind others. Of the quiet times between them. The fun times. Those remembrances stoking the heat radiating out from them both.

Mikel fought hard not to lose himself in the woman who had once held his heart. To prevent that from happening, he tasked his analytical mind with reviewing what Liria had placed on the table between them.

Was Liria speaking the truth?

Should he even consider the proposal she offered him in such a roundabout manner?

Was there an opportunity here that he had never considered?

A solution to many of the challenges he faced?

He couldn't say for certain.

Liria was the best liar he knew. He would need to talk to Teddy to make sure that whatever decisions he made, he made them with his brain and not another part of his body.

The moment he reached that conclusion, Liria pulled back from him, pushing his blade down as she did so. "You need to go. Now." Her voice was calm but insistent.

"Why do I ..."

Then he sensed what was coming toward him, relying on the connection he had to the Blade slung across his back. The Blade that offered him a power that he had yet to fully grasp or understand.

Pulling his weapon free, he stepped away from the alley and back toward the center of the small courtyard. Identifying what was approaching, he wanted more space to maneuver.

Several large shapes emerged out of the shadows.

Soldiers of the Ten Thousand.

Long thought lost to history.

Unfortunately found once more.

Their golden eyes glowed brightly in anticipation of the blood to be spilled.

Mikel's blood.

"SHE SAYS she didn't leave me to die," he muttered to himself as he glided around the courtyard. "Yet it seems that she always leaves me in situations where I could die."

Mikel moved with a surprising deftness for such a big man and one hindered by a knee that ached at the best of times. Though now, as he fought against the three Werebeasts who had cornered him in the courtyard, his pain was forgotten. His focus was on ensuring that none of his attackers got behind him. To do that, he kept the far wall at his back.

Pivoting, he raised the Blade of Light, the steel glowing brightly in the presence of his attackers. A shriek raced around the enclosed courtyard when claw met steel. The Were stumbled back after the slash, licking at his scorched flesh. Then growling in anger. Eager to repay the injury he received.

The wounded Werebeast didn't continue his attack, however, waiting to see if his diversion worked.

It didn't.

Mikel expected just such a play. Spinning swiftly, he slashed with the Blade of Light. The Were tasked with taking him from the other side bent backward at an almost impossible angle to avoid losing his head, then scrambled away on all fours before rising to his full height and placing Mikel in shadow.

The third Werebeast watched it all from the entrance to the courtyard. Growling softly the entire time, his eyes never left Mikel as he searched for the shortcoming he hoped to exploit.

Mikel ignored the Were's scrutiny, concentrating on the two attackers who sought to come at him from his flanks.

He should have assumed this would happen. Magnus warned him about Malor Dragoran's Werebeasts earlier that morning when he stopped by The Fox's Lair while making his way home to his pregnant wife.

But Mikel had allowed himself to be distracted by other matters. Liria just one of them.

That was an error he could ill afford to make again, the situation in which he found himself a great deal more complicated than he initially imagined. And not just because of the conversation he had just engaged in with his former partner.

Clearly, the Battle Lord's efforts at the Splintered Bridge to prevent those fighting for Malor Dragoran from reaching the Crux hadn't been as successful as he thought. He didn't seek to lay blame at the feet of Henri Dengannon, however. How could he? Who could have prepared for the reemergence of monsters long thought lost to the mists of time?

This trio of soldiers somehow made their way across the Trench and then the Churn to the Crux. If they could, so could more of the Werebeasts. He would need to get Teddy working on this new threat, assuming he survived this combat.

Of course, if facing three hardened soldiers wasn't bad enough, the trio had shifted before engaging with him. Half man, half animal. The one poised at the entrance to the alley resembled a wolf. The one on his right who towered above him was a bear. The last, licking his burned claw, gave into his instincts since he had been bred with a tiger.

The Werebeasts were devastatingly fast and dangerous.

Yet they couldn't make the most of those traits as they sought to kill him. The assassins found it difficult to get in a good strike, the small size of the courtyard constraining their movement and aiding Mikel's skilled bladework.

As he prepared to defend against the Werebeasts' next attack, he thought again of what the Battle Lord had hinted at in his missive. It would have seemed preposterous, though Mikel had no cause to doubt him. And he certainly didn't now as he stared at the truth with his own eyes.

Malor Dragoran had changed the game.

More concerning, Malor Dragoran wasn't what he seemed to be.

He was something far worse.

Mikel took one step to his right, sensing what his attackers had in mind. He could have used Liria's blade as he fought against the Werebeasts. Then again, it was probably best that she had scrambled over the wall behind him when these killers appeared.

No matter what she said, no matter what she promised, he couldn't trust her. Never again he had told himself after she betrayed him beneath the Ring.

That commitment wavered briefly during their discussion. The appearance of this trio of shifters slammed his belief back into place like the door of a crypt sealing shut.

She may have caught up to him because she wanted to warn him. That possibility continued to tease the back of his brain. Even so, she was just as likely to stab him as was one of his current adversaries.

Mikel ducked, avoiding the swipe of the Werebear, the assassin's claw slashing through the air above his head. In close to the shifter, Mikel couldn't slash or stab. So he did what he could. Rising up, he slammed the hilt of his sword into the bottom of the shifter's snapping jaw.

The Werebear snarled in fury, stumbling back. The hard strike snapping his jaws closed, the beast bit off a large portion of his own tongue, bloody saliva streaming from his maw.

Mikel didn't take the time to enjoy his partial victory. Pivoting back toward his left, he caught the Weretiger before he was ready and targeted the beast's wounded claw.

With an economy of motion, Mikel slashed, the Blade of Light cutting off two of the beasts sharp digits.

The Weretiger roared in pain as he glided back swiftly. Desperate to stay clear of Mikel and his bloody blade.

"You fight well, Broken Bear." The Werewolf standing by the alley nodded in appreciation. His words were only slightly garbled by the length of his snout.

"That's kind of you to say." Mikel could use the break, tired from his efforts. The downside being that he began to feel the pain in his damaged joint and leg now that his thoughts weren't consumed with how to stay alive.

He had proven successful so far. But how much longer ...

Mikel didn't want to think about that. He wanted to think about how to get out of the courtyard before these Werebeasts ate him alive.

"But it will do you little good."

"Why is that?"

"Our master sent us here specifically for you. Do what you will, you cannot defeat us."

Mikel nodded slowly, even as his mind worked swiftly, his suspicions hardening from theory to truth.

Just as she said, Liria hadn't tracked him that morning with the intention of killing him. She had known these three would be coming for him, and she had warned him in her way. Although he could have used more than just a few seconds to prepare for their arrival.

However, Liria had provided him with a gift, and perhaps unknowingly at that. It appeared as if there might be an opportunity here that Mikel had not considered. Because Assindra did not command the Ten Thousand. Only one dark creature of old could do that.

The Dread.

That conclusion confirmed one more truth for him.

The Dread could be but one person, just as the Battle Lord suggested.

The Dread was the King of the Tor.

Because, clearly, Assindra was doing Malor Dragoran's dirty work, although Malor wasn't telling her all that he had put into play. Not if the Dread wanted Mikel eliminated and Assindra desired first to engage with him.

Was there more than friction between the two supposed allies that he could use to drive a wedge further between them? Or better yet, into them?

Mikel offered the Werewolf a quizzical expression. "Why do you think I was trying to defeat you?"

"What are you ..."

The leader of the trio never got the chance to complete his question. A surge of energy blasted into the beast from behind, sending the Werewolf crashing against the far wall of the courtyard.

The soldier collapsed to the stone. Unmoving. As he breathed his last, the dark magic that made him what he was began to fade, his body slowly shifting back to his human form.

Several more bursts of energy followed. Each one struck a Werebeast.

The soldier who resembled a bear joined his leader, crumpling to the stone tiles of the courtyard, neck bent at a terrible angle after he struck the far wall with his head.

The wounded Weretiger was knocked skidding across the ground, fast enough to avoid the full brunt of the attack, though not fast enough to avoid his fate. The beast moaned softly as he slowly changed back to his human form, his leather armor melted, even more of his flesh charred and smoking. His death just a matter of time.

"Quite the entrance," Mikel murmured.

"It wasn't my work. Finn was showing me a new skill so he did the honors."

Nat walked into the courtyard, Finn right behind her. Both still touched the Talent, small spheres of power dancing around their fingertips.

"I'm grateful for Finn's thoroughness." Mikel offered his friend a nod of thanks. The Magus nodded in turn, clearly pleased. His success gave him the chance to forget his own troubles and pains for a brief time.

After surveying the damage Finn caused, Nat turned toward Mikel as she shook her head in disappointment. "This is getting to be much too common. It's almost like you need a minder."

8

## THE SPITFIRE

"A little angry this morning?" Mikel wondered.

He ducked to his left, whipping his sword up and around in a fiery arc, the steel blazing brightly when it connected with the white-hot spikes Nat threw at him.

"Not angry," Nat growled. "Just irritated."

For the last half hour, she and Mikel tested themselves against one another in the practice ring Finn created in his apartment, putting in place a dome of shimmering energy so that the magic employed didn't destroy his home.

Despite her best efforts, Nat had yet to break through Mikel's defenses. And he had not bothered to attack her. Not yet anyway.

A stalemate.

In the beginning, never before having tested herself against Mikel in this way, she was satisfied with that.

The Talent vs. the Light.

Now, she was growing impatient. Her natural desire to claim victory grew more insistent within her.

"Glad I could help," Mikel replied, offering her a wink after he said it.

Then he was moving again, shards of energy tracking him as he glided around the practice ring. Dodging several. Smacking away those that he couldn't with the Blade of Light. A sizzle of fiery sparks erupted and then faded just as quickly on those few occasions when his blade struck the Talent. Just not all the time, which was what the Magus observing the practice combat demanded.

"You cannot fight as you are used to," Finn commented with a gravelly aggravation. He sat on a stool within the bounds of the gleaming dome, a shield of energy hovering before him and moving as needed to defend against any stray bolts of magic that came his way. "Movement is still important in a combat of this type, I'll give you that. But it is not enough. It does not give you what you must seek."

"And what's that?" Mikel asked, standing his ground now as Nat sent a wave of energy streaming toward him from both palms.

"An agreement."

Mikel snorted as he held the Blade of Light up against his ward's attack. In truth, he had little to fear. Neither the Curse nor the Talent could harm him. The real purpose of this combat not just to refine Nat's skills, but also his.

"With Nat?" Mikel shook his head, the look of grim determination on Nat's face precluding that possibility. "She doesn't seem to be interested."

"With the Blade of Light, numbskull," growled Finn. "Are you purposely trying to get under my skin?"

"Is it working?" Mikel asked, adjusting the positioning of the Blade of Light in response to Nat's change in tactics. The young Magus was implementing a new skill. Letting go of her stream of energy, she held a whip of crackling energy in each hand. She flicked the tip at him, getting a feel for her new weapon.

"Of course not," Finn huffed. "Can't you focus for just a few minutes?"

Mikel smiled, hearing the lie in his friend's words. "It's just as much in the wrist as the arm," he explained to Nat.

"You're helping her?" Finn demanded.

Mikel shrugged as he dodged out of the way of Nat's first attack. The crackling cord of energy missed him by several feet. "That was good, Nat, just don't force it so much. A gentle motion." He mimicked what he wanted from her with his left hand. "A smooth motion followed by the sharp snap of your wrist. It's all in the wrist."

"An agreement," Finn said again, trying to recapture Mikel's attention. His friend apparently was more concerned that his ward master the new weapon she had crafted rather than he master the skill that was essential to him making full use of the potent weapon that had chosen him.

Nat didn't say anything, her face a mask of deep concentration. Then she did as Mikel suggested with her left hand, the whip snapping out toward Mikel, cord of energy sizzling through the air.

Mikel pivoted to the side. The tip of the whip slid right by him. He did the same again when Nat attacked with the whip in her right hand.

He smiled, pleased that Nat was smiling. She hadn't struck him, but she had gotten close.

Then closer and closer as she continued to attack, becoming more comfortable with the whips she had crafted.

"Well done," Mikel said as he dodged to the side. "Work on the snap with your wrist. Line your hand up with your target. That's how you'll ensure the tip strikes true."

Mikel slashed with his blade, knocking the sizzling cord to the side. "Well done!" He was impressed. She was aiming for his chest and she would have hit him if he hadn't turned sideways.

"Would you please focus on the reason that you're here," Finn pleaded, beginning to lose patience with Mikel. "Just as Cadmus explained, if you are to learn how to use the Blade of Light as it is meant to be used, you must reach an agreement with the weapon."

"Meaning?"

"Stop moving around like a fox trying to escape from the hen house with the farmer on your heels. Hold your ground. Use the power gifted to you. Don't run from it."

The next time Nat attacked, Mikel did just as Finn instructed. Watching the tip of Nat's whip come streaking toward his face, rather than skip out of the way or slash with his blade, he lifted his scimitar then curled his wrist to the right, allowing the first few feet of the blazing whip to wrap around the gleaming steel.

"Excellent!" Finn cried. "Now remember what I told you. An agreement must be reached. You and the essence of the blade."

"Easier said than done," Mikel murmured softly. He found himself in a battle not only with Nat, the young Magus tugging hard on the caught whip, seeking to free it from his steel, but also with the Blade of Light.

He sensed the magic contained within the scimitar, the magic surging within him as well. He needed to bring the two together. He needed to function with one mind. He couldn't allow the consciousness of the Blade to rule his thoughts.

An agreement, Finn had said. Still, not an easy thing to accomplish.

*"You seek to control the engagement. You can't. You must give a part of yourself to the Blade or the Blade will not give a part of itself to you. An agreement just as the Magus said, but more a negotiation."*

Mikel grunted. Standing strong, he prevented Nat from unwrapping the whip from his steel. Grateful to Knute for his advice.

He heard the former King of the Giants of the Rime's deep rumble in the back of his head, his spirit and that of all the other previous Bearers of the Blade linked to the weapon and now a part of him as a result.

*"A negotiation first before the agreement."*

"Exactly," Knute confirmed. *"In a sense a trading of gifts to prove intention and good will. From there the relationship grows."*

Mikel didn't doubt the truth in Knute's words, the process beginning the instant his fingers closed around the hilt of the Giant-crafted weapon when he claimed it from beneath the Citadel.

But now more was required. Now he needed to give more to the Blade in order to receive more from the Blade.

He needed to do something he rarely did.

He needed to share his true self with the ancient weapon.

He needed to demonstrate a vulnerability that he rarely ever did.

*"You're asking quite a lot."*

*"It's necessary, Steelheart,"* Knute grumbled. *"Think of it as a test of sorts. For the Blade of Light to do what's required of it, it must believe in you. But you must believe in yourself first."*

Mikel didn't reply to what he viewed as an almost circular argument. In part because it made a strange kind of sense. Then he recalled a conversation he had with Kaduna right before they made their escape from the Bitter Heights.

*"The greatest strength you can demonstrate isn't with Talent or blade. It's in your spirit. It's in who you are. Remain true to yourself. Always. Be who you are meant to be. Allow your spirit to show in your words and your deeds. It is from your spirit that your strength comes."*

Though he didn't quite understand it then, good advice now. He reached out to the Blade, the essence of the artifact always in the back of his mind.

A power that he didn't quite understand.

A power full of promise.

A power to be wary of as well.

A power that he needed not to master but rather to partner with if he was to have any chance of success.

Rather than seeking to employ that power, he opened himself to it and allowed the essence of the Blade of Light to sweep through him. Examining his wants and desires. The decisions he made. His perspectives. His dreams. His hopes. His morality.

A frightening experience. More terrifying than battling a Creeper or a cave spider.

Yet he withstood the Blade's scrutiny despite how uncomfortable it made him, permitting the Giant-crafted weapon to see him for who he truly was.

All his faults and foibles revealed.

All of his hopes and dreams divulged.

All of his loves and hates disclosed.

Satisfied, the power sweeping through him cleansed him. Burning away his fears and worries, it left behind a cool calm that he had never experienced before.

Mikel realized that calm came not just from him, but also the Blade of Light. The magic of the artifact had entwined itself with his spirit. Merging with it. Creating a stronger essence from the two. An unbreakable bond forming.

*"Good. Now on to the final step. You and the Blade must both function with one mind now."*

Understanding what Knute required of him, Mikel reached out to that essence that was so foreign yet at the same time so familiar. Tentative at first. Then with more confidence.

Understanding what the Blade truly was.

Understanding what he was now.

Understanding what would be demanded of him if he accepted this burden and its attendant duties.

*"It's a heavy weight you and the others accepted."*

*"A burden you face now as well, Steelheart,"* Knute intoned. *"Welcome. You are one of us now. A Bearer of the Blade."*

*"That may be. Even so, I sense the test is not complete."*

*"It's not. You have given yourself to the Blade. You must accept what the Blade gives to you."*

A jolt of electricity shot through Mikel the instant Knute finished speaking. The Blade of Light shared its history with Mikel and that of the Bearers who preceded him. It shared the knowledge gained since the Blade's creation. The lessons learned. Most important, the explanations as to why the Blade selected him and not a Giant of the Rime. Why the Blade believed that now was the time that he and no else should wield a weapon of such potency once more in the Natural World.

A heavy burden indeed.

*"Are you all right, Steelheart?"*

*"It's more than I anticipated,"* Mikel replied, wobbling a bit as he slowly regained his bearings.

*"It was for all of us. Dark times come. You know that now. You stand with us against that darkness. When it seems that you can no longer stand against that darkness, remember that the Blade selected you because it believed that you and only you could do what would be required. Seize on that when the darkness surrounds and know that if you do the Light will prevail."*

*"If that slips my mind, I'm sure you and the others will remind me."*

Knute chuckled softly in the back of Mikel's brain. *"Of that have no doubt. Now do what you have learned to do. Use your connection to the Blade. Open yourself to the Light and allow that power to work through you. Allow that power to become a part of you."*

It wasn't an easy demand for Mikel to meet, requiring a level of concentration and force of will that was difficult to manage when confronted by an angry teenage Magus who was less than pleased that she had not yet bested him. Nat continued to yank on the caught cord, about to send the whip in her other hand flashing toward him, viewing the tug of war as an opportunity.

Mikel smiled then, a new knowledge flooding into him as he recognized how his demonstration of vulnerability actually was a strength. The negotiation between him and the Blade complete, he realized that he need only think of what he wanted to do in order to accomplish that task.

And he did.

Much to Nat's and Finn's shock, the whip wrapped around Mikel's sword sparked then vanished, a streak of energy surging into the scimitar. The same happened to the other whip slicing toward Mikel's face.

This time he didn't feel the need to use the Blade. Instead, he caught the crackling whip in his hand. The energy flashed blindingly bright before surging into him. The power Nat had used against Mikel now a part of him and the Blade of Light.

"Enough," Finn said quietly. Amazed, pleased, and slightly frightened. Never having seen the like.

"But Finn ..." Nat was reaching for the Talent once more. She refused to acknowledge defeat and had every intention of continuing the combat.

"Enough," he repeated, releasing his hold on the Talent so that the protective dome faded away.

He was tired. He needed to rest.

Nat had mastered the skill he had taught her. Mikel had mastered the skill that he hadn't taught him, Finn sensing another presence in play during the time it took Mikel to learn how to work with the potent magic residing in the ancient scimitar.

"Fine," she growled. She sounded more like a grumpy teenager than the powerful young Magus she was. Muttering under her breath, Nat grabbed her books and placed them in her bag.

"You did well, Natalya." Finn offered her a proud nod. "I would hate to be the one opposing you on the field of battle."

That compliment brought a smile that cracked Nat's dour visage. She appreciated the praise even though she hated demonstrating so little success against Mikel. "Same time tomorrow?"

"Same time," Finn confirmed.

Nat nodded. "You ready?"

"Can you give us just a few minutes?" Mikel asked.

Nat offered him an expression filled with doubt, her mood already much improved. "Can I trust that you won't get yourself into trouble if I leave you alone for a few minutes?"

"Probably not," Mikel replied with a smile of his own. "If I need you, I'll shout as loud as I can."

Nat grunted, appreciating the thin layer of sarcasm lacing his words, then stepped out onto the balcony, the roar of the Churn just below assaulting her ears, unconvinced as to the verity of Mikel's claim.

"Quite the spitfire, isn't she?" Finn asked, a hint of admiration in his voice.

"That's one way to describe her."

"She's doing quite well. Whatever I teach her she learns astoundingly fast. I have not had a pupil like her in decades."

"That doesn't surprise me." Mikel glanced out onto the balcony, Nat watching the whitewater surging just below. "She's insatiable when it comes to acquiring new knowledge."

"That's a trait to be admired," Finn nodded. "A potential danger as well."

Mikel shifted his focus to Finn, seeing how haggard his appearance had become. His features more drawn than usual. Skin tighter around his skull. His eyes deeper in their sockets. "Getting worse?"

"What ails me is always getting worse," Finn replied. "It just seems to have increased its pace these last few days."

"Anything I can do to help?"

"No, there's nothing that anyone can do."

"What about Haven? Any word?"

"Nothing." Finn shook his head sadly. "And I don't expect to hear anything. I made a bad decision. I gave into my curiosity. Into my greed." He shrugged, as if to say that there was nothing to be done about it now. Because there wasn't. "Now I must pay the price."

"I'm sorry, Finn. I wish there was something that I could do."

Finn waved away Mikel's sadness, nodding toward the young Magus he had accepted as his student. "You understand why I worry."

"You fear for Nat."

"I do."

"As do I," Mikel admitted. About everything. Never having been a parent before meeting the teenager. Not realizing how swiftly she would become a part of his life and his heart. Not realizing how he would fear for her about the smallest of things. He wanted to protect her from any and every threat, understanding that at times he couldn't and shouldn't and not liking that one bit.

"Are you certain then that you want me to do this for the girl? Knowing what you know about me?"

Mikel studied the Magus for quite some time before he replied. "It's because of what I know about you that I want you to do this. Do you understand?"

Finn's frown slowly shifted to an expression of appreciation mixed with understanding. He nodded curtly, acknowledging the trust that Mikel was placing in him.

"Good. And you understand what I'll do if you step too close to the line with Nat?" Mikel's expression darkened. He wasn't making a threat. Rather he was making a promise. "I've grown quite fond of her."

"I do," Finn nodded again. "Have no fear of that. She will be safe with me."

"I don't doubt it," Mikel replied. He turned toward the entrance, having heard Teddy approach.

The giant bent his head upon walking through the doorway. Giving Finn a nod, he was all business when he spoke to Mikel. "All will be ready by dusk. Samuel is pulling together the crews you requested."

Mikel nodded, pleased to hear it. The Battle Lord requested his assistance, and he would give it. Particularly after his encounter with the three Werebeasts. "And you have what you need?"

"I do. Our eyes and ears are on the job."

If three Werebeasts could sneak onto the Crux, why not more? That question plaguing him, Mikel needed to plan for the likelihood that more of the Ten Thousand hunted in the streets of Innsbruck or soon would. Either for him or perhaps for the Queen, both of them a prize that Malor Dragoran would value highly.

Of course, there were other questions that kept dominating his thoughts. The most prominent?

How were the Werebeasts entering the Kingdom of the Crux? Were they risking the perils of the Trench and sneaking across the cavern floor? Or did they have a simpler method, such as making use of Assindra's unique skills?

Those were the queries for which he wanted answers. And he was worried that the answer was both. Because though he might be able to do something about the Ten Thousand if he located their route, he doubted that he could do much to hinder the Dark Magus.

"Learn anything yet?"

Teddy shook his head, disappointed though not surprised.

"It's too soon. All we know for certain is that the larger gondolas are not being used. We control all of those."

"So it could be much like what Hanover did for Dragoran before." As a part of his initial attempt to claim the throne of the Crux, Lucius Hanover had used his private gondola to transport soldiers loyal to Malor Dragoran across the Churn, seeking to kidnap Celindria Dengannon and then claim the throne of the Crux in her absence.

"I wouldn't put it past him." Teddy shrugged. Nothing would surprise him when it came to the grasping Lord of House Hanover. "We'll know soon enough, though not before we're gone."

"If you find that there are more of the Ten Thousand ..."

"Have no fear of that," Finn cut in. "If Teddy finds any more of those mongrels on the Crux, the spitfire and I will take care of them."

## 9

# RISE OF THE TITANS

The day had not gone as he wanted. That didn't surprise him, though it did sour his already bad mood.

None of the days of the last few months had gone as he wanted ever since Assindra's thief stole the Blade of Light and failed to deliver it as promised.

Malor Dragoran now feared this thief was the next Bearer of the Blade. And that shouldn't be possible. A sick twist of fate.

The Giants of the Rime crafted the Blade of Light, infusing it with its special and potent qualities, at the request and with the aid of the Order of the Magii. Just as was the case for all the weapons they made with the sole purpose of combating the Curse.

Yet in this singular instance, they crafted the Blade to fit the hand of a Giant. And ever since the weapon's birth, the line of Bearers were all Giants of the Rime or the Deep, unbroken for more than a thousand years.

Until now.

The magic in the Blade activated by the touch of Mikel Stahlherz, the steel adjusted its size to fit the hand of its latest wielder. All the while the magic contained within it remained as potent as ever.

It was as if the Blade of Light, so long hidden and dormant, had been waiting for its next Bearer. Malor unwittingly having set events in motion to make that happen. His need for the weapon putting the thief in place to take up the sword.

An interesting development from one perspective.

A disconcerting one from another.

Made even more so because ever since the thief with a seemingly endless supply of names -- the Fox, the Blade, the King of the Underworld, and, as the Queen of the Crux preferred, the Broken Bear – had claimed the Blade, all of Malor's carefully laid plans, so close to fruition, began to unravel.

His days transitioning from almost triumphant to bad to worse. With no end in sight.

Not until he acquired the ancient weapon for himself.

That left Malor with only one option.

He needed to seize the Blade of Light from the current wielder.

And as he had learned through a careful study of the histories maintained by the Magii, there was only one way to dispossess a Bearer of the Blade.

Kill him.

Only then could Malor twist the power and essence contained within the ancient weapon to his purpose.

Simple, yet as the Broken Bear demonstrated time and again, not so simple. The latest Bearer of the Blade revealed a unique ability to learn the ancient weapon's qualities, all of which helped to keep him alive despite the perils placed before him.

All those thoughts looped through Malor's mind. Distracting him. And he could not afford to be distracted.

Not now.

Not if he was to redirect current events back to the path that ensured the victory he deserved.

The victory that guaranteed the conquest and revenge that he craved.

Standing in his private office, Malor growled, shaking his head to clear it. Pressing his hands down onto the polished wood until his fingers turned white, he used the resulting pricks of pain to refocus his thoughts.

He stared down with a dark intensity at a piece of old, discolored parchment, ignoring the splatter of stains that marred its surface.

Blood.

That was to be expected, of course.

The map spread out before him was particularly valuable. The only one in existence in fact.

It had taken Malor years to acquire it and at great expense both in gold and lives.

However, the cost of acquisition meant nothing to him. All that mattered was that he had the piece of battered and worn parchment.

Most anyone else would not understand the peculiarity of the map. Only those few like him, those few touched by the Curse, could see what he was seeing thanks to his application of his tainted power. Thin streams of black drifted out from his palms and caressed the brittle surface, revealing the truth concealed within the map. Malor's focus on a section of the Frozen Waste.

For the hundredth time that morning, he traced with a single finger an anonymous river that curled through that frigid landscape. It had not been named when the map was drawn.

Why would it?

It couldn't be seen. The river was covered by thirty feet of ice and just as much snow. A hidden waterway masked by the Frozen Waste's unbroken white cloak.

Malor grunted in satisfaction, believing that single feature would be the key that unlocked his future success.

His Ten Thousand would serve their purpose. His Werebeasts already had created an unforeseen problem for the Crux that would ensure the Queen kept her focus on the Splintered Bridge and the threat of invasion from her east.

Although his Ten Thousand would play a key role, they would be no more than a diversion in his larger plan.

Keep the Crux and the Battle Lord looking toward the Tor, never thinking that another peril would emerge from the west and put the Kingdom that he desired for his own in an unbreakable vise. Assuming, of course, that the tool he planned to unleash performed as Malor required.

He hadn't studied the map for centuries. Yet he had little doubt that it remained accurate.

If it wasn't, those features displayed by the Curse would have adapted as that barren environment adapted over time. Perhaps the environment had in some small ways.

He didn't know. He didn't care. He did care that the site that was his goal was clearly marked.

The Lost Carcer.

Far to the north. Close to the Ice Forest. Invisible and hidden to all, unless you knew where it was tucked away.

And, thanks to the map, Malor Dragoran did.

Certain of his path, Malor crafted a portal made of the Curse, wispy threads of black flowing along the edge. As soon as he stepped through, his world shifted drastically to white and blue. The sky startingly bright with not a cloud to be seen. The ground covered by a thick layer of crunchy snow mixed with ice, the glare from the sun forcing him to squint until he used the Curse to protect his vision, deadening the brightness around him.

That done, he breathed deeply of the brittle air, letting out a long breath and relishing the brief spark of pain in his lungs.

He had not visited the Frozen Waste for quite some time, not having cause to do so. His strategies and goals had taken him in a different direction. Yet here, in this white waste, there was a peace to be found. If only for a time. And only if desired.

With the press of time and the burden of responsibilities on his shoulders, he desired nothing more than to complete the task that had brought him so far to the north.

He stood atop the wide channel of the hidden river that wound its way from north to south. Trudging across the packed snow, he tracked the river for a time before cutting to the right, his objective the icy cliffs that rose to his front and blotted out the sun.

Studying the ridge as he approached, the best word that came to mind for describing the landmass was imposing. The surface was craggy, jagged, sharp. The towering ridge made him think of spikes punching up through the surface of the earth.

Malor wasn't concerned, however.

When he was only a few hundred yards away, thanks to his use of the Curse he identified the imperfection that he sought. If he hadn't sent waves of the tainted power streaming out toward the cliffs, dancing and darting about with a strangely methodical freneticism, he never would have located the slim crevice that folded in upon itself at the very base.

The crevice was the only means for entering the natural barrier that shielded the Lost Carcer.

He didn't hesitate. Walking into the gap that was scarcely wide enough for his shoulders, he realized almost immediately that caution was required. This outer ring was made not of stone as he anticipated but rather ice. Razor sharp. Slicing him whenever a piece of his clothing scraped across it, the flesh on his upper arms paid the price for his initial lack of caution, several neat slices cutting across his flesh, blood dripping down from the shallow wounds.

He bit down on his anger at his own clumsiness brought on

by his eagerness, slowing his steps to avoid further injury and calling upon the Curse to mend his wounds. He could not afford to show weakness to the one he sought to summon, understanding the potential consequences if he did.

As he worked his way with greater caution through the narrow crevice that soon became a tunnel, the ice closing in around him, cutting him off from the outside world, Malor was struck by the remarkable clarity that allowed him to gaze dozens of yards into the cliff face before the ice's thickness clouded his perspective. The crevice narrowing, the ice pressing down upon him and forcing him to crouch, he recalled what had led the Giants of the Rime to partner with the Order of the Magii on the construction of this prison.

The War of the Brothers.

Beyond the gift he had granted Kronin, Malor had not involved himself directly in the conflict, having his own designs to play out that had nothing to do with the far northern Realms. Besides, he had not seen the need. Kronin and his Titans should have been able to manage their rebellion without further assistance from him.

Though his belief was strong in that regard, he had tracked the conflict that had raged across the Frozen Waste.

The betrayal.

The sundering of the bonds between the brothers, bad blood, literally and figuratively, flooding the frigid landscape.

A horrific number of Giants killed in epic battles that lasted for days.

The devastation wrought on what had been a pristine landscape.

How the younger brother sought to overthrow Karolingan Frost Lord, King of the Giants of the Rime, and failed.

The victory that Karolingan earned and what it cost him.

How Karolingan doomed himself, failing to kill Kronin and demonstrating a weakness that Malor viewed as anathema.

The King of the Rime allowed emotion rather than cold calculation to come before his own interests.

That weakness was now one that Malor sought to use to his own advantage.

It was said that at the behest of Karolingan, his smiths, so skilled at molding the Light and working in partnership with the Magii, constructed a prison that was impregnable. A prison that kept its inhabitants in stasis. More dead than alive. Their spirits severed from their flesh.

Another weakness that Malor planned to exploit. Better just to kill your enemies and be done with them.

Emerging from the gap in the ice, he took a moment to survey where he had arrived. Stretching his back to loosen his protesting muscles after walking bent at the waist for the last few hundred yards, what he saw made him think of a massive training circle restricted by the surrounding walls. In the very center stood a rectangular barrow much like the massive burial mounds in the valley not too far from the current capital of the Giants of the Rime.

Although this one was larger. A thousand yards long and several hundred yards wide with a height of several storeys. Even so, despite its size, the barrow appeared small because of the breadth of the ground upon which it had been built.

The Lost Carcer.

Even he had to take a moment to acknowledge the skill required for such a unique construction. But only a moment. Because one last challenge remained before he could put his plan in motion.

He had to gain entry to the ancient gaol.

The map that brought him here offered no guidance. Nor did the many resources he stole from Haven. The piece of critical knowledge he required forgotten with the passage of time. Or so most anyone but him would believe.

Because not all the artifacts crafted by the Giants of the

Rime were in their possession or had been lost. And oftentimes those items thought lost could be found when the right incentive was offered.

Reaching into a pocket, he extracted a delicately crafted broach made of gold, silver, and iron. The three metals were distinct, each one crafted into an arc, those arcs overlapping and interconnected to form a triquetra.

A symbol that represented not only eternity, but also connection and interdependence.

A symbol as well that signified the merger of effort between the Giants of the Rime and the Magii.

Assindra had failed to provide him with the Blade of Light. Yet in this at least she proved successful, finding the artifact buried deep in the vaults of the Aeyrie, another bastion of the Order of the Magii. A lucky twist of fate from Malor's perspective. He never could have acquired the item if it had been in the Giants' possession.

Striding across the crusty snow, he stopped in front of the narrower wall of the barrow that faced the crevice. Malor wasn't certain whether how he intended to use the artifact would work. Nevertheless, he was confident that he was on the right track.

Because before he chose to master the Curse, he was a skilled practitioner of the Talent. And it was that energy he called on now even as the effort pained him. The natural magic of the world protested at his touch, making its displeasure known, yet having no recourse but to obey the command of the one known as the Dread.

No longer a man.

No longer anything more than a physical manifestation of power.

In this case a dark power. One that had twisted his flesh and his spirit. One that he held back despite its insistent demands, enduring the worsening pain as he pushed the faintly glowing triquetra into the snow.

The energy emanating from the triquetra burned through the frozen crust. Half a foot. Then a half foot more. One more foot.

He cracked an evil grin when the artifact struck a hard surface and stuck there, Malor unable to push any farther.

He stumbled back a few feet, briefly blinded by the bright flash that erupted from the triquetra. The spark of energy shooting out from the artifact forced Malor to withdraw his hand, and he did so willingly, the sizzle across the flesh of his fingers a parting gift from a tool never crafted for use by one with such a dark spirit.

Although the pain remained, he ignored it. His injury was nothing compared to what he could gain.

He had done it, and he didn't have long to wait for the bounty that belonged solely to him.

A faint glow radiated from the hole in the snow. That glow swiftly became a pulsing brightness that blasted out in all directions along the barrow's sides, the lines of energy burning through the snow, melting it so quickly and with such an intense heat that the frozen substance converted into a scalding steam that forced Malor to raise a hand to shield his eyes and then turn away entirely.

When the hiss of the steam finally ended, Malor turned back around. Stunned. Pleased.

He had not touched the Talent in centuries. He had never had cause nor any real desire to since his true strength rested with the Curse.

But in this instance what he viewed as the weaker of the natural magics that circulated throughout the world demonstrated its value.

He stood before two doors made of ice. The surface of each was inscribed with runes designed to keep those who shouldn't enter the barrow out and those who shouldn't exit the barrow in.

A malignant smirk gracing his handsome features, the corners of his mouth dropped as a whisper of concern raced through him.

He was so close to achieving his goal.

Nevertheless, one more challenge remained.

Stepping up to the door, he placed a hand over the glowing triquetra. Uncertain if he would be able to proceed.

His smirk returned when the artifact came free in his grip and the two doors opened inward, granting him entry.

Wary, he didn't rush through the entrance. Though he didn't hesitate for long. The urge to complete his quest was too strong.

The instant he passed through the threshold of the barrow, the twin doors silently swung shut behind him. Even so, the darkness Malor anticipated never materialized.

The walls of the barrow were thick, ten feet if not more, yet the ice was perfectly clear and allowed the sun to stream through and create a false dawn within the prison, muted only by the snow covering the structure.

Malor would have been impressed by what greeted him if not for the insistent demand that he push forward quickly. That he do what he needed to do then leave, because though he had little to fear within the ancient gaol, being within its walls made him feel distinctly uncomfortable. This place a creation of the Talent and the Light, the Curse had no place here. He had no place here. At least not in his current capacity.

The massive barrow was empty except for one unforgettable feature.

A large pit sat in the very center of the floor that was wider than the gaping maw of a black dragon.

Approaching with a forced confidence, Malor stepped to the very edge and stared down into the darkness.

Slipping the triquetra back into his pocket, he seized the Curse. He ignored the angry buzz in his ears, the magic of the prison protesting but having little recourse as the corrupt energy flowed through his blood. Nourishing and filling him with a strength and a clarity that he could achieve in no other way.

Shifting his focus to the blackness below him, he unleashed the tainted energy that he had mastered, the tainted energy that had mastered him, so many centuries before.

Folds of corrupted power surged down into the gloom, piercing the magical shield set atop the pit with a bright flash and a contained explosion that set the entire barrow shaking.

The befouled magic then went deeper.

And deeper still.

Not stopping until there was no farther to go.

Malor's dark eyes flashed then. What he had come for remained locked away in the depths of the earth. The Curse confirmed it for him.

His confidence becoming tangible, he slowly motioned with his hand, bringing it in toward his chest.

The Curse responded swiftly, Malor not having long to wait before a Giant rose out of the darkness of the pit.

The figure resembled the Giants of the Rime. He wore the same garb. His flesh was a bluish white. His hair white and resembling icicles. Except for the right side. That side of his scalp was shaved.

A symbol from the time of the War of the Brothers.

A message.

A promise.

A warning.

The mark of a rebel.

The Giant hovered just above the edge of the pit. Frozen. Spinning slowly as Malor sent waves of darkness swirling around the massive figure. At the same time, he reached into the mind of the Giant, placing a compulsion upon him and requiring the Giant to serve him before he served even himself. A compulsion that could not be changed and could not be broken.

Only when that process was complete did Malor turn the Curse toward freeing the Giant from the stasis that had placed him in a strange and terrifying twilight for so many centuries.

"Who are you?" the Giant asked in a hoarse voice, his body and mind thawing slowly.

"Malor Dragoran."

The Giant did not say anything for quite a long time, pinpricks of pain shooting through him as his body came awake. Muscles that hadn't been used since he was imprisoned firing once more. His blood flowing again. Slowly at first. Thick in the beginning. Then thinning.

His thoughts, lost to him for so long, finally returned. Memories as well. Most of them bad. Those memories fixated on that terrible day when he stood across from his brother. Both of them bloodied and battered. His brother dying. Yet at the same time defeating him and consigning him to a fate worse than death.

"You are, but you are not," the Giant said when his mouth and jaw were working with greater ease, his words no longer painful to utter. He studied the man standing before him. The man who had freed him yet enslaved him at the same time. "You are more."

"You're correct." Malor didn't feel the need to provide a detailed explanation. Not to a creature he viewed as nothing more than a servant. A tool to be used then discarded when no longer of value.

"I remember you. Why have you freed me?"

"Answer my question first," Malor demanded with a quiet intensity, the bonds of the Curse set within the Giant ensuring that he would receive a truthful response. "Who are you?"

The Giant stared at him. His look of confusion slowly became a frown when he realized that he could not dissemble. He could not lie to the Dark Magus who had woken him from his purgatory.

"Kronin," the Giant intoned in a raspy voice, his vocal chords still stiff. "Rightful Frost Lord of the Giants of the Rime. Younger brother to the traitor Karolingan."

"What you claim, what you desire, is still within reach."

"What do you mean?" Kronin's look of confusion deepened.

"You can still be the Frost Lord of the Giants of the Rime. After all this time, the seat of power within the Frozen Waste remains within your grasp."

"If you allow it." Kronin was less than pleased to discover that he was trading one prison for another. The tainted bonds woven within him at the very edge of his consciousness stronger than steel. The bonds that he could not break. Though he would try. "If I remain your servant."

Malor snorted softly. He was amused that Kronin still had not yet comprehended the full extent of what Malor had done to him. But he would. "You will always be my servant ... until I no longer have need of you."

Kronin growled softly. The fire that had driven him to revolt against his brother slowly returned. "Am I alive?"

"In some ways," Malor replied. He was impressed by Kronin's question. Most in his position would simply be pleased to be drawing breath again. "In some ways not."

"I'm a Draugr."

"No, not a Draugr," Malor clarified. "A Draugr is undead. Unthinking. You are neither of those."

"Yet I must bend to your will."

Malor nodded in appreciation. Kronin was a quicker study than he thought. Not just brawn and fury but intelligence as well, and a cunning that Malor could use to his advantage. "You must. But you are alive. You can think for yourself. You are free to do what you believe must be done ... so long as I permit it as a part of my design."

"So I am a slave," Kronin hissed, his anger not only in his voice, but also in his eyes, which burned with a bright fire. The first emotion he experienced upon leaving his tomb, and the last he experienced before being placed within it. A symmetry that was not lost on him.

"You are my servant. Accept it. Trying to fight that truth will bring you and your kind nothing except pain and sorrow. You have a debt to me for your release. Pay that debt. It's as simple as that."

"And I can pay off this debt by doing as you require?"

"Just so," Malor confirmed with a sharp nod.

"And I can be free from the bonds wrapped around my mind once I have done as you require?"

"You can."

Kronin studied the Dark Magus. A man by all accounts. But not a man. More powerful. Filled with a greed that even he couldn't quite comprehend. Kronin would accept the lie for now, because there was little that he could do about it.

He was not a fool. He understood the application of power. He had done much the same himself many times before.

Once he got his hooks into someone who proved valuable to him, he didn't let that tool go. He used that tool until it was no longer useful ... or it broke.

A dilemma for another time. No more than a fact that he needed to make his peace with. For now. He could consider how he might change the dynamics of this new relationship once he gained more experience with the Dark Magus who had enslaved him.

Kronin nodded, hoping Malor Dragoran perceived the motion as acceptance of his fate. "Why have you done this?"

"You are familiar with the Crux?"

Kronin nodded again. Before his imprisonment it had been

a trading village surrounded by four wild rivers. He had not spent much time there, his focus on deposing his brother before expanding the reach of the Giants of the Rime beyond the Frozen Waste.

"I will claim the Crux, yet it is not an easy task. I have increased the pressure on that Kingdom from the east, though claiming the Splintered Bridge remains a challenge. You will increase the pressure on the Crux from the west by doing as you did before you were defeated."

Kronin frowned, not quite understanding. Until he did. He assumed that he would be required to conquer the Crux. However, the Dark Magus' plan was more far-reaching than that.

"You wish me to cause unrest on the Crux's western border. You want me to ..." He couldn't quite believe what the Dark Magus was demanding of him, because it was exactly what he desired. What he craved with every fiber of his being.

"The Frozen Waste can still be yours," Malor explained. "Your efforts to reclaim it aid mine with respect to the Crux."

Kronin considered the Dark Magus' command that was veiled in an offer. He couldn't quite believe his luck, so he would worry about the consequences later. "I cannot claim my homeland without my Titans."

"Your Titans will join you. Of that, have no doubt."

Kronin's gaze narrowed, finding it hard to make sense of the one who was both his rescuer and his jailer. "You give me a gift. Why?"

"For the reason I stated. Just like before, our partnership benefits us both. Claim the throne of the Frozen Waste. That will help me."

"You understand what I truly desire?" Kronin wanted to ensure that there were no misunderstandings between them.

"I do," Malor replied.

"I do not seek to rule. I seek to subjugate the Giants of the Rime."

"I know."

"Because that is your goal as well."

"Correct," Malor confirmed, his patience wearing thin. There was a great deal more he needed to do, and he could not afford to waste his time explaining matters to a servant.

"I don't really have a choice." Kronin felt the pressure of the Curse in the back of his brain, the insistent demand that he do as the Dark Magus commanded. A compulsion that he could not ignore. That he could not challenge. That pressure slid into the background when he did not question. When he did not push back. Then only there as a reminder so long as he played the role required of him.

"You don't," Malor confirmed, the curl of his upper lip narrowing. "As you said, I am not just Malor Dragoran. I am more. Much more. You cannot stand against me. You knew that when we bargained so long ago."

Malor's features changed then. Shadows swirled around him, revealing his true self.

Kronin's eyes widened, feeling fear for the first time since he was a boy.

"You will serve me," Malor continued. "Whether you like it or not, you have no choice. In this instance, however, you serving me now also allows you to serve yourself. If you choose to fight the restrictions placed upon you, you will experience a pain greater than that of being shut away for centuries from the world around you."

"Release my Titans and we will do as you require," Kronin said carefully, straining to ensure the fear that had settled within his bones didn't reveal itself in his voice. He had always been more pragmatic than idealistic, and the Dark Magus as Kronin chose to think of Malor spoke truly at least in this respect. What the Dark Magus purported to want with respect to the Frozen Waste and what Kronin wanted were one and the same.

"I will do so." Malor was pleased, though the outcome of this encounter was never in doubt. He had learned long ago that the easiest way to get what he wanted from those consumed by greed was to give them what they wanted. Then he could decide to allow them to keep what they claimed ... or rip it free like a bandage from a wound. It all depended on what he required for his own success. Because his success was all that mattered.

Kronin's lips curled. More a sneer than a smile.

Free but not free.

Enslaved though in a different way.

Free to return to the purpose that had led him to the Lost Carcer.

Free to claim his homeland.

To claim his heritage.

To claim his rightful place among his kind.

And to do that, he would offer the Giants of the Rime a simple choice.

Join him or die.

"Does Cadmus still rule?" It was his nephew who had placed him in the Lost Carcer, sentencing him to an eternity of darkness, silence, and insanity.

Malor nodded. "He does."

Kronin snorted. "Not for much longer."

**10**

# DEFENDING THE SPLINTERED BRIDGE

"Stand fast my friends!" Mikel shouted. He held the gleaming Blade of Light above his head. A beacon for all on the Splintered Bridge, including the monsters seeking to kill him. "We fight for one another! Our fates tied together by bonds of blood and bone!"

A resounding roar erupted from the throats of the men and women standing atop the strongholds positioned strategically along the causeway spanning the Trench.

The Crux soldiers battled with a savage urgency. Desperate to keep the parapets clear of the Werebeasts seeking to seize the mobile bastions for their own.

Worried about how the battle was playing out across the span, the Werebeasts making good use of their greater speed, strength, and agility as they pressured the Crux fighters, Mikel rushed forward, placing himself between Teddy and Samuel along the battlements.

His timing was excellent.

One of the Ten Thousand sought to gain a foothold atop the stronghold by slipping between Mikel's friends, each of whom was occupied with a Werebeast of his own.

Teddy held his ground, working hard to prevent the Weretiger roaring at him from getting a grip on the top of the wall with one claw. The giant's efforts ensured that his adversary didn't have the time to leap into the larger fray. Getting in close to the beast, Teddy forced the Were to focus solely on him and worry more about being dislodged from his perch.

The Werebeast who attempted to slide between Teddy and Samuel got no more than a claw atop the parapet. That claw swiftly removed by Mikel with a blindingly fast slash of his blade, the energy surging along the steel slicing through flesh and bone with little difficulty and chipping away a large piece of stone.

Howling more in rage than pain, the Werebear fell back from the spot he had claimed on the battlements, clasping the stump of his arm to his chest. Mikel aided the Werebeast on his way with a quick kick to the shifter's maw.

His section of the parapet momentarily clear of attackers, Mikel's first instinct was to aid his friends. His most skilled thief first.

Samuel didn't like swords. He preferred daggers. Because daggers were best for the close work with which he was most familiar. However, daggers weren't the best weapon to use against the monster he faced.

The Werewolf snapped at Samuel with his long jaws while at the same time lunging with the short sword he held in his claw. The beast howled and snarled, giving into his bloodlust, anxious to get a taste of the wiry man who impeded his ascent.

Samuel would be the first to admit that he was fighting a losing combat. However, that didn't mean the combat wasn't worth fighting. He hoped that he could delay the inevitable long enough for the momentum of the clash to shift in the direction of the Crux.

A futile hope, perhaps, still he held onto it as he danced out of the way of the Werewolf's razor-sharp teeth and the ragged swing of his sword. Stabbing and jabbing whenever he could, Samuel failed to find a home for his blade. Thankfully, he was doing enough to enrage the Werebeast and ensure he didn't claim a spot atop the battlements ... for now.

With a single stab Mikel placed a heavy hand on the scale of what he viewed as an unfair engagement. When Samuel glided to the right, the Werewolf turning his body and raising the sword in his left claw to bring down atop the thief's head, Mikel glided forward.

The instant he slid his flaring steel through the Werewolf's vulnerable armpit, the smell of burnt flesh and hair assaulted him. It was a small price to pay.

If he had not joined the combat when he did, Samuel would have crumpled to the stone, his head split open, the soldier fighting on his right side jostling Samuel and causing him to stumble at the worst possible moment. One of the Werewolf's rabid swings destined to strike true if not for Mikel's intervention.

The Werewolf's howl for blood became a gasp of surprise that turned into a whimper of agony. Wanting to make sure that the beast was well and truly dead, when Mikel pulled his blade free and the beast sagged against the parapet, Samuel went to work with a lethal efficiency, slashing the Werewolf's throat before punching a dagger through his heart.

Certain that Samuel had everything well in hand as the dying Werewolf slid back down the wall, Mikel shifted his focus to Teddy. With a grateful smile he realized that his friend didn't require his assistance.

The giant of a man had traded in his preferred cudgels for two three-foot-long maces much like the one nestled in the small of Mikel's back. The Weretiger climbing the parapet was no longer visible.

Mikel assumed that Teddy dispatched the beast with his well-practiced lethal efficiency, because now his friend was sweeping the battlements clear with a frenzied energy, the flow of Werebeasts seeking to claim the parapet slowing dramatically as a result. None of the monsters wanted to challenge the fighter who appeared to be more a force of nature than a man.

Mikel used the few seconds he had earned to scan the length of the Splintered Bridge. Clashes raged across the parapets of the several dozen strongholds situated across the span on the Crux side.

The barrier Leonardo commanded at the far end was still free of attackers. The Ten Thousand seemed to have little interest in pushing farther to the west until they eliminated the defenders on the bridge. To that end, more and more of the monsters created by the Dread swarmed up both sides of the span to take the places of their fallen brethren.

"This wasn't your best idea," grumbled Teddy. He had earned a brief respite as well. Perhaps a few heartbeats. No more. The Werebeasts at the base of the stronghold were regrouping, bolstered by the reinforcements coming up from below the bridge.

"On that we agree," Mikel muttered.

Nevertheless, Mikel had little choice other than to heed the call of the Battle Lord. Understanding just how precarious the Crux's hold was on their side of the Splintered Bridge, he had brought several hundred of his best fighters with him. Despite that, the aid he provided was no more than a temporary obstacle to be surmounted by the Curse-touched creatures swarming around them.

"We do what we must," the Battle Lord said with a grim finality. He stepped up next to Mikel and Teddy, bloody sword in hand. Having led the defense of the stronghold on the other side, he had no illusions about just how difficult their circumstances were and what the likely result would be if they couldn't seize the momentum. Swiftly. "We don't do what we like. Such is the way of war."

"Truer words have never been spoken." Mikel offered the Lord Dengannon a nod of respect. Then he was moving, the click of the claws digging into the stone of the stronghold grabbing his attention.

"The Ten Thousand seek the other side!" Mikel called in a strong voice, smiling as he said it, hoping that his display of confidence gave Samuel and the other members of his crew atop the stronghold the burst of energy they needed to continue the fight after more than an hour of battling for their lives. "We will help them in their quest!"

A shout of agreement swept across the top of the stronghold as Mikel and his warriors braced for another attack.

"THEY SEEM QUITE intent on joining us."

"Are you always so flippant with death so close?" the Battle Lord asked Mikel, astounded by how calm his ally was despite standing in front of the bodies of three Werebeasts. One resembled a bear, the other two panthers. All killed with a frightening efficiency by the one named the Broken Bear among his many other appellations.

Before Mikel could reply, he slashed down with his blazing scimitar, taking off several digits from the claw that had just appeared on the stone parapet. His efforts earned a string of curses from the Werebeast who dropped back down a few feet to consider his alternatives before seeking the battlements once again.

"Ignore him," Teddy suggested. "He's just being difficult. It's what he does best."

"So long as he makes life difficult for the Ten Thousand rather than us, I don't care," the Battle Lord growled.

This second attack by the Ten Thousand was worse than the first. The Crux fighters were wavering not only atop Mikel's stronghold, but all of them. The sheer number of assailants was beginning to resemble an unstoppable wave and likely to be the deciding factor in the bloody clash.

"It's going to take more than Mikel being difficult for us to win this battle," Teddy grimaced. Kicking out with a big boot, he caught a Werebear right in the face. Breaking the beast's nose and punching the bone back toward his brain, the creature slumped atop the parapet. Yet even with that small victory, more Werebeasts already were scrambling up the wall to take the place of their dead comrade.

The Battle Lord pivoted, allowing the sword wielded by a Werewolf to pass through the space in which he had been standing. Before the monster could pull back his blade, the Battle Lord struck with an admired precision.

Slashing down with his steel, he cut through the Werewolf's wrist to the bone. Rather than seek to complete the excision with his adversary turning toward him and snarling in rage, the Battle Lord slid his blade free and cut in a broad arc from knee to chest.

The Werewolf reared back, howling as he fell from the wall. The Werewolf seeking to clamp his powerful jaws on the Battle Lord misjudged the speed of his prey's counterattack. The Battle Lord cut deeply across the beast's maw and removed a large section of his nose and upper jaw.

Grunting in satisfaction, the Battle Lord heeded Teddy's words. The giant was right. They were fighting a losing battle. That meant there was only one strategy that remained to them that might give them any chance of surviving this onslaught.

"Rolf!" the Battle Lord called.

The Sergeant fighting right behind the Battle Lord didn't hesitate, ripping free the red flag from where it was locked in place by the trapdoor and waving it in the air. As he did so, praying that the fighters atop the other strongholds saw his signal.

He sighed with relief.

They did. And their response was immediate.

The soldiers defending the towers fell back, constricting their battle lines. Ceding the parapets to the attacking Werebeasts, they dropped through the trapdoors and took refuge in their brochs.

Mikel was the last to leave the roof of his stronghold, slicing and slashing with his scimitar to give the fighters at his back the few seconds they needed to escape the quickly advancing Weres. He caught two Werebeasts intent on following him into the tower.

One with a slash across the chest that nicked the artery in the monster's neck, the Werewolf dropping to his knees on the stone and scrabbling futilely at the blood pulsing out from the wound. Quickly lost to sight as the Werebeasts at his back knocked him down in their efforts to face his killer.

The second with a precise cut across the Werebear's hamstring, severing the muscle and almost taking the monster's knee off at the leg. Kicking out, Mikel knocked the floundering beast into his brethren and gained the few feet of space he needed to jump through the gap in the ceiling.

Teddy slammed the trapdoor shut and locked it before the Werebeasts could follow, leaving the frustrated attackers raging atop the stronghold.

Distracted as well, their emotions dominating their reason, many of the Werebeasts did not realize that the Crux soldiers had done more than escape them. They had cleared the battlefield.

Streams of liquid fire already were arcing toward them from the dragons placed along the top of the barrier that blocked the western side of the Splintered Bridge.

∽

Upon seeing the red flag being waved near the center of the Splintered Bridge, Leonardo didn't waste a second. All the while he hoped that the Crux soldiers gained cover in time, knowing he could do nothing for them if they didn't. The Battle Lord was very specific and very insistent with his instructions.

Don't wait.

Don't delay.

Do what must be done.

For the good of all.

"Fire!" the inventor shouted.

Leonardo had built nine dragons. He would have built more if he had the time. Each one positioned on a wheel that allowed the soldier manning the grips to spin in a full circle, the long tubes were connected to vats of boiling pitch with a small flame burning at the very end of the nozzle.

When the soldier responsible for managing the ingenious weapons pushed down on the foot lever, the effect was both impressive and terrifying. Pitch surged through the nozzles and erupted into streams of fire. The soldier then swept those flames across the span almost to the midpoint.

Those Werebeasts too slow to take cover became nothing more than charred husks, their screams of agony echoing in the ears of their brethren and their prey both.

Mikel peered through the slit in the stronghold's brick wall, prepared to close the thin piece of metal the instant one of the streams of fire came his way.

He had never seen Leonardo's latest creations at their devastating best. Or rather worst. The result terrible. And unfortunately necessary.

He was impressed.

Slightly sickened as well.

And then very worried.

Those Werebeasts not caught in the initial attack hid behind the towers, staying clear of the flames.

Waiting.

Seemingly unconcerned.

Every so often they dodged out from behind a tower, seeking to draw the fire of the dragons.

Why?

Clearly the Ten Thousand had learned from their previous assaults, taking cover behind the strongholds or slipping over the sides of the bridge to avoid the liquid fire.

But this?

Risking themselves in this way?

It didn't make sense.

Unless ...

He turned his body, placing his eyes up against the brick, struggling for a glimpse of the far southern side of the bridge through the slit. The northern side lost to him based on the direction he was looking.

He growled both in anger and resignation.

It seemed that the Ten Thousand benefited from the cunning that was innate within the species they were bonded with.

Leonardo had crafted a series of defenses to keep the Weres from advancing directly toward the barricade. Strings of razor-sharp wire draped the stone and wood barrier. Boiling pitch stood ready to be spilled and then set afire. Several more nasty creations that had proven incredibly useful during the battle to hold the Splintered Bridge at the ready.

Thus, the Ten Thousand's initial focus on seizing the strongholds before pushing across the span and into the Kingdom of the Crux. The Werebeasts hoped to force the towers up against the barricade to gain its height.

But the Weres had adopted a new strategy. Either they were

impatient or they decided that there was an easier way to seize the barricade. And if they did, the Crux soldiers on the Splintered Bridge would be caught in a noose. Slowly strangled as they kept to the safety of their strongholds.

For the Ten Thousand had taken a page from Leonardo's book of tricks. Having captured the springy ropes on both sides of the span that the Battle Lord and his men had used to such great effect against the Tor soldiers, they now turned those tools against Leonardo and the Crux soldiers manning the dragons. Gripping the ropes tightly, having no need of the harnesses, the Werebeasts swung up and over the streams of fire.

Leonardo was quick to respond to this new threat as he attempted to adjust his own tactics. But there was a flaw in the design of his dragons, and one that he might never get the chance to correct.

The soldiers using the dragons couldn't raise the weapons to the angle required to knock the Werebeasts out of the air.

Free of the flames, more and more Werebeasts landed atop the barricade.

The Crux soldiers rushed into the fight, attempting to contain the monsters so that their attackers couldn't extend the foothold they had earned.

A brave display as they challenged creatures half-man, half-beast who towered above them and relied upon a daunting strength and agility. Unfortunately it wasn't enough.

The Werebeasts were too fast. Eliminating two of the dragons on the far right side of the barrier in only seconds, they rampaged across the wall. The remainder of the lethal weapons their objective.

More Crux soldiers rushed up onto the battlements, trying to impede the Werebeasts' progress. They fought with an understandable desperation. If they didn't reclaim the parapet the path to the Crux would be open.

Mikel watched it all with a sinking heart. Desperation could only take the Crux soldiers so far. The claws, fangs, and steel of the Werebeasts already were proving to be too much of a challenge as another dragon sputtered out not long after the first two.

"Blast it!" Mikel growled.

Pulling his scimitar from the sheath across his back, the steel shining brightly in the shadowy insides of the stronghold, Mikel climbed to the top of the tower.

"What are you doing?" demanded the Battle Lord when he saw Mikel reaching for the lock. Aghast that he would open the trapdoor with the Werebeasts once again scaling the sides of the tower now that they no longer had to worry about so many streams of fire.

"What I need to do."

~

"CLEAR THE BRIDGE," Mikel ordered, locking eyes with the Blademaster. "I'll take care of the barricade."

Before the Blademaster could protest, Mikel pushed out of the trapdoor. He expected the worst and got it. The first Were to scale the parapet stalked toward him.

The Werewolf raised his snout and howled. Eyes bright, drool dripping from his fangs, he relished what he viewed as an easy kill. He got anything but.

The Werebeast towered over Mikel, who was half in and half out of the door. Mikel chose to use their distinct difference in height to his advantage.

A massive claw sweeping down toward him, the monster forgetting his weapon in his bloodlust, Mikel didn't bother to try to get out of the way. Because he couldn't. He had nowhere to go.

Instead he slashed with the Blade of Light, opening a long

and bloody gash across both of the monster's thighs that revealed the bone beneath. Before the Werewolf could adjust his howl from one of triumph to despair, Mikel struck again. Stepping up and out of the trapdoor, as he stood straighter the dagger in his other hand came up with him and punched into the monster's groin.

The Werewolf's howl died to a hoarse whisper. The beast crumpled, overcome by waves of pain and shock.

Mikel used his momentum to shoulder the stricken beast out of his way. Leaving the badly wounded Werewolf on his back to bleed out, Mikel only had eyes for the claws grasping the parapet to his front. The Werebeasts below were eager to claim the tower as their own.

"I'll take the one on the right," Teddy growled.

The giant followed on Mikel's heels when his friend emerged from the tower. His expression determined. Even more so, with the blood pounding in his ears, murderous. Teddy's desire for violence, usually so well controlled, freed.

Not liking to leave unfinished business at his back, Teddy crushed the whimpering Werebeast's skull with a single blow. Brandishing the maces he wielded in each hand, he advanced toward the Werebear just then pulling himself over the parapet.

The monster got no farther.

One hand still on the wall, the Werebear tried to bring his battle axe to bear. If he didn't strike the approaching giant he could at least force him back and gain the stability of the tower's roof.

Teddy didn't give his attacker the chance.

Ignoring the Werebear's snarl and the axe sweeping toward his head, Teddy smashed down with his mace. The steel crushed the creature's wrist, destroying the utility of his claw.

Teddy grunted in satisfaction as the Werebear fell away from the parapet, losing his grip. The pain of the beast's terrible wound not registering as the power of his swing pulled the shifter off balance and back toward the bridge below.

He didn't savor his victory for long. The clash of steel meeting steel ringing in his ears, Teddy turned swiftly toward the sound. He took one step toward Mikel, ready to assist him in his combat against a Weretiger. Then he stopped, holding his ground instead as Teddy realized that his concern was unnecessary.

Mikel had the combat well in hand, using his scimitar to deflect the Weretiger's axe. Having no desire to become trapped in a battle of strength with his much larger and bulkier opponent, Mikel moved in the direction the Weretiger was forcing him. Allowing his steel to slide off the axe, his lack of resistance pulled the monster off balance.

Fearing that he wouldn't be able to bring his Blade back around fast enough, and already in tight with the Weretiger, Mikel allowed his instincts to rule him. He punched with his dagger and drove the bloody blade into the monster's thigh.

A painful wound though not a debilitating one, the Weretiger already was shifting his weight so that he could reach for Mikel's neck with his free claw.

Mikel wasn't done, however. Calling on the Light that surged through his veins, a blast of energy burst from his hand and flowed through the dagger.

The Weretiger didn't make a sound. Offering Mikel only a brief look of shock as the fiery power sizzled through him, the monster's flesh and armor smoked as small flames flared from his mouth and his burning eyes.

Mikel ripped his dagger free, the Weretiger collapsing to the brick and stone. Dead. Charred and still smoking, the flesh flaked off and formed a ring of ash around the scorched corpse.

Turning slightly green, Mikel stared at the result of his work. Certain that if he hadn't used the Light as he did, he'd likely be the one lying dead atop the tower.

Still, the gravity of what he accomplished lay heavily upon him.

The power that he had harnessed and then applied with such a lethal purpose.

A power that was both seductive and frightening.

A power that he needed to master if he was to have any chance of ensuring that he didn't surrender to the temptations of the gift granted to him by the ancient Blade he wielded.

"That's quite an interesting new trick." With a wrinkled nose, Teddy snuck up next to Mikel, the smell too reminiscent of overcooked meat for his tastes.

"I guess what they say about old dogs isn't true."

Teddy snorted, his friend's humor not lost on him despite the fact that this latest act in the battle for the Splintered Bridge had only just begun.

"You still have some bite in you?" Teddy included a raised eyebrow with his question.

"Until the day I go to the other side," Mikel confirmed.

"Good. Then let's see what else you can do, because I'd hate to find out that you're only a one-trick pony."

"Down!" Mikel roared.

Teddy, Samuel, and the other fighters at his back reacted instinctively. Dropping, they hugged the cobblestones of the Splintered Bridge as an errant stream of fire sizzled above them. The heat of the flames much too close.

"Those hairy bastards are having too much fun," grumbled Samuel when he was back on his feet. His long curly hair, usually resembling a rat's nest, was now only big enough for a small bird. The heat of the fire singeing his scalp, his locks burned and smoldering until Teddy -- with more gusto than Samuel believed necessary -- beat out the last of the embers.

"Then it's time to take away their toy." Mikel scanned the length of the bridge to his front then studied the barricade that was now only a hundred yards distant.

Reaching this point had required both a great deal of skill and luck. Mikel and his crew put into practice all that they had learned while slinking about in the dark of the Crux on their various jobs. Along the way they used the strongholds and the scorched bodies of Werebeasts too slow to evade the flames to protect themselves as they advanced steadily toward their objective.

It was just as bad as he anticipated. Still, Mikel held out hope.

He and his crew were the closest to relieving Leonardo and the Crux soldiers battling to hold the parapet. Several more of his crews were working their way toward him from both sides of the bridge.

While Mikel led the attack, the Battle Lord assumed responsibility for ensuring that the strongholds remained in Crux hands while Mikel's fighters swarmed the few Werebeasts who remained on the span.

The primary question for Mikel was whether they could meet the challenge of removing the Werebeasts from atop the barricade.

Only five of the dragons were still functioning, the rest destroyed by the Ten Thousand. And of that quintet, the Werebeasts had claimed two for their own. Those dragons now were being used against Mikel and his advancing fighters as the Werebeasts sought to impede his approach.

"Move! Quickly!"

Mikel didn't think. He simply did as Teddy ordered. Just as everyone else with them did.

Scrambling to the right and the left, they reached the safety of two towers. Thankful for the brick and stone that protected them as the two streams of fire swept across the span, missing them by only a few feet.

"Now!" Samuel shouted.

Mikel and the others sprinted forward, gaining the back of the stronghold twenty yards closer to the barricade right before those two streams of fire swept by them again.

And so it went for the next few minutes. Mikel and his fighters, as well as the crews working along both sides of the bridge, jumped forward from one stronghold to the next. Avoiding the streams of fire directed toward them, they eliminated any Werebeast who got in their way.

All the while they ignored the fighting atop each of the brochs, trusting that the Crux soldiers could manage the Werebeasts attacking them. Because if they didn't, Mikel and his crews would be caught in a trap with no avenue of escape except for a mile-long drop over the side of the bridge.

"One last sprint," Teddy urged. He and Mikel were hunkered down behind the stronghold closest to the barricade. The wall only fifty yards distant.

"You know what to do."

Teddy nodded. "We fight for the Broken Bear!" While still enjoying the protection offered by the tower, he stood tall, brandishing his maces above his head. Teddy's yell drifted above the sounds of the battle -- the clash of steel on steel and steel on claw, as well as the sizzle of the streams of fire the Werebeasts atop the barricade guided toward the fighters hopping across the bridge from one stronghold to the next.

All eyes turned toward Teddy and with several sharp hand signals he relayed his instructions.

"Ready?" Mikel asked.

Teddy almost jumped back a foot when he was caught by his friend's gaze, stopping himself just in time. Not wanting to become a target to the Weres so happy to turn Leonardo's dragons against them.

Mikel's eyes. Usually, they were dark. Like the ocean deep. A blue that was almost black that helped to hide his emotions.

But now Mikel's eyes blazed with an infernal fire. The orange red more than unsettled Teddy. The flames in Mikel's eyes frightened him. Still, he held his nerve and nodded. "As ready as we'll ever be."

"Good." Mikel turned away from his friend, not understanding why Teddy seemed to be afraid of him.

A worry for another time. The Werebeasts first.

Peeking out from behind the stronghold, he surveyed the battlefield. It was fifty yards until they reached the barricade. No Werebeasts were in sight other than those atop the wall who were compressing Leonardo and his soldiers into a tighter and tighter ball. The momentum at the barricade clearly favored the Werebeasts.

Mikel wished that he had a better idea. But he didn't. Because he had very few options.

The strategy of attacking the wall directly didn't appeal to him, believing that such an assault was doomed to fail.

Even so, he knew something that the Werebeasts didn't.

Along the base of the movable barricade there were several hidden crawlspaces. Big enough for any of his crew to sneak through. Not big enough for the Weres.

If they could reach those crawlspaces, they could join the battle for the parapet and perhaps turn the tide by attacking the Werebeasts from behind and the flank.

And if not ...

Well, there was little difference whether he died on the bridge or atop the barricade other than a better view.

And just as always, his success would depend on speed, precision, and excellent timing.

"Now!" Mikel roared.

Pushing off the stone and brick, he sprinted out from

behind the stronghold. His bad knee protested from the strain, but he ignored it. Mikel needed to stay ahead of his fighters. His focus was on the crawlspaces in the center of the barrier. The streams of fire were currently directed toward his fighters along both sides of the bridge. His crews were taunting the Were-beasts and taking a great many risks to draw their fire, so he needed to make those risks they were taking worthwhile.

Teddy, Samuel, and the others were right behind him. Several more crews who had drawn closer while zigzagging from one stronghold to the next joined them from their hiding places.

Mikel was still twenty yards from the barricade when his eyes widened in fear and resignation. He and his fighters were fast and precise. But his timing for the attack was off. Only by a few seconds. But that was all it required.

Tightening the noose around Leonardo and his soldiers, the Werebeasts had claimed the last three dragons. And as Mikel stood out in the open those three streams of fire were converging on him.

Stuck in no-man's land, he and his fighters had nowhere to go. Too far from the wall to reach the crawlspaces and make it more difficult for the Werebeasts to direct their streams of fire because of the angle. Too far from the strongholds to regain the safety of the brick and stone towers.

"Mikel!" Teddy shouted. He skidded to a stop next to his friend. The fighters with him halted as well. All of them real-ized that they had failed. All of them understood the price that they were about to pay, the three streams of fire arcing toward them only a few feet away.

"Stand fast!" Mikel ordered. "Don't move!"

"But Mikel, we need to …"

Whatever Teddy was going to say was lost to Mikel. His focus instead on the Blade of Light.

The steel blazed even brighter, and he realized the energy to make that happen wasn't coming from the ancient weapon. It was coming from him. The bond between him and the artifact strengthened to the point of becoming unbreakable. The Light surging through Mikel, an almost uncontrollable tempest begging to be released, connected to the potency of the blade.

*"You know what to do,"* Knute Frost Lord growled. The former Bearer of the Blade spoke to him in his mind, Mikel not surprised that the Giant and the other Bearers had been watching the battle through his eyes. *"Don't think. Don't fear. Do what you know how to do. Do what you must do."*

Mikel nodded. Feeding off Knute's confidence, Mikel called on the Light within him, a nimbus of bright white forming around him and expanding swiftly to surround all the fighters with him.

For this task, his timing was perfect.

The glowing barrier took shape right before the three streams of fire struck.

The flames flared angrily against the power Mikel brought to bear but did little else. Even when the other two dragons were added to the mix the streams sizzled and flashed futilely, the flares of red turning orange where they licked against the blazing white of the magical shield that they couldn't pierce.

*"Well done, Steelheart,"* Knute said, his pleasure plain in his voice. *"But you can do more, and you know it. Don't fear what you can do. You can control it now. Don't hold back. Do what you must do. You are more than just the Bearer of the Blade."*

Mikel didn't understand all that Knute was telling him, but that didn't stop him from doing exactly as the Giant suggested.

"When the darkness surrounds the Light will prevail!"

Mikel didn't know why he roared the inscription inscribed on the Blade of Light. It just seemed like the right thing to do. At the same time, he crouched down swiftly and did exactly as he had done when he first faced Assindra and escaped her from beneath the Crux.

Slamming the hilt of his weapon against the cobblestones of the Splintered Bridge, this time the result was much more impressive. Also much more destructive.

A wave of energy blasted out, roaring past his shield and extinguishing the streams of fire. Killing instantly any of the Werebeasts caught out in the open, their bodies charred husks. The monsters crafted from the Curse unable to stand against the Light.

Nor could the movable barrier. The blast of energy devastated the section of the wall Mikel targeted. Stone and logs collapsed into a smoldering heap, the dragons falling in among the detritus along with the Ten Thousand who had claimed the top of the barricade.

The barrels of pitch that fed the dragons tipped over and were set alight, rivulets of fire snaking their way through the wreckage. A large segment of Leonardo's once imposing barricade was now no more than a smoking and burning pile of rubble.

Confident that their path was clear, Mikel released his hold on the Light. Shocked by what he had just done.

Still, it was necessary. As Knute had said, do what you must do. And he did.

The battle was not yet won, however. Not without a final push. And this would likely be his best and only chance.

Refusing to waste it, his bad leg screaming at him with every step he took, in a stumbling gait he advanced toward the massive gap in the barrier.

"The Crux first!" he roared, blazing sword lifted above his head. The white flames flashed and sizzled along the length of steel then sparked several feet into the air. Playing off his emotion, the Blade relished the anger and resolve that coursed through Mikel's blood, all that mixed with the desire for revenge on the monsters who had killed and wounded so many of his friends. "The Crux always!"

"You all right?"

"Those monstrosities used my own invention against us," Leonardo grated, shaking his head in defeat.

"They did," Mikel confirmed in a quiet voice. They stood atop the last section of the barrier that remained whole. The bulk of the structure was now no more than a smoking wreck. The eastern border of the Crux open with little in the way of a defense other than the few companies of soldiers standing a watchful guard and the strongholds, all of which remained in the hands of the Battle Lord after a hard and bloody fight.

"I can't believe you're dealing with this so easily."

Mikel didn't bother to correct his friend, recognizing how badly the battle for the dragons had affected Leonardo. "I have more experience in this than you do."

Mikel didn't need to tell Leonardo that he wasn't dealing easily with what he viewed as a defeat, and one that left the Crux open to invasion. But he understood that there was more to Leonardo's words than just bitterness at what he perceived as his own failures. Rather, the loss of so many of the men and women who had been working with him was driving the inventor's guilt and self-reproach.

Once Mikel and his crews cleared the last of the Werebeasts from the barrier's parapet, Leonardo had led the effort to aid the Crux soldiers wounded and caught in the wreckage as well as care for the dead. Not as many were lost as Mikel feared. Still, every death hurt.

With a great deal of reluctance they decided to leave the dead scattered about the Splintered Bridge for tomorrow, not certain if any would remain in the morning. Darkness was falling, and with it would come the Zaroi with the Werebeasts gone. Probably in greater numbers than usual because of the blood and death that waited for them above their nests.

It wasn't the decision that the Battle Lord wanted to make, but Mikel agreed with him. They couldn't afford to risk any soldiers on a burial detail with the Zaroi eager to claim their prizes. Not with the great many fires still burning on the Crux side of the Trench.

Pushing those dark thoughts from his mind, Mikel surveyed the Splintered Bridge from where he stood. The dire circumstances they faced stared right back at him.

True, the strongholds remained in Crux hands. That was a positive result after the daylong battle. But those towers wouldn't be enough. Not if the Tor soldiers joined the Ten Thousand in their next attack.

"I can't believe I was such a fool," Leonardo grumbled, streaks of tears running down his ash-covered face. "I could have accounted for what those monsters did. I should have." He smacked his hand against the battlements, then regretted it, shaking his bruised palm slowly because of the pain that radiated up and into his arm.

"Leonardo, you look at the world in a different way from everyone else. You see the potentials that others can't." Mikel reached out, giving his friend a warm squeeze on the shoulder. "But it's a big world. That doesn't mean you can see all the potentials and prepare for them. It's impossible. Even for you."

"I should be able to," he protested, pushing against Mikel's argument.

"No, you should expect to fail from time to time. You know that better than anyone from your experiments."

Leonardo started and stopped his rebuttal several times, hearing and hating the truth in Mikel's words. "Yes, but this was the first time my failures cost so many lives. We almost lost because of me, and good men and women would still be alive if not for me."

"If not for you and what you have done for the Crux, more people already would be dead."

"You don't know that."

"I do," Mikel replied with a calm assurance. "This wasn't your fault Leonardo."

"If not mine than whose?"

"Mine," Mikel replied very quietly, feeling the heavy weight of the many bodies laid out across the cobblestones at his back.

"Yours? How could that be? If not for you we would have …"

"I could have read the intentions of the Ten Thousand faster," Mikel cut in. "I could have assumed that they would use the ropes to turn the dragons against us."

"But that's absurd," Leonardo scoffed. "No one could have assumed that …"

"Exactly," Mikel snapped. "We try to plan for every possibility, every impossibility, but we don't always succeed. We can't. We're human, no matter how painful it might be to admit that."

He nodded toward the Splintered Bridge, the scorched strongholds fading into the darkness as the sun set behind them. "This is what happens in war. It doesn't matter how good your plan might be, it doesn't matter how good your weapons might be, as soon as the fighting begins the game changes. And then changes again. And again. No matter how hard you try, you cannot plan for every eventuality. All we can do is be prepared to adjust. To change as we need to according to the circumstances. Today, we did, and just in time."

"At a great cost," Leonardo whispered.

"At a great cost," Mikel agreed. "The challenge now is to ensure that the sacrifice made by those who died today is not wasted. They cannot have died in vain. That would be the greatest failure on our part."

Leonardo nodded, Mikel's words breaking through his

sorrow. "So planning for the battle is only one part of ensuring our success."

"Correct. More critical is how we respond when the circumstances change on the battlefield – because they always will – and how we react when we get hit in the jaw."

Leonardo thought about Mikel's advice and perspective. He still felt a great deal of guilt, but his friend was right. He couldn't allow that to weigh him down. He couldn't allow the men and women who fell today to have died for nothing. He had work to do.

The Crux had been hit in the jaw. The Crux needed to be ready to hit back when the sun rose again in the morning and the Zaroi returned to their nests. "Thank you."

Mikel clapped his friend on the back and offered him a warm smile. "All of us need a little help from time to time."

"You know, you're not as scary and intimidating as you're made out to be."

Mikel snorted. "You mean to say that the King of the Underworld is losing some of his mystique."

"You're revealing who you truly are, Mikel. Especially after what you did today." Leonardo motioned to the scimitar strapped across his back. "Word will spread. That's unavoidable."

"Try to slow it down if you can. I've put too much effort into building my reputation to lose it now."

Leonardo laughed softly at that, Mikel joining him. The first touch of humor either had felt since the battle for the Splintered Bridge began at the crack of dawn that morning.

It was short-lived, however. Leonardo's mind already was turning toward the new challenge that he faced, while Mikel acknowledged the danger of continuing as they had been and wanting to move the fight to territory more to his liking. As he considered the strategy that was forming in the back of his brain, Mikel grew more confident that he might be able to do what he had in mind.

"I feel like I'm running out of ideas."

"You?" Mikel scoffed. "That can't be possible."

Leonardo shrugged. "Well, not the ideas so much as the time to implement them. Before I can bring any new weapons to bear, we need to rebuild. The strongholds will serve us in that regard, but we are greatly weakened. And as we've seen, the Werebeasts have mastered attacking our barricade. What's left of it will do little to hold them back."

"You do what you need to do, Leonardo. Give us as strong a defense as you can by evening."

"And what are you going to do?"

"Try to change the game."

◡

THE BATTLE LORD looked at Mikel, who had been explaining some of what he had in mind for Malor and his Ten Thousand, with an expression of incredulity.

"I'm going to be blunt, lad, because I like you. What you're proposing is suicide."

They stood atop the barricade, staring off into the darkness that covered the Splintered Bridge. Grateful that the Crux soldiers were hunkered down into their strongholds. The shrieks and howls of the Zaroi claiming the dead setting their teeth on edge.

"No, it's not. It's risky. Not suicidal."

Henri couldn't help but smile. "You really think you can do it?"

"There's only one way to find out." Mikel tried to infuse his voice with as much confidence as he could manage.

"I can't argue that point." Henri decided to shift the topic. He wouldn't take the risk that Mikel was proposing, but he wouldn't get in the way either. "That was quite a display you put on during your rush toward the barricade."

"I was just doing ..."

"What you needed to do," Henri finished for him. "Yes, I know. That seems to be a common excuse for you."

Mikel shrugged. First Leonardo and now the Battle Lord? He got the sense that the world he had crafted so carefully was beginning to shift, uncertain if that was a good or bad thing, completely certain that the cause was sheathed across his back. "It's the truth."

"I don't doubt it." Henri studied Mikel with a keener eye. He was already quite familiar with the King of the Underworld, having worked with him ever since Henri assumed his position as the Battle Lord of the Crux. Yet the more he interacted with Mikel the more he learned about him and the more he liked him. Because the man standing next to him who was now being called the Broken Bear among the Crux soldiers had confirmed many times over a suspicion that had plagued Henri for quite some time.

Mikel rarely did anything solely for himself. His focus was almost always on meeting the needs of others.

Despite the risk.

To himself.

To his fortunes.

"You're giving me the same look your niece does."

"Is that so?" Henri asked with a small smile and a nod. "How do you usually interpret it?"

"As one to be wary of."

The Battle Lord chuckled softly. "You're smarter than I thought you were."

"I don't know if that's a compliment. Your niece has told me much the same, more than I care to acknowledge in fact."

"When it comes to my niece, it's definitely a compliment."

He offered Mikel a knowing nod. "I can see why my niece likes to call you the Broken Bear."

"Why?"

"Wounded or broken bears are often the most dangerous. And you, my friend, are the most dangerous creature I've come across in a very long time. Your roar on the Splintered Bridge won't be forgotten. I promise you that."

# ALLIES IN THE DEEP

"Do you really think that this is a good idea?"

Mikel didn't respond to Teddy right away. Instead, he concentrated on the small hollow below them. They were just under a mile away from the eastern side of the Splintered Bridge. The primary encampment of the Tor soldiers was located there.

With little time to reach their position, only so many hours before the sun rose and the battle began again, and not wanting to risk passage across the Trench, Mikel had again relied upon the knowledge shared with him by Knute and the previous Bearers of the Blade.

When he first confronted Assindra in the bowels of the Crux, he had escaped her by using the Blade of Light to craft a portal that allowed him to step through to a new location. His success left the Dark Magus to marinate in her failure.

He had done the same to bring Teddy and the several hundred fighters – who were now calling themselves the Broken Bear's Brigade despite his request that they reconsider the name, the title sounding presumptuous in his own ears – into the Kingdom of the Tor. They were arrayed along the top of the hollow, his application of the Light saving them a great deal of time and eliminating the need to challenge the Wyverns and black dragons that ruled the canyon that was only a quarter mile to their west.

Creating the portal hadn't been difficult, Mikel feeling more and more comfortable with his use of the Light. What proved to be most arduous was the strain he experienced while keeping the portal open long enough for so many of his crew to pass through.

But here, now, his exhaustion had no place. Pushing it to the side, promising himself that he would rest later, he reviewed in his mind the strike he planned.

The Ten Thousand fought as allies with the soldiers of the Tor. Yet that didn't mean they had any desire to mix with the men loyal to Malor Dragoran. Viewing the soldiers as inferior, the Ten Thousand made camp a good distance away from the bridge.

Having no need of fires because of the acuity of their vision, their site melded into the darkness. Invisible if not for Mikel's ability to employ the Light to see all that was around them, including that which desired to remain hidden.

Despite the advantage the Werebeasts enjoyed after the sun set, Mikel believed that he could turn their decision to remain apart from the allies thrust upon them to his advantage, preying upon their isolation if only for a short time.

"The proof is in the pudding, isn't it?" Mikel replied.

"Seriously? That's the best you can give me?" The tenseness in Teddy's voice suggested that he was feeling the mounting pressure as they prepared to take a substantial risk. But that wasn't truly the cause. After all he had done, much of it at Mikel's side, he was simply anxious to renew his acquaintance with the monsters of the Dread and gain some vengeance for the friends he lost atop the Splintered Bridge.

"This was the best idea that came to mind for what was required."

Teddy grumbled though he didn't argue. He understood just what waited for the Crux soldiers in the morning if they didn't prove successful now.

He knew as well that it wasn't so much what he was about to do that bothered him so much as the risk. He had been trained as an accountant, and as a result he had learned that risk was to be avoided. Having tied his fortunes to Mikel, he had adopted a more flexible approach with respect to that variable, although it chafed at times. So rather than worry, best to seize the initiative and hold it for as long as they could.

"Then let's get to it. The crews are ready."

"Two minutes."

"They understand that."

"You have command of the archers."

Teddy nodded then slid down from the lip of the hollow, sneaking along the deer trail to a position a few hundred yards farther along the crest. His archers moved to the crest. Those not holding a bow took their weapons in hand, ready if the conflict soured faster than they anticipated.

Once Mikel was certain that everyone was in place, he called upon the Light.

As soon as he did, the scimitar in his hand surged to life, white flames dancing along the steel. Mikel smiled as the natural magic roared within him. Calling to him. Wanting to be released.

Mikel was more than happy to accommodate that request.

Balls of flame that resembled comets shot from his left palm, streaking up above the hollow as he moved his hand in a slow arc. Those bursts of light hung in the sky and illuminated the ground below, revealing hundreds of Werebeasts bedded down for the night. All of them in their human form.

"Release!" Teddy ordered.

A flight of arrows whistled out of the darkness. The three-foot-long steel-tipped shafts slammed into the Ten Thousand with loud thwacks that were followed by groans and screams depending on where the barbs struck. And they all struck. The archers on the lip picked their targets carefully, heeding Mikel's requirement that they not waste a single shaft.

"Release!" Teddy commanded again.

Many of the Ten Thousand were still groggy from sleep and exhausted by the battle for the bridge. None of them had expected a surprise attack on their side of the span. So it wasn't until the third flight of arrows hit home that those not badly wounded finally began to form a ragged defensive line.

"Release!" Teddy had assumed that the Ten Thousand would respond with greater effectiveness after the first round of arrows. Still, even as his targets sought to defend themselves, some already preparing to counterattack, he was quite pleased with the results of their sneak attack as more soldiers loyal to the Dread fell every time a shaft whistled through the air.

And so it went for the next two minutes as Mikel maintained the brightness of the shining orbs that hung in the sky and illuminated the archers' targets.

With the Ten Thousand seeking cover behind the few trees and fallen logs in the hollow, the archers were more selective in their shooting, waiting for their prey to make a mistake. That often came in the form of a soldier unable to resist the urge to counterattack. The archers, firing swiftly though with a deadly discipline, always ready and willing to take down a charging Werebeast before the shift was complete.

When the bulk of the Ten Thousand finally relied on their reason and shifted, taking their more natural forms and preparing to race up the incline, the onslaught ended and the orbs in the sky winked out, returning the hollow to darkness. The only light came from the Werebeasts' golden eyes that flashed when caught by the moonlight.

Mikel and his crews already were well away from the hollow when the Werebeasts reached the crest. Moving at a ground-churning rate, Mikel led his Brigade toward the south, tracking the Trench and away from the Splintered Bridge.

He meant to keep this pace for as long as he could. Having little doubt that it wouldn't be long before the Werebeasts took up the hunt, he wanted to reach a more defensible location before the real fight began.

Still, he couldn't help but smile.

His archers had done excellent work, taking down a score or more of the Ten Thousand. And all that with no loss of life to themselves.

That was the kind of battle that he preferred.

The real challenge that Mikel faced now was ensuring that he got his crews to where they needed to be next. Before the Werebeasts caught up to them.

Probably more hope than reality, but in this he preferred to cling to hope.

His strategy had worked so far. It was just a matter of making sure that they kept a tight grip on the momentum. And he believed that he could make that happen.

～

"I hope there's more to your plan than just this," Teddy grumped.

The brief clash against the Werebeasts was less than an hour old. There was no sign of pursuit. Yet. Teddy anticipated that it wouldn't be long before that changed and they'd have another fight on their hands.

"What do you mean?"

"We took the Werebeasts by surprise. But this strategy of yours doesn't work if they catch us out here in the open. That's not the kind of fight we can win even with that blade of yours."

"Excellent point," Mikel acknowledged. He offered nothing else. Instead, he kept his focus on where he was placing his feet as he led his fighters toward the south along the eastern rim of the Trench.

Teddy waited almost a minute until he couldn't take the silence any longer, having expected more of an explanation from his friend. "That's all you've got to say."

"I was just agreeing with you," Mikel replied, calm as could be and seemingly unconcerned that a pack of Werebeasts would soon be snapping at their heels.

"The Ten Thousand are likely after us – angry, wanting vengeance, desperate for blood, yet it seems like we're out on a country stroll."

"I would describe this as more than a country stroll," Mikel grunted. A sharp pain in his knee made him stumble. A slip on the loose shale at the edge of the trail had almost been his downfall. Literally. That would have been embarrassing. Battling Werebeasts one moment, laid up on a stretcher because he was a clumsy fool the next.

"Fine, not a country stroll. What would you call it?" The pique drained from Teddy's voice as he removed his hand from his friend's forearm, grabbing him just in time to keep Mikel on his feet. He better than anyone understood the limitations imposed upon Mikel because of his old wounds.

"A strategic retreat."

"A strategic retreat?" Teddy's lack of belief in that statement was plain in his voice.

"Yes, a strategic retreat. Why so skeptical?"

"A strategic retreat assumes that we would have somewhere to go rather than tracking the edge of the Trench."

"That bothers you?" Mikel's smile couldn't hide the spark in the back of his eyes that confirmed he was having a great deal of fun poking at his friend and his concern. "The sense that we're only prolonging the inevitable."

"Of course it bothers me," Teddy grumped, his voice rising just a little louder.

"Why would it bother you?"

Mikel's tone of surprise and seeming lack of comprehension did an excellent job of getting under Teddy's skin and riling him up. "Why wouldn't it? Why doesn't it bother you? The Werebeasts are after us. We expected that. The next clash possibly coming sooner than we want."

"You're right, they are after us," Mikel confirmed. Unbeknownst to his friend, he had been tracking the Ten Thousands' progress with the Light. All of the Werebeasts not killed or severely wounded in the hollow had taken up the pursuit. And just as Teddy feared, they were closing the distance between them rapidly.

"That's my point," Teddy growled. Mikel was egging him on. He knew that. He didn't like it. What he didn't like even more was that he was allowing his friend to poke at him. The stress of the recent clash setting his nerves on edge.

"And as I said, you make an excellent point."

"Mikel ..."

Teddy's growl deepened, Mikel sensing his friend's anger rising. Good. He needed Teddy angry. He needed the Giant to emerge in the battle that was almost upon them. But he also needed that anger directed at their hunters rather than at him.

"I want the Werebeasts coming after us, Teddy. That's the plan. Even with our initial success in the hollow, we had no chance to eliminate all those monsters. All we could do was hurt them and shift their focus toward us."

"So we're bait."

"Exactly," Mikel confirmed.

"Why didn't you tell us?"

"Would you have in my position?" Mikel asked. "Better that the crews play from the edge they're used to. Better that they understand the challenges we truly face rather than rely on hope. And even better that the Werebeasts believe they have the upper hand."

Teddy tamped down on his temper. He considered what his friend revealed, having learned a long time before how Mikel thought and realizing that his friend would never permit his fighters to be caught out in the open. "You're luring them."

Mikel smiled. "That I am. Just like the Tartars liked to do. We're going to stay just close enough for them to focus on us and their desire for revenge rather than the Splintered Bridge when the sun rises."

Teddy couldn't find fault with Mikel's reasoning. If the Ten Thousand attacked the span before the Battle Lord and Leonardo had the chance to rebuild the Crux's defenses, the Splintered Bridge would fall to Malor Dragoran. "They're faster than we are. They'll catch up to us. They might even be faster than you planned for."

"They are on all counts. You're right."

"Then how will ..." Teddy nodded. Then he smiled thinly. He should have contemplated all this before complaining to Mikel. "You want them hungry for us. You want the Werebeasts believing that they have an easy and sure hunt."

"Now we're both on the same page."

"That's all well and good, but out here we stand little chance. That fact hasn't changed."

"On that we agree as well." Without another word, having reached the point along the trail that Mikel had been looking for, he turned sharply to the east. The Brigade followed him onto a game trail scarcely wide enough for a deer. The shadows of the Deep calling to him.

❧

"WHAT DO YOU HAVE IN MIND?"

Teddy was certain that the next clash was almost upon them. A sure sign? The hair on his arms sticking straight up.

The Werebeasts were minutes away. The archers nocked arrows to their bows while identifying the most obvious paths between the trees for the beasts to attack. Those without bows or out of arrows grasped their preferred weapons, whether long dagger, mace, or short sword, ready to defend the archers.

"Exactly this."

Teddy didn't bite this time. Instead, he surveyed their location with a closer eye, quickly understanding Mikel's larger strategy.

Mikel had positioned his Brigade with their backs against the heart trees, ensuring that they couldn't be attacked from behind.

But Mikel had been even more thorough with his selection. His efforts to narrow the battlefield aided by the roots running along both sides of the clearing. Thick as a man was tall, the roots twisted and curled off into the darkness at a rough angle that was close to forty-five degrees, effectively restricting or, if not that, at least hindering attacks from those directions.

To their front the ground was relatively free of obstructions. However, it wasn't a very large space. No more than fifty yards around before the trunks of the heart trees impeded once again, thereby limiting even more the number of Werebeasts who could attack Mikel's rough shield wall at the same time.

Teddy stood a bit straighter. Pleased with the decisions the Broken Bear had made.

Mikel was funneling the Werebeasts toward them. He wasn't trying to prevent an attack. He was attempting to guide it.

But there was more to it than that.

Even though Mikel had chosen an excellent space to continue the fight that didn't guarantee that they'd survive the battle to come. Not against the hundred or more Werebeasts who followed them from the hollow.

That could only mean ...

"We're more than bait," Teddy murmured quietly, a smile curling his lips for the first time since their escape began. "You've got a surprise up your sleeve."

"I usually do, don't I?" Mikel replied with a nod and a wink.

He turned away from Teddy then, his gaze shifting to their front. It was difficult to see in the gloom of the Deep even when it was day. With the night still upon them it was all but impossible. And his Brigade would need more than just the golden eyes of the Werebeasts to have any chance at striking their targets.

Calling on the Light, his scimitar blazed brightly. White flames licked along the steel, serving as a beacon for the fast-approaching monsters.

Then Mikel did as he had just a few hours before, comets of light streaking up from his free palm and into the air, the spheres taking their positions just below the lowest branches of the heart trees and illuminating the battlefield Mikel had chosen.

Mikel nodded in satisfaction. He had done all he could. Now it was time to rely on trust. And though he would rarely rely solely on trust when so many lives were at stake, in this instance he believed that he could.

Ignoring the pain in his knee, the joint feeling like it was filled with crushed glass after the long chase, he placed himself in front of his fighters. Blazing Blade of Light held at the ready, he served as a target for the Werebeasts who were now emerging from between the heart trees and crowding into the clearing.

The Ten Thousand had shifted to speed their pursuit. Massive panthers and bears, wolves and tigers, all wearing leather armor and grasping swords, maces, and battle axes, growled, clawed, and roared at the men and women who had the temerity to attack them and then flee.

All with golden eyes that flashed in the moonlight.

All strangely stuck in place rather than charging mercilessly toward their prey as was their wont and practice, a few lifting their noses to sniff.

Mikel had feared that it might come to this. He was quite aware of how acute a Werebeast's senses were. And he could understand why they hesitated now.

He couldn't afford to give them the chance to make a rational decision. He needed to play on their emotion and prod them into an attack.

"Archers, release!"

The men and women with bows drawn didn't hesitate. Steel-tipped shafts streaked through the air.

This time the Werebeasts had more of a chance to escape the quarrels. Despite being tightly packed together, they could see the barbs coming toward them. Their eyesight was that good.

Mikel eliminated that ability in an instant. A pulse of energy shot from his hand. Sizzling through the air faster than the arrows, the magic slammed into the ground right in front of the Werebeasts. Knocking the first few rows back into their brethren, his attack blinded the beasts.

Many of them turned away, the flash hurting their eyes. Many of them howled in anger when the shafts struck true. Few of the barbs did anything more than wound the monsters. Their broad and muscular backs absorbing the assault.

Even so that was all that was required to nudge the Werebeasts past reason. Their animal instincts surged to the forefront, drowning out the human intelligence that also resided within them.

As one the Werebeasts charged.

Howling and roaring.

Jaws snapping.

Drool dripping from their fangs.

Golden eyes blazing fiercely.

As the Werebeasts rushed toward him, Mikel stood his ground. Finding that of all the challenges he had experienced since taking up the defense of the Splintered Bridge the morning before, this was the most difficult that he had faced. The requirement that he demonstrate restraint when every nerve in his body demanded that he act.

"Mikel, what did you do?" Teddy asked in a tight voice, noticing the unease that rippled through the men and women standing with him and understanding the cause. Because he was uneasy as well, and he believed justifiably so. To calm himself, he gripped the maces he held in his hands a bit more tightly as he stared at the Werebeasts who raced toward him like an unstoppable wave.

Teddy had fought many different types of opponents. Some of them willingly, in fact. But these monsters were the only adversaries who truly worried him. Not only were they strong, resilient, and a good deal larger than he was, but they were also fast. Lethally so.

"I reached out to some friends."

When the Werebeasts were only twenty yards away and about to smash into Mikel's defensive line, he breathed a sigh of relief. Convinced that they would get no farther.

The rush of air that struck his back confirmed it. That was followed by a multitude of blurs streaking past Mikel. More appeared to the sides of the clearing, leaping over or sliding across the roots. Many more jumped down from the lowest branches of the heart trees that surrounded the battlefield.

Those streaks slammed into the Ten Thousand with the force of a tidal wave, stopping the Werebeasts in their tracks. Scythes crafted from unbreakable stone slashed and cut into flesh and bone, gleaming a bright red in the light thanks to the blood marring the razor-sharp edges.

The front rank of Werebeasts disappeared in seconds. The attack, which only had just begun, petered out swiftly.

The Giants of the Deep, brothers to those living in the Frozen Waste -- the only difference their coloring, their hair brownish green just like their skin and their armor a forest brown so that they could dissolve into the colors of the wood -- joined the battle with a jaw-breaking punch.

Maximus, their king, in the lead. His scythe slashed through the Werebeasts as if they were no more than stalks of wheat to be cut down for harvest.

The Peikkos under his command roared in rage and delight as they cleared their Kingdom of the creatures sworn to the Dread.

"THIS IS THE ONE?"

Maximus nodded. The King of the Peikkos stared down at the badly wounded soldier. Because of his injuries and blood loss, the Werebeast didn't have the strength to shift back completely to his human form. As a result, he was stuck. More wolf than man. Certain to die. His end just a matter of time. "He was a stubborn fool. He didn't want to surrender so we had to stick him."

Several Giants of the Deep surrounded the stricken Werebeast. Just in case.

Although he understood why the Peikkos chose to be cautious, Mikel didn't believe that their concern was necessary. Based on the severity of the Werebeast's wounds, Maximus was right. The last of the Ten Thousand still breathing in the clearing wasn't going anywhere except to the other side.

Mikel nodded at Maximus' comment as he studied the creature lying among the roots of a heart tree. "You're one of the Ten Thousand."

"I am," the dying Werebeast whispered hoarsely.

"The Dread made you what you are?"

"He did."

"By choice?"

The soldier didn't reply right away, unable to as he coughed up a stream of blood. He didn't say anything until the hacking stopped several long seconds later. "No. We didn't have a choice. We couldn't stand against our master despite our desire to do so. We still can't stand against him."

Mikel thought about that last revelation. Although not really a revelation. Really more confirmation. His suspicions about what was really at root within the Tor becoming undeniable truths. "The Dread still lives."

"That wasn't a question," the soldier wheezed. Smiling slightly, a thin trickle of blood ran out of the side of his mouth and down his jaw.

"It wasn't," Mikel confirmed. He had feared that the Werebeast would choose not to speak to him. But with his death approaching, the soldier who had survived for centuries as a shifter had little concern about revealing a fact that perhaps under less dire and inevitable circumstances he wouldn't.

"Smart. I'll give you that." The Werebeast groaned softly, a bolt of pain wracking his body. It took almost a minute for the agony to settle to the point where he could wheeze out a few more words. "Our master has always believed that he was cleverer than everyone else."

"That's led to many a person's downfall," Mikel countered.

"True, but you need to remember that my master is no longer just a man. And he's more than just a Dark Magus. He's …" Another coughing fit struck the soldier, the stream of blood now accompanied by several dark clots. His time was coming to an end, and he understood that. Accepted it. Even looked forward to it after all that he had suffered through since that fateful day when the Dread turned the Curse upon him and his brothers in arms. "I don't know what he is now. I don't know if even he knows what he is."

"That doesn't mean he can't be stopped."

"That doesn't mean you can stop him, however, now does it?"

"No, you're right about that," Mikel replied with a nod, acknowledging the truth of that statement. He was many things. Arrogant was not one of them. He understood the danger of adopting such an approach, preferring to see the world for what it truly was and not what he wanted it to be.

"Then again," the Werebeast murmured, nodding toward the hilt peeking over Mikel's shoulder, "that weapon you carry could help you."

Mikel stared down at the dying soldier, the Werebeast's body, already a horrible mess of blood and gore, appearing unnatural now that he was caught within the shift. An unexpected sorrow rose up within Mikel. This soldier of the Ten Thousand was his enemy, yet he had been forced to become a creature that he didn't want to be. He felt sorry for him. Along with that came a visceral anger at the thought of a person's choice being taken from them by someone who was stronger than they were. "It might not be enough."

"It might not," the soldier agreed. "There's only one way to find out. Besides, you were smart enough to rip us apart. That hasn't happened since the Wraiths attacked us during our retreat from Stronghold."

Mikel smiled sadly. Thanks to Kaduna ensuring that he was well versed in history -- and his own efforts to pursue his studies even after she passed, believing that any piece of knowledge he acquired might prove useful at some point in the future -- he was aware of what the Werebeast was talking about.

Specific to the Ten Thousand, the Dread killed the King of

Frisia, Julius Rache, and put the ruling family to flight, claiming the Kingdom and its capital, Stronghold, as his own. A remarkable victory, yet one that lasted only for a few hours.

Wounded in the duel against King Rache, the Dread watched helplessly as another of his creations rose up against him. The Wraiths were too lethal in the Murk, the Dread and the Ten Thousand having little choice except to retreat back the way they had come. Not gaining the safety they sought until they stepped free from the grasping grey the Dread ironically had crafted from the Curse to the benefit of the Wraiths. The ultimate and, in Mikel's opinion, quite fitting, betrayal.

"Any suggestions on how to improve my odds?" With the Werebeast and his brethren forced to become monsters, Mikel sensed there was no love lost when it came to the Dread. Mikel hoped that the soldier would exercise one last time the freedom that had been taken from him when the Dread first employed the Curse against him.

"You already know. You used it against me and the other Ten Thousand now lying dead within the Deep."

Mikel didn't say anything, instead allowing his mind to work over the puzzle the Werebeast set before him. The soldier wasn't talking about steel or magic. He was talking about something more basic.

More human.

A failing.

An often lethal characteristic.

Then he nodded knowingly.

Arrogance.

The Dread had become so powerful, so sure of himself, that there was little that he feared. Except perhaps the fact that Mikel held the weapon that the Dread believed belonged to him. That the Dread desperately wanted for himself. "Is there anything I can do for you?"

The Werebeast smiled one last time, appreciating the offer.

"I'm done with the world. Help me to the other side. I don't want to be like this any longer. I never wanted to be this."

Mikel nodded sadly. Pulling the dagger from the sheath on his thigh he limped toward the Werebeast. About to plunge his steel through the Werebeast's throat and give him the peace he desired, Mikel hesitated for just an instant, the soldier's last words chilling his heart.

"Thank you. And look to your Queen. Our mission wasn't just to claim the Splintered Bridge."

12

## BLOODY BARROWS

"It's been how long since you heard from Linus and his patrol?"

Cadmus stood where four barrows intersected, right in the middle of what the Giants of the Rime called the Great Barrow. League upon league of burial mounds larger than the ships that plied their trade on the Silent Sea ran from the base of the Dragon's Tail Mountains deep into the Frozen Waste to the very border of the Icehold.

"Linus was supposed to report back last night." Julia, closely resembling her father, though a head shorter, kept a wary eye as they and the squad of Defenders with them began to work their way down the trail that led south between the burial mounds.

All them were careful about where they walked, looking down at the crusted snow before they took a step. They were searching for the faint indentations that might be the only sign of the danger that lurked beneath. Using their scythes to test the icy crust to their front, they wanted to avoid falling into one of the sinkholes hidden among the barrows. A death sentence most of the time.

Following Linus' trail in among the barrows, they had reached the valley dedicated to the dead not long after the sun rose above the mountains. That trail faded as they made their way deeper among the burial mounds until it was lost entirely.

Cadmus and his squad had little choice other than to continue in the direction they believed their lost brethren had gone. Julia and several other Giants of the Rime had climbed the barrows to either side, seeking some sign of Linus' passage. But there was nothing to be found.

"Father." Julia called from where she knelt just a little farther down the trail. Several large shapes, invisible from only a few feet away, lay in the path covered by a thin layer of snow. Splotches of dried blood stained the pristine white terrain. "Linus and his patrol."

Cadmus walked over, having feared the worst. Angry that it had come to pass. But he didn't have time to be angry. He needed to figure out what had attacked so many of his Giants in their homeland.

To that end, he studied the ground surrounding his fallen warriors. The thin layer of snow hid much of what had occurred. But not all of it. He scraped away some of the white crystals with a boot, revealing exactly what he expected to see.

A great many prints crusted in ice. All the prints those of a Giant. Not all of them made by the Giants who lost their lives last night.

Then he turned his attention to Linus and his scouts, kneeling down to get a better look at the many wounds they had taken, most delivered with a frightening precision. The slashes could only have been made with a weapon common to the Frozen Waste. So not intruders. Not poachers. Not men.

That reality pushed Cadmus' thoughts down a dark path.

When his daughter told him that Linus had not returned when expected, strangely, rather than assuming bad weather or the multitude of other possible reasons for his delay, memories of the past had invaded Cadmus' thoughts. And no matter how hard he tried, he couldn't escape the nagging belief that something terrible had befallen the young Giant and his scouts.

No more than a feeling, true, nevertheless Cadmus always trusted in feelings such as this one. It's why he had ruled for so long. And it was because of this premonition that he decided to join the hunt for those late to return. Those now never to return.

Cadmus read the scene set out before him with a keen eye. Linus and his scouts had put up a good fight. Yet it had been a losing fight right from the start. Linus and those with him were overwhelmed by a superior force. The barely visible hints exposed by the crushed snow that had turned to ice revealed that.

Yet how was that possible?

The Giants of the Rime ruled the Frozen Waste. There was nothing in this Realm that could challenge a scouting party of ten of his best Defenders and expect to achieve this result. Nothing. Except for ...

The possibility that ran through his mind took his breath away. The memories that had been dancing in the back of his brain burst to the forefront. Those memories of a time that he would have preferred to keep buried in the past.

A time of blood and death.

A time when brother warred against brother.

While her father studied the scene of the clash, Julia grew increasingly worried. She understood why Linus was ambushed here. A narrow path and two steep slopes on each side that reached fifty feet into the sky limited his options and gave the advantage to his attackers.

An advantage that remained.

An inescapable urge rushed through her. They needed to claim the bodies of the fallen and find better ground. The belief that another assault was imminent weighed upon her.

And for good reason.

Their environment had changed from one moment to the next. A stillness had fallen between the two barrows. Made more alarming by the unnatural quiet that came with it, the usually gusting wind deciding to go silent.

And it was thanks to that silence that Julia heard the faint scrape that revealed what she feared was about to befall them. Peering up the side of the barrow on her left, she could see little more than shadows because of the angle of the sun. But she required no more than that to decide on her next course of action.

"Scythes at the ready, Giants of the Rime!"

The Defenders with her responded instinctively to her command.

Weapons raised and held deftly with both hands, they positioned themselves in a loose line of defense in front of the Frost Lord.

Prepared to challenge the several dozen figures sliding down the barrow on snow shoes.

"Hold the line!" roared Julia.

The Giants standing to both sides of her dug their spiked boots into the crusty snow. They kept their movements economical and precise as they had no space to slash wildly.

Their attackers slammed into them as they slid down the slope. Julia's warning just enough to ensure that the Defenders were ready and kept their feet.

Nevertheless, these renegade Giants didn't falter. They didn't care that they committed the crime of attacking the King of the Rime. They cared only about achieving their objective.

Killing the King and his daughter.

To that end, more renegades slid down the slope to join the push to break the line of Defenders.

Julia grunted with satisfaction when the Giant facing off against her was forced to step back.

Dark eyes boiling with anger, beard and hair a twisted mess, the renegade growled in anger as he reached for the deep slash on his forearm, a splatter of dark red following him in the snow.

She had caught him with a quick slice of her scythe, no more than the twist of her wrists, but that was enough. A warning that more of his blood would spill if the renegade came at her again.

She prepared for the next attack, breathing easier for a few seconds after having earned a brief respite. Their attackers' advantage in numbers hindered them.

Many of the renegades were getting in each other's way. The fighting space too constrained, restricting their movements and their options.

But that wouldn't last for much longer. Identifying the problem, several of the renegades already were seeking to flank the Frost Lord and his Defenders and take them from behind.

A smart tactic. Although in truth not the strategy she would have selected if the tables were turned.

She would have set ambushers atop both barrows, sending them down both slopes to place the Defenders in a vise.

Why the attackers hadn't, Julia didn't know. But she did know that if she and her Defenders were to have any chance of surviving this ambush she needed to adjust their strategy.

Swiftly.

"Circle!"

The Giants of the Rime responded to her command with a practiced efficiency. Shifting their formation despite the pressure the renegades applied, they negated their attackers' efforts to flank them.

Unfortunately, one crack appeared in what had been an impressive maneuver.

Marcellus fell at the worst possible time, slipping on the ice despite his spiked boots and giving the renegade opposing him the chance to gut him.

Marcellus' killer and two other renegades seized the opportunity presented by that momentary break in the line, joining Julia and her father in the center of the circle.

Having little doubt about what would happen if this trio attacked her Defenders from behind, Julia acted with barely a thought.

She charged the renegades from the left. Her father did the same from the right.

Steel screeched against steel.

Curses and insults flowed.

Blood splattered the snow.

The combats decided more by circumstance than decision.

Two of the renegades focused their attention on Julia. The third was pleased to challenge the Frost Lord. The desire to claim the suspect glory of killing the ruling family of the Frozen Waste dominated the trio's thoughts and was clear in their murderous expressions.

"IT HAS BEEN A LONG TIME, USURPER."

Cadmus frowned as he raised his scythe, blocking his adversary's slash and then moving with it. Spinning away and sliding his steel along the renegade's, he gained a nick on his attacker's hip when he stepped back. "You would dare to insult me?"

"Always, Cadmus Frost Lord," the renegade replied. "Do you not recognize me?"

"Recognize you?" Cadmus shifted to the left, allowing the

Giant's steel to slide ineffectually by his hip. "Why should I recognize you traitor?"

Cadmus was torn. He needed to defeat his opponent. Quickly if he could. Because he feared for his daughter's life. But this renegade's words tugged at those of his memories that brought him back to a time that almost destroyed the Giants of the Rime.

"It hasn't been that long, has it?" the renegade chuckled. "Maybe this will help?" Instead of slashing with his scythe, the Giant used the edge of the blade to lift his long white hair.

Cadmus' eyes widened. His expression, first one of shock, then horror, shifted almost immediately to a calm and cold purpose.

The renegade's scalp was shaven completely on the right side.

The mark from another time. Centuries past.

The mark of a rebel.

The mark of a Titan.

But how could that ...

He didn't have time to think about how the Titans could have freed themselves from the Lost Carcer. He needed to focus instead on how to defeat them. Because the stakes had just been raised. It was now a fight not only for his survival and that of his daughter and the Defenders with them, but also the survival of all the Giants of the Rime.

"I see it in your eyes, Cadmus. All your wonderful memories of victory burning to ash as you gaze upon me."

"Regulus." Cadmus' voice was tight, clipped. The Frost Lord clamped down on his emotions. Now wasn't the time to allow his rage to rule him.

The Titan let his hair fall back into place, chuckling softly as he stalked toward the Frost Lord. "The one and only. And now I'm finally going to do to you what I should have done so long ago."

For the next several heartbeats there was nothing for Cadmus except constant movement, having little time to think as he glided across the crusty snow. He stayed one step ahead of the Titan seeking to claim his head, having no chance to attack, focused on defending against Regulus' furious assault. Even so, the Titan's blue steel kept coming closer and closer to his flesh. Until finally, Regulus charging into him with his shoulder threatening to knock him off balance, Cadmus felt the blade slice across his arm.

Regulus stepped back then, staring at the dark red staining the blade of his scythe. "I was always a better fighter than you, Cadmus."

"You always thought so."

"I always knew. I just never had a chance to prove it. Until now." Surrendering to the urge, Regulus ran his tongue along the steel and tasted Cadmus' blood. He offered the Frost Lord a nod of appreciation. "Next time I'll take a much longer drink."

"Who freed you?" Disgusted by Regulus' action, Cadmus allowed his anger to drive away the sting of his wound.

"Does it matter?" Regulus shrugged. "What matters is that the Titans *are* free once more. And you know what that means."

"A new war begins."

Regulus chuckled softly. "The old war never ended, Cadmus." The Titan shrugged, an evil glint in his ice blue eyes. "Though I guarantee it ends here and now for you."

"My uncle sent you."

"Of course he did. He doubted that you'd be able to ignore the temptation of the trap he laid for you." Regulus strode forward confidently, scythe held loosely in his hands, murder and revenge dripping from his words. "And he was right."

$\sim$

"Come now, little one, do you really think you can stand against us?" The Titan laughed harshly, enjoying the game he and his partner played as they stalked around the daughter of the Frost Lord. "I don't think she can, Denzig."

"You're right about that, Orsin," Denzig confirmed. The one-eyed Titan lunged then pulled back just as fast, laughing at how he made their prey dance back a few feet. "If you begged us maybe we'd spare you, little one."

"Yes, we'd spare you," Orsin agreed, "but there would be a price." He faked a lunge, seeking to learn the rhythms of his quarry. He wouldn't tell her, not wanting to build her confidence, but she was fast. Very fast. And he had little desire to get poked by her. So best to see if he could throw her off before he and Denzig rushed her. "The thought of the heir to the Frozen Waste warming my blankets is almost too much to resist."

"That it would be," Denzig confirmed. "A dream come true, Orsin, though it appears the little one does not agree."

"Still fools after all this time," Julia scowled. "You'd think you would have learned after spending so much time in the Lost Carcer." She recognized who she was fighting before their blades met the first time. Not knowing these Titans, having been born after her father banished her uncle and his rebels. Nevertheless, she was well versed in the history of that time and the mark of those who fought and failed to bring down her grandfather, Karolingan Frost Lord. "No better than ice for brains."

"Watch it, little one," Denzig warned. "We'll only give you one chance. Warm blankets are always better than a cold grave."

Julia didn't respond right away. Instead she spun slowly as the pair circled her. Making sure that she could keep an eye on both, she worked hard not to be distracted by the combat her father was engaged in or the larger clash raging around them.

"That's right," Orsin added. "One chance and one chance only."

"You're both talking out of your arses," Julia chided. "My uncle wants me and my father dead. It's the only way he seizes the throne. So long as I breathe, I'm a threat."

Orsin and Denzig offered each other an evil grin then chuckled softly as they stepped in closer to Julia, tightening the snare.

"That doesn't mean we can't have a little fun first, little one," Orsin said. "Pleasure before blood I always say."

The Titan lunged quickly with his scythe then followed that with a slash. He didn't expect to strike the heir. Instead he sought to force her toward his friend and give Denzig the chance to make a killing blow. And he believed that was exactly what was going to happen ... until it didn't.

Julia wasn't thrown by the Titan's ruse. Responding exactly how her father trained her, she stepped away from her attacker and closer to the steel slashing toward her from behind before changing her direction and rolling to the right, having sensed the weakness of the snow beneath her the instant her heel touched down.

So caught up in the belief that he was about to kill one of their primary targets, Denzig had eyes only for Julia. His excitement led him to swing with such fury that it pulled him off balance. The instant his front foot touched down, the snow beneath him disappeared.

And so did he.

"Den ..."

Orsin got no more than that out of his mouth. Shocked as he watched his friend disappear through the thin icy layer and into the sinkhole beneath, his words became a gurgle as Julia slid her steel across his throat.

The Titan falling at her knees, hands reaching for his

ravaged throat, she kicked Orsin in the shoulder, certain that it was only a matter of time before he went to the other side.

Looking up, she growled. Her father was fighting for his life. The Titan challenging him demonstrated a skill rarely seen among the Giants of the Rime.

The urge to get to her father was too strong to resist. Even so, she still had one task to complete.

Her father had taught her a great many things while she was growing up. One of the lessons that he drilled into her time and time again rose to the surface in that moment.

She refused to leave an enemy at her back.

Stepping carefully to the edge of the sinkhole, she shook her head in disappointment. Denzig had survived the fall of seventy-five feet. Catching the side of the depression with his steel, the Titan was using his scythe to climb up and out of the trap.

With a quick flick of her wrist, a dagger appeared in the top of the Titan's skull, Denzig falling back into the sinkhole never to rise again.

That last impediment removed, Julia turned her frosty eyes toward the Titan about to kill her father.

~

"YOUR TIME on the throne has come to an end, Cadmus," Regulus roared.

On his back Cadmus pushed against the Titan's scythe, holding his own weapon with both hands and straining with every muscle as he fought to delay what seemed like the inevitable end. Despite his efforts, the steel tip drew ever closer to his eyes. Now no more than a knuckle away.

He didn't have the breath to offer a smart rejoinder to the Titan about to kill him. And he didn't have the strength to keep fighting. Regulus was too strong. Too determined. Too full of hate after being imprisoned for centuries.

The Titan, once the most feared of all the rebels for his fighting prowess, was proving that he had lost little of his skill and his fire even with the passage of the years as he attacked Cadmus with an unrestrained fury. Placing the Frost Lord in his precarious and almost certainly lethal position when Regulus swept his legs with his own while Cadmus blocked a slash that would have taken his head from his shoulders if it connected.

"I will bring your head back to your uncle," Regulus crowed as he pushed down on Cadmus' scythe with a burst of strength that came from his fury and desire for vengeance. That desire clear in the Titan's eyes as he forced his steel hair by hair closer to Cadmus' right eye, the first touch signaling the end of the combat along with the Frost Lord's reign.

"Yours first," a soft voice snarled from right behind Regulus.

The Titan never had a chance to turn around. Gasping as a bloody line appeared along his neck, Regulus' head rolled to the right while his body slumped atop Cadmus.

Ignoring the rush of warm blood that drenched him, Cadmus pushed Regulus off and climbed to his feet. Weapon at the ready.

For the first time since the clash began he took a deep breath as relief flooded through him.

Julia stood to his front, the steel of her scythe smeared with Regulus' blood. And, even better, his Giants were bringing the battle to a close with a brutal efficiency.

The Titans were formidable opponents. Especially with greater numbers. But so were the Giants of the Rime who formed the Frost Lord's personal guard.

Only two Titans remained alive, and they wouldn't be for long, both on their last legs. Cadmus was about to order that one be kept alive, then realized it was too late. Both Titans were skewered in the throat at the same time, dropping into the snow and staining the white a dark red.

He didn't regret the loss, doubting that they would offer useful information about what his uncle was doing and where he might be holed up in the Frozen Waste. Cadmus would need to dig that out some other way.

"Thank you, Julia. If not for you ..." Cadmus didn't finish his statement, not wanting to think about how closely he had come to dying. Instead, he surveyed the battlefield. Grateful that his Defenders had defeated the Titans. Saddened as well, because they had done so at a great cost. More than two-thirds of his personal guard had gone to the other side.

Julia nodded, not saying anything. Always uncomfortable with displays of gratitude or praise, her thoughts already were turned toward what needed to happen next. "What does this mean, father?"

Cadmus was slow to reply. What he had hoped was an impossibility had just become all too real. "That we are at war, Julia. We are at war with ourselves."

**13**

## UNWELCOME GUESTS

"Well done. Well done indeed." Drin stood off to the side, leaning back against the bar of the empty tavern. It was early morning, the festivities of the previous night having concluded in The Fox's Lair only a few hours before. She and her pupil would have the common room to themselves until the late morning. "Take your time. Remember, there's no rush."

"That's easy for you to say," Nat grunted. Sweat dripped down her brow. Her muscles quivered. She was having a hard time concentrating because of the strain.

She had been at this for almost an hour and had yet to earn so much as a crack in the magical defense Drin constructed to hold back her constant attacks. Her attempts at breaking through with delicacy and finesse failing miserably, Nat had adopted a more direct and blunter approach.

Nevertheless, manipulating more and more of the Talent and trying to pound her way past with brute force gave her just as much success as she had earned with her initial attempts. Now the strain of manipulating so much magic was wearing upon her, and she didn't know how much longer she could continue with her current tactics before she collapsed in exhaustion.

"You are doing well," Drin confirmed once more.

Drin had folded a thin shield of energy around herself. Then she had waited. Seemingly at ease. Unconcerned as Nat called upon more and more of the Talent to achieve her goal, Drin remained where she was by the bar. Each attack slid off her as if it was no more than rain trickling down a window.

Drin wasn't surprised in the least that Nat had applied a more brutal approach in light of her growing frustration. Drin had done much the same when she had been given this assignment while training to become a Magus at Haven under the tutelage of the venerable Rafia Riverstone. The only difference being that Nat had demonstrated a greater patience than she had, waiting longer to give in to her more animalistic tendencies.

"If you're attempting to get as close to the line as you can before you burn yourself out, you're doing quite well indeed," Drin counseled, her lips tilting up into a small smile.

"That's not what I'm trying to do," Nat growled. Taking in even more of the Talent, she fired several bursts of energy from each palm, striking Drin's magical shield with a resounding repetitiveness.

Nat hoped that the coordinated attack would weaken Drin's barrier just enough for her to locate the seam she required. But no such luck.

Drin didn't appear to have a care in the world, and her widening grin suggested that she was enjoying her pupil's struggles.

"Could have fooled me."

Nat didn't miss the trace of scorn that Drin offered her, the Queen of the Crux's lips now curling into a slight smirk. Angry at her failure, angry at Drin's prodding, Nat was about to reach for even more of the Talent, her desire to crush her instructor into a bloody pulp gaining traction within her. At the very last second, however, she held off.

That was odd, Nat thought. Not just Drin's expression, but also that she was goading her. Almost as if Drin was trying to push her over the edge.

The Queen of the Crux was many things. This behavior was out of character for her. Which could only mean ...

In an instant, Nat released her hold on the Talent. Placing her hands on her knees, she bent over and took several deep breaths before she pushed herself back up. Hands on her hips, she studied Drin.

Her instructor let her shield fade away. She wore a different expression now. Not one of scorn or disdain as had been the case just moments before. Rather, now one of expectation.

"Trying to break through your shield wasn't the only goal of this exercise." Nat was no longer angry. Only certain in her belief. "I'm not even sure it was the goal."

"It wasn't," Drin confirmed, although she offered nothing more than that as she waited to see where Nat was going to go with her supposition.

"In fact, you didn't expect me to break through your shield."

"I didn't, no," Drin agreed. Once again, she didn't offer anything more.

Nat could have surrendered to her anger, taking the path that she was offered. But she didn't. Instead she became thoughtful as she considered a host of possibilities. "You were teaching me something more important."

"That was the goal," Drin admitted. "Did I succeed?"

Nat stared a little longer at Drin. It had been an act at the end. Drin testing Nat, attempting to push her into a rash action. And she almost had with Nat balancing right on the edge. Nat hadn't fallen for it, however. She had recognized what Drin was doing and employed ...

"Restraint," Nat said in a soft voice, nodding her head

slightly, a small smile breaking free. "That's what you were trying to teach me."

Drin smiled broadly, her pride in her student plain. "And it only took an hour."

"Only took an hour," Nat glared, taking Drin's comment as an insult. "How could you think that ..."

"I went through much the same lesson when I was learning to make use of the Talent," Drin cut in. "I didn't realize the real purpose of this exercise until three hours had passed. So all credit to you."

Nat opened her mouth to offer the sharp words at the tip of her tongue then shut it quickly. What she had been preparing to say would not prove helpful to the conversation. Then she smiled reluctantly, pleased by Drin's praise. "Thank you for sharing that."

"We all make mistakes. We all fail. That's just the way of life. And it's often the only way to learn. What matters isn't that we made a mistake or fail at a task. It's what we do with that knowledge. How we apply it in the future."

"Now you sound like Mikel," Nat groaned.

"I don't know how to take that," Drin replied. A part of her wanted to view Nat's statement as a compliment. A larger part wanted to challenge her.

"However you like. But you two are more similar than either of you would care to admit."

Drin pursed her lips, thinking about Nat's claim. Not certain what she wanted to do with it. "Mikel does seem to offer useful advice on occasion," Drin offered diplomatically. She was willing to go no farther than that.

"On occasion," Nat agreed, not feeling the need to push again. Not yet anyway. Having caught her breath, she stepped up to the bar and poured herself a glass of water. Drinking greedily, when she was done she faced Drin.

"Going back to the topic of this morning's lesson, restraint. I need to understand that even though I can use the Talent, that does not make me all powerful. I still face certain restrictions that I can't ignore or avoid. Limitations in strength, skill, and knowledge. So I need to keep the implications of those limitations buried in the back of my mind so that the decisions I make are based on reality and not on what I might believe or perceive."

"I can see why Mikel relies on you so much. You're as sharp as a striking whip."

Nat blushed slightly, still not used to receiving compliments. Not after all that she had endured when she was a child. "Thank you."

"I'm just speaking the truth." Drin leaned in, wanting to make her point one more time. "All of us have our limits. Yours is almost as great as mine if not greater. Know your limits. Know what you can do. Know what you shouldn't do. You'll be more powerful for it."

"I'll remember that," Nat promised, blushing again. Because of her discomfort, she shifted the topic. "Can I ask a question?"

"Of course."

"I never had any chance of breaking through your shield, did I?"

"Not the way you were approaching the challenge, no."

"Will you tell me the secret?" Nat asked hopefully.

"You'll figure it out when the time is right."

Nat frowned, then chuckled softly. She could have pushed, but she realized that there was no point. Drin was remarkably patient. She needed to be. Otherwise, she'd never be able to manage Mikel as well as she did. "Another lesson on the same theme."

"As I said, sharper than a striking whip."

Nat snorted softly, becoming more and more uncomfortable from Drin's praise. Thus her desire to poke. Just a little bit.

To turn the focus away from her and onto her instructor. "You know it's all right with me."

"What's all right?" Drin didn't understand Nat's comment.

"You know." Nat offered Drin a shrug and a nod. "It's all right with me."

"Know what?" Drin was now thoroughly confused.

"That it's all right."

"Now you're definitely speaking like Mikel." There was a hint of exasperation in her tone. "You've been spending too much time with him."

"I like spending time with him," Nat replied with a wide grin. "He's full of surprises."

"That he is, and now apparently so are you." Drin pushed herself off the bar and faced Nat. "Now what are you talking about?"

"You don't know?"

"Nat!" Drin groaned, her exasperation becoming tangible.

Nat didn't bite back as she normally would, instead giving Drin a satisfied grin at having achieved her objective, which only served to elevate Drin's level of aggravation. Nat's expression was much like the one Mikel liked to give her whenever he succeeded in getting under her skin. A much too frequent occurrence lately.

Although Nat had a better sense than Mikel as to how far she could push. Having enjoyed her fun, she moved on to the more serious issue buried within. An issue that she didn't want between them any longer. "It's all right if you and Mikel ... you know." Nat gave Drin a suggestive look, Nat believing that would be enough for her to figure it out.

It wasn't. "Mikel and I do what?"

"You know." Nat didn't want to be too specific, the thought of adding color to what she was hinting at making her even more uncomfortable than she had been before.

"I know what?" Drin's cheeks reddened. At first because of

the difficulty of extracting whatever it was that Nat was talking about. Then because she believed that she understood exactly what Nat was talking about.

"If you want to spend more time with Mikel ..." Nat shrugged and nodded again, hoping that Drin would get the gist of what she was implying. "I don't mind."

"You don't mind?" Drin didn't know what else to say. Temporarily at a loss. Never expecting to discuss this topic this morning. And certainly not with Nat.

"I don't mind. I know you two have gotten ... closer." Nat looked down, her own face coloring and not wanting to reveal it to Drin. She was beginning to wonder if she was raising this topic at the right time. That perhaps she should have waited. And she probably could have. But there was something within her, an instinct, that made Nat feel as if matters could be moving faster between Mikel and Drin – that they should be moving faster -- and she didn't want to be an obstacle to what the two might be able to build together. "I don't want to get in the way of whatever it is that's between you and Mikel. That's all that I'm trying to say."

"I appreciate your concern, Nat, but you're not getting in the way," Drin explained in a soft voice, her aggravation fading quickly. She appreciated what Nat was trying to do. It took courage. And it revealed something more. A trust between them that Drin never was certain that they could achieve but that she was pleased that they had.

"I'm not?"

"No, you're not. Whatever happens between Mikel and me will happen. Either for good or bad. And how it all plays out ... well, the responsibility for that lies with me and Mikel. Although more with Mikel than me. You know how he is. Difficult. Very difficult."

Nat laughed at Drin's jest before blowing out a breath. "Good, because I was worried."

"You have nothing to be worried about. In truth, I don't know what the *that* between Mikel and me is."

"You don't know what the *that* is?" It took Nat a moment to realize what Drin was saying.

"I don't." It was Nat's turn to blow out a breath. "As I said, Mikel is difficult. And in this area, he has been even more difficult to pin down so I don't know ..."

Drin's posture straightened as she sensed the change in the room, Nat's expression hardening at the same time. A slight nod of her head turned Drin toward the entrance to the tavern.

The Fox's Lair had been theirs since the sun rose. It no longer was.

A fist of large men strode in, needing to bend their necks to avoid hitting their heads on the door head. Although they weren't wearing any identifying armor, how they moved, how their eyes scanned the room, how their hands were never far from the grips of the weapons at their hips, confirmed that they were soldiers.

The biggest of the quintet, much of his face except for his eyes hidden by his scraggly beard, approached the bar, not stopping until he loomed over Drin. Then he sniffed the air as he gazed down upon her, his eyes brightening as he did so.

"You are the Queen of the Crux."

It wasn't a question. The fact that this soldier knew who she was despite the disguise she wore and her efforts to leave the Citadel without anyone the wiser worried her. Even more concerning was that sniff. Why would he ...

The dispatches from her uncle and Mikel instantly crowded her thoughts.

She hadn't wanted to believe what they told her. She knew from hard experience, however, that there was a good deal of separation between want and believe.

Mind made up, she seized the Talent, glad that Nat already had done so. "Malor sent you."

The soldier nodded. He saw little need to engage in any subterfuge. Besides, that was not his strong suit. He was straightforward and decisive. Always. The result of the temperament forced upon him. "He did."

"Some of your peers already have tried their luck in my city, and they have failed. Are you certain you want to do the same now? I will give you this one chance to leave and return to your master. I suggest you take advantage of my generosity."

"And if I don't?"

"Then the lives of you and your friends are forfeit. I deal with enemy combatants in only one way." Drin's eyes turned colder than the Frozen Waste, emphasizing her point.

"I was told you were a feisty one, Queen of the Crux."

"I am more than feisty," Drin stated softly though in a voice as hard as stone. "I bow to no one. Not five soldiers of the Ten Thousand. Certainly not to the King of the Tor."

The soldier leaned back then, his shadow no longer falling so heavily upon Drin. "You know who we are. I guess I should not be surprised."

"I can tell by the smell."

A deep rumble of laughter erupted from the soldier rather than the anger Drin expected and actually wanted. Because anger was much easier to manipulate.

"Feisty indeed." The soldier took a step closer, leaning down even further so that Drin could see nothing more than his face. "This act might serve you well in your city with your Lords and Ladies. It will do you little good now, Queen of the Crux. If you know who we are then you know what we are. You know what we can do. You know what we will do to accomplish the mission entrusted to us."

"Is that supposed to frighten me?" Drin's eyes blazed all the more brightly now that she was in the soldier's shadow. Her lesson that morning with Nat had focused on restraint, however at that very moment she had little desire to exercise restraint. She hated nothing more than being bullied.

"I don't know that I can frighten you, Queen of the Crux. Credit to you for that. I am simply speaking the truth. You know what we are. You know what we can do. You know what we will do. Our master requests that you visit with him once again. He was disappointed that you left without asking for his leave."

"He wanted more than that from me."

The soldier nodded, not denying her claim. "Our master always wants more from anyone who can help him achieve his greatest desires. That's why he is who he is."

"And yet you fight for him?"

"We do, Queen of the Crux. Because we have no choice. We must fight for him. But that is not relevant to our conversation now."

"This is a conversation?"

"It is," the soldier confirmed.

"I thought it was an abduction."

"Be careful, Queen of the Crux. Otherwise your feistiness will cause you problems better left avoided." The soldier smiled then. Really no more than a thin split of his beard that revealed long fangs rather than teeth. A hint as to what would come if the Queen of the Crux demanded more from him. "Come with us now. Cause us no problems. We will leave the girl be if you do. You have my word."

Drin glanced over her shoulder. Nat's expression showed all that she needed to see to confirm her next steps. "I believe you, Were. But you must know that I won't go quietly. I am the Queen of the Crux. This is my city. My Kingdom. You have no place here. Go. Now. Or I will expel you myself." Swirls of energy began to cascade around her fingertips to highlight her obstinance.

The soldier stared at the Queen of the Crux. He had been

warned that this might happen. Malor Dragoran had been quite specific about how headstrong Celindria Dengannon could be.

It didn't bother him, however. Rather, it amused him. He had no time for the games that his master so liked to employ. This stalemate between him and the Queen of the Crux was something that he understood. Because the use of force was one of his most effective tools.

"You may not come quietly, but you will come," the soldier growled.

Drin's grin tightened. She had grown tired of the standoff. It was time to move on to the main event. "Then know the wrath of the Queen of the Crux."

A blinding white light exploded right at the soldier's feet, blowing the hulking figure backward and sending him and his comrades tumbling to the floor.

"Quite the speech at the end," Nat grunted. She spun swiftly. Swinging the baton of energy she had crafted with the Talent she missed the Werebear who tried to sneak up on her from her left side.

That didn't bother her, however, because she assumed that she was going to miss. Striking the Werebear wasn't her primary objective.

The Werebear glided backward, avoiding the blow after having already learned that Nat packed quite a punch when she hit her target. His fur and flesh burned in the several places where her weapon had struck true.

"I was in the moment," Drin replied. "The words just kind of flowed out of me."

Drin held a dagger in one hand, though she doubted she

would get much of a chance to use it. Even with their great size, their attackers were too fast and too disciplined.

The Werebears feinted now and then, looking for that opening that would allow them to break through her and Drin's defense. The fact that their current efforts were much the same as the exercise from earlier that morning not lost on either Drin or Nat.

Restraint.

No rash actions.

No rash decisions.

They wanted to maintain the stalemate that was no longer conversational in nature for as long as they could. Until they could find some means of escape.

That goal top of mind, Drin and Nat kept the bar at their backs. Ensuring that the five Werebears, snapping and snarling with their fang-filled maws, slashing with claw and battle axe, could not slide around their flanks.

Drin was grateful for that. Grateful as well that these Werebears had not sought to kill her. At least not yet. They were still intent on capturing her. But how long that would last as their bloodlust took them, she couldn't say.

Thus, the dilemma she and Nat faced. They had no good means of escape, and their kidnappers understood that.

Nat and Drin sent bursts of the Talent in every direction, seeking to knock a Werebear from the fight to improve their odds. Yet all to no avail.

Because though they could call upon the Talent, their skill in natural magic did not give them the advantage that it would in most every other situation. Crafted from the Curse, the Werebears had some resistance to the Talent that allowed them to absorb all but the strongest of attacks. And most of those they avoided because of the speed and agility gifted to them by the unnatural forms they had assumed.

"You need to be more in the moment now," Nat growled. "This isn't sustainable."

"I'm well aware." Drin hissed in anger. She thought she had one of the Werebears dead to rights.

The monster had been edging his way closer to her from the right, waiting to lunge at her once one of his comrades attacked her from the other side.

The strategy was a good one, but Drin was too fast for the Werebears.

The monster closer to the center of the line was caught off stride when she fired a bolt of energy right at him. Striking him full in the chest, the energy sent him flying backward and crunching into the far wall. Injured, perhaps, but not dead as he should be, the angry Werebear already was pushing himself back up with a smattering of curses.

An irritating failure, which was becoming much too common for Drin. Even so, her strike had been enough to dissuade the Werebear on her right side from continuing his advance, giving her a little more time to think before their attackers pressed them again.

"Any ideas?"

"If I had an idea, I'd offer it," Drin growled. Not angry with Nat but angry with herself for not having found some solution for relieving the pressure. "Why are you asking?"

Three spheres of energy shot from Nat's right palm, arcing through the common room. Destroying tables and chairs and charring the walls, and unfortunately doing nothing to their attackers, the Werebears scrambled out of the way just in time.

Nat didn't expect much joy from her effort. But that was all right. If the Werebears were more concerned about what was coming their way that ceded the advantage, however small it might be, to her and Drin.

"Mikel usually has an idea or two when the odds are against

him. Usually something dangerous and not completely thought out, but at least something."

Drin cursed under her breath. The concerns Nat raised with respect to her relationship with Mikel were of little consequence now. And she didn't need the reminder that he seemed to thrive when his back was up against the wall. The hard wood of the bar pressed into her spine poked her just as Nat had been before this fight began. "Since I'm all out of ideas, did you have something in mind?"

"You remember our discussion regarding restraint?"

"How do you want to do this?" Teddy crouched down next to Mikel, sticking to the shadows.

They and a crew had entered The Fox's Lair through a tunnel that Mikel had built so that they could move in and out of the tavern without being noticed. Samuel and several more crews were making their way toward the front entrance, but it was going to take a few minutes more for them to get into place.

Mikel peeked around the door jamb, or what was left of it. Drin and Nat were putting on quite a show with the Talent, doing all they could to keep free of their abductors.

He was impressed by their efforts. A little put out as well.

Neither of the Magii seemed to care that they were doing more damage to his tavern than to the Werebears facing off against them.

He could understand that. If he was in their position, he would do much the same.

Rather his anger was directed toward the Werebears, viewing them as the reason why the common room of his favorite tavern was being destroyed before his eyes.

Yet that anger couldn't hold a candle to the rage that surged through him, that he fought to contain, because of the five bastards who dared to attack people he cared about. The two women were more important to him than anything else he held dear in the world. A fact that he would readily admit to Nat. To Drin he wasn't so sure that he ...

Mikel shook his head to clear it of its less-than-useful thoughts, which only served to fuel his emotions. He would continue to think about his hesitancy with respect to the Queen of the Crux, but not at that moment. Instead, he studied the clash a few seconds more.

Drin and Nat remained in a precarious position.

Despite their best efforts, all five Werebears were still in the fight. And though Mikel was quite pleased that Drin and Nat were all right, he doubted that they would remain so for much longer.

Because if a quintet of Werebears wasn't bad enough, he sensed a more perilous threat approaching. Mikel didn't know why the premonition struck, and he didn't know what the cause was, but he was certain. The feeling was too strong to ignore.

Another skill that he had acquired since claiming the Blade of Light. He just hadn't worked with Knute and the other Bearers long enough to fine-tune this ability. But he would. Assuming he survived the next few minutes.

"I was going to say delicately ..."

"But that doesn't matter now," Teddy finished for him, reading the clash exactly as Mikel was.

"Precisely." Mikel cringed upon watching as several more of his tables were blasted into splinters by another errant throw from either Drin or Nat. He couldn't be certain who was responsible since they both were being so profligate with the Talent.

"If we rush in there we're just as likely to be struck by the Talent as the Werebears."

"My concern as well," Mikel admitted.

"What do you want to do?"

"You'll know what to do and when. Be ready."

Mikel pushed himself up then stepped warily around the door jamb. Setting himself, he pulled the Blade of Light from the scabbard across his back. The steel came to life at his touch.

"Five soldiers of the Ten Thousand squaring off against a woman and a girl and you can't do anything more than destroy my tavern! You're no more than a bunch of foul-smelling mongrels!"

THE CLASH that ripped apart much of the common room halted in an instant. The silence that descended thick with anticipation.

All eyes turned toward Mikel.

Blazing sword in hand. Dark eyes flashing. His scowl carved into his face.

He cut quite a figure.

At least he hoped he did.

Because what he had in mind next required that he hold the attention of five Werebears while their blood was up. Not an easy task.

"Mikel, what are you ..." Nat's hand on her arm stopped Drin from continuing with her question.

She leaned in close to Drin and whispered. "Buying some time."

"Who are you?" the largest of the Werebears growled. Clearly he was the leader, the other four adjusting their position in response to his. Two were focused on Nat and Drin. Two stared with heartless eyes at Mikel.

"The owner of this fine establishment that you're doing your best to level."

The Werebear grunted. "You don't like that, do you?"

Mikel shook his head, pleased to have gained the Werebear's attention so easily. "I don't."

"And you're going to do something about it? Stop us from completing our mission?"

Mikel smiled thinly, though there wasn't a trace of mirth in his eyes. His dark orbs flashed that much more brightly. "If that's what's required to send you fleeing from the Crux, then yes."

"Send us fleeing?" the Werebear chuckled, the sound a raspy rumble. His comrades joined him. "You've got some nerve, little man."

"I've been told worse."

"I don't doubt it," the Werebear said, nodding his head slowly before he motioned with a claw. "That's quite the sword you have."

"You like it?" Mikel asked. He lifted up the Blade, studying the blazing steel, making sure that when it caught the light from the few lanterns still in place, it flashed in the Werebear's eyes. "I quite like it myself."

"Do you know how to use it?" challenged the Werebear. "Just because you have a length of steel doesn't make you a Blademaster."

Mikel shrugged, ignoring the veiled insult. "I haven't cut myself yet if that's what you mean."

"This is not your business, tavern keeper. Leave. Now. You can reclaim your common room when we're done. We don't care about you. Only the Queen of the Crux."

"And that's the sticking point right there," Mikel said, offering the Werebear a sad shake of his head.

"How so?" The Werebear was less intrigued by the interruption now and more annoyed. His desire to complete his task added a stronger note of urgency to his deep growl.

"The Queen of the Crux is my business."

Drin was about to add a few choice words to the dialogue,

protesting what Mikel claimed. Nat squeezing her forearm again made her hold her tongue. For now.

The Werebear snorted. "Why would that be, little man?"

"I'm her champion."

"Champion? You?"

"Her champion, yes." Mikel offered the Werebear a confident grin. "Don't let my appearance deceive you."

"You're a tavern keeper," scoffed the Werebear.

"Among other things," Mikel agreed. "I have more than one interest in life."

"Is that so?" The Werebear was less than amused now, swiftly tiring of the conversation that was going nowhere.

"It is, indeed."

The Werebear lifted his massive head, looking down on Mikel with a skeptical eye. "You hear that lads. We have a warrior in our midst. Do you think he prefers to fight wearing nothing except his apron?"

The Werebear earned another round of harsh, guttural laughter from his comrades. It did nothing more to Mikel than harden his already flinty expression. It was almost time. The last piece of the game soon in place.

"I could be wearing nothing at all and still best you," Mikel stated with an absolute confidence that silenced the rough chuckles that seemed out of place coming from the maws of bears.

"You would dare to challenge me, little man?"

"I dare nothing," Mikel explained. "I do." Mikel's grin turned grim in a flash, his eyes sparking with a menacing fire. "And I don't challenge you, Werebear, I challenge all five of you."

Blazing scimitar in hand and raised above his shoulder, Mikel sprinted toward the Werebears.

At the last second, before he swung at the leader of the Werebears, Mikel slid across the floor. Left foot extended, he crashed into the Werebear's front leg, forcing the knee back at a terrible angle.

The Werebear crashing heavily to the ground, Mikel was on him before he could rise. Blade slashing down swiftly, he separated the Werebear's head from his shoulders.

He was about to make a play for another of the Ten Thousand, seeking to build on his momentum. Instead, he glided back and placed himself in front of Nat and Drin. He wanted to ensure that they weren't vulnerable to an attack as Teddy led his crew into the fight from the back storeroom and Samuel raced through the main entrance with a dozen fighters at his back.

It was an unfair clash.

Exactly how Mikel intended it to be.

His crews swarmed the four remaining Werebears.

The Ten Thousand demonstrated a martial prowess to be admired. But even with their monstrous size, strength, and speed, they couldn't avoid all the blades thrust toward them.

One Werebear fell.

Then another.

A third.

One remained, his back turned toward Mikel. Desiring to escape the daggers and swords that were seeking a home in his body, the Werebear spun swiftly and lunged toward Mikel. Perhaps believing the gleaming blade could be of use to him in his defense. Perhaps simply desiring to eliminate the ringleader who had brought on this bloody massacre.

Mikel would never find out.

Before he shifted his feet to take on the monster, a bolt of white-hot fire raced over each shoulder and slammed into the Werebear's chest, sending the soldier flying backward. Not convinced by the Werebeast's smoldering mess of charred flesh, several of Mikel's fighters made sure that the beast went to the other side by sliding their blades through the smoking corpse to ensure his swift passage.

Leave it to the two most important women in his life to make a point when he had everything under control.

About to sheathe his Blade and check on Drin and Nat, Mikel refrained. The voice coming from behind him sent a spike of ice down his spine.

"We need to have a talk ... my child."

"WHY AM I NOT SURPRISED?" Mikel squared off against Assindra, who had walked out from his office behind the bar, placing himself in such a way as to ensure that she would need to go through him before she could make a play for anyone else.

"You know the truth." Assindra could see it in his eyes. "Yet still you choose to ignore the connection between us."

"The connection between us?" Mikel snorted, more shocked than amused.

"Mikel ..." Drin's voice trailed off when she saw his expression. Colder than the Frozen Waste. Although not directed toward her.

Clearly, this was his battle. She didn't understand the Dark Magus' comment. Nevertheless, she feared for him and what could come of this encounter.

"You give yourself too much credit," Mikel said. "You are nothing more than a former client who tried to use me."

"Use you?" Assindra scoffed. "You betrayed me."

"Only because you were going to betray me."

Assindra bit back the words on the tip of her tongue, then offered Mikel a cunning smile. "True. I should have given you more credit. For that failure, I apologize." She took a step closer, more gliding across the floor than walking. "I give you credit now. Defeating soldiers of the Ten Thousand. And with such ease. More than just impressive. Enlightening as well."

The mysterious expression Assindra gave Mikel tightened his own. He was certain that she was trying to play him, and he didn't like it. "You came here for a reason, Assindra."

"I did."

Mikel studied the Dark Magus. She was difficult to read. Though not impossible. He caught several hints that presented him with a few paths for dealing with her. If he could.

Because not only did he sense that she was the greater evil that had teased at his consciousness before he challenged the Werebears, but he could also tell that the power she wielded could bring The Fox's Lair down upon all of them if she chose to surrender to her vindictiveness. Therefore, he needed to tread carefully, at least for a time.

"You weren't certain that your Ten Thousand would succeed."

"When I heard that you were returning to aid the two Magii, I sought to protect my investment."

"Your investment is gone." Mikel nodded to the five bodies on the tavern floor. In death the Werebears had shifted back to their human form. Their grimaces of pain and anguish joined with what Mikel could only interpret as relief. Understandable. The five were finally released from the horrific prison forced upon them by the Dread.

Assindra chuckled softly at that. "My investment is standing in front of me." She took another step closer to him, now only a few feet away. She nodded appreciatively. Pleased.

Mikel didn't flinch. He didn't try to step back. He held his ground.

She smiled then, appreciating his backbone. "You seem surprised. You shouldn't be. You should have assumed that this was my true end. That you are why I came."

Mikel's gaze narrowed as he stared into Assindra's eyes. Not losing himself as might have been her goal. Instead he searched for a characteristic that a small part of him wanted to find. Only a few seconds passed before he realized that what he wanted to see never had been and never would be there. That realization crystallized his perspective. "I'm just another of your tools. Nothing more."

"You are much more than that, Mikel." Assindra smiled warmly, then offered him her hand. He didn't take it. "We are of the same blood."

"That doesn't matter."

"Does it not?" The warmth in Assindra's voice dissipated in a flash. "What do you know of blood and the power that it contains other than how to spill it?"

"I know that this connection you claim to have with me is nothing more than blood." He stepped forward, looming over Assindra even though he doubted that it would affect her. Regardless, he wanted to make the point that he wasn't intimidated. "Kaduna raised me. She taught me that blood doesn't matter when it comes to most things in this world. The connections we feel to other people are not based on blood. They are based on more important and binding qualities."

"Kaduna betrayed me," Assindra hissed. "She was a fool and a traitor."

"Was she?" Mikel nodded, then tilted his head to the side. "To trust you perhaps."

"Watch your tongue. I will not have you ..."

"Have me what?" Mikel interrupted. "You gave up the right to claim blood ties when you gave me up. When you left me to die in the Bitter Heights. Kaduna was there. She raised me. Not you."

Rather than offering the rage that Mikel anticipated, Assindra gave him a sly smile. "It seems that not all that Kaduna taught you was worthless. I'm glad to see that you have a backbone."

"Your compliments will get you nowhere." Mikel was growing tired of the conversation. Disappointed as well. Because he had yet to identify how to extract himself from this confrontation in a way that didn't put his friends at risk. "You didn't come here just for your Ten Thousand. You didn't come here just for the Queen of the Crux. And you didn't come here just for me. What is it that you truly want?"

"You don't know?" Assindra challenged. "If not, I truly am disappointed and blame Kaduna for the foresight you lack."

"The scimitar." It's what had brought Mikel into Assindra's presence the first time. And now it had done so again. Though now he knew more about the Blade. What it could do and why she wanted it. Also who she wanted to give it to, unless she planned to betray him as well. In his opinion, the most likely scenario.

"Blood or no, I will have the Blade of Light from you."

Mikel set himself, preparing for the combat that he believed was a foregone conclusion. "If you want it, you'll need to take it."

"Brave words." Assindra offered Mikel a nod of respect.

"True words."

"They are," Assindra agreed. "I believe you."

For the next several seconds, Mikel and Assindra stood across from one another. Neither made a move. Assindra was the one to finally break the impasse.

"If you continue to refuse me, I could take from you what you love the most," she murmured.

A bolt of fear shot straight through Mikel's heart. He forced himself not to look over his shoulder and reveal the truth in Assindra's words. "You could try."

Assindra nodded, seeming to have reached a conclusion. "Kaduna would be proud of you. But are you really ready to pay that price if you don't have to?"

"We all must make hard decisions. I learned that from Kaduna. Lived it as well."

"Even for those important to us?" Assindra lifted an eyebrow when she asked her question, curious about his reaction.

"Another lesson from Kaduna. Some choices are not really choices at all. They are already determined."

"You are a hard man, Mikel Stahlherz."

"No harder than anyone else."

"We will see," Assindra mused. "I have enjoyed this conversation, and there is more to be said. However, it needs to be said privately."

With a wave of her palm, a cloud of roiling black swept down from the shadows above, encircling Mikel and Assindra and blotting them both from view.

Drin, Nat, and the others in the common room were forced to turn away. The wisps of the Curse poked and pricked at them, sending sparks of pain through their bodies until the mist dissolved.

Revealing ...

Nothing.

Mikel was gone.

Taken.

Lost.

**14**

## FAMILY TIES

"Back here again?" Mikel chided. "After our last encounter I assumed this would be the last place you would want to meet. Bad memories and all that."

Assindra had whisked him away to the cavern on the very lowest level of the Crux where they had contended against one another once before. The remnants of that first dialogue – large boulders and piles of stone littered the rough ground that was spiderwebbed by several flows of lava moving sluggishly across the floor – reminders of that less-than-pleasant initial encounter.

"It seemed like the best place to continue our conversation." Assindra studied Mikel. She was impressed. Pleased even. Despite all the challenges he presented to her, much to her surprise she felt a very, very faint sense of ... pride.

She didn't quite understand why. Nevertheless, she had to give him credit. He hadn't flinched upon being forced through a portal crafted from the Curse. His hardened exterior remained in place, not a crack to be seen.

"It guaranteed the privacy we needed," she explained further. "I wager that young Magus of yours has a mean streak, and I wouldn't put it past her to try to find you and exact her revenge upon me. I don't have time to teach her a lesson."

Mikel ignored Assindra's comment. She was watching him carefully, gauging his reaction, and he couldn't afford to reveal the closeness he felt to Nat. If he did, he feared that she would become a target. Nothing more than a lever that Assindra would try to use against him. Therefore, he hoped to nudge her thoughts in another direction. "Returning to where you were defeated can't be easy."

"Not a defeat, simply a setback," Assindra explained, eyes tightening at the slight. "I have a harder skin than you might imagine ... my son."

Mikel wasn't impressed by her play, her words washing off him. Not like the gentle touch of a stream, however. Rather more like the roil and boil of the Churn.

Seeking to maintain his composure, and understanding that Assindra would gladly twist any sign of weakness he displayed for her own benefit, he kept his disdain to himself. Maintaining his mask of equanimity, he treated this conversation much like any other negotiation he might engage in. "Try to play me all you want. It will do you little good. If we're to talk business, then let's get to it. Much like you, I don't have time to waste."

Assindra nodded. Even more impressed. Although she kept that to herself. She didn't want him puffing up and making this dialogue even more difficult than it needed to be. "You know who I truly am?"

"I do."

"And you don't want to give your mother a hug?" Assindra teased, a devilish glint in her eyes.

"I'm afraid that if I did I might end up with a knife in my gut ... or perhaps something worse."

"So cynical," Assindra scolded in a mild tone.

"My cynicism is justified. You've tried to kill me how many times now?"

"You can't hold that against me," Assindra declared. "That was before I knew who you were."

"And that's supposed to make me feel better?" Mikel shook his head. His small smile didn't reach his eyes, which remained just as hard as the stone of the cavern wall.

Assindra grunted. Not bothering to argue, she decided to change the direction of the conversation and come at what she truly wanted from a different angle. "You've carved out a big piece of the pie here on the Crux. The Tor as well."

"I've had a good bit of help."

"You give yourself too little credit."

"I don't, and I don't need credit."

"No, you need something else." She stepped closer to him, lips twisting into a small smile when he didn't budge from where he was standing. "Success. Yes, I see that. But that's only a part of it. That's only one aspect of what drives you."

Assindra's eyes narrowed. "Not revenge, though that emotion is not foreign to you. No, I think it's a deeper trait. One that you not only like to hide from others but that you also try to hide from yourself." Her smile widened. Eyes sparking with delight, she clapped her hands softly. "Redemption. That must be it. But redemption for what? Your past? What you've done to get where you are? Or is there more to it than that?"

Mikel maintained a strong grip on himself, keeping the dozen and more emotions raging through him from becoming visible on his face or in his voice. His only tell was how his eyes darkened slightly.

For just a second he felt untethered from his world much like a cargo gondola breaking free in the Churn. Assindra was hitting much too close to home for his tastes. Still, he regained control of the vessel before it crashed against the rocks. "What do you want ... mother?"

"That was hard for you to say, wasn't it?" Assindra poked.

"It left a bitter taste in my mouth. Yes." Mikel stepped forward. Seemingly at his ease, he wanted to make a point. And he believed he did, because when he stepped forward, Assindra retreated, wisps of black drifting out from her fingertips revealing her concern.

Mikel stopped then, his countenance still as hard as the rock at his back. Although Assindra believed she held the upper hand in this dialogue, he made her nervous. That was good to know. That was a fact that he could use. "But you're not here because of this *connection* between us."

"I'm not." Assindra didn't feel the need to help him, wanting Mikel to work for it. She was disappointed that it didn't take much effort on his part.

"This isn't so much about me as the scimitar. You've made that clear."

"You're selling yourself short. I do want the scimitar, you're right. Best if you gave it to me. Then we can discuss what happens next, because the Blade of Light is just the beginning of the relationship that can grow between us."

"And give up what little leverage I have?" Mikel asked. "I think not."

"Think harder," Assindra warned. "I understand that you and the Blade of Light are one. That I can't have one without the other. At least for now. We need to talk about that."

"I'm not giving you the Blade of Light. Not so long as I'm still breathing."

"If such an extreme action is required ..."

"You have no trouble taking it," Mikel finished for her. "I'm well aware. You needn't threaten me. I understand who you are and what you're capable of. If you were desperate for the Blade of Light, if you truly intended to take it from me and give it to Malor Dragoran, then you would have already tried to do so.

The blades back in my common room wouldn't have stopped you."

Assindra smiled again and nodded in appreciation. She was more than impressed now. After her earlier engagement with Mikel, she had spent some time learning more about the King of the Underworld.

He was quick. She knew that. However, the reports she received on Mikel Stahlherz weren't as accurate as they should be. He was much sharper than she anticipated. Mikel had a good head on his shoulders. And for that reason, he could keep it there for a little while longer. "You hit on the key point, my son."

"Malor Dragoran."

"Exactly."

It was Mikel's turn to nod, his suspicion becoming fact. He had expected as much, Assindra having just confirmed it for him. "You had no intention of giving him the Blade."

"I did not." Assindra didn't say anything more, waiting to see what else Mikel would offer. Curious as to how far down the road he had traveled.

"And you see a use for me."

"I do."

"Because I'm a Bearer."

"Correct."

"You want to use the power of the Blade of Light for your own designs. Unfortunately, you can't. That's why you had me steal it. You need me to wield it for you since you've given yourself to the Curse."

Assindra clapped her hands softly one more time. "Well done, Mikel. You have the right of it."

"You want me to be your blade, figuratively and literally."

"That's one way to put it." She took a step closer again, wanting him to understand that he was many things but he was not a threat to her. "Another would be that I want to help you reach your full potential."

"*Be wary, Steelheart*," Knute Frost Lord murmured softly in the back of his mind.

"*Are you enjoying the performance?*" Mikel asked.

"*I enjoy how you are dancing, yes. But you must remember that this performance is filled with more peril than facing off against a band of poachers in the Frozen Waste.*"

"*That wasn't lost on me, have no fear.*"

"*You understand that to her you are a piece to be played, yes? No more than that.*"

"*I do,*" Mikel confirmed. He was gratified that Knute thought so much of him to offer the warning, even though it wasn't necessary.

Mikel was well aware that Assindra didn't care about him. That she only viewed him as an avenue to power. And that she would do or say anything at his expense if it got her closer to that power she craved so desperately.

Kaduna had never told him how it was that she had come to raise him. She never had to. Mikel's mother had given him up because of all the Caledonii, he was the one, the only one, devoid of the Talent.

It was only after learning of his link to the Blade of Light -- that connection unlocking the potency within him -- that Assindra decided that he could be of use to her. Assindra never realized, however, that Kaduna was the one to hide his potent magic even from him so that Assindra couldn't discover it and turn him into someone he didn't deserve to be.

"*Good,*" Knute murmured. "*Remember, not just as strong as steel. You must be as strong as the Light. Always. Bending but never breaking.*"

"*A big ask.*"

"*True. Nevertheless, one that you can manage. Keep faith in yourself, Bearer of the Blade. The greatest challenges are not those that we don't expect, but rather the challenges that we don't see."*

With that, Knute drifted back into the recesses of his mind. Still observing though no longer engaging.

"And that's why you left me," Mikel said, taking Knute's advice to heart. "So that I could reach my full potential. That's your excuse?" He kept the disdain that wanted to break through out of his voice, though it proved to be quite a challenge.

Assindra said nothing for quite some time. Eyes fixed onto Mikel. Her façade unreadable even as she struggled for a reply.

She could tell him the truth. That she gave birth to him then left him when she failed to sense the Talent within him. A child who was a failure and wasted effort in her eyes.

She could tell him that she couldn't afford to be weighed down by him. She had too much that she wanted to do. Too much that she needed to do. And she stood little chance of doing all that she wanted and needed to do if she had to care for him as well.

She could tell him that his father didn't want a child in the first place. That much like her, his father viewed Mikel's birth as an unwanted encumbrance.

She could tell him that she already was too far down the path she had selected. That she was too consumed by her desire for more knowledge, too consumed by the Curse, to have any wish to waste her time on him.

But would admitting those truths aid her in her current quest?

She doubted it.

"I wasn't a good mother. You have every right to believe that." She looked down at the rock beneath her feet for just an instant. When she lifted her eyes, there was a sadness deep within. Even the trace of a tear at the very edge. "I couldn't be. I would tell you why, but I won't. I can't. All I can say is that the world does not always appear as it seems."

"I learned that lesson long ago," Mikel interrupted.

Assindra nodded sagely. "I'm sure you did. And I'm sure that you learned as well that the face that someone puts forward in the world does not reveal who they truly are. That their actions and decisions often are misinterpreted because others in the world don't understand what they are truly about. What they are truly doing."

"And you're an example of that?" Mikel challenged. "Of someone who has been judged badly? Misinterpreted?"

"I am," Assindra confirmed with a sad nod. "When I accepted the task that fell to me, I had no choice other than to acknowledge that truth. That is why it was best that Kaduna raise you. She could give you what you deserved. What I wanted to give you but I couldn't."

"Do you believe your own words?" Mikel wondered. "Because if I've learned nothing else, it's that those who claim to be misinterpreted are not fooling anyone except for themselves." He didn't expect an answer. Although he received one, Assindra's sadness appearing to deepen.

"I would not offer you my words unless they were the truth." She took a step closer to him, a pleading look in her eyes. "I never thought that I would see you again. I never hoped that I would because I feared the pain that accompanied that hope."

"I doubt your hope had anything to do with me."

"It had everything to do with you, Mikel. I allowed my hope to die so that I could protect you, and now it seems that my decision was premature. That I was wrong. And for that I apologize."

Mikel studied Assindra with a cautious and questioning eye. He didn't need Knute to offer another warning. He had taken the first to heart. He had little doubt that Assindra was trying to play him.

Assindra was correct. The face that someone put forward in

the world did not always reveal who they truly were. As well, their actions and decisions often were misinterpreted because others didn't understand what they were truly about. What they were truly doing.

With respect to Assindra, Mikel felt in every bone in his body that wasn't the case. With her, what he saw was who she was.

She had no interest in him after he was born because she believed that he couldn't touch the Talent. Therefore, Assindra viewed him as defective. She didn't want to have anything to do with him.

And seeing who Assindra truly was, her decision actually played in his favor. With Kaduna hiding his potency from her, Assindra couldn't sense what he could do for her.

Kaduna's decision to do that put them both in a difficult position, and it made Mikel an outcast among his own people. Yet her decision saved him as well, offering him a protection that he could not obtain in any other way.

From Assindra.

From his mother and the designs she would put in place so that she could harness whatever she could from him all with the goal of increasing her own power. Of achieving her own objectives. No matter the cost to him.

He saw through her words and her suspect emotions.

He saw her for the person she had become. Who she had always been.

And it wasn't a pretty sight.

"Say what you want," Mikel said softly, a tiredness seeping into his voice, suddenly growing weary of the confrontation. "I know the truth. I know what you are. I know what you want, and the Blade of Light is only a small part of that."

Assindra tensed. The sadness in her eyes vanished in a heartbeat and was replaced by a demanding will that few if any could stand against. "I am sorry that you don't see the world for what it truly is. I am sorry that I don't see you for who you truly are."

"It's because I do see the world for what it is, I do see you for who you truly are, that I don't believe you," Mikel countered.

"You are allowing your emotion to cloud your vision, Mikel. That is a dangerous failing."

Mikel smiled then. The first time since the confrontation began. "I'm seeing more clearly than I have in quite some time, Assindra."

"You are making a grave error, perhaps even a fatal one, by allowing your emotion to guide you."

"Emotion has nothing to do with this, Assindra. You should know that better than anyone." He laughed softly then, just beneath his breath, as a surge of relief swept through him. He had passed the test. "You said it yourself. We share the same blood. There is a connection between us. And in all things, especially the decisions that we make, emotion is never a variable that we consider. It all comes down to cold calculation. Always. Does it not?"

Assindra pursed her lips. If Mikel wasn't being so obstinate and preventing her from gaining what she wanted, she'd almost be pleased that he was standing up for himself. Almost. "So this is a negotiation." She nodded, believing that she finally understood the man who was her son.

"Everything in life is a negotiation, Assindra. You should know that better than most."

Assindra nodded then, a tight smile gracing her lips. "We have yet to reach a meeting of the minds. Even so, that doesn't preclude us from doing so."

"I didn't say that, Assindra."

"You didn't need to." She lifted her head, tilting it slightly to the right. As if doing so gave her a better perspective on the man she was sparring with. "The past is the past, Mikel. We cannot allow it to drag us down. Our futures depend upon it."

"Our futures?" Mikel almost snorted out a laugh, holding it back. Barely. "There is your future and there is my future. I would prefer that we kept to separate paths and that our futures never mixed."

"What you want rarely matters, Mikel. You should know that by now. All that matters is what we do. All that matters is whether we have the courage to fight for what we want and hold strong against those seeking to take what belongs to us."

"Speaking with you now confirms the truth of that."

Assindra either missed or ignored his hidden jab. Allowing her true nature to guide, she continued to push. "Blood may mean little to you. Fine. But you can't ignore the fact that we have a common enemy, Mikel. If we work together, we can remove him from the throne and protect what is most important to both of us. Or perhaps I should say for the sake of clarity who is most important to us."

Mikel frowned, not appreciating her comment, which he interpreted as a threat. "And what is it that you seek to protect yourself from?"

"Kaduna has taught you quite a lot, of that I have no doubt, but she has not taught you all. It would serve you well to remember that."

"Spit it out, Assindra. I tire of your games."

"Be careful, Mikel," Assindra growled, her temper sparking as she flexed her fingers, the curls of black mist spinning with greater force. "I am still your mother."

"Believe what you want, Assindra. But you were never my mother. Blood matters little when you're a child. All that matters is love. And Kaduna displayed that to me in a way that you never could."

Mikel's statement sent a chill through the cavern warmed by the flows of lava crisscrossing the floor. It also reset the tone of the engagement, as both Mikel and Assindra stared daggers at the other.

Much to Mikel's surprise, it was Assindra who backed down first. And he understood why she did.

"There are powers in this world, ancient powers, against which even I must fear," Assindra explained, deciding to play another angle and offering him no more than that because she was certain that Mikel knew exactly who she was talking about. What he said next confirmed it for her.

"Malor Dragoran."

Assindra nodded in confirmation. "You know the truth about the King of the Tor."

"Malor Dragoran is more than just Malor Dragoran."

"He is. He is a power unto himself. Or at least he believes that he is."

"You were working for him," Mikel accused. "You still are."

"I have no choice," Assindra claimed.

"You always have a choice."

"Don't be naïve, Mikel. You know better than most."

"You want us to do this together? Despite the lack of trust between us?"

Assindra smiled. A warm smile this time. The usual deceptive curl of her lips nowhere to be found. "I do. If I make an attempt on my own, he smells it out with ease. If we work together, we stand a better chance."

"And you remove his boot from your neck."

"From your neck as well, Mikel. Your Queen of the Crux would be free too. You would be taking off the board the greatest threat to her rule ... and to her personally. You know that he wants more from her than just the Kingdom." She shrugged. "A fair deal anyway you look at it. We both get what we want."

"I have no cause to trust you, Assindra."

"You don't. But you have little cause to trust most of your business partners. The only piece holding those deals together is common interest. And I state here and now with complete honesty that in this we have common interest."

"You're speaking honestly?" Mikel scoffed. "Really?"

"Think about it, Mikel. You ignore the blood we share, but to do so is a disservice not only to yourself but also to those who came before you. We are Caledonii. That still means something even among those who would keep us down." Her sharp gaze challenged him. "Kaduna taught you a great deal. Did she ever teach you the Caledonii saying, 'Better the pain of death than the pain of failure.'"

Mikel didn't respond, and Assindra didn't need him to. She saw the truth in how his eyes softened. "You know what it is to be Caledonii. The stigma. How we are looked down upon. Do you not want to get past that? Have your revenge? Take your rightful place in the world that you have been building around you?" Her voice became more strident. More urgent. "Do you still wish to be viewed as an outcast? As someone who is tolerated because of the wealth and power that you can bring to bear? Discarded the moment your wealth and power are no longer needed?"

Mikel didn't need specifics from Assindra. He knew to what and to whom she was referring.

"What you have done to prop up the Queen of the Crux truly is remarkable, Mikel. However, you are too smart not to know that there will come a point when all that you have done, all that you have earned, will not be enough to protect her. Not when the one who puts himself forward as Malor Dragoran decides to push down on your neck just as he is doing to mine now."

Assindra stepped back then, the sparks of black that had been dancing across her fingertips becoming longer streaks that swirled faster and faster behind her, a circle of darkness forming. Expanding. "Think about that, Mikel. Think about what is most important to you. Our interests have not aligned in the past. They are now. Do not miss this chance to protect the ones who are most important to you."

With that, Assindra was gone. Stepping into the portal of black mist, she vanished.

The chamber beneath the Crux returned to darkness except for the flows of lava that streamed across the cavern floor, the orange red playing across Mikel's eyes as he stood there.

Thinking.

Worrying.

Deciding on what he needed to do next.

No matter how much it could cost him.

15

# A NEW DYNAMIC

"Where have you been?" Drin demanded, pressing her palms into the top of her desk as she pushed herself up from her chair. Eyes sharp, incisive, she assumed in a heartbeat the persona of the Queen of the Crux to hide the worry and other deeper emotions that roiled within her.

Mikel emerged slowly from the secret tunnel in the back of Drin's private office. The fact that a Dark Magus pinched him with a remarkable ease seemingly of no concern to him.

She watched him walk toward her. His limp was slowing him down. The clash in The Fox's Lair and then whatever had occurred between him and Assindra clearly still affected him.

She was glad to see that other than for his old injury, he appeared to be little the worse for wear.

Drin had been worried about him. More worried about him than she was willing to admit. Not just to Mikel but also to herself.

As soon as she returned to the Citadel under Teddy's protection, she had sent out members of her personal guard to search the Crux for any sign of Mikel even though Teddy told her it wasn't necessary. Samuel and the crews already were on the job. Besides, he'd turn up like a bad coin because he always did.

She should have listened to the giant. Mikel had just proven Teddy true.

Her angst almost getting the better of her, for just a moment she considered telling Mikel what it was that had been going through her mind after he disappeared. The worries and fears that she preferred not to acknowledge.

Drin held back, however. Based on the expression Mikel was giving her, he had already moved past his kidnapping even if she hadn't. His next words confirmed that for her.

"Some business that I needed to take care of."

Drin waited for more of an explanation. When Mikel didn't say anything after several seconds passed, she sat down very slowly, placing her elbows on the table and interlacing her fingers. "That's all you're going to tell me? A Dark Magus snatches you and you have nothing else to say?" Her voice was calm and controlled. "Nat was worried sick. She wanted to go after you."

"That doesn't surprise me," Mikel murmured. "She is a bit hotheaded after all, though I do appreciate how she prefers to keep an eye on me." He offered Drin a wink, a signal that he understood Nat wasn't the only person who had been worried about him. "And you need not worry about Nat. I visited with her first."

"Very considerate of you," Drin said in an approving tone.

"Nat deserved to know. Besides, I didn't want her running off seeking revenge."

"A valid concern," Drin admitted.

"It is."

"You're going to need to offer more than what you've given me. I've had patrols scouring the Crux for you. What happened?"

"That was very kind but unnecessary."

"Kind but unnecessary," Drin repeated, her voice as frigid as the wind that gusted across the Frozen Waste. Why was Mikel hedging? "Mikel ..."

"Isn't it enough that I'm here and whole. What happened doesn't matter as much as what we need to do."

Drin's expression tightened even more. "We will discuss what we need to do after you tell me why you're being so evasive."

"Family matters," Mikel said with a shrug as he settled down in the chair in front of her desk, realizing that no matter how much he wanted to avoid talking about this topic, he couldn't. Drin wouldn't allow it. She was too tenacious. One of her many characteristics that he found quite appealing, except when it was being applied to him.

"Explain." Her regal tone and posture demanded a response.

At first Mikel grimaced, not enjoying the taste of her order. His expression shifted swiftly as a result. Becoming flinty. Drin was the Queen of the Crux -- that was undeniable since he had helped her claim her throne -- and she meant even more to him than that. But the approach that she was taking now rankled. He didn't like being pushed, and he thought that she realized ...

A knowing smile creased his lips as understanding dawned.

There was quite a lot that Mikel wanted to say to Drin, that he probably should say, but he knew it was for naught. He was from the Underworld and she was the Queen of the Crux.

Besides, now wasn't the time. Not with the risk he was thinking about assuming. He didn't want to add that stress to the challenges that Drin already was wrestling with.

Mikel clamped down quickly on his unexpected desire for a new openness between them. The conversation they needed to have would have to wait for a little while longer.

He was beyond tired and he couldn't concentrate on Drin and the issues between them as he wanted to. The snippets of his conversation with Assindra continued to play through his mind. Distracting him. Much of it no more than flotsam and jetsam.

Though not all.

Digging through all that he and Assindra had discussed, just as much unsaid as said, the question was, should he take the road that lay before him? And, if he did, was that decision more likely to harm or help Drin?

That last was the key question. And as he looked across the desk at the Queen of the Crux, he realized that at least in one respect, Assindra had gotten it right.

Mikel would do everything in his power to protect Celindria Dengannon.

No matter the cost to him.

Of course, Drin didn't need to know that. Not when he couldn't commit to her in the way that she deserved.

"I'd prefer not to, but in the spirit of releasing some of the tension in the room," Mikel said, offering Drin a lift of his eyebrow that made her frown, "let me just say that my discussion with Assindra provided me with a boatload of information. Some of which I was aware of and would prefer not to acknowledge. Some of which is directly relevant to the conversation that we need to have now, because time is of the essence."

"You could have sent word once you were safe," Drin said quietly, not yet ready to let go of her anger. Also wanting to make her point, although she was willing to stop pressing him on his engagement with Assindra ... for now.

"I was always safe."

"In the hands of a Dark Magus?" Drin scoffed.

Mikel allowed what he believed was a humorous response that was just on the tip of his tongue to die unspoken, wisely concluding that now wasn't the time to offer it. Drin's fierce expression confirmed the rightness of his decision as the end of his conversation with Assindra ran through his mind one more time.

*"Do you still wish to be viewed as an outcast? As someone who is tolerated because of the wealth and power that you can bring to bear? Discarded the moment your wealth and power are no longer needed?"*

Of all that Assindra had said those questions had buried themselves the deepest within his heart. Yet looking at Drin now, her true concern for him revealed despite her efforts to mask it. Her true ...

He smiled and spoke softly, never anticipating that he would reach this point with her after all that had occurred between them. "I know it sounds strange, yes, but at least then I was."

"How could you be so certain of that?"

"She needs me," Mikel responded in what he hoped was a tempered voice, glad that some of the fire in Drin's eyes faded as she released most of the anger she was feeling toward him.

"She needs you? Why would she ..." Drin leaned back into her chair, Mikel's previous reference about the necessity of this conversation finally making sense to her. "It's not just about the Blade." She nodded toward the hilt that rose above his shoulder.

"No, not just the Blade of Light." He could have offered more, but he didn't. It was clear that Drin understood.

"That's quite a burden."

Mikel shrugged. "Only if I allow it to be. It's much like any business deal."

"The requirement for caution."

"Exactly."

"That's a very mature decision," Drin nodded appreciatively.

"Thank you." Nat had said much the same, although her voice had dripped with sarcasm when she did.

"A risky one as well," Drin challenged.

"On that we both agree."

"You're looking for a way to change the dynamic."

"I am. I'd prefer to play rather than be played. I want the upper hand."

"So would I." After the attempt on her life, Drin had reached much the same decision Mikel did upon his encounter with Assindra. Despite Malor Dragoran's obvious move, the King of the Tor disclosing the real power at his beck and call, she wasn't scared.

She was furious.

But she was realistic as well.

She had to be. Because too much was at stake.

She couldn't hold the Splintered Bridge while also seeking to defend the Crux from attacks within. Whether on her person or in other ways. It required too much energy and too much in the way of resources.

She was stuck in a vise and she needed to relieve the pressure.

And for that, she needed to rely on Mikel to find some way to blunt Malor and his designs. Actually, she needed him to go farther.

She needed Mikel to remove Malor Dragoran from the Tor throne. That was the only solution.

So long as he ruled, the Crux would be his target. She would be his target. And, eventually, Dragoran's pressure would gain him what he wanted.

Would give him her.

And she wasn't sure what she found more intolerable. Losing the Crux to such a hateful person as Malor Dragoran or her becoming nothing more than his plaything.

"You have something in mind?" Drin was certain that Mikel did. He couldn't be the King of the Underworld otherwise.

"I do."

"You're not going to share?" The quirk of Drin's eyebrow suggested that his holding back was a bad idea.

"Once it's fully baked, I will." He lifted his hands, seeking to head off her protests. "I promise. In the meantime, I have some information that might be of use to you." He leaned forward. "And I think you might even enjoy putting this information into play."

16

## A FITTING END

"**M**ikel didn't want to be here?" Drin strode down the curl that led from the Royal Ring to the one below. Her ultimate destination just then coming into view. "He has a bone to pick as well."

The mansion that rose before her was more a compound built to resemble the Citadel that towered above it.

A testament to power and wealth.

A testament to ambition.

Also a testament to overwhelming greed and overreach. Betrayal as well.

Teddy stayed right at her side. Perhaps it was a bit risky for the two of them to be walking through the light fog that hung over the city without the Queen of the Crux's soldiers at their backs. But he wasn't worried. They were well protected.

And he understood the Queen's logic.

Drin demonstrated greater power doing what she had in mind without a company of blades following behind her. The blades would enter the picture later.

Of course, just to be on the safe side, Samuel and several of Mikel's crews already had claimed the shadows as their own, watching them and watching for any threats that might come their way.

"He did," Teddy clarified, "but he wasn't certain the business he needed to conclude would allow him to return in time. He didn't want to slow you down."

Drin nodded, accepting Teddy at his word. Still, a niggling suspicion wormed its way through her mind.

Mikel always had more than one game in play. Always. That's why he was so good at what he did. Running almost all the nefarious enterprises on the Crux as well as just as many legitimate ones.

Yet even knowing that, what game could be more important than this one?

"Care to tell me what this other business entails?"

"Mikel didn't tell me."

"So that you couldn't tell me."

Teddy snorted out a brief laugh. "Now I see why you two get along so well." He glanced to the side, catching the faint hint of movement in the misty grey at the very edge of the marketplace that had closed just a few hours before. Not Samuel. Although he knew that Samuel was close. Which meant there was no need to worry. "Two peas in a pod."

Not wanting to travel along the path that Teddy had opened before her, in large part because she still felt conflicted about her partnership ... friendship ... relationship – she wasn't sure what it was that had grown between her and Mikel -- Drin chose a new direction.

"Mikel is Caledonii."

"He is," Teddy confirmed with a sharp nod.

"Yet here on the Crux he does business without the many impediments that are often put in place in the other Realms."

Teddy shrugged. "Those impediments appear here as well on occasion. None of them legitimate. All of them based on bias, greed, jealousy, usually a mix of all three."

"Then how does Mikel get past all that? It can't be easy."

"What do you mean?"

"From what I've been able to learn, he has a strong grip on the City Below and much of the City Above."

"The King of the Underworld has a long reach, that's true."

"No longer than mine." Drin felt the need to make a point. However, she wished she hadn't. Her words sounded defensive.

"Very true indeed, Queen Dengannon." Teddy certainly wasn't going to challenge her on that.

"Are you humoring me, Teddy?"

The giant fought hard not to smile. "Of course not, Queen Dengannon."

"You do that very well, Teddy."

"Do what, Queen Dengannon?" His countenance reflected an innocence incongruous with his size and the set expression of his features.

"Speak the truth even when it doesn't seem to be the truth."

"Thank you, Queen Dengannon."

Drin smiled, only for a second, not wanting Teddy to know that she was enjoying the exchange just as much as he was. "Will you answer my question, Teddy?"

"Do you really want to know?"

"I doubt you could tell me anything that I don't already suspect," Drin replied.

"Probably not," Teddy agreed. "The truth is quite simple. There are people here on the Crux who seek to use the fact that Mikel is Caledonii against him. They try to play off the prejudice ingrained by history and the hatred that still plagues the Realms."

"You're not answering my question."

"You're not giving me the time to do so, Queen of the Crux."

"Point taken. My apologies. Please continue."

"Apology accepted." Teddy smiled then. He understood why Drin was pushing on this matter. And truth be told, her doing so raised her to an even higher level in his estimation. And she had attained quite a high level already. "The natural intolerance against the Caledonii remains, but here it's muted or not a factor at all. Not anymore. Not after what Mikel has done for the city that your predecessors didn't." He gave her a knowing look. "It's hard for people to hold onto that intolerance when a Caledonii does so much for them."

Drin didn't reply right away, mulling his response. Hearing the logic. Unable to ignore the subtle dig about the failure of her forebears, Teddy's complaints justified based on what she had discovered regarding the King of the Underworld and her family's own failures. "That certainly makes sense. You don't bite the hand that feeds you. But what about the competition he faces? Don't they use his background against him?"

"Many have tried. All have failed."

Drin nodded in understanding. There were a great many similarities between politics and business, the two inextricably intertwined on the Crux. "The carrot and the stick."

"Exactly, my Queen. Mikel uses both with equal skill. Much like you do." He gave Drin a nod of respect as he said the last.

"Yes, I've seen him in action. Still, there is more that I would like to know about him and his heritage."

"It'd be better if you asked him. I can't speak to that like he can. Nor should I."

"I was just curious about ..."

"How he's Caledonii and can't use the Talent?"

"Yes," Drin admitted. The Blade of Light had chosen Mikel, instilling within him a magical power that was almost unimaginable. That, in itself, wasn't so curious as the fact that throughout history the use of Giant-crafted weapons usually was dependent upon the individual's ability to employ the Talent. So if Mikel couldn't use the Talent ... Teddy's response drew her from her thoughts.

"Again, not something that I can speak to. However, having

gotten to know Mikel better than most, of all the wounds he carries, that's likely the deepest cut."

"Does it hinder him in any way?" Drin had seen firsthand what could happen when someone was denied what they believed was theirs by birth. That natural anger becoming toxic. A visceral motivation in and of itself. A weakness as well. A malignant worm working its way through the individual's thoughts and decisions. The man they were about to visit a prime example of that failing.

"Hinder, no," Teddy snorted in amusement. "It drives him. It always has."

"His inability to use the Talent? Really? That's a difficult ask of anyone."

"For most, yes, you're probably right," Teddy agreed. "I think what drives him more is not his inability to use the Talent but rather the repercussions of his inability to use the Talent."

Drin didn't understand the argument Teddy was making. Not at first. "You're slicing hairs."

"Am I? Maybe. Maybe not. The fact is, unlike the other founding tribes of the Realms, the Caledonii have been looked down upon for millennia. A few bad apples all that was required for those seeking power or seeking excuses for their own failures to shift blame to an entire people. Perhaps not with such vehemence or frequency on the Crux as in other places thanks to Mikel's efforts and successes."

"There is some legitimacy to that," Drin countered. Not because she wanted to disagree with Teddy. Rather because she believed it was necessary to engage in the argument. "Not all the Caledonii are blameless."

"The Caledonii carried the blame for the supposed actions and decisions of their ancestors even after the passage of thousands of years," Teddy argued. "Convenient. Particularly when you consider all the terrible things that have happened in the

Realm since the Caledonii were first blamed, all committed by people who are not Caledonii."

"A fair point," Drin acknowledged.

"Thank you," Teddy said with a sharp nod. "A great deal of scapegoating has occurred over the centuries, but that's the way of it, isn't it?"

"Unfortunately so," Drin agreed. The Caledonii were only one example of that sad fact, though certainly the most obvious.

"We are not lacking in those who are more than willing to place an entire people in a bad light for their own personal gain."

"That's why he came here to the Crux? He believed he had a better chance here than in the other Realms?"

"Mikel has never really said," Teddy shrugged. "I can only assume that it was difficult for him where he was. If you're the only Caledonii who is not truly Caledonii that's likely worse than being Caledonii among those who are not Caledonii. In all likelihood, he didn't have much choice but to come here." Teddy sighed, reaching a point in the conversation where he didn't want to go any further. "Regardless, he's here, and I view that as a good thing for more reasons than you likely imagine."

Drin nodded. "On that last we are of the same mind." She couldn't argue with Teddy's reasoning. And based on what little history she knew regarding that original tribe of Caledonia, being ostracized for not being able to use the Talent might not be the worst punishment that could have been meted out for his perceived inadequacy.

"Everything ready?" Teddy asked. They had arrived at their destination. Ornate double doors that resembled those on a castle, a retracted portcullis even hanging overhead, though this one primarily for ornamentation, barred their way. The personal guards usually stationed there nowhere to be seen thanks to the man who appeared right next to them. A host of shadows at his back.

"We going to knock first?" Samuel asked.

"No." Drin nodded toward the doors as the squad of Crux soldiers materialized out of the mist, battering ram in hand.

MIKEL SLIPPED into the overly ornate room at the back of the mansion. He could navigate any of the many secret tunnels that cut through the Citadel that rose above this ostentatious home meant to impress with its undisguised display of wealth and largesse. And he had. Many times.

He also was familiar with the tunnels built into many of the other mansions lining the Ninth Ring, courtesy of his friend-ship with a well-respected architect who was the brother to one he had once worked with, and still did in fact, on the Tor.

For just a moment he had to stop, shaking his head in a disgusted wonder at the gold gilding applied to the wood-work that crisscrossed the ceiling and spread out into a confusing design meant to dazzle the eye and the mind. The display doing nothing more for Mikel than making him feel slightly sick as he considered how many people in need could be fed for a year with the precious metal used for orna-mentation.

Advancing on silent feet past the priceless furniture and trophies of the past, the heads of exotic animals lining the walls along with spears, lances, and other weapons from battles fought centuries before, he was drawn toward a demanding, slightly shrill voice that blasted out from the chamber just beyond.

Stepping between the painted stone columns designed to mimic the Citadel's throne room, Mikel waited a few seconds more. Using the power of the Light to extend his senses throughout the mansion, he confirmed that he had nothing to worry about other than the men crowded before him.

Lucius Hanover, lord of the most powerful House on the Crux, at least in his own mind, stared down at several large maps spread across a table that ran from one wall to another, hands pressed into the wood, back turned to Mikel.

He was giving orders to the two fists of soldiers who stood across from him. Or rather the same orders. Lucius kept repeating his instructions with different words, either not trusting himself or not trusting the men he was tasking.

Having learned a great deal about Lucius Hanover after their frequent encounters of the last few months, Mikel assumed that it was both.

Studying the men surrounding the table, Mikel smiled. Pleased that he had arrived when he did.

All the soldiers who listened with feigned interest to Hanover's commands were unnaturally large, a primitive menace radiating off of them.

He was more familiar with these fighters than he cared to be.

Men of the Ten Thousand.

Just as Mikel hoped would be the case.

These soldiers being here made life much easier for him. It meant that he wouldn't have to hunt these Werebeasts in the streets of the Crux. He could deal with them all in one fell swoop. Of course, that assumed that upcoming encounter went the way he hoped it would. And he was worried about that because he'd expected at least one or two obstacles to present themselves before the night's drama came to its climax. But that was all right. That was just the unavoidable cost of doing business.

"That's a good plan," Mikel interrupted. Stepping out of the gloom, his smile widened upon hearing the growls and soft curses from the Ten Thousand that accompanied his appearance. Probably because they hadn't sniffed him out beforehand. "But it's not going to work."

"What in the blazes are you doing here?" Lucius demanded, unable to prevent his shock from seeping into a voice he fought to keep unnaturally low, believing that the tone he had adopted made him come across as more commanding and capable. "How did you even get into my home?"

"This isn't a home," Mikel snorted. "This is a museum." He stopped when he was no more than ten feet away from Lucius. Obviously unconcerned by the looming soldiers standing on the other side of the table. "And there's a better question to ask."

"What would that be?" Lucius cursed under his breath. He should have kept his mouth shut, ceding control of the conversation because he couldn't.

"Why am I here?"

Lucius didn't take the bait this time. Not at first. His expression, beginning as one of cold anger, slowly turned more calculating. Having the King of the Underworld slip out of the darkness like a monster in a children's fairy tale was unsettling. Not frightening, however. Not with the resources available to him. Not with the men standing at his back.

He nodded over his shoulder.

The soldiers of the Ten Thousand glided around the table, positioning themselves for whatever havoc might be coming their way. Or better yet, the havoc they planned to author.

All of them knew who Mikel was. Some of them had fought against him on the Splintered Bridge. They had no illusions regarding what the one named the Broken Bear was capable of.

Mikel didn't mind the attempted display of dominance. It was the obvious move on Lucius' part. In reality the only move, and he had anticipated it. "I would think that after your last attempt to seize the throne you wouldn't be so foolish as to make the same mistake again."

Lucius laughed, primarily to hide his discomfort. "Last time I made a play for the throne that rightfully belongs to me I brought Tor soldiers onto the Crux. That was my only mistake. Not the plan but rather the tool I was forced to employ. Now I have the right tool for the plan. Putting these monsters of old to work in furtherance of my birthright ensures my success. Even you won't be able to stop me this time."

"Very confident, aren't you, Luscious?"

"I always am," Lucius replied, biting out the words and struggling to ignore the insult the King of the Underworld offered him.

"And that's what I was waiting for. The key trait that will ensure your disastrous failure. Again."

"What would that be?" Lucius didn't want to ask, but he couldn't help himself. His ingrained insecurity worming its way to the forefront.

"Your overarching arrogance."

"Strong words from a man about to die."

The soldiers took a step closer toward Mikel at the prompt. He held his ground, not even bothering to draw the scimitar sheathed across his back.

"So certain are you?"

"Completely certain," Lucius confirmed, infusing his voice with a false confidence. "As you can see, I have ten reasons to be certain."

"Then you truly are a fool. Wouldn't you agree my Queen?"

"I would," a soft but commanding voice answered from the gloom.

Celindria Dengannon strode into the chamber. Regal and graceful. Her spine as straight as a steel blade. Her expression even harder.

Teddy followed a step behind her. And behind him came fifty soldiers who moved swiftly into a broad arc. All of them armed with crossbows. All of them targeting the Ten Thousand.

The soldiers enslaved by the Dread were fast when they shifted. But they weren't fast enough to avoid all the barbs pointed at them.

"And you heard his admission of treason?"

"We all did," Drin confirmed with a satisfied nod. She turned her attention to Hanover. "I have to agree with Mikel. I had hoped for more creativity from you, Lucius. This is truly disappointing and certainly not the actions of a man capable of usurping my throne."

The Lord of House Hanover glared at the Queen of the Crux. It was because of her that he was in this position now, being forced to scrape his way into the Citadel's throne room.

If she hadn't been a fool, all of this never would have been necessary. They had grown up together. His father placed him at her side so that when the time came they would bind their futures together and he would sit next to her on the throne. And then, eventually, he would be the only one sitting on the Crux throne.

But Drin had hesitated at the worst possible moment. Ignoring their past, she negated all the work he had done to position himself so close to the Crux crown.

Why had his efforts failed?

Lucius wasn't certain. Although his demise coincided with the King of the Underworld stepping out of the shadows and taking on a larger role in Celindria's life.

He had tried to show Drin the error of her ways. He had tried to educate her on what she needed to do to ensure not only her success but also the success of the entire Kingdom. Tying her fortunes to the King of the Underworld was a recipe for disaster.

His disaster Lucius soon came to realize.

Despite his best efforts to reignite the flame between them

she had parried his advances. Time and again. Shunting him to the side and taking instead the advice and assistance of the man who had snuck into his home.

A Caledonii.

A member of that tainted race who had brought the Curse into the Realms.

If anyone had committed treason, it was her.

She was the one who deserved to die.

He wasn't seeking revenge by seeking the throne.

He was seeking justice.

He was serving the Crux and its residents.

He was simply claiming what truly belonged to him.

What she didn't deserve to have.

The Crux was his.

Celindria was the usurper. No more than that.

A traitor to the Crux.

And Lucius was going to rectify that.

He was going to pull her from the throne with his bare hands if necessary.

This very moment.

Knowing who he was, none of the Crux soldiers aiming their crossbows at the Ten Thousand would dare to fire on him.

"I have not spoken treason," Lucius snarled. He pulled a silver dagger from the sheath on his hip. "I have spoken the truth. I claim the right of challenge. Even you as the Queen cannot deny me that."

"I can deny you whatever I choose to, Lucius. The prerogative of the one ruling the Crux."

"You would have never been enough for me, Celindria." Lucius sought to incite her into taking up a blade against him. A decision that would ensure his success. He was certain of that. "But I would have suffered through it for the Crux. Now do the right thing. Abdicate. And if you don't have the courage to do that, fight me now and let the one left standing assume the throne. For once in your life show some courage."

Drin didn't reply immediately, instead assessing the situation in a calculated fashion.

It was a difficult task, because she would have liked nothing more than to pull her dagger free and put the Lord of House Hanover in his place.

She didn't fear the risk of fighting him in single combat. But she didn't want to give Lucius what he wanted. He didn't deserve it.

Lucius needed to understand that he wasn't a worthy opponent.

She glanced at Mikel then whispered to him. "I assumed that you would have jumped at the chance to cross blades with Lucius Hanover."

"I certainly wouldn't turn down the opportunity," Mikel replied just as quietly, "and it's not that I don't want to. It's just that I assumed that you would take a great deal of pleasure in teaching Lucius Hanover a lesson. I didn't want to get in your way."

Drin smiled, appreciating that Mikel recognized not just her authority but also her skill. Moreover, demonstrating that he knew and agreed with everything that she had been thinking. "Thank you for that. You understand that in this circumstance I must call upon you."

"I thought that might be the case." Mikel offered her a slight bow of his head in respect. "As you command, my Queen."

"I accept your challenge, Lucius," Drin said, turning her focus back to the Lord of House Hanover. She looked forward to his reaction when he discovered he would be dueling someone he perceived as his inferior.

"Hah!" Lucius cried. "Your rule ends today!"

"Perhaps, perhaps not. You'll need to defeat my champion

first. Can you do that, Lucius? Can you defeat the Broken Bear?"

~

THE SILENCE DEEPENED with each passing second. Not a word said. Not a sound made.

Drin stood ramrod straight as she and the others in the room watched Mikel face off against Lucius Hanover.

The King of the Underworld taking on the man who dreamed of being King of the Crux.

One a real ruler. His position earned.

The other believing in a destiny told to him since he was no more than a small child. A song stuck in his brain harping on his character and excellence. As a result, the position he craved one that he didn't believe needed to be earned because it was his by right.

"Afraid, are we?" Lucius mocked.

"No, not afraid. Just slightly disturbed." The curl of Mikel's lip hinted at his disquiet. Not because he was about to fight for his life and, more importantly, for the honor of the Queen of the Crux, but rather because his opponent was putting on a display that threatened to curdle his stomach.

Hanover held a dagger in each hand. He was poised on his toes. Well balanced. Yet for this duel he had stripped down to his breeches, leaving his chest bare. And on his chest was a tattoo that Mikel couldn't quite make out.

At first he thought it might be some kind of mythical animal. But the more he looked at it, the more it appeared to be a tattoo of Lucius Hanover riding ... he didn't know what. And he wasn't sure that he wanted to find out.

Lucius snorted, his natural arrogance seeping out of him. "Come now, Caledonii, do you really believe you can defeat a Lord of the Crux?"

Mikel smiled, a menacing look. "Have no fear, Luscious. I'm not going to defeat you. I'm going to kill you."

"With that?" Lucius ignored the jibe thrown his way even as it burrowed under his skin just like every other insult he had ever acquired.

Mikel lifted the weapon he held in his right hand. His smile broadened. The Blade of Light had become a part of him. But this ...

The mace with the blade on one end, hammer on the other, was like an extension of his arm. He had been fighting with this weapon ever since he escaped the Bitter Heights, Kaduna his instructor. "It's not the weapon that makes the victor, Hanover. It's the person wielding it. I thought that you would have learned that by now."

"Philosophical words from an outcast and a thief!" Hanover lunged, only rushing forward a few steps before gliding back just as fast. He wanted to judge his adversary's reaction. He expected Drin's favorite to scuttle back and avoid what he likely perceived was a potentially fatal blow. "I never thought I'd live to see the day."

The King of the Underworld didn't scuttle back. He didn't move at all.

Instead, he studied Hanover's movement, seeing exactly what he expected to see. A lord trained to fight just like every other Lord of the Crux was trained to fight. "Then it's a good thing you have, because this is the last day you'll be among the living."

"Brave words," Lucius snorted. "Foolish as well to antagonize your better." He nodded toward Mikel. "I've heard about that bad knee of yours. Seen you in action as well. Is that why you didn't scramble back like the coward you are? You can't?"

"I only move when the threat is real, Hanover," Mikel explained in a soft voice while his expression began to darken. He would have ended this farce already. But he couldn't. Not yet. "I'm not skittish ... like some others who I know."

"So not just an outcast but a cripple as well." Lucius snorted again, adopting the approach he had used so many times before and seeking the chinks in his adversary's armor before the real clash began. Holding onto the latest insult to stoke the fire raging within him, he sensed that his time was coming. That all that he had been striving toward since he was a child finally was coming to a head.

"Is there a point to this, Hanover? Or are you trying to talk me to death? No real desire to test yourself against me?" Those comments drew snorts and chuckles of disdain from the Crux soldiers at Mikel's back.

Lucius' face tightened even more. Unused to being abused by someone so beneath him, he found it difficult to hold his temper in check as he sought to worm his way into his adversary's thoughts and break him down from the inside before he cut him open with his daggers.

"I don't understand what Celindria sees in you." Growing more frustrated, Lucius attempted a new point of attack. Yet to identify any real weakness that he could make use of. "Caledonii, so a people not only looked down upon, but also despised. Add to that a cripple for life with one more good blow to that weak knee of yours."

"It's likely my effervescent personality," Mikel suggested.

"Definitely that," Drin interjected. "Because it's not his looks."

Even Mikel joined in when the soldiers and fighters loyal to him laughed heartily at the Queen of the Crux's joke.

Lucius scowled deeply as the laughter echoed around the walls. His latest lack of success was driving him closer to the edge.

"It has to be, doesn't it," Lucius agreed, seeking to play off what he perceived as an opening that Celindria mistakenly gave him. "I look like a king." Lucius lifted his arms and spun slowly so that everyone watching could see every inch of him. "You ..." Lucius sighed, taking in Mikel's hulking appearance and then nodding at his less-than-handsome features and the nose that had been broken one too many times. "I don't know what to say about you. Homely is too kind."

"We're not in the schoolyard, Hanover. Do you really believe that your words matter to me." Mikel glided forward with an unsettling speed. Lucius stepped back in response, his confidence wavering at the swift advance. "You know what the real difference is between you and me, Hanover?"

"I can't wait to hear it," Lucius snorted in disgust as he tried to hide his increasing discomfort.

"Everything I have I've earned. I've had to work for it. And I know that I couldn't have attained my success if I hadn't worked with other people who were willing to work with me, just as hard, all with the goal of improving our lives and the lives of the people important to us."

"You're a thief!" Lucius raged. "If you're trying to make yourself sound better than you truly are, then you ..."

Mikel rode right over Lucius. "It's all about you, isn't it, Hanover? You were born with everything. You've always had access to everything, except the throne of course, which really must rankle." Mikel enjoyed how Hanover's lips twisted into a scowl. "Because of that, you expect everything to be given to you. You always have and you always will. You've never had to work for anything in your life that held any real meaning. And, as a result, you don't want to work for it because you don't believe you have to."

"You don't know of what you speak you larcenous ..."

The heat of indignation was driving Lucius at that moment, prodded forward by Mikel. Exactly how Mikel wanted it.

Because right then Mikel caught the movement to both sides of the chamber. All of his fighters were now in place, crossbows trained on the Ten Thousand from the wings so they had no options for escape.

The time for games had come to an end.

"I know exactly of what I speak, Hanover," Mikel cut in. "And that's what you fear the most. The truth. About whom you really are."

"I am quite happy with who I ..."

Lucius never had the chance to finish his statement. Stumbling backward until his hip hit the table, he dodged to the right and then again with no time to raise his daggers to defend himself. His only thought was to stay clear of the mace that slashed through the space he had been occupying only a heartbeat before.

Almost a minute passed before the sound of steel striking steel echoed in the chamber, and that more luck than anything else. Lucius guessed from where the next attack was going to come and crossed his daggers above his head just in time to prevent the King of the Underworld's mace from crushing his skull.

The next minute was filled by a stream of curses. All from Lucius. The slice of Mikel's blade painful. Not just across his flesh, but every slash cutting into his ego as well.

And there was little that Lucius could do to prevent it.

Mikel was a whirlwind, moving with a dexterity that even the Ten Thousand acknowledged was intimidating, only their eyes betraying the truth of their perspective. As he cut at Hanover's edges, Mikel's mace was a grey blur while he maintained his attack, waiting patiently for that one opportunity that he expected would come his way.

He found the crack he desired at the beginning of the third minute of the combat.

Lucius ducked Mikel's slash then tried to roll free, yearning to gain the space so he could take his feet once more.

Mikel ensured that he couldn't, kicking out with his bad leg and catching Lucius' foot with his own.

Lucius landed heavily on his back, his breath knocked out of him. When he tried to push himself up, he realized that he couldn't. The cold steel of Mikel's mace against his throat prevented it.

"Kill him!" Lucius squealed, directing his order to the Ten Thousand who were only a few feet away from him. "Now! Kill him!"

"They can try, Hanover," Mikel replied in a lethally quiet voice. "But they know better. They'd prefer to stay out of a losing fight."

Lucius couldn't move his head. Not without drawing blood. But based on where he lay on the floor, he could see why the men loyal to Malor Dragoran didn't obey his command. The King of the Underworld's fighters, all armed with crossbows and spears, had crowded in from both sides.

Even he had no choice but to acknowledge the futility of the Ten Thousand intervening in the combat.

He let loose a string of curses in his mind. The King of the Underworld had set up an excellent killing ground, and Lucius had stumbled right into the middle of it.

"Besides, that would not be honorable on their part." Mikel lifted his gaze, his dark eyes catching those of the soldier he assumed led this contingent of the Ten Thousand. "Yes, these men working for you have been touched against their will by the Curse. Even so, they have not given up their honor. That they still maintain as best as they can. I have seen it with my own eyes. And I hope that I continue to do so."

The soldier didn't say anything. He didn't need to. Feeling the spark of energy among his comrades, the King of the Underworld's words having a real impact upon them, he nodded.

The Dread had taken much from them. Free will the most

painful of their many losses. But their honor remained theirs so long as they chose to hold to it.

"Honorable! What do you know about honor you mongrel! You have no place here. You do not belong here! This is my world! Not yours you Caledonii scum!"

Mikel's expression stiffened, his face a mask, all emotion draining from his features. Except for his fury. There was only so much he could take before he gave into the drive for revenge on those who slighted him.

Pulling the blade from Lucius' throat, he twisted his wrist, about to bring the hammer down on Hanover's head.

At the very last instant, he stopped.

Feeling the gentle hand on his shoulder, he sighed as his rage flowed out of him. Then he pushed himself up, his bad knee cracking as he did so, and stepped back next to Drin.

A grim smile split her lips. "Soldiers of the Crux, seize the Lord of House Hanover. He is guilty of high treason and must pay for his crimes."

**17**

## PAST LEADING TO THE PRESENT

"Why am I not surprised?" Cadmus shook his head slowly in amusement after Mikel relayed all that had occurred on the Crux during the last few weeks. Some of which he was aware. Most of which he was not.

The King of the Giants of the Rime sat in a large chair positioned close to the fire. It was the only source of illumination in the Great Hall, the flames dancing along the walls and creating captivating shadows that brought back a great many memories for the ruler of the Frozen Waste. Several of the remembrances he would have preferred to have kept buried. But he couldn't. Not with how the world around him had changed so drastically and quickly.

"You know how I like to keep busy." Mikel shrugged, a cunning smile gracing his grim countenance. Usually he enjoyed spending time with Cadmus in Icehold. Especially when a blizzard raged beyond the stoutly built stone and timber walls that were insulated by a layer of ice and snow that was several feet thick. But not right then. Not when so much was at stake. Not when Mikel felt the need to accede to the urge that pulled him to the east.

"Keeping busy? That's how you describe it?" Cadmus leaned forward in his chair, a smile breaking through his thick beard.

"How would you?"

"Protecting Queen Dengannon and her throne for the second time if not the third and along the way helping to take down the primary internal threat to her rule," Cadmus challenged, hearing beneath Mikel's words the tension that his friend was trying to hide with his casual demeanor.

"That last part really was just a bonus for me. I had a score to settle with Lucius Hanover and it worked out the way I wanted. He got what he deserved."

"I have no doubt that he did, and clearly you enjoyed doing that to him."

"I won't deny it." Mikel's smile revealed the true pleasure he felt because of that success. He had little love for the grasping First Families of the Crux who believed that their wealth and power that came to them through birth granted them certain rights and benefits that those less fortunate didn't deserve.

"And if defending the Queen and the Crux wasn't enough, you decided to engage with the Ten Thousand as well, smoke out an evil that has haunted this land for centuries and is only now revealing itself again, while also challenging a Dark Magus whose ties to you are born of blood."

"When you put it like that ..."

"You're taking this seriously, I hope," Cadmus cut in. He said it more for himself than for Mikel. He knew the Steelheart better than most. Well aware of what he was made. He knew also that despite the challenges and threats he had named, Mikel would stand strong much like the pingos that littered the Frozen Waste. "Lucius Hanover is nothing compared to Assindra. And Assindra is nothing compared to the Dread."

"Thank you for that reminder, Cadmus, and I thank you for your concern." He nodded toward his friend, then gave him the look that he usually reserved for when he was taking someone into his confidence. "Actually, that's why I'm here."

Cadmus leaned back then, blowing out his mustache. "I'm glad your senses haven't left you entirely."

"Not yet. Let's hope it stays that way." Mikel's broad smile helped to lessen the deepness of Cadmus' scowl. His friend was worried about him, and Mikel appreciated that. It hinted at the strong connection between them, a rarity when it came to Giant and man.

"If it doesn't, you die," Cadmus stated bluntly. Not taken in by Mikel's attempt at humor. "You understand that, yes? Even with the Blade of Light, one misstep on your part and you go to the other side."

Mikel nodded soberly. "Yes, I'm more than aware of that possibility. In fact, Queen Dengannon made that point several times before I made my way here."

"You told her what you had in mind?"

Mikel chuckled softly. "Of course not. If I did, I wouldn't be here. She'd lock me in a cell. I just told her that I needed to visit with you so that I could acquire some necessary information."

"The Queen of the Crux is a smart woman. She sees the game for what it really is. And she likely sees more of you than you would like her to."

"A fact that I have grown used to though I can't say it pleases me," Mikel replied. "And she sees multiple games all at one time and has the skill to play them all. That's why she's on the throne."

"High praise." Cadmus offered Mikel an appraising eye. "Not because of you?"

"I just gave her a little nudge. That's all. She's done the rest after I got out of her way."

"I will never understand how you've managed to stay humble after all your success, but I'm grateful for it." Cadmus had little doubt that Mikel was giving himself too short a shrift in all that he'd accomplished since Celindria Dengannon claimed the throne of the Crux. Not only for her but also for the Kingdom.

"You have Kaduna to thank for that."

"The woman who raised you?"

"Yes, my mother in everything but name." A warm smile graced his rough features as he thought about her.

"It seems to me that it was a good thing then that Assindra left you as a babe. I'd hate to see what would have become of you if she had taken an interest in you before you acquired the Blade."

"You and me both."

Cadmus nodded, not saying anything for a time. Staring into the flames, memories that had become nightmares played behind his eyes.

He was glad to have his friend with him on this night. Mikel the only one he could speak to about certain matters. Understanding as well that Mikel being here at this very moment, a Bearer of the Blade of Light, prophesied more dire things to come. And sooner than he would have preferred.

"I knew that trouble was coming when you claimed the Blade of Light," Cadmus murmured when he came back to himself.

"It wasn't my intention to be the cause of the threat you face now."

"You're not the cause," Cadmus corrected. "The threat was coming. True, you taking the Blade put this entire series of events into motion, but it also gives us a chance."

"How so?" Mikel was intrigued. Cadmus came across as straight-forward. Yet there was a craftiness to him that had served him well during the many centuries he had ruled the Frozen Waste.

Cadmus gave Mikel a lift of his eyebrows. "Perhaps there is a way to knock our true enemy's plans off kilter."

Mikel smiled. He should have expected this. He rarely had any success trying to slip something by the Frost Lord. "You know what I want to do."

"What you always want to do, my friend," Cadmus said, a touch of pride in his voice. "Protect those who can't protect themselves."

"That's a very broad statement."

"That doesn't make it untrue," Cadmus argued.

"Before we go down the path of ethics and philosophy and the connection between self-interest and the greater good, I can tell by the gleam in your eye that you've been waiting for this moment in the conversation."

"I have," Cadmus replied, reaching down to the ground. "And I believe this would be of use to you, assuming that I'm correct in what you have in mind."

Mikel opened the intricately carved box that Cadmus held out to him and pulled out a bracelet that flashed brightly in the firelight. Made of iron, gold, and silver, the three strands of metal were wrapped around one another in a dizzying pattern that was equal parts pleasing and disturbing.

When Mikel first acquired the artifact while on a job beneath the Tor years before, he had sensed the power within the beautiful piece of jewelry. He had no clue as to the artifact's significance. Now, thanks to his connection to the Light, he understood exactly how the exquisite piece crafted by the Giants of the Rime could prove helpful to his larger endeavor.

"I have to be honest," Mikel said as he turned the bracelet, examining how the metal flashed and seemed to change color based on how the flames played off the strands. "I had a hard time giving this back to you."

"I can understand why." Cadmus leaned in closer, as if he feared they were being spied upon even though they were the only two souls in the Great Hall. "You know how to use the bracelet?"

"I do," Mikel confirmed.

"Why am I not surprised?"

"You know I like to look into my marks before I accept the work."

"I'm quite familiar with your methods, yes," Cadmus grumbled. "That's why you're here? Not just to visit with an old friend?"

"I am here for many reasons, Cadmus."

"You see the larger game that's in play."

"I think I do. But it's more than that. A game within a game within a game ..."

"And a game within a game," Cadmus concluded. "Yes, with the players involved, it is hard to discern what is really at stake and for whom."

"Which is why I wanted to get your perspective." Mikel leaned forward in his chair, enjoying the warmth that emanated from the fire. "I assume that what I must do is connected to the threat you now face."

"It is. Frozen solid, in fact, the two threats one when looked at it from the right angle."

"So we must shatter what it is that is connecting the two. Reduce the number of games that are being played and we reduce our opponents' options."

"Correct," Cadmus confirmed with a sharp nod. "And if we remove options, we have the chance to remove players. But you understand the risk, yes? What is truly being asked of you though it hasn't been put into words?"

Mikel didn't reply immediately. Instead, he rested his forearms on his thighs. Soaking in more of the warmth from the fire, he rubbed his aching knee, which never enjoyed the cold. Then he nodded. "Kaduna had a lot of sayings that she used to share with me when I was younger. They've stayed with me all this time, and they've always proven to be right on target."

"Get what needs to be gotten then get gone," Cadmus said softly. That had always been one of his favorites.

Mikel smiled warmly. "Yes, that one has always appealed to me since it applies directly to one of my stronger skills. A mantra for how I approach my business and my life."

"And it applies now?"

"Yes, though it's not the only one. Another saying comes to mind that I believe is just as appropriate."

"Are you going to share or make me ask?" Cadmus was growing impatient. The sense that the challenges he faced were approaching with greater speed than he originally imagined weighed him down.

"Fight the battle you need to fight. Not the battle your opponent wants you to fight."

"That's good advice," Cadmus stated, nodding in appreciation.

"I thought so."

"You need something more from me than the bracelet." Cadmus was certain. He could tell by the hard set of his friend's jaw.

"The two threats we face are connected just as you said. Finn was able to only tell me so much. As I said, before I go after a mark, I like to know all that I can. It helps to reduce the number of traps I could fall prey to."

"You're looking for any piece of knowledge that could help ensure you don't go to the other side. Even though that's the likely result with the madness you're planning." Cadmus leaned forward again, now shaking his head in a way that hinted at pride and exasperation. "Queen Dengannon doesn't know what you have in mind? You're sure of that?"

"She does not, and we're going to keep it that way."

"I could tell her."

"But you won't because doing so doesn't serve the interests of the Giants of the Rime."

"Unfortunately you're right about that."

"I have my moments. Queen Dengannon does not know what I have in mind and she will not. That's how it needs to be." Mikel didn't want Drin getting in his way, although that was a harsh way of looking at it. Rather, he didn't want what she might feel toward him to get in the way of what he must do. No matter what that might cost him ... and her. The Crux first, the Crux always. She would understand that. But better she not need to understand that until he was beyond her grasp.

"That's a good decision on your part."

"I make them on occasion, although based on the look you're giving me you don't agree."

"I've known you for a long time," Cadmus said, a sparkle of amusement in his ice-blue eyes.

Mikel ignored the gentle jibe. "Can you help me?"

"Where would you like me to start?"

"Kronin."

"Not my favorite topic," Cadmus murmured, his deep voice still a low rumble. "A necessary one, nonetheless. What do you know of the War of the Brothers?"

"Only the basics. The most salient fact being that your father sacrificed himself to ensure that you could defeat your uncle."

Cadmus nodded sadly, more memories from that terrible time flooding back to him. "Yes, my father accepted a fate that I would have gladly suffered for him."

"Why did he do it?"

Cadmus didn't reply right away. Still caught in his memories, a deep sadness filled him. "The trap my father set needed to be real. He needed my uncle to be pulled in. It only worked with him as the bait. I was of little interest to Kronin compared to him."

"What happened?"

"To take you through all that occurred would require most

of the night. The short of it? My father lured Kronin and most of his Titans to the Lost Carcer. The prison crafted of the Talent with the aid of the Order of the Magii that was designed specifically to catch my uncle and his rebels in its web. My father attempted to escape the end my uncle had in mind for him, Kronin seeking vengeance for what my father did. And my father almost succeeded. But he was betrayed."

"How so?"

"It was supposed to be a single combat. My father Karolingan against my uncle Kronin. A way to bring an end to the War of the Brothers once and for all with a minimum of bloodshed."

"How was your father betrayed?"

"Kronin and his Titans had turned to the Curse. What my father didn't know was that my uncle's weapon of choice, a scythe made of black steel, was infused with that insipid evil. My father was more than holding his own during the combat. He was winning the combat, keeping Kronin on his back foot. However, the instant my uncle gained a touch on my father, and a lucky one at that, the tenor of the combat changed. The Curse imbued within Kronin's scythe infected my father and affected his ability to fight. To think. That blasted evil consumed him with the speed of an avalanche sweeping down the mountain."

"A true betrayal indeed."

Cadmus nodded sadly. "We all saw it, but we could do nothing about it. The combat was protected by a magical dome. Only the victor able to emerge from the shield that settled into place right before their blades met for the first time. My father knew what was happening to him, that he was doomed, so he tried to end the fight before he lost his life. Kill Kronin before the Curse killed him. And he almost succeeded. He wounded Kronin badly, but my father died before he could inflict the finishing blow."

"Kronin claimed victory?"

"He tried to. He could barely stand. Even so, he said that he won the combat. That the Frozen Waste belonged to him."

"You disagreed?" Mikel prodded.

"Most vehemently. And the Talent that the Order of the Magii infused within the Lost Carcer did as well. Before my uncle could press his false claim, the Talent latched onto Kronin and many of his Titans and pulled them down into the pit that opened right below my uncle's feet."

"Not all of the Titans were captured in that way?"

Cadmus shook his head at the memory, his face twisting into a grimace. "There were some on the outskirts of the magical trap my father set. They were too far away to be taken."

"You took care of them," Mikel said. Not judging, only stating. A necessary and deserved action in his opinion.

"Kronin and his Titans will say that they were betrayed. That their supposed victory granted them rule over the Frozen Waste and that it was stolen from them. But they will not say it was a tainted victory. They will not say it was earned by the Curse."

Cadmus squeezed his fists together, knuckles turning white, his anger at past events made plain. "We fell upon those few dozen Titans with a vengeance. All of them touched by the Curse. All of them former friends or family. All of them slaughtered in minutes, the Defenders of the Rime fighting with me letting loose their rage at the terrible loss and destruction brought upon our Realm by the greed of my uncle and his rebels." Cadmus leaned back into his chair, sighing and shaking his head sadly. "It was not the end that my father envisioned. But it was an end. Until now."

"Kronin must be dealt with once more."

"He must," Cadmus agreed. "And for good. The threat he presents must be removed entirely."

"Can you?" Mikel saw the doubt in the back of his friend's eyes not long after he asked the question.

"I don't know. He is just as strong as he was when he was imprisoned. And he has the numbers to challenge us. Though it's not Kronin who I truly fear."

"The one who freed him."

"That's right," Cadmus confirmed. "Kronin and his Titans are a threat. They will be a threat until they are eliminated. And my Giants certainly will do all that is required to make that happen."

"I'm sensing a but here."

"But the Titans are only a symptom of the disease that threatens to consume the Frozen Waste and the lands that touch it."

"The Dread."

"Yes, the Dread." Cadmus sighed, almost as if he were responsible for giving Mikel what he viewed as an impossible task. "You must destroy the disease first. You must cancel out the Dread's power. Only in that way do we stand a chance against Kronin and his Titans."

"How is the Dread connected to Kronin? I understand that he freed your uncle and his rebels, but is there more to it than that?"

"Always seeing more than the obvious," Cadmus murmured.

"Another of my unique skills," Mikel replied with a grin that would have earned a sharp rebuke from Drin but only gained a soft chuckle from Cadmus.

"It's just another example of the Dread seeking the best tool for the goal he seeks to achieve. He was the one who turned Kronin against my father. He was the one who used my uncle's discontent at his place among the Giants of the Rime to corrupt him against his own kind. He was the one who convinced my uncle and his followers to revolt. And he was the one who enhanced the Titans' power through the use of the Curse."

Mikel took in all that Cadmus revealed. Unable to imagine what it must have been like for Cadmus and Karolingan to address that betrayal. And for Cadmus to now have to address it once more. "How were your uncle and his Titans affected by the Curse?"

"Not in the way they anticipated," Cadmus said with a smirk.

"They were tricked by the Dread?"

"They were. The Dread does for the Dread. Again, Kronin and his Titans were no more than tools. To ensure that my uncle and his followers did what was required of them, he used the Curse to link them to him just as he has done with his other creations. They were dependent on him because he used the Curse to change them."

"Change them? How so?"

"The Titans are no longer Giants of the Rime," Cadmus explained. "They have certain abilities, qualities might be a better word, that have made them more than they were before – the ability to stand against the Talent except for the most potent applications of that power, for example -- but it has come at a cost."

"I'm going to need details."

"Kronin and his Titans cannot use the Curse themselves, but they are strengthened by it. And they have been changed by it. They are stronger. Faster. Unaffected by the cold. More volatile. And a bloodthirstiness has consumed them that was not there before. No remorse. No pity. Just blood and pain."

"They sound more dead than alive."

"They very well could be," Cadmus agreed.

"It's almost like the Dread was using them to test his power."

"That's an excellent way to describe it."

"And the cost of being touched by the Curse in this way?"

"Besides the loss of free will?" Cadmus asked.

"A terrible loss right there," Mikel said.

"I couldn't agree more." Cadmus leaned forward again, almost whispering. "Kronin and his Titans are stronger than they ever were before because of their connection to the Dread. They are weaker as well."

Mikel thought about that, his mind already moving down the path Cadmus laid out before him. "They are tied to the Dread. Weaken the Dread and we weaken the Titans."

"Their power is his power. Exactly so."

"Which is why you're supporting the play I'm going to make."

"For that and other reasons."

"More than cunning," Mikel said. "Some would say cold-hearted."

"Would you do it any differently if you were in my position?"

Mikel bit his lip, holding back the several curses that sprang to mind. Instead he examined the situation with the calm calculation that was so much a part of who he was. "I wouldn't. I would do exactly as you are."

"Thank you, my friend."

"For what?"

"For understanding, and for being willing to take on this risk."

"It serves both our purposes," Mikel acknowledged.

"It does," Cadmus confirmed.

"The Dread has the power to free your uncle? It seems that would be quite a challenge even for him if the Lost Carcer was constructed with the Light and the Talent."

"The Dread may be an old evil we thought long banished, but he is an evil whose power is not forgotten by those who lived during the War of the Brothers. What he can do with the

Curse ... it is unimaginable. Freeing my uncle and his traitors no more than sleight of hand for him."

"You're not filling me with a great deal of confidence."

"It's not my intention to do that." Cadmus shrugged, understanding that Mikel preferred the truth above all else. Even if it was a truth that he didn't want to hear.

"Why now? Why after all this time has he chosen this moment to make his move?"

Cadmus gave Mikel a sly look. "You know why."

"The Blade of Light."

"Correct."

"Why? What's the connection?"

"Do you know much about the Dread?"

Mikel frowned. "Not as much as I would like. There's little about him in the books I have, and Finn could provide only so much information."

"Because he lost his position at Haven?"

"He was lucky to lose only that," Mikel grumbled. Then he shrugged. "It wasn't his area of study, so there was little that he could give me that wasn't common knowledge."

"Then I will try to fill in the gaps, and if I say something that you already know ..."

"Stay quiet and listen," Mikel replied with an impish grin.

"That would be appreciated." Cadmus settled back into his chair. Closing his eyes for a moment, he enjoyed the heat washing over him as he gathered his thoughts. The shrieking of the storm just beyond the Great Hall no louder than a low buzz in his ears. "Finn likely told you that the Dread was not always the Dread."

"Rickard Riverstone," Mikel offered.

"I barely get started and you're already interrupting?" Cadmus growled.

"Sorry, couldn't resist."

"Try harder."

"I will. I promise."

"Steelheart ..."

"Sorry. Go ahead, my friend, I'll stay quiet."

"I doubt that," Cadmus grumped beneath his breath. Then he began again. "Rickard Riverstone became the Dread. A former member of the Order of the Magii, and a man consumed by his greed and his desire for knowledge, he allowed his arrogance and cravings to take him down a terrible path."

"He became a Dark Magus, twisted by the Curse."

"Mikel ..."

"Sorry." Mikel held up his hands in apology. "I'll stay quiet. I promise." And he would. He knew that he could only have so much fun at his friend's expense before Cadmus lost his temper, which was never a pretty sight. Not because it burned brightly, but rather because it was as cold as ice.

"I'll believe it when I see it," Cadmus muttered. Still, he began again. "You're right. It's not an original beginning. All too common, in fact. Arrogance and the quest for power guided the promising and powerful Magus down a road that he shouldn't have traveled despite the many warnings given to him along the way."

"Finn suggested there was more to it than just that."

"There could have been. From what my father said, Rickard believed that he was just a breath away from learning how to destroy the Curse. Because that was Rickard's original goal and the reason he provided for taking the path that most every other Magus avoids. Not realizing all the while that the Curse was destroying him. A fact that he discovered much too late in his quest."

"Not a demonstration of strength on his part," Mikel murmured.

"Correct. Just as with all the others who followed that path, the ultimate demonstration of weakness. Yet in this case

Rickard was the strongest of the Magii ever to be seduced by the Curse."

"How did he become the Dread?"

"My father didn't know," Cadmus sighed, disappointed that he had to reveal that fact. "No one of the Rime knew. All we can assume is that it happened over time, the Curse turning Rickard into what it wanted him to be. Giving him the power that he desired, though at a cost that I doubt even he comprehended at the time."

"When did he seek the lands to the west of us?"

"It seems that Finn knew more than most." Cadmus pushed himself closer to the fire to ward off the chill that trickled down his spine. He wasn't superstitious by nature. Nevertheless, talking about the Dread, believing that this monster of old had returned, or rather had never gone away, instead finding a way to hide himself in the world, filled Cadmus with an apprehension that overwhelmed that of knowing his uncle and his Titans stalked the Frozen Waste once more.

"That's what he likes to tell himself," Mikel replied with a soft chuckle.

"On that we agree. The Dread sought to exert his power and increase his domains not long after becoming one with the Curse."

"Becoming one with the Curse?" Mikel frowned, eyebrow quirked. "Is the Dread the Curse?"

Cadmus shrugged. "I don't know. Why do you ask?"

"Because if the Dread is the Curse, it makes it that much more difficult to defeat him."

"Fair point," Cadmus acknowledged. "I can only share what I know."

"I wish you knew more that you could share."

Cadmus didn't take Mikel's comment as a challenge. "Nervous, my friend?"

Mikel nodded toward the sheathed scimitar leaning against his chair. "If you were a Bearer of the Blade, wouldn't you be?"

"I would be," Cadmus admitted, "but perhaps you're looking at all this in the wrong way."

"How so?"

"There is the Talent. The Curse. The Spirit. The Light. Several other concepts, consciousnesses, sources of magical power that need not be named that are in the Natural World or have been. How many still exist, how many can still be harnessed, how many are yet to be discovered, isn't for me to say."

"You've lost me already."

"That's because you're so impatient."

"That's your perspective. Mine is that the Dread, a man ... creature ... monster with an almost incalculable potency in the Curse has an interest in me and the Blade I carry. You understand my apprehension?"

"I do, but that's my point. There are different types of power, and they often come in pairs. Usually one to negate or challenge the other. A balance of sorts, which is one of the rules of the Natural World." Cadmus leaned toward Mikel then, catching him with his ice-blue eyes. "The Blade of Light selected you. Why is that so?"

"That's the question I'd like answered."

"Who can say, other than the fact that the Blade chose you for a reason. It wouldn't have done so if it didn't believe that you had within you what was required to face this challenge."

"You really believe that?"

"I do."

"Why?" Mikel challenged. "I admit, my link to the Blade allows me to see a place in the world for myself that is larger than anything I could have possibly imagined. But with it comes responsibilities and dangers that give me nightmares."

"And that may be why the Blade of Light selected you. That and another reason."

"And this other reason?"

"You're the Steelheart, my friend. Made from the stone of the Bitter Heights, molded by the ice and cold of the Frozen Waste. Implacable. Unbreakable. You do what you must even when you know what that will cost you."

"Are you trying to make me feel better about all this, Cadmus?"

"Is it helping?"

"Not really."

"It was worth a try." Cadmus shrugged then leaned back, offering Mikel a wry grin. "Now instead of asking questions to which I do not have answers, allow me to continue. Otherwise, we'll be here all night. And though I enjoy your company, I enjoy my sleep more."

"Harsh," Mikel chuckled, catching the glint in his friend's eye. He then motioned for Cadmus to proceed.

Cadmus' smile tightened. He and Mikel had been friends for quite a long time. That was true. Few would dare treat the Frost Lord as he did, which was one of the reasons why Cadmus believed that the Blade of Light was in good hands. "Back to the topic of the Dread seeking the Realms to the west of us. West Lurangia. East Lurangia. Frisia. The plan he put into motion was both ingenious and marred right from the beginning."

"The Murk."

"Exactly," Cadmus nodded. "A terrible creation of both power and limitation. And the tool of his own demise at the end of that ill-fated expedition. As you probably are aware, the Dread crafted the Murk to conquer those Kingdoms, hiding his killers within that grasping grey when they invaded Frisia, which was then ruled by Julius Rache. The King of Frisia was a Magus as well, and he knew Rickard Riverstone before he turned to the Curse. Moreover, he was a more than competent ruler. Perhaps most important, he was a man who refused to bend to the will of the Dread. He knew what would happen to his people if he surrendered as his former friend demanded."

"Even so, despite his efforts to defeat the Dread, the Wyld is what remains of Frisia."

"True, but we cannot prove victorious in every battle," Cadmus intoned. "If you were in Julius' position, would you have handed over Frisia to the Dread?"

"No, of course not. He had to fight."

"He did, you're right. And he fought well. All the while understanding that defeat was inevitable against the Ten Thousand. No one had come up against those terrifying warriors until they invaded Frisia. Merciless shifters. Supposedly they couldn't be killed."

"They can be killed," Mikel stated with a lethal intensity. Not bragging. Simply stating a fact.

"Yes, another of the skills that you've acquired from the reports I've received about the battle for the Splintered Bridge. Back then, the Murk a tool for their use, without the Talent or a bit of luck, the Ten Thousand couldn't be killed. Keep in mind as well that the Ten Thousand weren't just soldiers. They were handpicked by the Dread. He needed a particular kind of servant for what he had in mind."

"Complete domination of the Realms," Mikel murmured.

"That's right. And that's why the Dread used the Curse upon them. He sought to change them. Mold them into what he wanted a soldier to be. He wanted to make them stronger. Faster. More dangerous. Yet all the while chained to him with a leash because the Dread trusts no one but himself."

"That remains the case to this day. Those Werebeasts are still doing the Dread's dirty work."

"You're more familiar with them than you care to be." Cadmus nodded, thinking for a moment. "I can understand how that wears on you. But have you ever considered the Ten Thousand from a different angle?"

"What do you mean?"

Cadmus tilted his head down, brow furrowing, before he offered his idea. "The Ten Thousand were not willing participants. They still might not be willing participants."

Mikel didn't say anything for a long while as he stared into the flames, considering what Cadmus was suggesting and weighing the advantages and disadvantages of the possibilities that statement opened to him. "Do you really believe that's an option?"

"I don't know what to believe," Cadmus replied in a judicious tone. "Who can say at what level the resentment remains? Who can say where that resentment and yearning could lead?"

"A fair point."

"I'm glad you see it just as I do," Cadmus said, nodding in approval. "Something for you to consider then."

"To consider, yes, but not commit to. Not yet. I prefer not to take such a risk unless completely necessary."

"Agreed. There's no need for me to touch on the Werebeasts in great detail. How their ability to shift enhances them. The forms they can take – wolf, bear, panther, tiger – and how those forms bring with them the attributes and even some of the characteristics of those animals. I seek only to make one point that is often lost."

"Another point?" Mikel mused.

Cadmus ignored the good-natured jibe. "I wouldn't offer it unless I believed it was something else that you should consider."

"What would that be?"

"It is said that the Ten Thousand, what's left of them anyway, are now no more than animals."

"You don't believe that?"

Cadmus shrugged, unwilling to offer a strong opinion. "I

haven't decided. I just find it difficult to believe that who they were before the Dread changed them with the Curse was lost entirely."

"That would be quite a risk I would be taking," Mikel noted. "And as I just said, I don't like taking risks such as that without having some confidence that it was a risk worth taking,"

"Very prudent," Cadmus acknowledged, "which is why I would suggest that you only take it if there is no other course."

"Another fair point," Mikel admitted, all the while wondering if based on his encounter with some of the Ten Thousand while arresting Lucius Hanover whether he could read anything more into their restraint other than their desire to not waste their lives on a lost cause. Or perhaps on a cause that was not in their interests as well.

A useful discovery?

Maybe.

Then again, maybe nothing more than a useless hope. Nevertheless, that musing would have to wait.

"I do try my best," Cadmus replied. "Now allow me to return to the story."

"You're the one who led us onto this tangent."

"Now you're just nitpicking," Cadmus scoffed. "We have seen and engaged with the Werebeasts of the Ten Thousand once more. We have not seen the Dread's other creation, and I doubt that we will. Still, useful to the story."

"The Wraiths."

"Yes, even harder to kill than the Ten Thousand. Touched by the Curse just like the Werebeasts though crafted in a different way by the Dread. Essentially invincible within the Murk. The Dread sent the Ten Thousand into Frisia. Julius Rache knew that he was going to lose as soon as that happened. Even so, he and his people resisted. They put up a fight that is worth remembering."

"So it wasn't the Ten Thousand who defeated the Frisians." Mikel gathered as much from Cadmus' tone.

"Not on their own, no. The Wraiths were the final weight on the scale that shifted the balance in favor of the Dread."

"Although in this case not as effective or as well thought out as when he crafted the Weres," Mikel noted. "The Wraiths were flawed. Or rather how the Dread created the Wraiths was flawed."

"Correct, my friend. The Wraiths were the Dread's first attempt to make soldiers who were invincible. When he realized that he had made some terrible and unforgiving mistakes with the Wraiths, he shifted his focus in another direction, adjusting his approach in a way that led to the Werebeasts of the Ten Thousand. Because, again, for the Dread, it all comes down to control. Every tool at his command must function exactly as he requires."

"A useful fact," Mikel murmured, his thoughts already taking into account how he could turn that weakness to his advantage.

"That's why I shared it with you."

"From where did the Wraiths come?"

"They were the elite of the Ten Thousand. The shock troops. The assassins. Because that was one of the Dread's primary tactics when conquering a land. He would send the Wraiths across the border first with a simple yet critical mission."

"Kill the leaders and weaken from within. A tried-and-true tactic throughout history." Mikel would have said more, but he didn't. Distracted. He turned his head slightly, allowing his eyes to drift toward the darkness that consumed the back of the Great Hall.

No one was there.

Even so, he was beginning to feel uneasy. As if something

was wrong, and it had nothing to do with the howling wind and falling snow just beyond the walls.

"The Wraiths were incredibly skilled at their work," Cadmus continued. "They killed with impunity. Few could offer any defense against them. Even so, the Dread wanted more from them. He always wanted more. He was never satisfied. And that proved to be a key factor in his downfall."

"How so?"

"In an attempt to give the Wraiths greater advantages in the bloody work that he demanded of them, with his application of the Curse he turned them into something worse. In fact, he turned them into something he had not anticipated. It was because of what he did to the Wraiths, changing them physically, that he was able to perfect his use of the Curse to create the Weres. But in other ways he failed because of the mistakes that he made with that tainted magic. He was arrogant. He thought that he could do no wrong." Cadmus straightened his spine and brought his shoulder blades together, seeking to ease the ache in his lower back. "A common belief among those convinced of their own power and ability. He didn't make mistakes ... until he did."

Mikel chuckled softly as he caught the sparkle in his friend's eyes, a sparkle that didn't come from the flames before them. "You're enjoying this, aren't you?"

"I was told that I would have made an excellent storyteller if I had not been my father's son."

"You were told many things because you were your father's son."

"That feels like a dig, my friend."

"Perhaps. That doesn't make it untrue."

"Another reason I like you, Steelheart," Cadmus smiled. "You have little trouble challenging authority or ensuring that ego does not run amok."

"One of my unique skills."

"We will refrain from discussing the other reasons, many less than savory."

"My thanks."

Cadmus struggled not to laugh. To aid him, he returned to his story. "Just like the Werebeasts that came after them, the Wraiths were transformed against their will."

"Shocking that they weren't happy about what was done to them." Mikel's words were thick with sarcasm.

"Quite right. They were enraged. Even so, they understood the nature of their circumstances and the power that their master employed. Therefore, they obeyed the Dread without question, hiding their true feelings and their simmering intentions. And, because of who they were and what they did, their master gave them a freedom that the rest of the Ten Thousand didn't enjoy."

"There had to be more to the Wraiths' anger than just that," Mikel charged.

"There was. The Wraiths didn't understand why the Dread did this to them even though they were so successful, never having failed on an assignment. They killed their targets with impunity, nothing able to stop them." Cadmus hmphed. "Even the Seekers miss a kill from time to time, but never the Wraiths."

"So when the time was right they rebelled."

"They didn't want to go through the change caused by the Curse after seeing what happened to some of their comrades. But, again, the Dread was too strong for them. For a little while longer."

"How so?"

"The Dread did what he wanted to with the Wraiths. They couldn't stand against him with any hope of success. But in his anger at their resistance, the Dread made another mistake. Giving in to his desire to ensure his control over the Wraiths, he made the Wraiths stronger in the Curse than he intended."

"The Dread lost power over them," Mikel mused. "That makes sense. Kind of fitting as well."

"I thought so," Cadmus murmured. "The Wraiths wanted Frisia for themselves. And that's where the Dread's next mistake proved quite useful to them."

"The Murk," Mikel said in response to the lift of Cadmus' eyebrow, his friend expecting him to push the lesson forward. "So focused on what he wanted to achieve that he never considered the full consequences of his actions."

Mikel would have said more but didn't. That sense of unease that had been plaguing him was becoming more urgent, though the cause remained a mystery as he saw and sensed nothing out of the ordinary within the Great Hall.

"Indeed. The Dread used the Curse to create the Murk, believing that his tainted creation would aid the Wraiths in the work that they did for him. That the Murk would make them stronger. More effective. And it did. Just not in the way that he expected."

"The Wraiths mastered the Murk," Mikel chuckled, finding himself in a strange kind of humor.

"That they did," Cadmus replied. "The Murk nurtured the Wraiths. Became a part of them. As a result, no one could challenge the Wraiths in the Murk. Not even the Dread."

"A strength but also a weakness."

Cadmus nodded in agreement. "The Wraiths thrive in the Murk, but they cannot leave the Murk. A terrible strength and a terrible weakness, both at the same time."

"A strength for the Dread to begin, his greatest weakness in the end."

"A good way to describe it," Cadmus agreed. "Julius lost his Kingdom to the Wraiths. Not before he wounded the Dread and eliminated a good number of his Ten Thousand, however, thereby weakening the Dread right when the Wraiths struck with deadly intentions. Having no choice, needing to heal and regain his strength, the Dread withdrew with what was left of his Ten Thousand. With the King of Frisia dead along with most of his soldiers, the Dread believed that he would consolidate his hold on the Kingdom when he returned and paid back the Wraiths for their betrayal. The Wraiths had other plans, taking advantage of his weakness. As a result, the Dread disappeared from history."

"Until now," Mikel said in an ominous tone.

"Until now," Cadmus repeated. Not wanting to dwell on that dark topic, the Frost Lord shifted to a matter that had been stuck in his mind ever since he saw the Blade of Light in Mikel's possession. "How did you master the Blade? You are the first not of the Giants of the Rime or the Deep to wield that ancient weapon."

"It wasn't easy."

"Nothing worthwhile ever is," Cadmus stated in an even tone designed to elucidate a response.

"One lesson after another. Storyteller some would say, but I have no doubt a better teacher you would have been. If you were not your father's son."

"I'll take that as a compliment."

"You should," Mikel said. "I learned that you can't master the Blade."

"What do you mean?" Cadmus frowned, revealing his confusion. "At first I was worried that you claiming the artifact would only earn you an early death. Yet you have joined with that ancient blade just as all the previous Bearers have."

"How can you tell?"

"You're still alive," Cadmus replied with an infectious laugh. "A good many have been chosen to be Bearers. Only a dozen have succeeded. Those who did lived. Those who didn't died."

"I wasn't aware of that." Mikel would need to have a longer conversation with the Bearers when the time was right. This would have been worth knowing before he began the long process of learning the Blade and what it could offer him. Both the good and the bad.

"Back to you carrying the Blade. How did you do it? Again, only a Giant has wielded it until now."

"It's not a matter of mastering the Blade of Light, it's more like a negotiation," Mikel explained.

"With which you are more than familiar," Cadmus prompted.

Mikel nodded in appreciation at the compliment. "Yes, and this negotiation was the most demanding in which I've ever engaged." Mikel's businesses and resulting success depended on the agreements he made. Partnering with the Blade was much the same. Once they had come to terms -- more a battle of wills at the beginning as Mikel and the artifact tested one another -- he learned to unleash the full potency of the Blade.

Yet that required as well that he and the Blade join together completely, heart and soul, body and spirit. Each powering the other. Each protecting the other. An agreement of sorts but more than that. And more than a meeting of the minds. An acceptance. A gifting of one to the other. Mikel and the Blade understanding that together they were stronger than they ever could be apart.

"It couldn't have been easy," Cadmus prodded. "Of all the artifacts that the Giants of the Rime have crafted for the Order of the Magii, this is one of the most powerful. The most temperamental as well."

"You've got the right of it," Mikel said. "The weapon is too strong, in will and power, to be treated as a stallion to be broken. The Blade of Light can't be broken. It can only be persuaded. Thankfully, I was able to persuade the Blade that I was worthy of what it offered."

"And it persuaded you to take it up."

"It did, though it was a prickly start." Mikel chose not to explain how the Blade tried to force its power upon him at the very start of their partnership, making it feel like the artifact was using him rather than him using the artifact.

"More detail would be appreciated. The last Bearer of the Blade was lost to us before I was born."

Mikel nodded. Knute Frost Lord. One of Mikel's guides. That was a topic for later when they had more time. "No matter what I tried to do, the Blade kept pushing back. Steel meeting steel and you know what results when that happens."

"I do."

"Thanks to my time in your forges and my experience working steel and the Light, I realized that I was employing the wrong approach. So I applied the same tactics as I did with Eisa. Calm. Controlled. I allowed the Blade to make the first touch."

"There had to be more to it than that."

"There was," Mikel admitted. He said nothing more on it, however. The connection, the partnership that he had earned, too personal to be shared with anyone, even the Frost Lord, who had not experienced the same as he had.

Therefore, he had no desire to discuss the terms of that partnership. What each would bring to it. What each would do to maintain it. What would be required of them both. And the terms of separation if either faltered or were found to be lacking.

Nor did he want to reveal how he communicated with the former Bearers of the Blade. Even though Mikel would be the first to admit that the guidance and advice provided by Knute and those who came before him was integral to his success, mentioning how the consciousnesses of the former Bearers of the Blade were tied to the ancient weapon would add hours to their current conversation. And he couldn't let that happen.

The uneasiness he had been experiencing now felt like a constant pounding in the back of his skull. His skin prickling, his senses sharpened. Just as was usually the case before he engaged in a combat.

What was it that was bothering him so much. "I'm sorry."

"You're not paying attention," Cadmus grumped. "You just said I was a good storyteller and teacher."

"Teacher yes, storyteller is still to be determined."

"Unfairly harsh," Cadmus grumbled. "I was explaining that Kronin is a terrible threat. That is undeniable. But as I said you must focus on the cause of the disease. Cut away the cancer and we have a chance. If you don't ..." Cadmus didn't feel the need to complete his thought.

"I'm glad you're so confident," Mikel chided.

Cadmus smiled, enjoying his friend's dark humor. It was a sign of the steel in his spine. The greater the threat, the more sarcastic he became. "I'm just being realistic. I know that's a quality that you value. The Dread first. After that, we deal with the other challenges we face, assuming you succeed."

A difficult task indeed. But Mikel much preferred to go to the heart of the matter than nip at the edges, cutting off the head of the snake directly relevant to his current thinking.

Besides, Mikel knew where to find the Dread. It was just a matter of getting close to him, and he believed that thanks to Cadmus he had a remedy for that challenge, which provided even more of an incentive for him to make a play for Malor.

"So while I do what I can against the Dread ..."

"The Giants of the Rime will hold the Titans."

"A big ask for both of us."

"But a worthy goal, nonetheless."

"And if I can't?" Even with the Blade of Light in his hand, Mikel had no illusions after speaking with Cadmus and Finn as to exactly how dangerous the Dread was and the power he could bring to bear against him.

"Then the Frozen Waste and the Splintered Empire and all the Realms beyond are doomed."

"Uplifting proclamation, Cadmus. Thank you for that unnecessary reminder." Mikel was going to say more, but he couldn't ignore the edginess any longer. Every nerve in his body warned him that danger was close.

*"You are not alone, Steelheart,"* Knute Frost Lord whispered in his mind. *"Beware."*

Mikel didn't hesitate. Reaching for the Light, the magic surged through him. His senses functioning at a level beyond the natural. The presence that had disturbed Mikel, that had slipped into the Great Hall, gained clarity. The danger it presented demanded action.

Mikel sprung up from his seat, pulling the Blade of Light free from its sheath as he did so. The steel blazed with a white light that not only illuminated the Great Hall but also the two shadows that sought to make their kill before revealing their presence.

Mikel didn't bother to attack the Titan closest to him. He sensed the movement behind him, certain that Cadmus was ready.

Instead he ducked the Titan's swing, the black steel of the scythe passing through the space just above his head. Kicking out with his foot, he smiled grimly when the Titan grimaced, the assassin's knee bending too far in the wrong direction.

Mikel pushed his success from his mind, having eyes only for the second Titan. This brute was the biggest Giant Mikel had ever seen, his head almost scraping the ceiling of the Great Hall.

Understanding what would happen if he tried to parry the sharp steel streaking down toward his head, Mikel surrendered to his instincts. Kneeling down swiftly, he slammed the hilt of the blazing scimitar against the stone tile of the floor.

A blast of light erupted from the blow. Sending the Titan flying backward, the assassin crashed against the far wall.

Before the Titan could rise, Mikel was there. Instead of

slashing the assassin's throat, he used the hilt once more, bringing his steel down onto the rebel's hard skull and sending him to a less-than-blissful unconsciousness.

"You didn't kill him." Cadmus stepped up next to Mikel, blood dripping from his scythe.

"I thought you might like to have a talk with this one."

"I would. The other was less than amenable."

"Then I'm glad to be of service."

"You were more than that, my friend. My thanks, Lightcrafter. If not for you, these two assassins would have succeeded."

"Lightcrafter? You've said that before."

"It's a term that's a part of our lore. Literally, it means that you can craft the Light, manipulate it, in ways that others can't. Different from our smiths. Just as you demonstrated. A unique and rare skill. Also one that reveals the strength of your partnership with the ancient weapon."

Mikel thought about that, Cadmus' explanation sparking a memory of one of the many nights he stayed up into the early hours of the morning with Kaduna, who was always willing to talk and teach so long as it was on a topic that she believed was important to him.

She had mentioned the Lightcrafter.

Once.

At the time he had found the reference interesting because it seemed more story or myth than real.

Until now.

Kaduna had explained that the Lightcrafter didn't just manipulate the Light. The Lightcrafter destroyed the shadow. The Lightcrafter revealed the truth within the darkness. Which with respect to the Dread could mean ...

"*What else can the Light do?*" Mikel remembered asking Kaduna.

"*Almost whatever you want, little one,*" she had replied. "*Just remember. The Light is a two-fold blade. It can be used to create. It can also be used to destroy."*

"Why does the Dread want the Blade?" Mikel asked in a voice barely above a whisper, still partially caught in his memories.

Cadmus gave Mikel a sly look. "You already know the answer to that my friend."

Mikel nodded, because thanks to Kaduna, he did.

"You're walking into a pit of ice vipers," Cadmus continued. "The only chance you have for defeating the Dread is to use the Blade of Light. But if you fail and he claims the scimitar, he claims the Frozen Waste and any other Realm he chooses. So best that you don't fall in."

18

# FIRE AND VENOM

"You're having too much fun, Eisa!" Mikel shouted. Grateful for the saddle that Cadmus had made for him when he recognized the affinity between the Bearer of the Blade and the ice dragon, the rush of air threatened to dislodge him and send him tumbling to his death if he lost his grip.

Eisa responded with a throaty rumble, clearly enjoying the pursuit as they flew across the Trench. The trio of Wyverns snapping at their backs were of little concern to the ice dragon and only added to her fun.

Mikel had hoped that with darkness falling, and his decision to cross the Trench much farther south and well away from the Splintered Bridge, that they could avoid the Wyverns.

Once again, Mikel learned the futility of putting too much faith in hope.

Of course, though he might not be enjoying the bumpy flight, powerful gusts of wind pushing them from one side to the other, or dipping down or up on a whim, Eisa was in her element.

The ice dragon was relishing her youth. Her power. Her strength.

But with all that came another trait.

She was becoming more and more impatient.

That only stood to reason.

She was young. Less than a year old.

Even so, she was three times the size of a Wyvern, and Mikel was certain that she would have little trouble challenging the much larger black dragons that claimed the canyon floor as their own.

Eisa wanted to fight.

She wanted to demonstrate her dominance.

She wanted to show him what she could do.

Still, Mikel held her back, only allowing her to evade their attackers. And she did so with a unique pleasure, though that pleasure was fading. Twisting and turning, corkscrewing and diving, the Wyverns struggled to stay with them. Mikel was glad that he was flying on an empty stomach, sure of the result if he had eaten something before they left the Frozen Waste.

If Mikel gave into his caution, he could have kept them on course. Eisa would have been disappointed, but she would have understood. They were almost to the far side. Only one Wyvern still hounded them. The other two had ducked back beneath the cloud cover, tired of participating in a fruitless chase.

"Make it quick, Eisa!" Mikel shouted, moved by her grunt of displeasure.

Eisa roared, at the same time dipping her right wing. Allowing her momentum to take her, Eisa cut to the right and down swiftly, then curled her body and held her place in the sky as the Wyvern streaked by, the beast shrieking in fury as it missed its prey with an outstretched claw.

With a few powerful beats of her wings, Eisa was right on the Wyvern's tail. Literally. Snapping with her jaws.

The Wyvern, sensing its peril, made the right decision. Diving down, it sought the safety of the clouds and the Trench beyond.

Eisa refused to allow her quarry to escape. Yet she had no intention of following through the misty grey, not wanting to risk what might be waiting for her when she emerged.

Instead, she demonstrated another reason why she was coming into her own.

Closing the distance to the Wyvern with a few more flaps of her powerful wings, the clouds only a hundred yards away and coming up fast, Eisa opened her jaws and shot a blast of icy mist from her throat.

The whitish blue spray that resembled a comet slammed into the Wyvern. The intense cold ate through the Wyvern's scales and into its flesh. Freezing muscle and bone, the cold was so crippling that the Wyvern lost control of its own body. The beast's blood turned to ice while its wings froze to its sides.

Before it dropped into the grey, the stricken Wyvern was no more than a dead weight.

Eisa screeched in triumph as she veered away from the clouds, her claws kissing the grey before she curled back toward the east and the far side of the Trench.

"Well done, Eisa," Mikel said with pride, rubbing the ice dragon's neck. "Well done, indeed."

A deep rumble emanated from Eisa's throat, pleased by Mikel's compliment and even more with his affection.

The dangers of the Trench past them, Mikel needed to decide on the best path to take now that they were only a few flaps of Eisa's wings from crossing into the Kingdom of the Tor.

Eisa could land right atop the highest tower of the Ring.

Quite an entrance that would be, Mikel announcing himself on the back of an ice dragon. It might even catch Malor Dragoran off guard and put him on his back foot.

However, Mikel needed to remember that Malor Dragoran was no more than a name. A skin to be shed when the time was right.

The Dread was Mikel's true opponent.

An ancient evil.

That truth required a delicate touch. One that allowed him to approach from the shadows until the time to strike was right.

And that meant for him to have any real chance of defeating the Dread, Mikel had to get close. So rather than a grand entrance, subterfuge was the better course.

It was also one of his stronger skills.

Yet even with that decision made, he needed to make another.

His first choice for entering the Tor would have been the hidden path that he had used to help Drin escape.

That path was no longer hidden, unfortunately. Assindra was aware of it. And he assumed that if Assindra was aware of it, the Dread was aware of it as well. Such a risk wasn't worth taking despite the potential ease of access.

He would need to take another risk, accepting the additional peril involved as the cost of the stealth he desired.

"Let's keep our distance, Eisa," Mikel said, speaking into her ear.

Eisa screeched her agreement before tilting her wing and curling sharply to the south.

"Stay safe, Eisa. And stay close. I will see you soon."

Eisa offered a deep rumble, rubbing her large head against Mikel's chest and shoulder, purring as he scratched below her chin, before she stepped back and launched herself into the sky.

She would use the last of the night to find shelter at the tip of the Spine. If Mikel needed her, she could return to the Tor in less than an hour.

Watching Eisa disappear among the stars, Mikel felt a touch of nerves much like he did before he began one of the jobs that had served as a starting point for his gradual transformation into the King of the Underworld.

The unease didn't bother him. He would have felt more uncomfortable if the butterflies weren't flitting about in his stomach.

What bothered him was a new emotion that came along with it and he rarely experienced.

Guilt.

He had left Drin on the Crux without telling her his plans.

Of course, if he had told her what he had in mind, she would have nixed his plan and then done everything in her power to ensure that he didn't take up this mission. Or, worse, and the more likely result, she would have demanded to come with him, putting herself in even greater peril than she already was.

That would only increase the difficulty of the task he had given himself. And, she would have been a distraction. He would have been more worried about her than in what was required of him.

She would have been an impediment. Nothing more than …

Who was he kidding?

Every excuse playing through his mind was valid.

None was the primary reason he chose to assume this task on his own. None was the reason he was trying so hard not to acknowledge.

Shifting his gaze to the dark trail to his front, and thereby adjust his focus, he told himself that he would deal with the guilt and second-guessing later.

If he actually survived the next few hours.

Now, he had to concentrate on getting what needed to be gotten, then get gone.

In this case, not an item.

Rather a life.

If that life still was a life that could be claimed after being so deeply corrupted by the Curse.

Grumbling under his breath, Mikel began the treacherous descent down the steep path that would take him to the bottom of the Ravine.

FEARING injury because of the ruggedness of what any sane mountain goat would avoid, Mikel didn't rush his climb down the rock-strewn trail while his knee protested every step he took.

And now that he was in the Ravine he moved even slower. Steep cliffs rose up on both sides to a height of several hundred feet, those jagged walls making the nighttime darkness even more acute but for the few feeble rays of the moon that touched the ground whenever the thick clouds permitted.

He was careful with each step.

Avoiding the sand and dirt whenever he could.

Seeking to make his way across the rock.

Even then, placing each foot with a good deal of caution.

Slowly.

With the greatest delicacy.

Attempting to mask his movement.

Not wanting the Ravine's lurking residents to learn of his presence until he was well past.

He knew what would happen if the hunters hiding in the sand discovered that he was there before he reached the tunnel that was located at the far end of the cavern.

Every few seconds he stopped.

Listening.

Waiting.

Hearing nothing.

Not even the faint stir of a breeze.

A deathly quiet enveloped the Ravine.

That was to be expected, however.

Not even the mountain goats that climbed the steep heights of the Tor came this way, well aware of the risk and likely result of making such a foolish decision.

And that was why traversing the Ravine was not Mikel's first choice for sneaking into the Tor. Rather, it was his only choice because he was unwilling to test the deception he had planned until the very last moment. Not until he could put himself in a position to strike a fatal blow.

Though thinking about that now could lead to his early demise. If he wasn't careful, if he made a single misstep, the Ravine's residents could and likely would strike and end his hunt before it even began.

The need for caution ever present in the back of his mind, Mikel advanced once more along the rocky floor, placing each foot as if he were sneaking up the creaky steps of an old house and doing everything he could to not give himself away.

To not disturb the ground in any way.

To not relay his location to the creatures hidden around him.

The narrow tunnel that was his objective – from his current distance of a hundred yards no more than a dark splotch on the rocks at the far western end of the Ravine – appeared to be impossibly far away. Nevertheless, he continued on his course. Slowly. Ever so slowly as he drew closer with each silent and cautious step he took.

He had traveled along this route before. Once and only once. And then solely because he put in play a diversion that allowed him to avoid the dangers of the Ravine.

Now he was on his own with no tricks up his sleeve.

He felt naked, and he hated it. His unease was fed by his uncertainty about whether he could get past the perils of this route unscathed.

He had placed himself in a dangerous position. Yes, he was the one to do it. He could admit that freely. He was where he was because he had made the decision to be here.

And if he really unraveled it, it all started because of a woman who had twisted him into ...

Mikel halted abruptly, his right foot just above the ground. Standing stock still, he held his breath and listened for the whisper he thought that he had heard.

The quiet somehow had deepened. Thickened.

Then his ears picked up what had unsettled him.

The faintest sound of a scrape. He could have put it down to his imagination, but to ignore his instincts in the Ravine ensured his death.

And that faint scrape was right below where he wanted to place his boot.

A cold liquid fear entered his veins. He was no longer alone. Worse, he was balancing on his bad knee. The pain shooting through the damaged joint then up and down his leg started his body shaking.

He couldn't hold his position for much longer. The reason he kept his foot elevated had not moved.

As a result, he was trapped.

And the instant his knee gave out, which it would, he was dead.

Any movement on his part, no matter how small, no matter how silent, would still capture the interest of the creature beneath his boot. The likely cause of his death could sense any movement when so close to its prey, even just a whisper through the air.

Mikel considered the only idea that came to mind for escaping his fate. He needed to weigh his desire to remain anonymous so close to the Tor against his desire to remain alive.

He decided that it was better to risk alerting the Dread that he was close than to go to the other side.

With his knee on fire it was a risk worth taking. He couldn't hold his position for more than a few seconds more.

Decision made, he called upon the Light. With the flick of his wrist Mikel shot a tiny spark right into the ground a few feet to his right.

The animal beneath his boot acted exactly as Mikel hoped it would.

Lunging with an angry hiss, the serpent exploded out of the gritty soil, fangs snapping toward the light.

Mikel responded instinctively. Pulling the mace free from the scabbard nestled in the small of his back, he slashed with a sure grip, the blade at the end cutting through the thick body with little resistance.

One threat removed with a great many more in his way.

The floor of the Ravine came alive before the separate pieces of the snake's corpse hit the sand. The hisses and scrapes of scales across rock threatened to freeze the cold that had found a home in Mikel's blood.

Now he had no choice except to build upon the risk he had taken. Sweeping his free hand in a wide arc, sparks of light flickered then crackled through the air. Snapping loudly when they hit the ground, the sparks burned blindingly bright before sizzling out.

In those few seconds of illumination, the sparks gave Mikel exactly what he required.

A path.

And he was quick to make use of it.

Stumbling more than sprinting because of his knee, Mikel made for the gap in the rock.

Out of the corner of his eye, he glimpsed more movement through the gloom and shadows of the cavern floor.

That movement sidewinded toward him before the last of his sparks fizzled away.

Blast it!

They were faster than Mikel remembered.

He just needed a few more steps.

But would he get them?

He felt more than saw one of the animals slithering toward him from his right.

His objective just to his front, Mikel leapt off his good leg, reaching up as high as he could before he slammed the blade of his mace into the ravine wall with a stone-crushing force.

Mikel thought he had a good hold, his cold fear surging when the blade slid a few knuckles out of the stone, tilting him back toward the roiling mass of hissing serpents below his dangling boots. He didn't breathe again until the steel caught in the crevice he created.

For a heartbeat, he scrambled futilely with his feet, his desperation intensifying, grateful when his left boot finally found purchase on a small ledge.

Bunching his shoulders, he lifted his body and pulled himself up.

Just in time.

The dark shadow streaking toward him fell short of his boot. Smacking its extended fangs against the rock wall, the serpent tumbled to the ground.

Placing his forehead against the cool stone, Mikel took a deep breath to calm his racing heart.

His hunter missed him by no more than a hair.

He had gotten lucky, avoiding the agonizing death that fate held in store if the animal had taken a bite of him.

And all it took was a single drop of venom to do the deed.

Just then, moonlight shone brightly into the Ravine, the clouds clearing.

Mikel looked down even though he really didn't want to see what was revealed on the canyon floor.

Dozens of poisonous serpents waited for him.

Their venom the most powerful in the world.

Rock vipers.

He couldn't tell how many slithered around near where he made his leap. Several waited patiently, coiled up, their dark eyes reflecting the light. A few of the more aggressive beasts extended up the canyon wall toward him, snapping their fangs, but only able to reach so far.

Mikel was grateful that the snakes couldn't climb the vertical surface.

Still, a key question kept playing through Mikel's mind.

How long could he hold on before he fell to his death?

Mikel studied with a wary eye the serpents he had hoped not to encounter.

Despite his efforts to proceed quietly without disturbing the ground, no such luck.

He'd wakened the entire nest of rock vipers.

All because one snake had decided to emerge from its burrow along the path he had chosen at the worst possible time.

And now he was stuck.

The serpents slithered and snapped at him and their brethren. A few of the more adventurous ones lunged at his boots every so often, falling short so long as Mikel kept his knees in tight to his chest.

Mikel wasn't their usual prey. The rock vipers lived off other snakes, lizards, and the birds that nested along the Ravine's walls.

Nevertheless, they were territorial. And they were the reason no one in their right mind traveled through the Ravine.

Seven or more feet long with thick bodies, they appeared to be slow and moved like the sidewinders found in the deserts far to the south. They were anything but, however. The serpents slithered with a deceptive speed and attacked with a viciousness born of both hunger and a nasty streak, which was currently on full display.

With the rock vipers riled up, he had no chance to sneak by.

Worse, he couldn't hold his place along the rockface for much longer. The effort to stay above the hissing and snapping serpents was draining him of his strength. His knee was on fire. And his hands were wet with sweat.

He needed to move.

The floor of the Ravine now off limits, Mikel had only one choice. A fact that was really beginning to gnaw at him.

The lack of choices.

Mikel always preferred to have more than one option in every scenario. In this instance, he didn't, and that grating truth was becoming much too common in recent days.

He could berate himself for his decisions later. Now, he needed to get clear of the vipers that were eager to sink their fangs into him.

Grunting from the required effort, he began his slow trek along the rockface.

Taking his time.

Understanding the danger of rushing, he didn't slide across the stone until he punched the blade of his mace into the canyon wall and found a grip for his free hand and feet.

It was slow-going. Made all the more difficult as he tired. The strain on the muscles in his back and shoulders turned into a slow fire that soon mimicked the heat in his knee.

His hunters helped him to ignore much of his discomfort.

Many of the rock vipers followed along the base of the cliff as he scrambled for the tunnel that was his only way out of his predicament.

His progress slowed all the more because of the sheerness of the rockface, the stone worn down by the torrents of water that rushed through the Ravine during the spring. That challenge required Mikel to make several hard decisions about where he would tempt fate with a handhold or foothold.

Nevertheless, slow though it was, he was moving in his desired direction.

Until he couldn't go any further. A ten-yard gap in the rock wall prevented him from reaching the tunnel.

He cursed himself for a fool. He had picked the wrong side to make his initial escape from the first rock viper.

Then again, thinking back, it was the right decision. Because it was the only decision he could have made.

He had picked the side that he was closest to. If he hadn't, he would be lying dead on the sand and stone, his insides liquefied by the rock viper's venom.

Worn down by time and water, the gap was too far to leap across.

Once again, he didn't want to put into practice the only plan that came to mind. Still, better that he risk detection than die at the bite of a rock viper.

This time, he allowed more of the Light to surge within him, savoring the power and using it to strengthen his weakening body. His eyes opened in delight as his pain and weariness faded away. Even his knee no longer barked at him.

Revitalized, he turned his attention to the rockface beneath his feet. With a delicate touch, he sent several precise threads of natural magic slicing into the stone.

Although he employed very little of the Light, the result was exactly what Mikel had envisioned. Large shards of rock sheared off and tumbled to the ground, crushing and burying the rock vipers at his feet.

He didn't hesitate. Jumping down, he slashed with his mace and beheaded the sole rock viper that had evaded the pile of rubble.

Then he was gone, sprinting into the tunnel. Already certain thanks to his use of the Light that the way was clear.

*"Your skill is improving,"* Knute Frost Lord said in his mind.

*"You and the other Bearers deserve the credit,"* Mikel replied in a humble tone, thankful that he had escaped what should have been his certain death.

*"It takes excellent instructors and a willing pupil. A true partnership."*

*"Another lesson, Frost Lord?"*

*"Always."*

MIKEL STOOD BARELY BREATHING in the massive cavern beneath the Tor. Eyes transfixed by the shadows flickering along the walls.

Much like in the base of the Crux, channels of magma criss-crossed the floor. Some were too wide for him to cross. Others were little more than narrow rivulets he could step over with ease. The spiderweb of orange red provided enough light to illuminate the enormous hollow in a dull glow.

He had escaped the rock vipers. He was glad for that.

Now, though, he faced an even greater challenge.

And that challenge didn't involve him choosing which tunnel to take.

The three dark openings beckoned to him from the far side, each one branching out and heading deeper within the Tor. Then branching out again and again, forming an almost indecipherable maze. Anyone foolish enough to attempt to navigate the convoluted web guaranteed a singular and torturous fate.

A slow death.

Except for him.

Mikel knew the route that he needed to take, having made the journey once before.

That wasn't what made him stop rather than continue on his journey, however.

No, the last and most dangerous confrontation before he slipped into Malor Dragoran's fortress waited for him. It was just a question now of how difficult this latest challenge decided to be. His last obstacle obstreperous at the best of times.

"Show yourself," Mikel called, his voice echoing softly in the cavern.

A quiet broken only by the slow flow of the lava at his feet greeted his demand.

"You know that I am here, my friend. And I know that you are here. There is no game to play nor the time for it. Only a negotiation to be undertaken. Just as was the case the last time we met," Mikel chided.

The quiet settled around Mikel once more, though it did not last for long.

A dark shape that grew greater in size with every silent stride emerged into the light.

"You're taking all the fun out of this, Steelheart." The voice was as hard as the stone of the cavern. Raspy as well, as if she drank from the magma that flowed through the channels cut into the floor. "And I have yet to decide if we are friends."

"I've been accused of doing worse." He offered the Giant a slight bow. No more than was required to demonstrate a mutual respect between them. His action earned a brief grunt of approval from the figure blocking his way.

She was as tall as Julia, the Frost Lord's daughter, yet there the resemblance ended. Her skin had a reddish hue that matched her hair, the thick, braided strands a mix of red and orange that were similar in coloring to the lava flowing beneath her feet. Her clothes were black and brown, the color of the earth that was her home.

A Giant of the Flame.

Kin to the Giants living in the Deep and in the Frozen Waste, Giants of the Flame tended to be more solitary than their brethren, usually not living together unless they were family. And they were rarely seen, unless they chose to reveal themselves.

For the Giants of the Flame had mastered the many hidden paths beneath the earth that allowed them to travel throughout the Realms and beyond without having to step above ground. As a result, often they were thought of as no more than a myth or, for those who believed the tales, an extinct branch of Giant lineage.

Although clearly that last wasn't the case.

Giants of the Flame lived near volcanos. Live and dormant, the Crux and the Tor the latter.

Mikel had come to know the Giant who lived beneath the Crux, finding him in a chamber much like the one he stood in now. They had become friends, exchanging information, gifts, and favors, such as introducing Mikel to the Giant standing before him who's wry grin was at odds with the harshness of her features and her gravelly voice.

Aurelius' passing had saddened Mikel. The Giant of the Flame had a good and generous spirit. Even more important to Mikel, he was a Giant of honor and integrity. Age had taken him, and Mikel had done all that he could to ensure he was comfortable when he passed to the other side. A fact that the Giant blocking his way had appreciated.

"I did not think you would come this way again after our last meeting." The Giant flipped her long hair over her shoulder with her free hand. Her other hand grasped a scythe made of a red steel that resembled glowing lava.

"I didn't have much choice, Teine."

"A poor decision on your part, Steelheart. I am not in a magnanimous mood today."

"The only decision," Mikel sighed. Then he offered her a cunning grin meant to challenge her. "And when have you ever been in a magnanimous mood?"

Teine almost smiled at the question. But she didn't, refusing to give Mikel the satisfaction. "Rarely. And not since Aurelius passed. He was a good friend."

"He was," Mikel agreed.

"And it is because of Aurelius that I stand here talking with you rather than killing you on sight."

"That's very magnanimous of you," Mikel stated with a respectful tilt of his head.

Teine barked out a sharp laugh that she quickly crushed, refusing to reveal her pleasure at his quip. "Why are you here, Steelheart? I know you have other ways to enter the Tor."

"I am seeking to avoid a host of potential complications."

"You don't view me as a complication?"

Mikel didn't reply right away, recognizing the trap in her words. "I view you as many things, Teine. But as a complication? Never."

"As smooth as ever," Teine snorted. "A unique skill with words you have, Steelheart, and a dangerous one."

"I'm just being honest."

"What do you truly seek in the Tor?" Teine asked. "Do you finally wish to claim it for yourself?"

"Why would you think that?"

"I may reside beneath the Tor," Teine explained, "but still I know much of what is going on atop it. You have expanded your holdings."

"Quietly. I was hoping that no one would notice."

"Yet I did."

Mikel nodded to her in respect again. "I'm not surprised. You have always seen more than others."

"Yet I do not see why you are here. If you sought to claim the Tor, you would do so from a different direction."

"I do not seek to claim the Tor, Teine." Mikel shrugged, as if her claim was of little matter. "I admit that I have expanded my holdings, but that's just business."

"And you being here now isn't business?"

Mikel bit his lip before replying. After a few seconds of deliberation, he decided to tell Teine the truth. Whether she chose to believe him would be up to her. "Not business, no. My being here is personal."

Teine studied Mikel, her red eyes blazing brightly as she measured him. Then she spoke in a soft voice infused with a mystical quality that sent a cold shiver down Mikel's spine despite the heat emanating from the lava that was all around him. "You do not seek to claim the throne. You seek to claim the one who sits upon it."

Mikel's eyes hardened as his features tightened. "I had heard that there were a few Giants of the Flame who could see with more than just their eyes. You never told me that you were one."

"Why would I?" Teine replied with a shrug.

"I'm just disappointed." Mikel took a deep breath, seeking to calm himself. Not wanting to forget himself or why he was there. Teine was Teine. That's what Aurelius said in the moments after he introduced the Giant of the Flame to him. Best to acknowledge that fact and work with it rather than against it. "I thought we were better friends."

"Friendship has nothing to do with it, Steelheart. Why do you take such a risk knowing the likely outcome? What do you hope to gain?"

"You have a great many questions, Teine. I'll not answer them all."

"I didn't expect that you would." She glided forward then. Two big steps to close the distance between them. Mikel now in range of her scythe. "And because of that, I am not of a mind to let you pass."

"Can we not negotiate, Teine? It would make both our lives easier."

"You promised me the last time we met, Steelheart."

"I did," Mikel replied in a solemn tone. Among the Giants, a promise was an unbreakable bond. "I remember. I am simply seeking to delay that promise until next we meet."

"Your business is so pressing?" Teine lifted her head and tilted it as she stared down at him. Not doubting him. Just not pleased that he sought to delay what she truly desired.

"It is."

"Why?" Teine refused to be put off.

Mikel didn't want to provide all the details, but he couldn't avoid the heart of his interest. "I promised that I would do all that I could to protect a woman."

His response drew a loud and harsh bark of a laugh from Teine. "I never expected such sentimentality from you, Steelheart."

"Not sentimentality. I am simply seeking to keep a promise to myself."

"And promises are important to you?" she asked with a raised eyebrow.

Mikel sighed. Teine had trapped him. "To the death?"

"To the death," Teine growled, her red eyes sparking with delight.

Mikel jumped over the channel of lava to his left and kept moving as Teine slashed with her scythe. The red steel slammed into the ground where he had been standing just a moment before. Following him as he ran and jumped in a ragged circle around the spiderweb of channels, Mikel always stayed a hair in front of the blade that sought his flesh.

"You cannot escape me, Steelheart," Teine stated with a frightening certainty. "You know that. So stop trying."

"I'm not trying to escape you, Teine," Mikel called over his shoulder. "I'm just trying to reach a more defensible position."

And he did only a heartbeat later.

Spinning swiftly, he pulled the scimitar from the scabbard across his back. The Blade of Light came to life at his touch, blazing white erupting down the steel and sparks flying when the Giant-crafted weapon met Teine's scythe.

"A new toy?" Teine grunted as she pressed down with all her strength. The tip of her scythe was only a few knuckles above his head, yet it moved no further. The Giant of the Flame not understanding how the Steelheart was able to stand against her.

"Something like that," Mikel replied. His dark eyes flashed as he leaned to the side, Teine's scythe sliding off his steel.

Caught off balance, before she could recover Mikel cut across her thigh. Not deeply. Just a thin slice. A warning.

Teine ignored the fire of the cut and the trickle of blood as it flowed freely down her leg. "Lucky, Steelheart. No more than that."

"We'll see," he replied. His voice was as stern as his eyes.

Teine was stronger than he was. Bigger. More durable. Therefore, Mikel had little desire to get drawn into a long combat. So he didn't.

The more he used the Blade of Light, the more he understood the true properties of the ancient weapon. Just as important, the more the ancient weapon understood him.

The cavern wall at his back, channels of lava marking off a space similar in size to the practice ring in The Fox's Lair, Mikel seized the initiative. Feinting to his left, he cut with a quick backslash and opened a long slice across Teine's other thigh.

"Are you sure you want to do this, Teine?" he asked as he stepped back.

Mikel avoided her retaliatory swing, red steel crunching into the cavern floor once again.

She growled an angry response. "More than ever."

"Then your blood is on your hands."

Rather than spinning away from Teine's latest overhead attack, he stepped forward. Getting in close to the Giant, he slashed once, twice, a third time with his scimitar. Each time he opened a shallow gash. Twice below the ribs, one on each side, and a third across her hip. Then he disengaged, attacking for only a few seconds before putting the cavern wall at his back once again.

"You think you can best me, Steelheart?" Teine demanded.

"I have to, don't I?" Her voice didn't reveal the rage that Mikel anticipated. Rather, she sounded ... excited. It was as if she were enjoying herself despite not having earned a cut on him.

Mikel moved again. A blur of motion. His bad knee not bothering him as he continued to benefit from his application of the Light. Four more efficient slices and he was back against the cavern wall.

"Are you having fun, Steelheart?" Despite her many bloody wounds, Teine wore a broad smile. "I certainly am. I have not fought someone as worthy as you in quite some time."

"That's kind of you to say, Teine. But I do need to be going."

"And end what is happening between us?"

"Unfortunately so," Mikel replied. "As I said, I have a promise to keep once this promise has been kept."

Before he completed what he wanted to say, Mikel charged straight at Teine.

Momentary astonishment clear in her eyes, she tried to bring her scythe up in front of her to defend against the killing blow she anticipated.

The Giant of the Flame was too slow, her eyes growing wider more in shock than fear.

The Steelheart missed her entirely despite being so close.

Instead he slammed the hilt of his fiery blade against the ground.

A blast of rock and magma exploded into the air and sent Teine flying through the air.

Struggling to push herself back up after she crunched into the ground, the touch of the Steelheart's blade to her throat stopped her.

"I could kill you."

"Why don't you?" Teine murmured. She had lost, and she had loved it. For the first time in decades she had tested herself against a worthy opponent. "You have earned the right."

"You've grown on me."

Teine snorted out a very brief laugh, the steel slicing into her skin preventing anything more than that. "You want something."

"As I said, I prefer to negotiate rather than draw blood."

"What do you desire, Steelheart? I will consider it."

"Your life for a favor to be named at a later date."

Teine didn't reply immediately as she mulled the Steelheart's proposal. He could kill her now. With honor for them both. A good ending from her perspective.

Still, was she ready to go to the other side? Would it not be fun to challenge the Steelheart once more when circumstances permitted? "Done."

"Good." Mikel pulled back the Blade of Light then offered his hand, helping Teine to her feet before sheathing his scimitar and pulling the small pack from his back that contained the medical supplies he always carried.

"Will I regret this favor?" Teine rumbled.

"I expect so."

19

## A TRUE TEST

"I was expecting you." Nat didn't bother to look up right way, finger still scanning the page. She was well aware that she was no longer alone.

She sat in the back of Mikel's bookshop in the City Below, reading several of the latest texts he had set out for her that would be part of their next lesson. These books offered a more in-depth history of the lands surrounding the Crux, reviewing not only the ruling families, but also the strategies they employed to maintain their power.

She understood why he had given them to her. Nat already had identified several of the tactics Mikel used on a regular basis to undermine the First Families to the benefit of Innsbruck's general populace, and of course himself. Tactics that she needed to learn as well.

"Is that so?"

Nat turned then pushed herself up, book in hand. Her gaze was sharp.

She wasn't the least bit intimidated by the woman standing in front of her. The woman who had snuck into the shop without opening the door, which revealed who she truly was and what she could do. The woman who bore a striking resemblance in several ways to the man who had taken Nat in and given her the tools to build a life of her own.

"That surprises you?"

"Not with Mikel having trained you."

Nat grinned. With an obvious cunning, tilting her head slightly to the right, her eyes narrowed as she measured the woman who had come for her. "He believed that you wouldn't be able to resist what I might offer you."

"It's not what you offer me, but rather what I offer you." Assindra stepped farther into the bookshop to the very edge of the candlelight. "I'm here to present you with an opportunity that you could not gain in any other way. An opportunity that you will neither be able to nor will want to resist."

Nat's lips quirked into a small smile. Brief flashes of the conversation she had with Mikel before he went to visit Cadmus passed through her mind, Assindra saying almost word for word exactly what Mikel said she would. "To join you. To learn from you. That's why you're here."

Assindra nodded. Her smile widened, making Nat think of a king cobra rising up, its hood flaring as it prepared to strike. "You have a power in the Talent that few can match, young lady. There is much that I can show you. There is much that I can teach you. If you apply yourself, you could be one of the strongest Magii to ever walk the Realms."

"Thank you, but I already have an excellent instructor."

"For the Talent, yes. I am aware. But there are more potencies in the world than just the Talent. And there is so much more you could make of yourself if you explored them as I have. The power you wield now is nothing compared to the power you could wield if you demonstrate the courage so few have." Assindra bent down, as if she were sharing a secret with Nat. "Why be satisfied with only that single skill when you can explore and employ so many more? Clearly you have an interest in learning." She motioned toward the book in Nat's hands. "Why limit yourself?"

Nat didn't respond right away. "You're offering me a chance to become someone like you."

"Like me?"

Nat nodded knowingly, her own smile becoming more of a smirk. "Like you. Weak."

"I am not weak ..." Assindra growled. Her rage burst to life in a flash, unused to being spoken to in such an insolent manner, and by someone so far beneath her in skill and experience.

"You gave yourself to the Curse," Nat explained. "You didn't fight it. You acquiesced. You surrendered. You ..."

"How dare you! You don't know of what you speak."

"You demonstrated a weakness of character that remains with you today," Nat finished, unconcerned by the Dark Magus' rage. "Yes, you exercise a great deal of power. That's undeniable. In fact, I can sense it. But truly how much of what you do is you and not the Curse doing what it wishes through you? Have you ever asked yourself that? Explored it?"

"You dare to challenge me?" Assindra spat, her glare fiery enough to melt a path through the Frozen Waste. "I came here to help you. I came here and offered you an unimaginable gift. I will not be disrespected by a girl barely out of adolescence."

"You came here to corrupt me," Nat clarified. "Just as Mikel said you would. What you want for me you want for yourself."

"And why would you believe him?" Assindra scoffed. "He understands little of the Talent. He does not have the skill. Devoid of the ability and an embarrassment to his people. To me." Assindra clenched her fingers, wisps of black energy beginning to drift up from her fists. "Why would you believe that he knows so much about the Curse?"

"He knows more than you believe, Dark Magus. That is why you're here."

"You think you're so smart. Standing up to me. Yet at the same time having no clue as to what I am truly capable."

"No, not smart," Nat corrected. "Just perceptive. A skill that Mikel helped me to hone. You seek to bring Mikel under your sway. You want to use me to do that because you have yet to find the right lever to make him dance as you want him to."

"I misjudged you, girl," Assindra barked through clenched teeth, the wisps of black flowing more freely from her fists and beginning to swirl around her forearms. "You're not just smart. You're too smart for your own good."

"No, I'm just being honest. Just as Mikel taught me to be."

"You give Mikel too much credit."

"He said the same just recently," Nat admitted with a smile meant to irritate Assindra. And it did, the Dark Magus' brow furrowing. "I disagreed with him then, and I disagree with you now."

Assindra took a deep breath and let it out through her nose. She needed to calm herself. This negotiation was not yet lost. There was still a chance that she could gain what she wanted. And if she couldn't, she would do as she needed to do. "The offer still stands, girl. Will you explore where the power you wield can take you? Will you seek to become something more than you already are? To become truly great? Truly powerful?"

"What you're really asking is will I place myself beneath you. Will I serve you as you want Mikel to."

"There is a great deal to gain by doing so," Assindra admitted. "Much you can learn if you stay in my good graces."

Nat didn't need more than a heartbeat to consider her answer. "No."

"Don't be too hasty, girl. You are making ..."

"No, I will not serve you." Nat placed the book on the table at her back, then squared up to Assindra. "You only serve yourself, Dark Magus, and the Curse that flows through your veins."

"You're making a terrible mistake, girl."

"The only mistake I could make would be to align myself with you." Sparks of white danced across Nat's palms, which she held close to her sides. She was ready. Even so, she would do as Mikel suggested. She would continue to provoke. She would continue to poke. She would push the Dark Magus away from reason and toward emotion. A lesson learned from *The Art of War*, the first book Mikel gave her to read.

"You know so little, child," Assindra murmured, her tone laced with a sad disappointment. As if Nat didn't really know what she was doing.

"I know that you are a slave to the Curse, Dark Magus. I will not become one myself."

"You will regret your obstinance," Assindra hissed. Her attempt to sound conciliatory was gone in an instant.

"Prove it."

The attack was fast.

Deceptively so.

Assindra sent whips of black energy from each hand. Those thick and spiky strands strove to wrap themselves around Nat and dig into her flesh. Contaminate her. Turn her.

Nat was ready.

Spinning around completely and waving her arms in a broad circle, a swirl of white energy formed. Flowing around her. Protecting her. Preventing the whips from latching on.

But Nat wasn't done.

If she had learned nothing else from Mikel, it was that you couldn't win a combat if you spent all your time defending yourself. So she didn't.

Certain that she had Assindra's first attack well in hand, she decided to give Assindra a taste of her own medicine. She sent a thin thread of the Talent streaking across the floor, seeking to entangle the Dark Magus' legs then bind her and take her to the ground.

It didn't work.

Assindra dodged out of the way just in time.

Nevertheless, it was enough to halt the Dark Magus' attack. And that's when Nat struck again. And again. And again.

Shards of magic screamed through the air.

Waves of energy warped toward Assindra, the goal to wrap her in unbreakable bonds.

A cloud of energy that was designed to confuse and distract followed.

Nat cursed at each of her failures.

None of her plays worked.

None of them gave her the traction that she desired and needed.

And she realized at that very moment that she had lost the initiative. For a streak of power that resembled a comet as dark as night blasted right toward her.

She was defenseless.

She could never shield herself in time.

And even if she did, the Curse would smash right through it.

But it didn't.

The comet of tainted magic slammed into a glowing shield of white that gained shape in front of Nat a heartbeat before it corrupted her.

"You dare to attack my pupil!" The deep voice sounded even louder in the small space of the bookshop.

A silence descended that lasted for almost a minute.

Assindra scrunched up her features into a hate-filled mask, less than pleased to come face to face with the Magus who obstructed her.

"We had an agreement, Finnelaus."

"That agreement ended a long time ago, Assindra."

"The agreement between us can never end, old man. Except in death."

Before Finn could reply, Assindra acted. A surge of the Curse rolled through the shop right toward him.

The Magus didn't bother to craft a shield, knowing that he could never stand against such power.

Instead, he used the Talent to form a wedge that resembled a farmer's plow, setting it to his front at the last possible second.

The magical implement sliced through the wave, the tainted power flying up and over the creation on both sides and slamming against the walls.

The store rumbled from the intensity of the strike, a cloud of dust forming as small pebbles clattered down from the stone ceiling. Thankfully, Assindra's Dark Magic did no more damage than that.

Finn was inordinately pleased with himself. He had not engaged in a combat for years, yet he had not lost a step.

He realized too late that he shouldn't have allowed his ego to get in the way of the real challenge he faced. Because Assindra wasn't done.

Following right behind the wave, hidden within it, came a small spike of the Curse.

Virtually invisible until the very last second.

Unable to defend himself with the Talent, he twisted his body to the side. Finn avoided the full brunt of the attack. Nevertheless, the tainted spike sliced across his ribs.

That was all that was required.

The Curse contained within that spike flooded into his body. Contaminating him in a heartbeat, the tainted power called to the Curse that Finn had locked away within himself. The taint that he had fought to control for so long awakened once more.

Assindra laughed softly upon seeing the terror that passed across Finn's face. "Still the same after all these years. Still so easily tricked."

Finn staggered against the bookshelves as he struggled to gain control over the tainted magic that raced through his blood. Time short, Finn attempted to employ what he had learned from Kaduna so long ago. The process difficult. Painful. And not a cure. Only a temporary respite from the inevitable end.

But it didn't appear that he would have the chance to do even that.

A ball of black energy spun just above Assindra's palm, the Dark Magus striding toward him.

"You can't save yourself this time, Finnelaus. No one can." About to flick what would prove to be the fatal blow at the old man so foolish as to get in her way, she held back at the last instant. The sharp cry behind her locked her in place.

"You can't have him!"

Assindra turned swiftly, a lance of blazing white energy streaking toward her chest.

She didn't have time to move.

To think.

She just did.

Growling in anger and dismay, instead of throwing her death blow at Finnelaus, she slammed the tainted ball of energy into the floor. The explosion of magic sent a tremor through the cavern, a cloud of shimmering black forming right before the lance struck. The rumble expanded out from the cavern and into the City Below, a reminder of the power once wielded by the dormant volcano that was the Crux.

"You heard her before she disappeared?" Nat asked as she rushed up to Finn.

Assindra was gone. The ground where she had been standing scorched a dark black.

"How could I not," Finn muttered as he staggered. The pain in his side was almost too much for him.

Nat nodded, remembering the words that she would not

soon forget. "This is not over. You will both pay for your insolence."

Pushing her fears to the side, Nat caught Finn under a shoulder and eased the Magus down into one of the few chairs that hadn't been destroyed during the magical battle. "Are you all right?"

"I will be." He was more than tired. More than exhausted. Almost every ounce of his strength was drained from him. And he could feel the Curse raging within him. Desperate to break free. A token of how close he had come to the horrifying end that he had avoided for almost two decades.

He had blocked off the Curse. Slowed its progression. But now ...

Now he needed to think about someone other than himself.

"You did well, Natalya. But you have much that you still need to learn."

"She'll be back."

"She will. She does not handle defeat well, and she will want her revenge."

**20**

# SIZING UP THE COMPETITION

"Please, Drin. You don't need to do this. You don't. Let your anger go, Drin."

"You will address me as Queen Dengannon," Drin stated in an unyielding voice. Her eyes matched her tone. Her face a mask. Unreadable.

"Drin, this is getting ..." The hard knock to Lucius Hanover's back not only took the breath out of him but also sent him to his knees, groaning in pain and wheezing for air. "Queen Dengannon. Queen Dengannon, I'm sorry. Truly." He wanted to glare over his shoulder at the soldier who had taken the liberty of striking him. He didn't, however, exercising what little discretion that still remained to him.

"You are wasting the Crux's time," the Battle Lord growled harshly. "Back to your feet while in the Queen's presence so we can be done with this."

Lucius nodded, trying hard to make sense of what was happening to him and finding it almost impossible to comprehend.

He was the Lord of the strongest House on the Crux. The Hanovers had once sat on the throne now occupied by Celindria Dengannon. Almost two hundred years, in fact, until a Dengannon took it out from beneath a Hanover who enjoyed his drink more than his power.

And, in truth, he, Lucius Hanover, should be the one sitting there now, passing sentence on the young woman who refused to learn her place in his world. "Dr ..." He caught himself just in time, sensing the soldier at his back tensing. Prepared to offer another lesson. "Queen Dengannon, please accept my apology. Clearly I have offended you in some way. That was never my intention. All I have ever done has been for the Crux. Always for the Crux."

Drin's lips curled into an expression of disbelief. "Lucius, all that you have ever done has been for yourself. You view ruling the Crux as your opportunity to enrich your House and do whatever you desire, not as a responsibility that must be valued and respected."

"That's an unfair characterization ..."

"It is an honest characterization, Lucius," Drin cut in sharply, though not loudly. There was no reason to raise her voice. The authority she exuded filled the throne room.

There was so much Lucius wanted to say to bolster his argument. So much that he wanted to do. But he couldn't.

That harsh truth pushed his simmering rage at his treatment close to the boiling point. Nevertheless, he maintained control over his temper. Finally he was beginning to understand the real tenuousness of his position ... as well as the associated consequences.

His fear guiding him now, he offered Drin his best and most winning smile, trying to evoke memories of when they spent time together while they were younger. Only a few short years in the past. When marriage was not just a distinct possibility, but was perceived as an inevitability.

"Please, Dr ..." Lucius caught himself again just in time. "Queen Dengannon, please," he pleaded. "You know me." He tried to step closer to the woman who held his future in her hands. He wanted to create a sense of closeness and remind her of what they once had. He couldn't, however, stumbling instead before he halted entirely so that he didn't fall. The chains around his ankles a testament as to how far he had fallen. "Queen Dengannon, this is all a misunderstanding. We were so close once. Almost married. There's no reason that we can't …"

"Enough, Lucius. I tire of your begging." Drin pushed herself up from the throne, hands clasped in front of her. She looked down at Lucius with a steely-eyed glare. "Lucius Hanover, you are a traitor to the Crux. You brought Tor soldiers across the Churn so that you could seize my seat."

"Queen Dengannon, you can't believe what that coward in the shadows tells …"

Drin spoke right over him. "Then, that attempt having failed, you brought across soldiers of the Ten Thousand. Werebeasts, Lucius. You dared to bring the monsters of myth fighting Crux soldiers on the Splintered Bridge across the Churn. An absolute disgrace."

"That's not entirely …"

"All for your benefit. All for your greed. All because you are so desperate to claim the throne upon which I sit. As I said, you care nothing for the Crux. You care only for yourself."

"That really …"

"Enough, Lucius." Drin spoke with such force that it strengthened the spines of those in the throne room who supported her and sent a cold shiver down the spines of those who feared her. "The Werebeasts were found in your home. You tried to use them against me. You then challenged me to a duel when you realized that you couldn't kill me as you hoped that you could."

Lucius tried to snort out a laugh and lighten the dark mood that had settled over the Crux throne room. Somehow, he needed to change the narrative. Fast.

But his snort came out more a whimper, the full implications of what was happening finally breaking through his delusions. "Queen Dengannon, again, just a misunderstanding. You caught me when I was trying to negotiate ..."

"I caught you red-handed, Lucius. You cannot escape the fate that awaits you."

"You have no right to do this!" Lucius roared, his reason slipping away. The rage that had been building within him finally free to roam. His emotion ruling him now. "I am Lucius Hanover! The Hanovers rule the Crux! Not ..."

When Lucius could finally see again, a darkness having draped itself over him, he reached up with a hand, his fingers coming away red from the trickle of blood running down his brow. A large gash on his forehead. And he was back on his knees. Pants torn and knees scraped.

He couldn't believe it. The soldier had ...

Before he could comprehend fully the insult he had suffered, Lucius was back on his feet. His knees weak. His head still in a fog. Held in place, a soldier on each side supported him.

"I was just trying to defend my family's honor, Drin," Lucius sobbed. His voice was weak and filled with terror. "Truly. That's all that I was doing." He could say no more, his voice breaking at the end. "I'm so sorry, Drin. So sorry. I was just trying to do what was right by my family just as you are doing what's right for your family." Lucius hoped with a ragged desperation that with this one last chance he could fix things between them. Never conceiving that he could fail in this his final and most important endeavor.

"There is a difference, Lucius," Drin said in a lethally bitter voice that brought to mind for many in the chamber the frigid gusts of wind that blew across the Frozen Waste and often blasted the Crux from the west. "My uncle and I are all who remain of our House. My father was murdered. By the man you are allied to."

Drin waited for the full import of her words to strike Lucius before continuing, the silence in the throne room deafening. "You are done, Lucius. Your House is done. The Hanovers are no more. Your name will be reviled on the Crux for centuries to come. The only word affixed to the name Hanover will be that of traitor."

"Drin, please, you can't do this," Lucius sobbed, his mask finally cracking then breaking entirely. His terror plain on his face and pouring out of him. "You can't …"

"Take him away, Sergeant," the Battle Lord ordered. "He has wasted too much of the Queen's time as it is."

Ronnie, who held Lucius Hanover by the right arm, nodded to the soldier holding the prisoner's left arm. As one they turned, lifting Lucius off the ground so that he couldn't slow them down by dragging his feet.

For the first few steps, Lucius did just that, struggling mightily, using the last of his strength and sanity. Both fled him swiftly, the reality of what was to come numbing him. Destroying his reason. In an instant he became nothing more than a shell of the arrogant Lord he had been, carried from the throne room, only the sounds of his whimpering audible.

The moment Lucius was through the doors, Drin turned her attention to the many Lords and Ladies gathered in the throne room. Some stood with pride at her action. Others with a hunch in their shoulders. Fearful.

"Do you understand what is expected of you? Do you understand the cost of betraying the Crux?"

All the heads of the great Houses of the Crux fixed their eyes upon Celindria Dengannon. The Queen stood with a composed confidence, the throne at her back a reminder of the power that she wielded. The power that she would not hesitate to wield to defend the Crux and herself.

Behind her stood her Battle Lord. His expression was unreadable just as always. Although his hand rested comfortably on the hilt of his sword, and the gleam in his eye hinted that he would relish the opportunity to draw his blade.

While along the sides of the chamber stood several ranks of soldiers. All of them loyal to the Crux. All of them loyal to the Queen.

But what truly unsettled several of the Lords and Ladies tied most closely to Lucius Hanover were the men and women mixing with them. They had not a clue who they were, though they were certain that these intruders did not come from any of the great Houses. None of them carried weapons, at least openly, yet they glared at the Lords and Ladies as if they were no more than meat to be cut. A menace radiating off all of them, their cold eyes chilled an already frigid atmosphere.

"We do, Queen Dengannon," the Lady Kendillon replied in a strong voice.

A smile graced Lady Kendillon's features. She had quite enjoyed the spectacle put on by the Queen, never having liked the Hanovers. More, she had always been an ally of the Dengannons, having grown up with Drin's father, the murdered king. And though she saw the Queen in her now, Lady Kendillon still remembered Celindria from when she was a child, and she was quite pleased to see the young woman she had become.

"And though many of you have businesses interests on the Tor, do you understand the penalty for allying to Malor Dragoran? He is a man who wants nothing more than to claim the Crux as his own and that I will not permit."

Many of the Lords and Ladies nodded meekly, having a difficult time expressing themselves in any other way. Not just because they felt like sheep herded together for the slaughter, but also because they understood that Lucius Hanover had brought his end upon himself. Worse, several of them, thanks to their ties to House Hanover, could have joined him. Would join him. If the Queen decided that more examples needed to be made.

Yet Queen Dengannon had chosen to grant them an implied mercy.

At least for the moment.

For that they were grateful. Even so, their amazement at how swiftly Lucius Hanover had fallen after being just minutes from claiming the throne was forcing them to experience an emotion they rarely felt.

Fear if not outright terror.

Because Lucius Hanover wasn't just going to lose his life.

Perhaps even more frightening to all those who lived on the Crux's Ninth Ring was the forfeiture of all Hanover property and businesses to the Crown. A penalty that would be applied to anyone who betrayed the Crux. A penalty that could be applied to them if they set a foot wrong again. And with that single misstep centuries of power, wealth, privilege, and position would be ripped from them. A sentence not only galling but also bone-chilling.

"Clear as the ice in the Frozen Waste," Lady Kendillon confirmed in a strong voice. Her smile broadened. More than pleased by Celindria's firm hand on the reins of power. The Queen's spine made of the steel required to sit the Crux throne. "Just as it should be."

"Good. If you remember nothing else from today," and Drin was certain that the Lords and Ladies who had just watched the scene with Hanover would remember every second of it, "the Crux first. The Crux always." With a sharp nod she released the Lords and Ladies from their audience with her.

Many of them left quickly, almost scampering through the doors, eager to be away from the young woman who had rattled them to their very depths. The Lady Kendillon, the Lady Becerra, and a few others who had long been allies to House

Dengannon made a more stately exit, offering nods of respect before leaving the throne room.

"Will they cause trouble?"

"They always cause trouble," the Battle Lord replied. Henri Dengannon stepped up next to his niece.

"You know what I mean."

He frowned, watching the last of them file out. "The few that we should be concerned about have been sufficiently cowed. For now."

"So we can focus on other matters," Drin stated with a confidence that she had rarely felt since she took the throne. "For now."

"Correct."

"Good, because there is much to do to keep the Crux free of Malor Dragoran."

"To that end I return to the Splintered Bridge tonight," the Battle Lord said, "with your permission, of course. Leonardo is to implement several new ideas that I'm looking forward to testing."

"How do matters stand there?" Drin asked. "Truly. From all reports it was a close thing when the Ten Thousand assaulted our fortifications."

"Well ... for now."

"Not an uplifting report."

"An honest one. Leonardo is proving his worth, and the soldiers stationed there know their business. And they know how to fight those shifting beasts now, so it's a more even engagement. Moreover, the aid the Broken Bear has provided and is still providing is invaluable. But ..."

"Malor Dragoran has more fighters to throw at us than we have to defend our Kingdom. And the Werebeasts of the Ten Thousand remain a threat. We just don't know how large a threat after what the Broken Bear did to them."

"Unfortunately true."

Drin considered all that. "Safe travels, uncle. Perhaps there are some things we can do to lessen the strain Malor Dragoran is placing upon us." She was quite aware of Mikel's exploits against both the soldiers of the Tor and the Werebeasts of the Ten Thousand. She hoped that he had a few more ideas that they could implement that might improve their odds.

"Give my best to the King of the Underworld," he said as he strode off.

"I will," Drin replied, watching her uncle until he turned a corner, not bothering to deny what she had in mind, her uncle knowing her much too well. Then she made her way to her private suite, already thinking about how best to connect with Mikel and looking forward to when that time came. Sooner rather than later she hoped.

That hope was crushed the moment she walked into her apartment.

"I had a sense that I wasn't done with you," Drin grumbled as a shadow stepped out of an alcove in the back of Drin's office, placing herself in the light.

"It is indeed your lucky day." Liria was impressed. Reluctantly. She was aware of the Queen of the Crux's skill in the Talent. Though she didn't believe the woman standing before her with a regal bearing and a hard edge had used natural magic to identify her. Heightened senses more likely, which testified to her skills as a fighter.

"Another assassination attempt?" Before Liria responded, Drin held a dagger in one hand, a small ball of fire in the other.

"Not today," Liria replied in a soft chuckle. She really was impressed. The same fire radiated from the Queen of the Crux as did the last time they contested against one another. She could understand Mikel's interest, though she didn't like it. "Perhaps another time."

"Then what do you want?"

"I wanted to size up my competition."

"Competition?" Drin realized that the thief's decision to come here now was more personal in nature and not just an attempt to frighten her.

"You think ..."

"I know," Liria said in a tight voice. "I can dig out information almost as well as Mikel can."

"I doubt that. There are certain things that Mikel can do that you clearly cannot." Drin's raised eyebrow left it to Liria to determine to what she was referring, a very broad spectrum of possibility open to her.

"Where is Mikel?" Liria refused to be put off even as Drin's words rankled.

"I thought you could dig out information almost as well as he could."

The Queen's response irritated Liria, though she refused to show it. And for just a heartbeat she considered challenging the Queen, wondering if she could best her before she used the Talent.

The purposeful glint in the Queen's eye unmistakable, Liria decided against it. "I'll find him. Mikel and I have unfinished business. And you, Queen of the Crux, be careful. If you haven't figured it out already, the Broken Bear can be quite a handful. Often more wild than tame. Best to enjoy him while you can. Because soon I will lure him into my trap just as I did before. And once I have him again, I won't let him go."

**21**

## CONFUSING CONFRONTATION

"General Booruz, I did not expect you back in Graz so soon." Malor Dragoran stood atop the highest tower of the Ring, staring out at the Barbed Path. The glass sculptures crafted by lightning gleamed brightly whenever struck by the moonlight that was playing with the clouds drifting slowly overhead. "I would think that your responsibilities would require that you remain at the Splintered Bridge. Doing as I ordered you to do."

"A necessary visit," Booruz replied in his usually gruff voice, not put off by the hint of menace contained in the King of the Tor's voice.

"Tell me."

Booruz stepped closer. He stopped when the King of the Tor glanced over his shoulder. Blowing out his sagging mustache, he replied. "The King of the Underworld has been causing more problems than we imagined possible. All has not gone as we planned."

"Yes, this king who prefers the shadows has proven difficult. More difficult than I anticipated. Specifics. Now."

"The battle at the Splintered Bridge continues," Booruz

reported. "We have not lost ground, but we have not gained the span."

"Despite the unique resource I gifted you?" Malor barked. His fingers, clasped behind his back, turned white as he squeezed in irritation.

"Despite that resource, yes," Booruz confirmed. "Many of the Ten Thousand originally assigned to that task are no longer with us. In fact, thanks to the fighting that has taken place, I would suggest that the Ten Thousand can no longer be called the Ten Thousand. Not after the losses they sustained. The Thousand sounds more reasonable, and even that might be a stretch."

"What happened?" Malor's voice was little more than a deep growl that strangely shifted to a lighter tone in barely a breath. The King of the Tor's head lifted slightly, as if he had discovered something amusing or unexpected despite the dire nature of the news his general was relaying.

"The King of the Underworld slipped across the Trench and attacked the Werebeasts' encampment. Hit and run."

"And my Werebeasts could do nothing else except take the bait."

"Correct. Their instincts got the better of them."

"Then the King of the Underworld hit them again," Malor stated with complete confidence, having little doubt in which direction the tale was going. More than familiar with the blood-lust of the Ten Thousand. A strength most of the time. But not always. Not against an adversary with a knack for identifying and then playing off an enemy's weaknesses.

"He did. He led them right where he wanted them. Then slaughtered them."

"So we now lack our vanguard." Malor nodded his head slowly, digesting the information. Also beginning to under-stand that more was at play here than a report from a subordinate. And, strangely, he was enjoying the encounter in spite of the loss of several companies of his best troops.

"We do," General Booruz confirmed. He slid forward a few feet as if he wished to speak with greater privacy though there was no one else atop the tower. Almost where he wanted to be.

"Very clever of you," Malor stated calmly. "As I just said, you're more of a challenge than I anticipated." Turning around, the King of the Tor wore a malicious grin. Then he offered Booruz a nod of respect.

"Me?" Booruz replied, his confusion plain. Almost palpable. Just as he believed it needed to be. All the while a tremor of trepidation ran through him.

"Your deception may have gotten you here undetected – an accomplishment in and of itself -- but you could not fool me for long. Not with you so close to me. Since you know that I am more than I appear to be, you had to assume this would be the result. That I would know you are not who you pretend to be even with the magic you employ."

General Booruz didn't say anything. Then, eyes narrowing, he smiled. The grin of a little boy caught trying to swipe a slice of freshly made pie from the bake shop. "I must admit that I was curious as to how long it would take." Booruz reached toward his wrist. Pulling off the bracelet hidden beneath his sleeve, he pocketed it. The moment he did, his appearance shifted. The shimmer of magic faded, the illusion gone and revealing who he truly was. "And I do know who you truly are."

Malor smiled thinly. He nodded, giving Mikel permission to continue.

"You are Rickard Riverstone." Mikel understood that the real combat had not yet begun. More so that the next few minutes were critical. If he acted out the scene correctly, he might find some way to achieve his goal and still not lose his life in the process.

"A name I have not heard for quite a long time," Malor

replied in a quiet, reminiscent tone. "I congratulate you. I had heard that you were tenacious when you set your mind to a task. Whether it involves sweeping my Ten Thousand from the battlefield or finding out who I truly am."

"That's very kind of you. Thank you." Mikel clasped his hands behind his back. The hilt of his scimitar poked above his head. Even so, he felt more comfortable with the feel of the mace hidden in the holster strapped to the small of his back. An old habit, nothing more, the mace useless against the adversary standing before him. Nevertheless, the cool steel of the weapon helped to maintain his focus even as his fears rose. "What do you prefer? You have so many names. Rickard. The Dread. Malor. There are likely others but I had only so much time to dig before I felt the need to visit you."

"I could ask you the same." Malor's eyes sparked. A sign that he was enjoying the conversation or that his anger was building, Mikel wasn't sure. Though he leaned toward the former. "The Fox. The Knife. The Broken Bear. The King of the Underworld. You seem to pick up names faster than I do."

"Not by choice."

"Nevertheless, a mark of our success," the Dread said. "Names are power, and not just in how we use them." The Dread's expression became shrewder. "And I can tell from your expression that you knew that already."

"Perhaps it is a mark of success," Mikel mused, "or it could be something else."

"Respect."

"A distinct possibility."

The Dread studied Mikel for a time, then nodded after identifying the colder characteristic in the King of the Underworld that he had missed during his first inspection. "Fear."

"That likely as well," Mikel conceded.

"The more we talk, the more I sense that we are more similar than not," the Dread mused.

"Perhaps just in our ability to acquire names," Mikel replied with a short laugh, not sure that he liked being compared to a creature with such a terrible history as the Dread.

"You give yourself too little credit, King of the Underworld. We both understand how to exercise power."

"I won't argue with you about that."

"Though I sense you want to," Malor stated in a confident voice. Always sure of himself and his beliefs, he folded his hands in front of him. Intrigued by the man who stood with a straight back, not a hint of fear wafting from him. The man who had taken a huge risk by coming here. A man who still could prove useful if he was willing to bend. "In one key aspect, however, we are not the same."

"And that would be?" Mikel prompted. More than just a little curious because he believed that he already knew the answer. He could read it in the Dread's dark almost hypnotic eyes.

"The power you exercise does not compare to mine."

Mikel smiled at that, nodding to himself. He had been right. "I didn't know that it was a contest. That we were going to be measuring our ... power. If I had known, I would have come better prepared."

The Dread stared at Mikel for quite some time. Not even blinking. Then he barked out a harsh laugh, his image flickering before gaining substance once more. For just a heartbeat Malor Dragoran disappeared and was replaced by a figure wearing a dark shroud of black. Eyes even blacker. Face a sickly grey. Wisps of dark mist drifting around him.

"There is another key way in which we are distinct."

"Do tell," Mikel prodded. Despite the danger he was in, Mikel was at ease. He had run through a variety of possible scenarios before deciding to give himself this assignment. His chances of success minimal to begin with, though still worth pursuing despite the likelihood of his demise. That undeniable fact now established for him, Mikel felt as if a weight had been lifted from his shoulders. His newfound clarity sharpened his thinking.

"You came here to kill me even though you knew you couldn't. I, on the other hand, know that I can and will kill you."

"I did, you're right." Mikel saw little point in denying the truth. And he was glad for the supreme confidence the Dread had in himself. He hoped that he could use that. Turn that confidence into a reckless arrogance that influenced the Dread's decision making.

"Yet I don't take you for a fool," Malor murmured, examining Mikel with a closer eye.

"I appreciate that."

"What drove you to accept such a suicidal mission? It does not seem a part of your character."

"Who knows why we truly do what we do?" Mikel replied with a seeming lack of concern.

"Your attempt at humor might work on others, but not me."

"A hard habit to break. My apologies." Mikel offered the Dread a short nod.

"You came here to kill me, yet I feel drawn to you for some reason. It's the most unique feeling."

"I try to ignore feelings such as these," Mikel said with a wink. "You might want to as well. They rarely lead to anything good."

Malor stared at Mikel, ignoring his humor. Instead struggling to get a better feel for the man standing against him.

Was the King of the Underworld here to kill him? That was Malor's original belief. Now he wasn't so sure, and his confusion in that regard bothered him.

"You thought the artifact made by the Giants of the Rime would allow you to get close enough to me to do the deed, and it did," Malor murmured, "but you hesitated."

"It did." Mikel shrugged then, his lips curling slightly. "And did I?"

"What do you mean?" The Dread was even more confused now. He had assumed that the King of the Underworld would have attempted to strike by now. Yet he seemed more than happy to engage in conversation instead. Why take such a risk? Unless ...

"You think I came here to kill you, but you know as well that I do my research before taking on a job. Based on that research, I confirmed that I can't kill you. Even with the sword on my back, it's not possible." Mikel took a half-step forward, leaning toward Malor as if he was about to share a secret. "I didn't want to kill you. I just wanted to get into the same room with you. I did. In that respect, I succeeded. I'm exactly where I want to be."

The Dread didn't say anything, never considering the possibility laid out before him, the moonlight disappearing for quite some time while the clouds smothered it, Malor not talking until several beams of light shone through again.

"I heard you were clever. Intelligent. I just never realized how clever and intelligent."

"If you keep going on like this, you'll make me blush," Mikel replied with a wink meant to nudge Malor's thoughts in the direction they already were headed.

The Dread nodded as if all was finally coming to light. "You see an opportunity."

"I always see opportunities. Especially when other people don't see any. When other people are so stuck in their ways or their perspectives that they miss the obvious ... and most profitable ... play. That's why I'm so good at what I do."

The Dread studied Mikel with a keener eye. "You wish to partner with me. Not Celindria Dengannon. You've decided to change course."

"The thought had crossed my mind," Mikel replied with a

shrug. "As I said, there's always more than one path open to us. It's just a matter of whether we have the courage to take it. And, I can say unequivocally that unlike Lucius Hanover, when I do a deal, I get it done. Always."

"What was holding you back?" Malor wondered. "Why go through the risk of fighting my Werebeasts? Why fight for the Crux? You could have reached out many times before. You didn't need to go through with this scheme of yours."

"I did have to go through this with scheme. I needed to show you that I could get close to you. I needed to show you that whether with my wits or my steel, I know not only how to fight, but also how to win. I needed to show you all that you would gain."

"If I what?" Malor asked. He needed to hear Mikel say it.

"If you decided to partner with me. Because if you do, I can give you the keys to the Crux."

## 22

## FULL OF FIRE

"I still can't believe he kept this from me," Drin growled. Her hands tightened on the rail, knuckles turning white, her anger close to the boil that was the Churn.

The giant standing next to her wasn't enjoying his dialogue with the Queen of the Crux. Teddy shrugged, not having much more that he could offer than that. "He thought it was best that you didn't know."

"He thought it best because he knew I wouldn't let him take on such a foolish quest. Who does he think he is? My knight in shining armor?" Drin bit her lip, shaking her head, a heat rising within her. And not just because she was put out by the man she had come to trust with more than just her life.

"Not that, no," Teddy chuckled, amused by the image that came to mind of his friend trying to don anything more than leather armor. Of course, even that was asking for more than Mikel was willing to give. He preferred not to be encumbered during a combat, skilled at using his deceptive speed to negate his lack of protection. "You wouldn't catch him dead wearing armor like that."

"That wasn't my point, Teddy." Drin bit out the words as if she were chewing on leather.

"I'm sorry, Queen Dengannon," Teddy replied with all haste. Still, he couldn't keep his lips from quirking into a small smile. He understood where the Queen's displeasure really was coming from, though he would keep that knowledge to himself. Not wanting to make himself the target of her wrath. "Mikel is never impulsive about the decisions he makes, unless he's got a ..." Teddy stopped himself, realizing that saying anything more than he already had would be a bad idea. To that end, he wiped the smile from his face.

The Queen of the Crux stared up at him, her hard eyes catching his. Mouth set in a tight line, her words were more a demand than a question. "What were you going to say, Teddy?"

"I've said enough already." He pulled his eyes away from hers despite the difficulty of doing so. Shifting his attention to the darkness around them, he looked over the side. Their objective should be coming up on them soon.

"Teddy ..." Drin's expression somehow got even harder. Her head barely reaching his chest, with a steely resolve the Queen of the Crux squared up to a man who put her in shadow.

He replied in a quiet, calm voice, though he refused to look at her. "Your business with Mikel is with Mikel. Not me. I'm not putting myself in a position where the both of you blame me for something I may let slip by mistake."

"Is not your loyalty to me and the Crux, Teddy?" Drin demanded. "Is that not why you are here and taking this risk?"

Drin waved with her hand in exasperation at the exact moment a strong gust of cold air struck, filling the sails almost to bursting and sending the flying ship through the night at an even greater speed. Leonardo's latest creation, the airborne vessel was as large as a schooner. Supported by six balloons made of a newer, thinner, lighter sailcloth and filled with hot air, two affixed to each mast, the vessel sailed through the sky with a deft grace. Two other ships flew with her. Both at the stern, one to the port and the other to the starboard side.

Leonardo only had enough time to build three of these new weapons of war, but three were more than enough for that evening's test. And completed just in time for what Drin had in mind. Assuming, of course, that all went as she hoped it would.

"It is. I wouldn't be here otherwise. Nevertheless ..."

"Your loyalty to Mikel comes first." Drin frowned at him. She understood his reasoning even though it chafed. "How do you manage your split loyalties?"

"I don't have to," Teddy explained, glad that this was a point he didn't need to argue. "At least I haven't had to. When it comes to you and Mikel, my loyalties are not split because of your ..."

"Be careful what you say, Teddy," Drin warned, her eyes flashing dangerously.

"Connection?" Teddy offered, his response more question than statement. He wasn't sure how far he could go without getting himself into trouble.

Drin nodded, willing to accept how the Giant described her partnership with Mikel. The term relationship popped into her mind but stayed there only long enough for her to quash it.

She looked at the giant then, brow furrowing, thinking about what had pushed her to where she now stood. She had not originally intended to fly across the Kingdom of the Crux toward the east at this time of the night, the full moon peeking through the clouds with greater regularity as she approached the Trench. "He told you to tell me." She snorted in disbelief. And she thought she had dug the information out of Teddy on her own. "Are you serious?"

Teddy grinned, then didn't. The Queen of the Crux's face was a thundercloud. "He told me I could tell you this evening. But he didn't want me to make it too easy for you."

"Why not?" she growled.

Teddy shrugged again, realizing that once more he was on dangerous ground. "You know how he is."

"I do know how he is." She stepped closer to him, which made Teddy nervous. His size not much of a defense against the authority and sense of purpose she projected. "You're not answering my question."

"I feel like if I do I'd just be jumping into the Churn, and I'd prefer not to do that."

Drin didn't respond. She didn't push. She waited.

Staring at Teddy, she was impressed. Despite her focus, despite the hard look she gave him, he didn't crack. And, admittedly, she expected no less from the King of the Underworld's second in command. So she allowed him his small victory, promising herself that she'd take a piece out of Mikel's hide when next she saw him.

"He expected me to come after him," Drin murmured, shaking her head in ... anger ... wonder ... pleasure ... all three and more? She didn't know. Nevertheless, she had to give Mikel his due for how he had played this, although she would never tell him that directly. The angst she was feeling only served to keep the chip squarely perched on her shoulder. She didn't want him doing this to her again ... if he survived the mess in which he had placed himself. "I can't believe this. It's like he's playing me as he would anyone else."

"That wasn't his objective, my Queen. Truly."

"I don't doubt you, Teddy. It's just hard to view it in any other way."

"That's understandable, and I fully admit that Mikel is a master at running schemes within schemes within schemes. But in this, his decision to reveal too late what he had in mind, he had no scheme to play. Not a good one anyway."

"I can see that, Teddy," Drin sighed, a deep sadness filling her. She had been using her anger to hide her fear. For Mikel.

For what he was attempting to do without asking her for permission. "Why would he do this?"

"You know why, my Queen." Teddy's reply was little more than a whisper, feeling as if he was intruding by staying with her as she pulled her gaze from him and looked out at the clouds that passed off the starboard side, the full moon setting them alight.

"I do," she admitted finally. A hint of defeat snuck into her voice.

"Please keep in mind, my Queen, that Mikel had no expectation that you would come after him, though he did think you would consider doing so. Thus, the timing of our conversation."

"He doesn't want me coming after him?"

"He didn't say that, though I could tell that he was concerned."

"For me," Drin said very softly. The warmth that had been surging through her, fighting the effects of the biting cold wind, changed. No longer filling with her anger, instead it came from a deeper place within her. A place she had never truly explored until Mikel had forced his way into her life.

"For you, my Queen. With what he's doing, I doubt he would turn down any assistance you provided. However, I know with absolute certainty that he did not want you to place yourself in danger because of him. He did not want you doing as you are."

"Too late now." She leaned her forearms against the railing, studying the terrain below as best as she could through the darkness. It wouldn't be long now. "Why did he want you to tell me when you did?"

"Putting aside the slim possibility of going to his aid – keep in mind Mikel wasn't aware of how matters stood with Leonardo's latest creations, even Leonardo uncertain that they were ready for what we're about to do – he wanted you to know what he was doing so that you could plan appropriately."

"You mean plan for his death."

"Hopefully not that, although it's a strong if not likely possibility." Teddy leaned down, offering her a sympathetic smile. "As you know, in every situation there are opportunities to be had. In this, there are opportunities that you can use to the benefit of the Crux. He wanted to give those to you in case he doesn't ..." Teddy had little desire to complete his thought.

Drin couldn't argue with Teddy's logic. Still, she couldn't quite believe Mikel's audacity. When next she spoke with him – if she spoke with him – he was going to learn once and for all how matters needed to be between them. How they would be between them.

No more of his gallivanting around thinking that he could solve her problems for her. They would work together. As a team. Whether he wanted to or not. Or not at all. He could return to his cell in the dungeon and she would make sure he couldn't pick the lock if he failed to obey.

"I still can't believe he wouldn't tell me." She knew Mikel would never ask her permission. And not just because of any concern he might have about her trying to impede his efforts. Even though she had the authority to stop him, she doubted that she could. He was too slippery.

"He didn't want to worry you. He didn't want to ..."

"It's time," Leonardo called from the tiller. Samuel stood next to the inventor, sure hands on the wheel. Putting into practice his experience from his previous life as a former navigator, the thief was controlling the wings that mimicked those of a bird and extended from the sides of the flying ship by manipulating the ingenious foot pedals Leonardo had crafted. Only one skilled navigator was required to control a ship like this one, which allowed the rest of the crew to do that night's bloodier work. "Soldiers to the gunwales!"

Teddy was grateful for the timing. Before he could move to his position, however, Drin grabbed his forearm. "This conversation is not over, Teddy. And I promise that you won't enjoy the rest of it."

Teddy nodded after gulping. Glad to be away from the Queen of the Crux as she strode toward the helm. The Splintered Bridge coming up beneath them.

"Why haven't we made another push?" General Booruz demanded. "We've brought up five additional companies from the encampment near town. There's no excuse for the delay."

The commander of the Tor army stood atop the battlements of the redoubt that extended across the Splintered Bridge on the Tor side of the Trench. It was strangely quiet that evening. Then again, it had been quiet ever since the King of the Underworld's attack on the Ten Thousand at their refuge at the edge of the Deep. The defeat of King Dragoran's shock troops an unexpected turn for him and the soldiers tasked with fighting their way across the span and into the Kingdom of the Crux.

Since then, the Crux soldiers had used the time granted to them to strengthen their defenses. That blasted inventor working hand in hand with Henri Dengannon demonstrated once again a lethal ingenuity that required Booruz to rethink his strategy. Because at that moment his plans that had almost led to victory were in tatters.

None of the officers standing with him responded at first. Most kept their heads down, hoping not to be noticed. The youngest finally had the courage to speak and if not that at least the impatience to break the silence. "We have sent several scouting parties toward the Crux lines, General Booruz."

"I'm well aware of that Captain Dovik. That doesn't answer my question. Why are we employing a caution that in a certain light more closely resembles outright fear?"

"None of the scouting parties have returned, General Booruz," Dovik replied in a very quiet voice, hating to be the bearer of bad news.

"None?"

Dovik shook his head upon lifting it, deciding that if he was about to be upbraided by his commanding officer, or worse, it would be better if he was staring his mentor in the eye. "None, General Booruz."

"The Zaroi?"

"Perhaps," Dovik acknowledged. He shrugged, unwilling to agree to the easiest answer.

"But you don't believe so."

"We ..." Dovik corrected himself quickly, catching the looks his fellow officers gave him. They didn't want to be associated with his theory. "I don't believe so."

Rather than engaging in the dressing down that so tempted General Booruz, he took a deep breath instead. Before he let his temper loose and made a decision, he required a better sense of what was going on since he had returned earlier that evening from South Lienz due to conflicting reports. The small town was just a few miles to the east and served as his headquarters when the fighting wasn't too fierce on the Splintered Bridge ... and where he preferred to spend his nights when his mistress made the journey from the Tor to visit with him.

"Why is that, Captain Dovik?"

"The Zaroi have done little different ever since I took up my station here. Every night we heard them on the span. Every night we might even catch a glimpse of those beasties on patrol. But ever since the Ten Thousand's failure to break through, there has been no activity on the part of the Zaroi. Nothing. We've seen neither hide nor hair."

"That seems more than suspect, don't you think?"

"It does, General Booruz. And we ..." Dovik corrected himself again, once more catching the looks that shot his way.

"I believe it's not because the Zaroi aren't interested in coming after our scouts. They're hungry. They're always hungry. Rather I believe that they are ..."

"Being prevented from doing so," General Booruz finished for him, "that Crux inventor likely having something to do with it."

"Correct, General Booruz. That was my thinking."

"But why would the Battle Lord want that done? The Zaroi aid his defenses when darkness falls. With those beasts roaming the span, it limits what we can do when we can't call upon the Ten Thousand."

"Absolutely right, General Booruz. And that makes me think that perhaps the Battle Lord wishes to adopt a new strategy in which the Zaroi do not hinder his plans."

"A new strategy?" Booruz pondered. "You mean ..."

The rest of Booruz's words got caught in his throat. Captain Orban, a man who had served with Booruz for several decades and stood right next to him, collapsed, a soft groan escaping his lips.

"What the ..." Booruz reached for Orban, grasping his arm.

The man's dead weight pulled Booruz down to one knee. Then he saw it. An arrow. Though different from what the Tor soldiers used. This one had a much longer shaft, which suggested a much larger bow. That made sense if the Crux soldiers were shooting from the Splintered Bridge. They would need the additional range.

Yet to strike Orban from beyond the skirmish line?

Even with a new weapon that would be asking too much. That couldn't be skill. That could only be luck.

"General, we need to get you ..."

Dovik gasped, his words dying with him as he dropped on top of Orban, a steel-tipped shaft punching through his back. The shaft reached out from the dying man's chest and missed Booruz by no more than a knuckle, Dovik taking a half step toward Booruz to help with the stricken Orban, thereby ensuring his own death.

"Take cover!" Booruz ordered as he crouched down against the parapet, lifting his head just enough to peak over the top.

Where could the archers be?

And how had they gotten past his skirmish line without a warning being raised?

Just a small group?

That made the most sense since he didn't hear the tell-tale sounds of troops advancing across the span.

All was still quiet on the Splintered Bridge.

That in itself made this attack that much more difficult to comprehend.

With the bright moonlight, Booruz could see well beyond the first of the many Crux towers that stood defiantly just a half mile away on the Splintered Bridge. There wasn't a hint of Crux soldiers sneaking across.

If not from the span, then where was the attack coming from?

Booruz dropped back down, keeping his back to the stone.

A soft whistle that was slightly louder than an arrow streaked through the air.

If not from the Splintered Bridge, then there was only one answer.

General Booruz looked up. Eyes widening, his shock froze him in place.

Visible thanks to the bright moonlight, a dark object hurtled down toward the redoubt just a few hundred yards to his left.

The dimness of the night was eliminated entirely by a blinding flash when the object exploded atop the parapet, a ball of fire erupting. Reaching dozens of feet into the sky, the flames spilled and splattered in all directions, scorching stone and soldiers.

His men caught in the attack were dead. Those on the periphery screamed and ran, several on fire, desperate for the flames to be put out. All of them learning the horrific truth when their comrades' efforts to douse the fires did nothing more than spread the flames that much faster.

The sticky substance that engulfed them burned through flesh and muscle to bone. It couldn't be extinguished. Rather, it slowly died on its own when there was nothing left to burn. A truly horrific end.

Hearing more soft whistles coming from above, Booruz forced himself into motion. "Clear the wall!" he ordered as he crawled along the parapet and then slid down the ladder. Blistering his hands because of the swiftness of his descent, he ignored the pain, grateful when his feet touched the ground.

And not a moment too soon.

Another explosive struck. Right where Orban and Dovik lay wrapped in one another's arms.

The explosion deafened Booruz and eliminated the rest of his officers who were too slow to move. Sticky globs and strands of fire bursting out in all directions, the flames ate through anything they touched except for stone.

That blasted inventor!

It had to be. Some variation on the pipes of fire he used to defend the Crux side of the span.

But that still didn't explain how these new weapons could be used against his forces here.

How could the span remain free of attackers?

It couldn't be catapults.

Even the inventor couldn't build one that shot explosives across a mile-wide gap. And Booruz was certain that he would see and hear a monstrosity like that being pulled across the Splintered Bridge.

More whistles assaulting his ears, Booruz looked up as he ran from the redoubt and tried to judge how close he was to the falling explosives. Anxious to discover in which direction he could find safety, his fear threatened to get the better of him.

He skidded to a stop, his flight forgotten if only for a moment. Peering into the sky, he saw what he never thought he would.

Flying above him.

A shape resembling a ship.

That's when he realized that his soldiers weren't fighting to invade the Crux. Not any longer.

On this night they were fighting to ensure that the Crux didn't invade the Kingdom of the Tor.

His redoubt destroyed, Booruz's first instinct was to rally his troops in the town just to the east.

That thought was drowned out by the pounding of thousands of marching feet on the Splintered Bridge mixing with the screams of pain and terror that came from his soldiers as they sought refuge from the fire erupting all around them.

Then a more unnerving sound demanded Booruz's attention. Looking up, he couldn't identify it in the gloom. But he could hear it. The sharp whistle that was screaming down toward him.

"THE CRUX FIRST! THE CRUX ALWAYS!" Drin shouted.

The soldiers manning both sides of the flying ship took up her cry as they dropped canister after canister of the sticky substance Leonardo used with his dragons, flames bursting to life the instant the gel came into contact with the air.

The results of just a few minutes of their work were devastatingly obvious.

What had been a professional and efficient defense centered on the Tor's stone redoubt was no more. Destroyed by fire and the terror associated with an attack from above.

The battlements were in flames.

The redoubt was scorched, a dark smoke pouring out of every window all along the span of the Splintered Bridge.

Strands of fire flared along the stone and all across the ground, making Drin think that this must be what it would look like if a volcano erupted and sent streams of magma flowing in every direction.

Fires burning wherever she looked, it was difficult for her to make sense of it all as a sick feeling settled in the pit of her stomach.

All the while, Tor soldiers scurried away from the Splintered Bridge and the redoubt, fleeing toward the perceived safety of South Lienz's stone buildings. Consumed by fear, the soldiers proved to be little more than sitting ducks. Not a tree in sight that could impede an attack from above.

The Tor soldiers cleared the wood that used to run from the redoubt to the town to create a killing ground against the threat of a Crux attack.

That killing ground now was being used by Drin and her flying ships to ensure that little prevented them from advancing on the Tor. The soldiers' odds of gaining safety lessened all the more by the archers in the rigging who were quite pleased to use their longer bows, which gave them a greater range and even more stopping power.

Drin hated the death and destruction.

Nevertheless, she couldn't escape it.

If Drin had learned nothing else while preparing to serve as Queen of the Crux, it was that she needed to do what was necessary.

For the good of the Crux.

Always.

No matter the cost.

To others.

To herself.

Her responsibilities had to take precedence over any other considerations.

Always.

And from Mikel she had learned that she needed to do the unexpected. Thus her decision to put into play Leonardo's flying ships.

Although that was only a part of that night's game. The first move. Several more were to come before she met her objective. Preferably by sunrise.

Several companies of Crux soldiers already were advancing across the Splintered Bridge. Her uncle in the lead. The undefended redoubt was the only obstacle preventing her troops from claiming Tor territory for the first time in more than five centuries.

Once the Battle Lord conquered the bastion, he would expand the Crux's foothold by pushing farther to the east. Toward the Tor. More Crux soldiers coming up right behind the vanguard.

And with the Battle Lord drawing the gaze of Malor Dragoran, that would leave Drin with the opportunity to deal with Mikel.

## 23

# KEYS TO THE CRUX

"The keys to the Crux," Malor murmured softly. "Quite a gift. And how do you expect to procure them?"

"I already have them."

Malor tilted his head to the right, left eyebrow rising as he considered the claim. "I would say that you are arrogant, but I know that you're not. Confident instead."

"That's how I do business," Mikel replied. Feeling the need to move, he began to walk slowly around the circular tower. Staying close to the edge. Hands clasped behind his back, he kept to a steady pace. "I only say what I mean and I do what I say. And I say I have the keys to the Crux in my hand and that I can give them to you. If you believe that we can reach an agreement that best suits both our interests."

"An intriguing offer." Malor spoke scarcely above a whisper. His black eyes flashed, though whether from distrust or real interest, Mikel couldn't say.

"More than that," Mikel clarified. "The best offer you're going to get. Why fight for what you absolutely must have when you don't have to?"

"Sometimes you do it just for the fight," Malor murmured,

"because you can." He was trying to get a feel for the man who demonstrated a composure that almost impressed him, and he was finding it difficult to do. An uncommon occurrence for him. A worrying one as well. "And sometimes the fight is necessary."

Mikel nodded, understanding the sentiment. "Sometimes. But that costs more time and more money, and why waste either when the fighting we're discussing usually involves more than just a blade? Besides, I already did the fighting for you, so why bother?"

"Keep talking," Malor ordered. His lips twisted into a questioning grin. He was curious as to how the scene he found himself in was going to play out. Once again the King of the Underworld had caught him by surprise, and he wasn't sure how he felt about that.

"There's a better way to do this. A faster way."

"Don't waste my time, King of the Underworld. I sense that you're enjoying dragging this out. Or rather dragging it out because doing so allows you to continue to draw breath. Get to the heart of the matter quickly before I take yours."

"It's quite simple, really. The Queen of the Crux trusts me. I'm close to her. And I can get closer." Mikel shrugged as he came back around Malor's shoulder, interpreting from the look in the King of the Tor's eye that he had hooked him like one of the spinefish that resided in the rivers that led into the Churn. Now all Mikel needed to do was reel him in as he slowly cut the distance between them. "I help you remove her from the throne. You gain what you want. You build what you want." Mikel stopped right in front of Malor, staring him straight in the eye. "I'm assuming that your plans go well beyond the Crux and the Tor?"

"Of course they do," Malor murmured quietly, unconcerned about revealing his larger strategy. For there were only two ways the King of the Underworld was leaving the tower. A slave ... or dead.

"Then you do whatever you want to do. Do what you do best. And you let me do what I do best. I serve you, of course. But in every other way, you leave me alone. You let me conduct my business without impediment from you or any of your servants."

"You ask for a great deal, King of the Underworld." Malor crossed his arms over his broad chest when Mikel began to walk around him again. "You seek to make a bargain when I don't require a bargain to gain what I most desire."

"I ask for no more than I deserve. I'm offering you the catalyst you need to put the rest of your plans into motion. The one piece that removes any obstacles that remain."

"I understand greed, King of the Underworld. But I don't fully understand this. You are not known for being greedy."

"I'm not greedy," Mikel stated in a quiet voice, his expression just as firm as his voice. "I'm practical. And I have a broad and long perspective. I see which way the wind is blowing. I would prefer not to be caught in a bad storm if I can avoid it."

He shrugged when he started walking around Malor again, pleased to see that his opponent's gaze stayed on him as he skirted the battlements. "And based on what you've said, you've done some digging on me. You know that what I do I don't do for myself. I have others who depend upon me. I need to consider their interests as well. Based on the current reality, discovering the truth about you, that necessity tilts me in your direction rather than that of the Queen of the Crux. As you've likely surmised, I'm not an idealist. Far from it. I'm a realist."

"Quite the argument, King of the Underworld," Malor replied, his doubt obvious in his voice and his expression. "It seems like you've thought of everything."

Mikel chuckled softly. "I have thought of everything. That's why I'm good at what I do. But I'm not making an argument as you seem to believe. I'm stating facts. Hard truths. You can see them just as well as I can. The Queen of the Crux … she has struggled to do so." He shrugged again. "She is young. She is new to her throne. Her lack of foresight is understandable. Although I would like to stand with her, because I do like her, in good conscience I can't. I must think about those who are already standing with me and depending upon me. The many before the one."

"Yet it was you who helped her gain the throne of the Crux. And it was you, as you say, who put the interests of the one before the many." Malor was quite enjoying how the King of the Underworld was trying to thread the needle.

"Only temporarily," Mikel replied, "and you miss the point. I did all that, I did everything since then, to get where I'm standing now. All of it was designed to give me this chance to speak with you."

"You are quite convincing, King of the Underworld. Is that how you got the Queen of the Crux into your bed?" Malor stared intently at Mikel, seeking to judge his reaction to an incendiary query.

A flash of anger burned through Mikel. He suppressed it, swiftly, as he came back around Malor's shoulder. Mikel was there for a reason. Now wasn't the time to allow emotion to muck up all that he was working toward. "That's neither here nor there. All that matters is that I am in a position to do this deal with you. It benefits me and the people I'm responsible for. It benefits you. Where do you stand? Have I wasted my time by coming here or shall we see if we can close this bargain?"

Malor didn't say a word for quite some time, Mikel circling him twice more at his deliberate pace before he finally spoke, the entire time his eyes fixed far off into the distance. Beyond the gleam of the Barbed Path. Beyond the Plains that led to the Trench and the Splintered Bridge. The two primary barriers that had prevented him from advancing as he desired. "Why would you trust me?"

"I don't trust you," Mikel snorted out in a soft laugh. "Why would I?"

"Then why do this? As I said, you helped Celindria Dengannon claim the Crux throne. Now you seek to give it to me despite your lack of trust. That is not the decision of a rational man. That is the decision of a man with an underlying intent."

"You're right, I do enjoy a good scheme from time to time, but just as you've looked into me, I've looked into you. At least as best as I could."

"You will find little that can help you," Malor growled.

"Very true, but the little I found was enough. And it's because of what little I learned that I decided on this approach. I could tell you that I'm not running a scheme, but why bother? You wouldn't believe me if I did. So I don't care what you might be worrying about. I only care about what you think."

"As I said, I think that you are intelligent, cunning, and perhaps too smart for your own good."

"Perhaps you're right, but as you know, any agreement involves assuming some risk. In what I've proposed, I've mitigated your risk. Because in this, what I'm offering you benefits me as well. From my perspective, this is nothing more than a business decision. Although, admittedly, on a somewhat grander scale than I usually must make."

"That's what all this is to you? Business? No more than that? I still find that hard to believe."

"Everything is business," Mikel explained, "and the reason that I'm so good at my business is I know which way the tides are shifting before they do." Mikel lifted his hands as if he wanted to clear the air before clasping them behind his back. His slow rotation drew him ever closer to Malor. "We are having a circular conversation. We need to move forward or not at all."

Malor's lips twisted into a slight curl. So the real dance had just begun. What was presented during a negotiation wasn't always what was. "I will admit that you offer an interesting proposal."

"And admittedly a profitable proposal for me. I won't deny that. For you, not only a profitable proposal when measured in ways other than coin but also one that simplifies your task and ensures that you're working with someone who can get things done."

Malor's twisted lips curled higher. Now close to a smile. "You have a low opinion of Lucius Hanover?"

"How could I not?" Mikel responded as he continued on his wandering path. "Your Dark Magus as well."

"Assindra?"

"Was she not supposed to bring you the Blade of Light long ago? Yet that same weapon is strapped to my back rather than in your possession. I would say that's quite the failure."

"She failed because of you, King of the Underworld. You broke your deal with her."

"I did. You're right." Mikel knew that there was no point in denying the truth. Better to meet Malor's accusation head on.

"And why did you do that? Was it spite for your own flesh and blood? Or did you crave the weapon for your own?"

"It has grown on me," Mikel admitted in a glib tone. "How could it not?"

"You're not answering my question."

"Trust. It comes down to trust. I didn't trust Assindra. I had an inkling as to what she planned to do if I gave her the weapon, and I didn't want to take that risk. Learning more about her, learning what she did to me when I was scarcely off her tit, only confirmed the rightness of my decision."

"You feared that she would eliminate you?"

"Knowing what she was, of course I did," Mikel confirmed. "The fact that I'm her flesh and blood is of little concern to her. My guess is that she planned to challenge you as well."

"Challenge me?" Malor scoffed. He couldn't quite believe the claim, though the King of the Underworld's words did contain the ring of truth.

"With the Blade of Light in her possession, I believe it was a reasonable concern, and it's one that I still have. She is not known for her trustworthiness, so I assumed that if she proved successful she would use the ancient weapon against you after she killed me."

"You did?"

"I did."

"Why would that worry you?" Malor had to admit that the King of the Underworld was quite skilled at weaving an enthralling narrative. Yet a narrative that he believed as well was built on little more than shifting sand.

"I do well in business because I have a deep knowledge and understanding of the players and the playing field. Assindra is a wildcard who would have affected my playing field in ways I never could have conceived and therefore could not have prepared for."

"You're saying that I'm a known quantity?" Malor was still smiling, although his eyes sparked again. Whether out of amusement or indignation at what he perceived as an insult remained a mystery.

"Not well known, I will admit that. But better known than Assindra. Based on your past history, your goals are more obvious. Thus my decision to keep the Blade." Mikel offered Malor a broad smile as he came back around his shoulder, only a few feet away from him now. "A way of protecting myself. Only fair under the circumstances, wouldn't you agree?"

"I still find it hard to believe that you would treat Assindra in this way despite the connection you have with her."

"I didn't know who she was when she came to me with the job."

"Even so," Malor challenged.

"The connection with Assindra is blood, that's true. Nevertheless, that means very little when you're abandoned in the Bitter Heights and left to the mercy of the Caledonii, your own people looking down upon you through no fault of your own." Mikel spoke with a keen acidity, the taste souring his tongue but certainly not curbing it. "Blood does not guarantee love. Blood does not guarantee safety. Blood does not guarantee trust."

"Quite bitter, aren't we?" Malor mused, nodding his head in feigned sadness. "An apt description considering where you're from."

"If you were in my position, wouldn't you be?"

"I would," Malor confirmed without hesitation. "Yet there is a wrinkle that we must work through before we can reach an agreement."

"That would be?"

"The Blade of Light. It is what stands between us. You have it. I want it."

Mikel nodded, anticipating that this issue would raise its head during the negotiation, just not sure when. "You can't do as you truly desire without the Blade of Light."

"How do you know what I truly desire?"

"You seek vengeance on those who betrayed you," Mikel stated with complete confidence. "You can't gain that vengeance without the Blade of Light. Even with the tremendous power at your fingertips, only with the sword on my back can you enter the Murk and have any hope of meting out the justice that you believe your former servants deserve."

"Cunning and intelligent as I said. I'm glad that you understand the challenge I face. That will simplify our negotiation, assuming that I can trust you."

"I do understand the challenge, which is why I find it so interesting that you want the Blade of Light to begin with. You can't wield it yourself. You are more than just touched by the Curse. In some ways you are the Curse. For that same reason, you can't even touch the weapon on my back. Whether it would destroy you ..." Mikel shrugged, not knowing the answer to the possibility running through his mind. "Probably not based on your strength. Your dark magic would protect you. Though the Blade probably would harm you. And you don't want to take the risk. Not with all the work you've done to reach this point."

"But you can use the Blade." Malor had expected to reach this point. The King of the Underworld was correct. Taking up the Blade of Light himself was a massive risk.

Mikel nodded to himself as he continued. "I can, I have, and I will wield it, just as I did against your servants and allies. But if we reach an agreement, I will wield it for you. There's the key distinction."

"You failed to mention one aspect of your proposal that is the tipping point between us," Malor claimed.

"I didn't think it was necessary. It was too obvious."

Obvious or not, Malor raised it. "Keeping the Blade in your possession gives you the protection you desire. A way to ensure I don't come after you. A guarantee of sorts that the terms of any agreement we reach are upheld."

"Correct. The easiest solution to a potentially thorny dilemma."

"And what prevents you from coming after me?" Malor wondered. "As you admitted, you have not hesitated to use the Blade of Light. You have eliminated many of my servants with it, the latest example one that you offered. My Ten Thousand seeking to conquer the Splintered Bridge. And I won't deny the risk I face with respect to that Giant-crafted weapon. I don't like the idea of having you at my back with that piece of glowing steel in your hand."

"If we reach an agreement, I won't be at your back. I'll be your partner. Right at your side. Hard to drive a blade through your back when I'm standing next to you."

"Even with the vivid imagery you've provided, I have my concerns, King of the Underworld."

"Why would I break any partnership we enter into? That's not a good business decision."

"Everyone gets greedy once they get a taste of real power," Malor challenged. "I've seen it. I'm certain you have as well."

"The greedy die," Mikel stated unequivocally. "The cautious live."

"Well said."

"Well learned," Mikel clarified.

"I'm tempted," Malor grumbled.

"But you're hesitating."

"Wouldn't you?"

"I probably would, yes." Mikel shrugged. There was nothing else that he could do or say to persuade Malor. There were no other arguments or points to be made. In the end, it came down to risk and how much Malor was willing to take. "You will need to decide. No bargain is ever perfect. Nevertheless, the best bargains are those that require each party to give a little to get what they truly desire, understanding that they will not get all that they desire. You may not gain the Blade of Light yourself, and you will never hold it in your hand. Even with all the power that you can call upon, you cannot without putting yourself at mortal risk. However, I can not only carry the Blade of Light, but I can also be your Blade. You will need to decide if such an arrangement suits your interests. Moreover, whether you can adhere to the terms."

Mikel said no more than that. But he did stop his pacing right in front of Malor. He stepped a few feet closer, though not so close as to make the King of the Tor question his intentions.

In Malor's dark, mesmerizing eyes Mikel recognized the

conflict that he was struggling with. Mikel was pleased by that. He hadn't anticipated getting this far into the dialogue before Malor lost patience with him.

It was then that he decided to take a risk. Cadmus had told him that Malor could not sense the use of the Light, or at least he believed that Malor couldn't, and past practice suggested that belief was correct.

While Malor contemplated the proposal and the risk entailed, Mikel reached out to the Light. Connecting to the unique power that surged through him, he extended his senses.

He sighed with silent relief, Malor not moving a muscle, which confirmed that the Dread may have complete control over the Curse, but when it came to the Light for him it was an unknowable power.

Mikel had come to the Ring with one purpose in mind, resigned to his fate the moment he left the Frozen Waste. Yet now another avenue could be opening to him. An opportunity he dared not consider until this very moment.

Should he take the risk that he was contemplating? Mikel realized it was too late to ask himself that question. He had decided already.

Mikel almost took a step back when Malor glided toward him. Then his grin became a smirk. The King of the Tor who was so much more than just that clapped his hands together in appreciation.

"Quite the proposal, King of the Underworld, but it complicates my plans unnecessarily."

Malor didn't want a partner. He loathed the very idea. "Do you really believe that you're my equal? That I would deign to work with you? *Partner* with you?"

Mikel shrugged. "It was worth a try."

Malor used the next few seconds to study the King of the Underworld. Trying to read him. To better interpret his aims. Yet his effort was stymied.

He could read most anyone with barely a glance, learning not only their intentions but also their desires. Their weaknesses and larger failings. The pressure points that would give him the opportunity to wraps his strings around them and make them dance like a marionette.

But not the King of the Underworld. Most likely because of the Blade on his back that truly belonged to Malor. But it wasn't just the Blade, now was it? There was more at play within this negotiation. He had known that from the start.

"As I said, you weave quite a narrative. Allow me to separate fact from fantasy."

"By all means," Mikel allowed. He had little doubt that they would reach this point, surprised that it had taken so long.

"You have no intention of giving up the Queen of the Crux."

"I don't. You're right."

"You came here to find some weakness that you could exploit."

"Guilty."

"But you're discovering that I have no weaknesses."

"Other than being quite full of yourself," Mikel offered.

"I will allow you that indiscretion because of the courage you demonstrated by coming here."

"Very kind of you."

"So here is my proposal. You will serve me. You will be my Blade."

"Why would I do that?"

Malor smirked. "You know why."

"Because if I don't you'll kill the Queen of the Crux."

"Wrong. I'll kill her and everyone important to you."

"You drive a hard bargain."

"It's not a bargain," Malor stated harshly. "You will be my servant. You will do what I require when I require no matter what I require."

"You're very sure of yourself," Mikel mused.

"I have reason to be." Malor stepped closer. His eyes burned fiercely. "Decide now. Serve me or the people important to you die."

"You don't give me much choice."

"That's because unlike you I don't negotiate. Now tell me. You said that you stand before me now because you see a business opportunity. And you know what I truly desire. But you have not revealed what you truly desire."

"I haven't. You're right."

"The story you wove was filled with half-truths and false trails," Malor stated with absolute certainty. "Why?"

"Because I assumed that you would have figured it out by now."

"Tell me," Malor demanded. "You will serve me. You have no choice."

Mikel nodded, accepting that truth. "What I truly desire is really quite obvious. What I truly desire is to be standing right here. Right now. With you."

Before he even finished speaking, Mikel pulled free the Blade of Light in a smooth, blindingly fast motion and swept the blazing weapon down toward Malor Dragoran.

He doubted that the Dread could be killed. He was too powerful. Too skilled in the Curse. The Curse too much a part of him. Where Rickard Riverstone and the Curse began and ended could not be determined, the lines blurred by centuries upon centuries of contamination.

Even so, the Dread was alive, as was the Curse, and if there was any weapon that could do the deed, it was the one that had chosen Mikel.

If Mikel could not kill the Dread, he should be able to wound him. Weaken him. And if he could weaken the Dread enough ...

As a result, just as in everything that Mikel did, it came down to risk.

How much was he willing to accept?

Or perhaps the better question was whether he was willing to risk his life based on a belief that was both hope and truth, which aspect was stronger unknown until he took the fateful step?

Then perhaps he stood a chance.

Drin as well.

He needed to do this for her.

It was the only way to keep her safe.

He had never thought it possible, but his connection to the Queen of the Crux had only grown stronger the more time they spent together. So much so that what he defined as a connection had transformed into a relationship, and that was a great deal more terrifying.

Yet rather than run from what was both an opportunity and a risk as he had done ever since Liria's betrayal, he wanted to embrace it. He wanted it to grow and flourish. To become stronger and more than it already was. He wanted it to gain a solidity from which a foundation could be built.

And it was that disorienting and stirring thought that was running through his mind that scared him more than the Dread as he stared into the evil being's eyes, his scimitar screaming through the air.

If Mikel had struck true, he would have cleaved the King of the Tor in two.

Not unexpectedly, he didn't.

Mikel was fast, just not fast enough.

Right before his steel sliced into Malor Dragoran, a deadening black light flashed before his eyes. Mikel realized that he was flying backward, the sound of the ancient weapon striking the magical shield the last sound to play across his senses.

Dazed, his head feeling as if he had placed it on an anvil in the Icehold, a Giant of the Rime pounding it into shape with a hammer, it took Mikel a few seconds to push himself back to his feet. When he did he was more than just a little unsteady, his bad knee not helping him.

When he could see again, the flashes and dots of black gone, the image in front of his eyes finally clear and no longer double, a rush of disappointment flooded through him. He had placed too much of his faith in hope.

He had not killed his enemy.

He had not wounded him.

All he had done was reveal his true adversary.

The figure of Malor Dragoran, King of the Tor, was gone. That skin ripped before Mikel's eyes. Dissolving. Flaking away.

In Malor's place stood what Rickard Riverstone had become. What Mikel had glimpsed for just a heartbeat only minutes before.

The true essence of the evil plaguing the Tor.

The Dread in his true and unnatural form.

Greyish skin stuck out from the sleeves of his wispy black robes. His hands were spotted by age while his features were sharp, angled, and almost skeleton-like. His skin was pulled tight across his hairless scalp. Eyes a black darker than the darkest night flashed and moved much like the Churn. All while wisps of the Curse swirled around him, making Mikel wonder how much of the Dread was substance and how much was spirit.

That thought sticking with him, the monstrous being radiated a menacing potency that made it difficult for him to breathe. The Dread's very presence consumed the space atop the tower and drained it of air.

"As I said, clever, though not clever enough," the Dread cackled. "Your impetuousness is going to cost you more than your life. You will serve me, King of the Underworld. You will be my Blade."

A blast of tainted energy shot from the Dread's palm.

Mikel slashed with his scimitar. Scarcely thinking, his

instincts guided him as he cut through the Curse before it slammed into him.

Lucky, he believed, his senses still askew and slow to return to him. Still, he would take lucky.

"And I'm sure you already know who your first target will be if you do not obey me now," the Dread hissed. "Your lovely Queen of the Crux. She will die by your hand, our partnership, such as it is, sealed with her blood."

For the next several minutes, the Dread attacked with a terrible ferocity. Forcing Mikel this way and that, he blasted energy toward him with a frightening rapidity. None were larger than a crossbow bolt, though each contained a devastating power.

The parapet atop the tower attested to that. Wherever one of the Dread's bolts struck the stone the resulting damage was much like that caused by a huge rock flung by a ballista. Large sections of brick shattered and fell away.

As he danced around the tower with an awkward grace, his knee impeding him, Mikel began to fear that if he wasn't careful, the Dread's unending attack would be the least of his concerns. The gusty wind tugged at him and then he felt his foot slide on a loose piece of rubble at the worst possible moment.

All it would take would be a slip. Lose his balance, lose his focus only for a split-second, and he would lose his free will. The Dread would press his advantage. He wouldn't kill Mikel with the Curse because of his natural resistance, but the Dread could enslave him just as he promised.

Anxious to rectify the imbalance, understanding that if he didn't his death would be the best possible outcome, Mikel considered one possible avenue of attack after another.

He discarded them all, not having the time or the opportunity to do anything else except defend himself.

The Dread was too strong.

Too certain in himself.

Too focused on crushing Mikel's will just as he was crushing the stone of the tower.

Stumbling, Mikel dropped to his bad knee. The fragmented rock behind him gave way when the latest of the Dread's corrupted bolts slammed into the Blade of Light and pushed him back closer to the fringe, his back foot slipping off the edge of the tower.

He didn't look over his shoulder, worrying that if he did his slide would shift into a fatal fall. A drop of almost a thousand feet waiting for him.

For a heartbeat, he considered sacrificing himself.

But not yet.

Not until he was certain he had no other choice.

For even if the Dread lost the chance to use the Blade, no one else but Mikel could stop him from killing Drin.

That concern driving him, Mikel held his position and set himself as best as he could, Blade of Light gleaming brightly as he prepared for what he feared would be the Dread's final attack.

Yet, inexplicably, the Dread halted his assault. Hovering above the stone, swirls of tainted energy played across his claw-like fingertips.

Mikel was grateful for the reprieve. Though he doubted it would last long. Thanks to the Dread's sneer this mythical monster who finally had stepped free from the illusion hiding him appeared to be confident that he could deal with the Bearer of the Blade at his leisure.

"Now that we finally stand against one another and we see each other for who the other truly is, do you believe that you can defeat me?"

Mikel smiled wearily as he pushed himself back to his feet. As he did, he ignored the pain that radiated from his knee and made his leg feel as if it was on fire. He then shuffled a few feet closer to the Dread and away from the broken edge of the tower. If he was going to die, a thousand-foot drop wasn't the way he wanted to go to the other side unless he had no other choice. "Defeat you? Who can say?"

"Even now you press me. I have barely touched my power. I have done nothing more than play with you just as you tried to play with me during your negotiation. Yet still you challenge me. Still you seem to believe that we are equals."

The Dread's eyes flashed with an all-consuming hate, his indignation laced into his voice. "We are not equals, Bearer of the Blade. We are not negotiating now. I am demonstrating that you are nothing more than another in a long line of failures. All of your brethren in the position you are in now, fighting for their lives against a power that exceeds your own. All of your brethren dead! You, on the other hand, have a different fate. You will yearn for death. I promise you that. For you will no longer be the King of the Underworld or the Bearer of the Blade. You will be my slave."

"I was simply answering your question," Mikel replied in a calm voice, his lips unavoidably twisting into a small smile. Pleased that he could aggravate the Dread with such ease. "Can I defeat you?" Mikel shrugged as if the matter was of little concern to him even as a small voice in the back of his head screamed in fear. "At the moment, probably not. That much you have made clear, and though I am many things, I am not a fool. Still, so long as I breathe, I have a chance. So if you're waiting for me to capitulate, if you're waiting for me to bend the knee, you're wasting your time."

"You have no chance, Blade Bearer. You should know that." The Dread smiled then. A disturbing expression. His face more resembled a disembodied skull as the threads of the Curse swirled around him with greater intensity. "And you do know that. Thus your decision to try to charm me. Ingratiate yourself with me. Hoping that your cowardly first strike would prove to be the only strike necessary." The Dread cackled even louder this time, the sound making Mikel's ears hurt. "Such a terrible thing when hope is lost, is it not, Blade Bearer?"

"I still have hope," Mikel replied with what little confidence remained to him. Struggling for some way out of what had become an untenable predicament, back to a fall that ensured his death, he stood against a monster who was more powerful than he was, even the Blade of Light seeming to agree, its brightness dimming as the hope he spoke of faded slowly. "Until my dying breath I will always have hope."

"Before I described you as cunning, intelligent, and impetuous. Foolish belongs there as well, because you fail to see the truth despite it being right in front of your eyes. I should have also said maddening."

"I get that a lot."

"I will make you mine now, Blade Bearer. The rest of your days will be misery and sorrow as you aid me in conquering the Realms."

"Are you certain?" Mikel taunted, not sure where his newfound confidence was coming from except perhaps from his desire to continue to fight back any way that he could. His reason told him that his enslavement would come soon even as what little hope remained to him told him to push. To prod. To prick. To buy whatever additional few seconds that he could. "Because I'm still here despite you telling me several times that you will kill me."

"Maddening, just as I said."

"Think of it more as me being consistent in how I approach the world."

"How you approach the world is flawed," the Dread snorted.

"I can't wait to hear why," Mikel nudged. "Please. Tell me."

The Dread's dark eyes became even darker. He knew exactly what the Blade Bearer was doing. Confident in the power that he exercised, the Dread didn't care. "The world you see is the one that you've created, King of the Underworld. I will give you credit for that. However, it's a small world. Tiny in the grand scope of the Realms. The world I see is the one that I can create. One in which all the Realms fall under my sway. Not just the Crux or the Tor or what was once Frisia. You seek a small piece of the pie. I want the entire pie, and I will have it. That's the difference between you and me."

"Not really an original dream. There are others who have tried to do as you are."

"True, but none of them had the power that I do," the Dread replied with an absolute confidence. "None of them could do what I can."

"All of them just as arrogant and misguided as you are, and all of them gone."

"A pity that we can't work together willingly," the Dread rasped, tiring of the conversation between them. He had little desire to give the King of the Underworld more opportunities to poke at him and delay the inevitable. "You understand what must come next?"

"I do."

"Then there's no point in wasting any more time. All the Realms will be mine, including the one you have worked so hard to create."

Before Mikel could argue, twisting and curling ropes of the Curse shot out from the Dread's hands. Shocked by the speed of the attack, Mikel didn't bother to fight back. He did the only thing that came to mind.

Calling upon the Light, he wrapped himself in a thin layer of energy as he sought to protect himself from the contracting bonds of the Curse.

The pitch-black strands that had a mind of their own surged around him. Swirling. Churning. Wrapping around his body. Constraining him. Binding him.

Mikel growled in anger.

He couldn't move.

He could scarcely breathe.

And he couldn't use the Blade of Light. Though the steel was still in his hands, it was pressed against his chest, the Blade vertical to the stone he stood upon. The tip of the Blade pressed against his forehead as the tainted strands tightened their hold.

Mikel struggled to free himself, yet doing so was exactly what the strands of black desired. Every time he moved was an opportunity for the Dread's creation to tighten its grip.

His fear rising to the surface, not wanting to look at the grinning visage of the Dread, the glowing steel pressed right up against him, Mikel closed his eyes and remembered the inscription that ran down the length of the weapon. Written in the old tongue it was an ancient saying and one filled with real power. If he could harness it.

*"When the darkness surrounds, the Light will prevail."*

A nice thought, Mikel admitted even as it became harder and harder for him to breathe, but not very useful when he was gasping for air and stuck within a tightening cocoon of tainted energy.

*"You are trying too hard, Steelheart,"* Knute grumped, the former Bearer of the Blade unable to stay silent in Mikel's head when he faced such dire circumstances. *"You must let go."*

*"Let go? What do you mean let go?"* Mikel couldn't believe he was having a conversation with a long-dead spirit at a time like this, Knute's advice not what he anticipated. He had hoped for something more direct. More aggressive. More immediate as the pain in his chest worsened.

*"You are the Blade and the Blade is you. But now, because of your fear, because of the weight of what is demanded of you, you and the Blade are not one. You are still fighting one another. You have not found the required balance. To defeat the Dread, what you are with the Blade, what the Blade is with you, must be what battles this*

*plague that seeks to consume the Natural World. Two become one. That one stronger than the two. That one stronger than the Dread."*

Mikel thought about Knute's logic. In a strange sort of way, what the Frost Lord said actually made sense. Perhaps the Frost Lord was right. Perhaps he was thinking too much. *"How do I do that?"*

*"I just told you, Steelheart. Let go. Don't do. Don't think. Just be. You and the Blade. Together. One. You've done it before. Do it again now."*

Not knowing what else to try, his options limited as the bonds of tainted energy stiffened around him, seeking to crack his protective shell of natural magic, Mikel moved in the only way that he could. He tilted his forehead down until it touched the glowing steel.

His breaths no more than irregular gasps, eyes still closed, Mikel focused on the brightness of the Blade that burned through his eyelids. The dim glow became stronger, burning with a new strength. A new purpose.

Clearing his mind, Mikel concentrated on the power that slowly began to flow within him. That flow increased in pace and became an overpowering surge, boiling and rolling through every cell in his body.

The true essence of the Blade of Light.

The source the Giants of the Rime melded with the steel.

The Light.

Untainted.

Hotter than the sun, the heat warmed him.

Filled him.

Guided him.

Changed him.

Scalded him.

Showed him who he truly was.

Revealed to him what he could be, what he needed to be, if he had the courage to follow that path.

"What are you doing, King of the Underworld?"

The Dread's question was only asked in part because of curiosity. Included within it was a strong pinch of concern.

The Dread's strands of darkness that surrounded the Blade Bearer had stopped moving. They were still in place, but what had once been a solid shell of the Curse no longer was.

Blasts of light fought through the gaps that began to appear in the shell of tainted energy. Pushing back, the natural magic craved to be free.

Mikel didn't hear the Dread. No longer concerned with the Curse wrapped around him, he focused on himself. On the power within him. How the Light was releasing him from the bonds first set upon him when he was no more than a babe.

His true self emerging, the Light bonded with him. Learned him. Merged with him.

And without a second thought, Mikel accepted the responsibility offered to him, comprehending what was expected.

What only he could do.

What he needed to do.

In that instant, Mikel truly understood who he was, what the Blade was, and how they fit together.

Two pieces.

Stronger as one.

Unstoppable as one.

The two becoming one.

A new confidence raced through him, and he relished the power that was his and his alone.

When he opened his eyes, the Dread stared back at him. Stunned. That look replaced a moment later by alarm.

For a brief moment, the Dread disappeared. Mikel was blinded as he released the energy surging through him, the Light burning with a white-hot fire through the strands of darkness.

The bonds fell away as they were ripped apart. Disintegrating and releasing Mikel from what would have been a terrible fate.

"Shall we finish what we started?" Mikel asked. His smile not only confident, but also certain, his eyes flashed with a fire that mimicked the Light.

"I don't know what you have done," the Dread hissed. "But it is not enough." Pointing his palms toward the tower, he sent a bolt of black blasting into the stone.

The tower shook dangerously from the force of the strike, a massive cloud of crushed stone and grit mixed with the Dread's tainted magic swirled up, hiding him from view.

Through it all, Mikel waited. The Blade of Light in hand. Unconcerned by the Curse, which swirled around him but refused to touch him.

When the cloud finally dissipated, Mikel realized that the shape of the battle had changed.

The Dread had moved to the far end of the tower, joined by several score soldiers.

"Seize him!" the Dread ordered. "I will have him alive!"

As the fighters of the Ten Thousand raced to obey their master's command, they began to shift.

Their true selves emerging.

Their golden eyes promising pain and suffering before Mikel was made to serve their master.

**24**

# ATOP THE TOWER

"Do you see it?" Drin asked.

"Hard not to," Teddy replied.

Sailing in from the northeast, Leonardo took control of the wheel, freeing Samuel to engage in the activities that he excelled at when darkness settled over the land. He and the rest of Mikel's crew waited expectantly at the side railings, long ropes in hand.

The night that still covered the Tor wouldn't last for much longer. A hint of orange brightened the eastern horizon. That glow was muted by the display coming from the top of the Ring's highest tower.

"Do you think it's him?" Drin asked.

Teddy chuckled softly, his expression of bemusement unable to hide the intensity of his gaze. His desire to be off the flying ship and back at work an urge he couldn't wait to surrender to. His friend needed help. That's all that mattered to him. "It has to be. He's the only one I know who can cause so much trouble so quickly."

Teddy and Drin stood at the helm of the flying ship, streaks of magic illuminating the sky. Some disappeared in the blink of an eye. Others lasted for several seconds.

"At least we know that he's still alive," Drin murmured, not caring that her concern was apparent in her voice.

"That we do, but for how much longer ..."

That was the question that had been playing through Drin's mind as soon as they drew close enough to observe the battle taking place atop the crumbling tower, the magic in use taking a heavy toll on the structure.

"Signal the other ships," Drin ordered. "We stick to the plan. Hopefully, Mikel can hold out a little while longer."

"This is not what I wanted to be dealing with right now," Mikel grumbled to himself through gritted teeth.

Against the Dread he scarcely stood much of a chance in a fair combat. Thus, his decision to try to end the contest before it even began.

*"Get what needs to be gotten then get gone."*

Words to live by. But he hadn't struck true with what he had hoped would be a blow that balanced the playing field.

His failure still smarted. Both his ego and his body, the resulting blast making every part of him ache.

And now he stood no chance at all. The Dread the furthest target from his mind because he couldn't get to the evil bastard without fighting his way through the whirlwind of claws, teeth, and steel seeking to tame him.

Of course, he could take some solace from the fact that he was still free of their grasp after battling against two dozen Werebeasts, the soldiers of the Ten Thousand shifting to their Curse-crafted forms before engaging in the fray.

Now? He wasn't sure how many were arrayed against him.

It was all that he could do to stay clear of the scrum of

monsters that sought to chain him, though not without inflicting some punishment first. Blades and maces slashed toward him. The jaws of men with the maws of wolves, tigers, bears, and panthers snapped at him.

How long he could keep this up, his body and mind tiring, his knee screaming at him, he didn't know.

And he didn't want to think about what that meant.

Because he refused to surrender to the inevitability of serving an evil he despised. A bloody and painful end preferable.

When the appropriate time came, he would seek that end.

But not yet.

Not until he was certain there was no more that he could do.

Mikel glided around the tower with a grace brought on by desperation. His blazing steel more often than not finding a home in the flesh and bone of an overzealous Werebeast. The Light bursting from his free hand to protect his blind side and create what little space he could to maneuver among the many assailants who scrambled to take him down.

Not choosing in which direction to go. Rather pushed. The Werebeasts' frenetic efforts to seize him made that decision for him. Their assaults uncoordinated and chaotic, which at that moment served Mikel's purpose and gave him a few more seconds to ponder how to escape what appeared to be a snare snapping closed.

His odds of breaking free poor to begin with, despite his efforts those odds only worsened as more Werebeasts joined the clash. With each opponent Mikel forced from the fight, another appeared. Or two. Or three.

The supply of attackers seemed endless as more and more of the Ten Thousand rushed out of the four doors that led to the top of the tower. Any avenue of evasion he created with the Light and his Blade closed in a heartbeat.

"You cannot escape what fate holds in store for you, Blade Bearer!" the Dread roared. "Your service to me is certain. You are wasting your efforts seeking to achieve the impossible!" Even though his soldiers had failed to claim the prize that belonged only to him, the Dread was enjoying the King of the Underworld's performance, having little choice but to offer a grudging respect. That magnanimity resulted solely from his belief that it was only a matter of time before the King of the Underworld faltered.

"Fighting you and your servants is never a waste of time," Mikel growled, more than irritated by the Dread's arrogance. Infuriated. Yet having no good answer for it and no good way to release his rage on the one who most deserved it.

Especially when the Werebeasts swarming the tower finally began to work together, rushing at him from all directions at the same time. Mikel certain that the narrowing circle would prove to be the final noose around his neck.

Mikel recognized immediately that he couldn't take on so many attackers all at once.

So he didn't.

He gave into his instincts.

Crouching down swiftly, just as he did in his combat against Assindra, he slammed the hilt of the Blade of Light against the stone at his feet.

The effect was immediate.

The sound deafening.

The blast blinding.

The Light erupted from the ancient weapon, a tidal wave of natural magic surging out in all directions.

The tower shook and swayed. Its very foundation at risk of failing.

The charging Werebeasts were knocked from their feet and sent tumbling head over heels backward, giving Mikel the lane he desired.

Pushing himself up, gritting his teeth at his protesting knee, he raced for the closest door. If he could get into the tower the stairway would limit how many Werebeasts could attack him at one time. That restriction just might give him a chance to slip the trap.

But it wasn't to be.

His hope was crushed a heartbeat later when just a few paces from his objective, a ball of cold black fire slammed into the doorway that offered Mikel his best chance for escape. With a single throw, the Dread destroyed the threshold, the ceiling collapsing and the walls caving in, killing the soldiers who were racing up the stairs to join the fight. The Dread unconcerned about the loss of more of his Werebeasts if it meant removing the thorn that was the King of the Underworld from his foot.

"You will not escape me, Blade Bearer!" promised the Dread. "You can't. You will serve me. But do not fear. You will not be alone for long. That I assure you. Your Queen will follow closely in your footsteps. She will serve me as well, in ways that you cannot even imagine, and there is nothing that you can do to prevent that fate from befalling her."

Mikel skidded to a stop, one hand reaching toward the rubble to halt his progress before he slammed into the crushed and crumbling rock and brick. When he turned back around, his eyes blazed with a bright fire.

Perhaps the Dread was correct.

Perhaps he wouldn't escape his fate.

So be it.

Mikel would not serve the Dread.

He would meet his end as he chose.

Like the gladiators of old, he would be dragged across the white sand. And he would take as many of the Ten Thousand to the other side until it was his time.

Fighting until his very last breath.

Though he was certain that the breaths remaining to him were numbered.

The Werebeasts were back on their feet and more soldiers of the Ten Thousand were streaming through the three remaining doorways. All the while, the Dread floated just above the stone on the far side of the tower. His devilish grin revealed his pleasure, all but certain that his victory was only moments away.

Mikel had been close. So close. But it wasn't to be.

Still, even with the number of adversaries increasing by the second, he was in a better position than he was before. Seeking whatever faint glimmer of hope he could find in the despair that threatened to crush him, he rationalized that with the barrier now at his back the Werebeasts gathering around him had fewer avenues of attack.

It wasn't exactly the position that he wanted to be in, but it would have to do.

Mikel stood straight then, flexing his shoulders and working out the kinks.

Then he set himself on the stone, one foot in front of the other. The Blade of Light held loosely in his hand and against his leg, he prepared himself for what was to come.

He glared at the Werebeasts now stalking toward him.

Their howls, barks, and roars suggested that the conclusion to the melee had come.

Maybe they were right, Mikel mused.

Then again ...

Glancing back over his shoulder, Mikel smiled.

A spark of hope flashed in the back of his dark eyes when he glimpsed the shadow hidden within the fading night that approached from above.

It seemed that Leonardo's flying ships actually worked.

∽

"Come on boys and girls!" Teddy roared from his perch along the outside of the flying schooner. He jumped backward off the vessel grateful for the leather gloves that protected his hands as he slid down the rope. "Looks like there's still some fun to be had!"

Samuel and several dozen fighters standing on the running boards built along both sides of the vessel followed right behind the giant. The score of archers firing from the rails protected their descent down the dangling cords.

The Werebeasts, so focused on their master's obsession, didn't know what hit them. Releasing his fury in a roar that put a Weretiger to shame, Teddy entered the fray like a boulder rolling downhill. Knocking a fist of Werebeasts to the ground, his battle axes sang through the air, bloody and covered in gore just seconds after his boots touched the tower stone.

Samuel and the men and women behind him rushed into the gap that Teddy created, daggers and short swords stabbing and slashing with a lethal accuracy as they expanded the wedge and left bodies in their wake.

Their objective was simple.

Get to the boss before the Werebeasts got to him.

The sudden attack sent a shudder through the unsettled ranks of the Ten Thousand. Many of the monsters attempted to turn and face this new threat.

They couldn't, however, caught in the crush of their comrades, the bulk of whom struggled to break through the dynamic barrier of steel and magic the King of the Underworld wove just a few dozen yards to their front.

Drin watched it all from the helm, Leonardo at the wheel and ensuring that the flying ship curled gently with the winds and maintained its position several dozen yards above the tower. She was more than pleased by Teddy's early success.

The ferocity of his attack eased some of the pressure on Mikel.

But not all of it.

And she was certain that the shift in momentum would be short-lived.

Her assumption proved correct just a few minutes later when the battle atop the tower was reduced to a melee of dozens of distinct combats. Close quarters fighting the rule.

A result that benefited Mikel's fighters, who were trained for such engagements. Yet even that advantage would turn against them eventually because of the constant flow of Were-beasts coming through the open doorways.

For a moment Drin considered using the Talent to collapse one or two of the Werebeasts' means of reaching the tower. She held back, however. Despite the battle's momentum teetering on the edge, her smile broadened when she looked toward the base of the tower.

The two other flying ships were exactly where they were supposed to be. More of Mikel's crews were disembarking from gangways and entering the tower through the main gates as well as the windows halfway up the soaring stone, bent on their mission.

The raiding parties were charged with clearing the lower levels of the tower then working their way up. The corridors and passageways perfect for the bloody work the crews loyal to Mikel specialized in.

That additional pressure should reduce to a trickle the flow of new combatants joining the clash. But that still left a more perilous threat that Drin couldn't ignore.

She assumed that the black-clad figure hovering on the other side of the tower was the Dread. The ancient evil masquerading as Malor Dragoran finally had removed the illusion he had used to conceal his true nature.

That truth sent a shudder of revulsion through her. Gripping the rail tightly, her fingernails digging into the wood, she refused to allow the terror that formed in the pit of her stomach to gain hold.

To help with that, she shifted her gaze to Mikel.

He fought with a ferocity and precision that was a wonder to watch.

His steel and magic swept through the ranks of the Werebeasts.

All the while the Broken Bear roared defiantly against his attackers.

Releasing her grip on the rail, she turned her flinty gaze to the Dread.

Deeply engaged with the swarm of Werebeasts seeking to draw his blood with blade or claw, Mikel had no way to defend against the sphere of black energy flickering above the Dread's palm. The ancient evil sought to take advantage while he could. That sphere of energy meant for Mikel's unprotected back.

Drin refused to permit such a cowardly act.

Mikel had saved her life before. Now it was her chance to return the favor.

Her eyes sparking with a deadly fire, she sent spike after spike of the Talent streaking toward the Dread.

Drin muttered a silent curse. Disappointed. Believing that she might get in a good strike before the Dread was even aware of her attack.

A vain hope on her part.

The Dread turned at just the right moment and defended against her assault with a wave of his hand, a shield of swirling black energy blocking the spikes.

Nevertheless, she achieved her objective. And she meant to prevent the Dread from sneaking another jab at Mikel by maintaining her attack.

To do that, she called upon all her knowledge in the Talent to occupy the Dread and keep the ancient evil focused on her.

Her goal not to defeat the Dread. She doubted that she could do that.

Rather, she sought only to distract him long enough to give Teddy the chance to reach Mikel and turn the tide of the battle before the Dread could intervene.

MIKEL PIVOTED TO HIS RIGHT, allowing the Werebear with the battle axe in his claw to slide by him. The monster pulled off balance by the power of his own swing, Mikel used his opponent's momentum against him. Kicking out with a boot he tangled the Werebear's legs, the beast's growl of surprise cut off by the crunch of his maw against the collapsed stone of the doorway.

That sound brought a brief smile of pleasure to Mikel's grim visage. That was all that he would allow himself as this combat was far from done.

Before the Werebear could turn back toward him, Mikel punched backward with his Blade, sliding the steel through the back of the Werebear's neck.

Certain that his most recent adversary would no longer be a threat, he ripped his blazing scimitar free, the smell of cooking meat coming with it, and turned to defend against the movement he sensed on his left.

Already slashing with the Blade of Light in a sweeping arc, he sighed with relief, halting the intended blow just in time.

"This is fun and all, but how do we win?" Teddy stood next to Mikel, body, face, and axe covered in blood, little of it his own, finally having reached his friend after cutting a gory swathe of destruction through the Ten Thousand.

For the first time since the clash began, Mikel didn't have any opponents. Grateful, he used the brief respite to survey the battlefield.

The Ten Thousand remained a problem. Though not as big a one as before.

Samuel and the rest of Mikel's crews had stemmed the flow of new entries onto the tower, which suggested that there was more going on in the Ring than just what was happening on the battlefield with which he was familiar.

Good.

That gave them a better chance.

But only a slim one at best so long as the greatest threat remained.

"The Dread has to go."

"Then you need to hurry," Teddy said, "because I don't know how long our very angry Queen of the Crux can hold off that bastard."

"Keep the Werebeasts off me and I'll take care of it."

"Done." Teddy jumped back into the fray with a murderous intent. His goal to provide Mikel with the time that he required.

And Mikel was quick to make use of the gift his friend gave him.

Drin was doing well against the Dread, keeping him on the defensive as much as she could by sending bolts of the Talent streaking toward him. Ensuring that the unmasked ruler of the Tor focused solely on her.

At least for a time.

And that was the problem.

Because Drin was vulnerable while fighting from the flying ship, and the Dread clearly recognized that. He was no longer attacking her directly but rather targeting the large balloons keeping the vessel aloft.

That changed the dynamic of the combat in a flash, and not in Drin's favor.

She needed to devote all of her efforts to defending against the Dread's attacks by forming shields that bore the brunt of whatever dark magic was thrown at the flying ship.

A strong effort on Drin's part, and Mikel was proud of her. Nevertheless, eventually the Dread would break through. Because though she was skilled, though she was determined, though she didn't know how to quit, she didn't exercise the potent power that only the Dread could call upon.

Ignoring the pain in his knee, Mikel burst forward. A bolt of the Light shot from his palm. And then another. And one more.

The Dread, fixated on the flying ship and the Queen of the Crux standing at the helm, recognized the attack at the very last second. With a haughty wave of his hand, the Curse streaming from it, he knocked away each magical shard.

Still, Mikel kept to his plan, firing more bolts of the Light toward the Dread as he closed the distance to his target. Seeking to bear the full brunt of the Dread's attack, he earned that privilege just a moment later.

With no time to think, Mikel relied on his instincts. He held the Blade to his front, pommel toward the ground, as he called upon the Light and crafted a thin shield of energy.

When the tidal wave of the Curse slammed into Mikel's barrier, it sounded much like the roar of an avalanche.

Yet despite the potency of the blow, Mikel not only held his ground but also kept coming. Refusing to be denied, he shot more bolts of the Light at the Dread, who was now only a dozen yards distant.

Mikel's aggressive tactics were rewarded a heartbeat later. Drin joined the attack by sending streams of the Talent toward the Dread, hoping to distract him during Mikel's charge.

And she did.

The Dread was forced to defend against assaults coming from two different directions. The Queen of the Crux's efforts from aboard the flying ship's helm prevented him from halting the onrushing King of the Underworld.

Screaming in rage, unwilling to risk defeat as he sensed the tide of the battle atop the tower shift, the Dread realized that he would have to wait a little while longer for his victory.

Decision made, the Dread directed a stream of the Curse behind him. That stream quickly formed into the shape of a circle. The tainted power spun faster and faster, sparks of black flaking away at the edges as a large room appeared before him.

"We are not done, King of the Underworld! We will finish this, you and I!"

Promise made, the Dread stepped through the portal.

Only a few yards away, the spinning black fading but still spinning, Mikel dove after his enemy. Eager to continue the combat.

25

# RAGE AND ROAR

"You don't know when to stop, do you?"

Mikel scrambled up off the polished tile of the throne room, the white stone reflecting the myriad colors of the stained glass that ran from floor to ceiling behind the King of the Tor's seat of power.

He would have spent more time studying the interplay of the intricate design – scenes from the history of the Tor playing across the floor in blue, red, orange, green, purple, yellow – with the light of the rising sun if not for the figure hovering just above the raised dais.

"Another one of my failings," Mikel murmured. Once again ignoring the burning ache that radiated out from his knee and into his leg, he raised himself to his full height. Setting his feet, he held the Blade of Light loosely in his hand. The fiery steel created patterns of its own on the floor, a blazing white slicing through the flashing colors.

"A failing that will ensure my victory," the Dread promised.

"Perhaps," Mikel acknowledged with a shrug. "Perhaps not. You've had several chances to take me, yet here I stand."

The Dread's grim expression tightened, the flesh on his

bald splotchy scalp becoming more pinched. At first the King of the Underworld's obstinance had amused him. Now, he had little patience for it. Especially with the unrest surging through the Tor's tallest tower. All that he sought to accomplish upon seizing control of the Kingdom so many centuries before was now at risk. All because of the thief standing before him.

"You should have accepted my offer," the Dread warned. "Now I will rectify my error, and I will turn you to my purposes in the most agonizing manner possible."

"Promises, promises," Mikel teased, even as his voice deepened and his dark eyes shifted color. Becoming a pure white, the Light surged through him. Scalding him. Cleansing him. Begging to be released. "Just not yet I think."

Mikel understood just how foolish he had been to pursue the Dread on his own. He had allowed his emotions to get the better of his reason.

Still, what's done was done. He came here for a reason. His desire to protect Drin drove him into what even she would describe as a rash act. Yet to his way of thinking an act that was necessary.

Therefore, acknowledging that he was starting from a position of weakness, he followed the advice Kaduna gave him that was always top of mind when he faced difficult circumstances and challenges.

*"Get what needs to be gotten then get gone."*

The only distinction this time being that rather than seeking an item he sought the Dread's life. Or a piece of it. Some portion that would weaken the ancient evil.

Not an easy thing to steal. Likely impossible considering the power the Dread exercised.

None of that mattered, however.

He was here.

He was ready.

And the Light demanded to be released.

Still, if he was going to make a play, if he was to have any chance of success, he needed to strike first. Forcefully. With purpose and conviction.

"Your confidence betrays a deep arrogance ..." the Dread began.

Mikel wasn't listening. Relishing the potent energy raging through him, he directed his free hand down to the large white tiles and sent a strong burst of the Light surging through the floor. A brilliant flash erupted throughout the throne room, forcing the Dread to turn away for a split second.

That was all the time that Mikel required.

Pivoting back toward the upstart who dared to challenge him, the Dread glided to his left, avoiding the blast of magic that screamed through the space in which he had been standing only a moment before. The blazing white comet slammed into the granite throne, scorching the stone, several large cracks appearing in the centuries-old carving.

The Dread pulled on more of the Curse, yet before he could engage, he was moving again. To the other side. Avoiding another blast of magic. And then one more.

The King of the Underworld strode toward him. His flinty expression matched with the white glow of his eyes sent a hint of worry through the Dread's gaunt frame. An almost unheard-of feeling for him, yet one that he couldn't ignore.

Before he could rectify the inequity of the combat, threads of the Curse spinning around his fingers, he was moving again. Escaping the King of the Underworld's latest attack, the Dread drifted backward, seeking to keep some distance between him and the Bearer of the Blade who approached with a measured step.

And so it went for the next few minutes.

The Dread evading and unable to attack.

The King of the Underworld advancing.

As the one-sided combat continued, the Dread experienced

an emotion that he thought he had forgotten a long time before. A feeling that last ravaged him when he was still solely human.

Fear.

The King of the Underworld was dictating the duel, sending one blast of the Light after another toward the Dread. Forcing him to dance to his tune. Demanding that the Dread focus solely on defending himself with the Curse. Even that proving difficult because of the power and intensity of the Blade Bearer's attack.

"Enjoy your fun," the Dread hissed. "You can't keep this up forever."

Mikel ignored the Dread's taunt. Maintaining his assault, blast after blast of white-hot magic shot from his free palm. The very light in the chamber answered his call. Drawn to him, it mixed with the power surging within him.

Strengthening the magic that he commanded.

Strengthening him.

The Light scorched and scarred the tile floor. The throne. The walls. It blew out several panels of stained glass.

Mikel didn't care.

He only cared about keeping the Dread on his back foot.

Because if he was attacking, the Dread wasn't, which meant that Mikel was still alive.

Yet even as he relished his success, Mikel made an error.

He was too focused on what he was doing and not on all that was going on around him.

So consumed with his strategy, he didn't see his adversary's sneer. The Dread revealing that the tenor of the combat was about to change as a shadow emerged through the portal of black that took shape behind Mikel.

~

MIKEL HAD FORCED the Dread to the far side of the throne room. Stuck up against the wall, he couldn't stay there. The Dread would have to move, and there was only one direction he could go.

Eyes widening in anticipation, a ball of white fire formed on his palm. The early morning light shining through the broken stained glass joining with the potent magic, Mikel held out his hand, about to release what he hoped would give him the advantage that was so necessary to his success.

His plans were shattered a heartbeat later when his connection to the Light disappeared.

The compressed ball of energy fizzled on his palm and then vanished.

He stared down at his hand in shock.

The Light wasn't gone.

It was still there.

Within him.

Around him.

He just couldn't touch it.

Unbidden, his arms were pulled up tight against his chest and his legs were pushed together. His entire body rigid.

The Blade of Light still glowed dimly at his touch, but he couldn't wield the weapon. The link to the ancient Blade broken.

He couldn't do anything.

Somehow his bond to the Light had been severed, and with that loss he had been bound with the Curse. The thin wisps of black spun around him. Having no substance. Even so, as strong as steel. Teasing and taunting him as he stood stock still and ramrod straight.

It couldn't be the Dread. Even with his power, there was no way that ancient evil could do this while dodging Mikel's attacks. It had to be ...

"I would have thought that by now you would have learned your place, my son."

The fear that settled in his stomach the moment he lost touch with the Light was burned away in a flash by the rage that radiated out from his chest and filled every cell in his body.

Assindra emerged from the shadows at the back of the throne room. The last few flakes of the portal she had used to intrude upon the duel sputtered out as she appeared in front of Mikel.

Furious, Mikel struggled futilely against his bonds. A useless effort revealed only by the strain on his face, the rest of his body moving not an inch. All the while, Assindra peered at him with a smug grin gracing her beautiful features.

How had she managed to do this to him?

She wasn't stronger than he was in natural magic. It had to be something else. Perhaps his concentration. Focused so entirely on the Dread, he was unprepared for such a subtle attack.

Mikel promised himself that he would never allow himself to be placed in this position again. He would be ready. Assuming, of course, that he found some way out of his current predicament. A result that even he believed was more hope than reality.

However, instead of allowing his dark thoughts to take him down an ineffectual and terrifying path, he shifted his focus toward what Assindra had done to him. He could see the bonds. He could sense the bonds.

But it wasn't the Curse that held him in his grip so much as Assindra severing his connection to the Light and putting him into some kind of stasis.

Not bound by the Curse. The tainted wisps of power more for show. Instead somehow she had hidden his link to the Light from him.

The Light was still there. He could sense the power that he had been exercising just seconds before.

But he didn't know how to touch the Light again.

Every time he tried, it slipped away from him like water running through his fingers.

What had Assindra done to him?

The loss was more than irritating. It was devastating.

He felt as if he had lost a part of himself. He couldn't even hear the Bearers of the Blade whose consciousnesses resided within him, their angry protests muted to a furious though incomprehensible buzz.

"The rule of the King of the Underworld has come to an end," the Dread proclaimed. He stood in the center of the dais once more. The backrest of the throne destroyed by Mikel's attack, shattered granite lay about the folds of his cloak that hovered just above the floor. That was joined by stained glass, broken shards scattered across the tile. "We will end this farce now. You will serve me."

The swirls of black always present around his hands and forearms increased their pace as they raced around the Dread. His rule over the Tor still hanging in the balance, he was tired of this game. It was time to finish this and be done with the irritant who had caused him so many problems.

"Not yet. I would speak to my son." Assindra looked over her shoulder, earning a reluctant nod from the Dread having earned the privilege thanks to her timely assistance.

Mikel smirked. The only movement he could make. The rest of him stuck as if he stood naked in the Frozen Waste. "Now we're mother and son. Why?"

"You still have an opportunity to make amends for the damage you've caused," Assindra murmured quietly.

"The damage I've caused?" He frowned as he took in the shattered throne and broken glass. "You want me to pay for that?"

"Even now with your life hanging in the balance you are difficult," Assindra growled.

"One of my more refined skills," Mikel replied, his frown shifting to a grin. In his current condition, he could do little more than aggravate the Dark Magus who had severed his link to the Light.

"Yes, your skill in the Light is anything but refined."

"On that at least we both agree," Mikel admitted. He was disappointed in himself. He wished that he had spent more time with the previous Bearers of the Blade learning how to use the power gifted to him.

"Not an argument. Will wonders never cease?" Assindra studied Mikel for a time. Noting the resemblance, the memories that followed brought a soft curl to her lips. "Have you ever wondered why I wasn't there for you when you were a child?"

"I don't have to wonder why. I know why."

Assindra nodded. She had assumed as much. "Kaduna told you."

"In part. It's common knowledge, after all. Every Caledonii can use the Talent. I couldn't. There wasn't a trace to be found in me. I was an embarrassment. To the Caledonii of the Bitter Heights. To you."

"Not an embarrassment, Mikel. Never that."

"You say that, yet you still left me." Mikel spoke in a flat tone, not a hint of emotion in his voice.

"I did leave you, but not because you were an embarrassment. Rather because I sought the truth. About you and why the power that should have been within you wasn't."

Assindra's revelation surprised him, though it didn't ease the hurt he felt building up within him. "Did you discover the truth?"

"I did," Assindra replied, "although not for quite some time. Not until just recently when you came back into my life."

"You have quite the way with words," Mikel mused. "You come across as the aggrieved party."

"I am the aggrieved party," Assindra stated forcefully. "Just as you are."

"You'll have to explain that to me."

"Kaduna hid the power that belonged to you within you. She hid it from me."

"And that's why you killed her?" Mikel demanded. Terrible memories of finding Kaduna after that clash passed through his mind.

"We fought because she failed in the responsibility she accepted. She was to care for you. Protect you. But she told me that you died." Assindra's eyes softened just as her voice did. "What was I to do? I was your mother. I was upset. I was angry." She sighed sadly. "I did not mean for it to happen, but it did. I proved to be the stronger of us."

"Putting aside that you killed the woman who raised me, why would Kaduna hide the power within me?"

"The Light as you just used. With great effect, in fact." She nodded over her shoulder toward the destruction he had caused. "Of course, there is still a great deal more that you need to learn before you reach your full potential."

"And you can teach me? That's what you seem to be implying."

"I believe I can."

"Why?"

"We'll get to that," Assindra promised. "First, we must remove Kaduna from the story we're writing. If she had not betrayed me through some misguided purpose or desire, we would have been together, Mikel. I would have been there for you, not her. But because of what she did, what she forced me to do ..." She shook her head sadly. "I thought you were dead, my son. But you're not. I can't believe my good fortune. And I can't bear the thought of losing you again."

"You didn't seem all that concerned beneath the Crux," Mikel challenged.

"I didn't know who you were then," Assindra countered. "If I had, that scene would have played out much differently."

Mikel kept his emotions in check. Spending the last few minutes studying Assindra, he did as he usually did when he was negotiating. He learned the tells, the truths, revealed by the other person's words and movements. Building his knowledge all with the goal of finding a resolution that worked for him.

Though in this instance he had no choice but to admit the challenge Assindra presented to him. So he felt the need to push, hoping that with a little more time he might find a way to escape the fate he could see waiting for him in the Dread's dark eyes.

"Why do you believe that you can teach me how to use the Light?"

Assindra smiled then. Warmly. Her expression at odds with her cold eyes. "How many Bearers of the Blade have come before you? I know you know. Because I know they are with you now even though you can't hear them."

Mikel wanted to ask her how she did as she did, cutting him off from the Light and the weapon crafted with that power. But he knew she wouldn't answer. "Twelve," Mikel replied, not understanding where Assindra was guiding the conversation.

"And how many have used the Light as you can?"

"I don't ..." Mikel frowned again. Now that was a good question, and he had never wondered about that. Cadmus had said a Lightcrafter was rare, but never how rare.

Assindra's smile deepened. "Only a few people know, and I am one of them." She stepped in close to him, only a few feet separating them. "We are Caledonii. We were few in number to begin with. Even fewer now because the persecutions still continue."

"What does that have to do with ..."

"Patience, my son. Patience. There is the Curse. There is the Talent. There are other forms of natural power. Yet that's all they are. Natural power. Different forms of the same source. How that power is used defines it. Otherwise, there is little distinction among its various forms."

"That's quite the argument you're making, but I don't see how ..."

"Perhaps more listening and less talking. Doing so will get us both where we need to go that much faster."

Mikel didn't say anything as a flush of red raced up his cheeks. He felt as if he was back in front of Kaduna, who rarely looked kindly upon him when he interrupted one of her lessons.

"There is the Curse. There is the Talent. There are other natural powers. And of those there is the Light. The natural power that you can exercise. Only *you*. A power that some have said is stronger than any other."

"Is it stronger?" Mikel couldn't stop himself from asking.

"We shall see," Assindra murmured, believing, hoping, that she might be turning Mikel toward her cause, his dire circumstances aiding her. "It's important to note that your strength in the Light is not contingent upon the scimitar you hold in your hand."

Assindra nodded then, seeing the truth in Mikel's eyes. "Yes, you understand that, don't you? The Blade of Light amplifies the power you wield. It gives you an additional potency you could not attain otherwise. But the Light, the natural power, comes from you. And it was that which Kaduna hid from me. It was how Kaduna betrayed me. It was how she betrayed you."

"Kaduna was trying to protect me." Mikel spoke clearly, quietly, not appreciating Assindra's disparagement of the woman he had come to see as his mother.

"Is that what you believe? Have you never considered that she might have had other designs when it came to you and the

Light?" Assindra shrugged. "It doesn't matter now that she's gone to the other side. But the truth is that if I had known that you could touch the Light, that you could use the Light as you did so magnificently just now, I never would have been forced to leave you."

"So you say."

"So I do," Assindra confirmed, "and I wouldn't say it if it wasn't the truth." She leaned in even closer. Mikel worried for a moment that she might give him a motherly kiss on the cheek. "As I said, all Caledonii can use the Talent. But you were gifted with an even rarer power. Much like the Talent, but stronger. Older. More powerful. More dynamic. Uncorruptible. Almost unquenchable. A power reserved only for the Caledonii. No one else can use the Light as you can. Not even a Giant of the Rime, though they have learned to use the Light in their creations thanks to the Caledonii."

"No one has ever said that only Caledonii can use the Light."

"No one with knowledge of that fact likes to admit it," Assindra murmured. "Our greatest gift yet also a curse. Another reason we are hated and looked down upon by so many." She shrugged, as if that meant little in the larger scheme of things. "In all our history do you know how many Caledonii have used the Light?"

Mikel couldn't shake his head to answer in the negative, the bonds too tight, even as his curiosity intensified.

"Twelve."

"Twelve?" Mikel couldn't stop himself from confirming. "So few?"

"Twelve," Assindra confirmed. "All Caledonii. The first the sire of your line. Generations past. Generations gone. All Light-crafters coming from your forebear. The last ..."

Mikel didn't have any doubt. "My father."

"Correct," Assindra said with a hint of pleasure.

"How is that …"

"Possible? That the power of the Light has revealed itself only through your bloodline? How it didn't reveal itself in you when you were born?" Assindra stepped back, catching Mikel's eyes with hers. "I didn't leave you, Mikel. Your father and I went in search of answers. We believed that the Light was within you. It had to be. But we didn't know why it was undetectable. We didn't know why you couldn't touch it. We visited all the places that might offer some scrap of an answer. Haven. The Aeyrie. All the bastions of the Order of the Magii. Other vaults that maintained the hidden knowledge of the past. But we could find nothing. Nothing at all. And when we returned, Kaduna had taken you from us."

Mikel didn't know what to say. He was usually very good at pulling the truth free from the lies. But now, he could barely make sense of what Assindra was telling him. All of it plausible. All of it believable. Yet all of it …

"You are confused. I understand that. It is a great deal to take in."

"It is, but that's not why you're being patient with me."

"Mikel, we don't know each other. How could we? That opportunity was stolen from us. Yet still we are of the same blood. I am your mother. And I am here because of the bond between us."

"You are here because you want to use the power that I wield," Mikel stated with calm certainty. He might be confused, but he wasn't a fool. Assindra was very good at twisting together half-truths with lies, crafting a fabric of reality that seemed real – that he wanted to be real, but was far from it. "You want to use me."

"No, Mikel, not use you. I want to teach you how to use the Light," Assindra clarified. "I want to help you grow into your full potential."

Mikel chuckled softly then, the peril he faced not lost on

him but no longer his primary concern. "Make me use it, you mean. Just as your partner," Mikel swept his eyes over the Dread for just an instant, his nemesis' impatience plain, "wants me to. But not for the Dread. No. That's why we're having this private conversation. For you. Because you see an opportunity with me. An opportunity you could not pursue when I was younger thanks to Kaduna."

"You are too fixed in your misplaced convictions, my son. You do not know of what you speak."

"I know quite well of what I speak. If you had learned what I could do with the Light when I was younger, your world would have been much simpler. I would not have been able to stand against you as I can now. You would have been able to wield me just like I wield the Blade of Light. No one could challenge you. Not even the Dread."

"You think too much of yourself, Mikel."

"Rarely," he snorted in disgust. "You wanted to use me in the past and you seek to use me now. State it plainly. I tire of your lies."

Assindra said nothing for a time. Not angry. Not disappointed. Slightly impressed, in fact, though she kept that to herself. Mikel was made of steel. Of course, considering his lineage, that wasn't all that surprising. And that was something else that she might be able to use to her advantage.

"We will do a deal, Mikel." Assindra leaned in close again. "You're right, it would have been easier when you were younger, but I can still use the power you control for my purposes. Because there is another power at work here against which you are defenseless."

"I can't wait to hear what it might be," Mikel scoffed.

"You love Celindria," Assindra explained. "And that's very unfortunate for you. But it works to my advantage. Once you are enslaved, the Dread will kill Celindria Dengannon, though not until after he's had his fun with her. Do you want that?" She stepped in closer then. "That's why you came here, isn't it? This is why you took this risk? It wasn't about you or the responsibility you might feel as a Lightcrafter. It was about her. You seek to protect her."

A tremor of fear rushed down Mikel's spine. He would have shivered if he could have. "Believe what you want ... mother. You are quite far from the truth." He knew in an instant that he failed to keep his worry from his voice.

"Now who is the one telling lies," Assindra challenged. "You came here for a reason. You can still accomplish what you set out to do even though the parameters of the engagement have shifted. Do what you must for her, no matter the cost to yourself. Work with me and the woman you love will be safe. I promise you that. Together we can remove the threat the Dread presents. Remove him and Celindria Dengannon is safe. I give you my word."

Mikel didn't know what to say because he could scarcely think.

Worse, his mother was right.

He did love Drin.

But what would Drin say if he faltered and acquiesced to Assindra's proposal?

How would she react if she knew that he sold out the Crux for her?

Was her life more important than the destruction that could follow if he went along with his mother's plans?

"No."

"No," Assindra snorted, not believing her ears. "You can't be serious?"

"No," Mikel repeated. This time with even greater force.

"You will regret this, Mikel," Assindra hissed, threads of the Curse drifting out from her fingertips. Her intentions toward her son clear. The Curse itself had no effect upon him, though she could still use her Dark Magic in ways designed to shift his thinking in the right direction. Pain an excellent incentive.

Before she could make good on her promise, a massive blast erupted right between her and Mikel. The explosion sent him flying backward while Assindra tumbled toward the dais.

Mikel pushed himself shakily to his knees. Afraid to rush. His mind fogged. Clarity slow to return. A faint hint of nausea tickling his belly. Yet even with all that, he smiled.

Whatever Assindra had done to cut him off from the Light was gone.

He was free to move.

He was free to fight.

"The Broken Bear is mine," Drin glared. She reached down, offering Mikel her hand and hauling him to his feet. "You can't have him."

～

A BLADE of shimmering black spinning end over end toward Drin, she tilted the shield of natural magic that she wore on her forearm to an acute angle.

The Curse deflected off her barrier and slammed into the wall instead of her.

Unfortunately Drin had little chance to celebrate her success, because Assindra wasn't done. The Dark Magus sent three more spinning blades of tainted magic racing toward her. One right after the other.

Parrying each one with a deft touch, she grunted in satisfaction. Even so, the tenor of their duel was wearing on her.

"She thinks I can't handle her," Drin growled, once again talking to herself in times of stress and not caring a whit. She had to give the Dark Magus credit. Assindra was doing well to ensure that Drin never had the chance to seize the momentum. Still, she was quite predictable, favoring one particular method of attack. And Drin was beginning to believe that she could use that rigidness against her adversary.

Before Drin could try what she had in mind, three more blades of black cartwheeled toward her. Doing as she had done so many times before, she blocked each one, the result of her work leaving black scorch marks along the stone wall.

Rather than be pleased with her success, however, Drin cursed. She had almost been taken for a fool.

Assindra wasn't predictable. Rather, she was lulling Drin into a false sense of security. Right behind the trio of blades a wave of the Curse rolled toward her much like the chop of the Churn.

The Dark Magus' grin revealed her belief that her latest creation would wash Drin away. A gnat removed so that she could concentrate on her primary quarry.

Drin dissuaded Assindra of that notion a heartbeat later. Letting go of the shield that had served her so well, she put into play a trick she had learned from Nat, the young Magus becoming instructor rather than pupil for a brief time.

Forming a wedge with the Talent that resembled the prow of a ship, she held her ground. She wasn't interested in battling Assindra's latest creation. Instead, she sought only to divert it.

Her magical creation worked like a charm. When the wave of tainted energy struck, it split in half, the single fold now two, each half continuing past her before charring the wall at her back.

Drin smiled in satisfaction. Even so, she was more than just a little aggravated. Enough was enough.

Assindra might have more experience than Drin.

She might have greater knowledge of natural magic.

But that wasn't going to be enough for the Dark Magus on this day.

Cursing up a storm of her own and momentarily distracted

by her latest failure, before Assindra could attack again, Drin lashed out.

Remembering Mikel's advice the first time she met him in the Frozen Waste during their battle against the Northern Trolls, she employed the same tactic as she had then. Bolts of energy shot from her palms and slammed into the white tile right in front of the Dark Magus.

Drin wasn't trying to kill Assindra even though she really wanted to. Rather, she was intent on preventing the Dark Magus from fighting from her front foot.

And much to Drin's relief, her tactic worked.

Caught by surprise, Assindra not only turned away but also scurried backward, blinded and coughing because of the cloud of crushed stone that formed around her. Fearful of and not knowing from which direction Drin's next attack would come.

"This is more like it," Drin growled as spheres of energy formed above both palms. Striding toward Assindra, at that moment just a dim shape in the gritty cloud, Drin meant to force the Dark Magus from the clash for good.

It was the cackle that was bothering Mikel more than the feeling that he was being burned from the inside out.

No matter what he tried, he couldn't get in close to the Dread and use the Blade of Light as he desired. The ancient evil kept him at bay with a constant stream of attacks. The latest the most perilous for Mikel.

*"Victory does not always come from strength, Steelheart,"* Knute murmured in the back of his head. *"Sometimes victory comes from surrender."*

What did the Frost Lord mean by that?

He would have liked more time to think about it, but time was in short supply.

Mikel had been holding his own against the Dread. Yet the moment he began to feel confident, the moment he began to believe that he actually stood a chance against the ancient evil, the Dread caught him out.

Defending against the streams of corrupted power that the Dread so liked to employ, Mikel almost missed the surprise hidden within.

Invisible until the very last second.

Not revealing itself until it pierced Mikel's skin.

A tiny shard of metal no larger than a pin hidden within the Curse.

When he felt the pin's touch, a sizzling pain raced through him.

Because the Curse itself couldn't affect him. He was immune. His battle against the Dread's attacks more a nuisance than anything else, used as a means to prevent him from employing the Blade of Light in close quarters.

But the pin was another matter entirely.

Not tainted with the Curse.

Rather guided by it.

Right toward Mikel's heart.

And against this attack he had no good means to defend himself. Not with the Dread maintaining his assault while the pain he was experiencing threatened his ability to defend himself.

Understanding the real hazard he faced, Mikel had called upon the Light just in time. Using the natural magic that flooded through him, he held the pin in place and prevented it from sliding deeper into his chest. Yet as the pain streamed through him and almost took him to his knees, he was close to losing his grip on the Light as his concentration wavered.

The Dread grinned in delight, relishing the struggle and believing that his victory was in sight as he used the power at his command to punch the deadly sliver in between Mikel's ribs. Just a little farther. As soon as the pin pierced the King of the Underworld's heart, the battle would be done.

Mikel knew that. He could feel the sliver sliding through him. Slowly. Painfully. Despite Mikel's best efforts to hold the means of his death in place, he was failing.

The pain wracking his body was too much for him.

Hindering his efforts to defend against the Dread.

The Dread too strong and too certain in his actions.

Focused solely on bringing about Mikel's end.

Already certain that the Blade of Light soon would be his.

The pain Mikel was experiencing made his nerves pulse involuntarily.

Mikel's ability to think clearly faded, replaced by a reality filled with a searing agony and the certainty that it wouldn't be long before he went to the other side as the pin slowly pinched deeper into his body.

It was either that or surrender himself to the Dread. Become his slave. But he couldn't do that.

Drin was with him. If he gave in, the Dread would do as Assindra said. He would use her then discard her, and Mikel could do nothing about it. But he could still try to do something about the Dread's latest attack.

He wanted to scream, but he couldn't, gritting his teeth as he pushed back against the pin. All the while knowing that it was wasted effort on his part.

He couldn't do it.

He couldn't stand against the Dread.

The pin was past his ribs now. He could feel it moving within him. In just seconds it would slide into his heart. That thin piece of metal all that was required to kill him.

No more than a sliver.

But that sliver would be all that it took.

And then Drin would be the Dread's.

Mikel was trapped, having no good options, only one terrible result guaranteed.

Hating that truth, his thoughts and memories cascading wildly through his mind, the pain threatening to send him to his back, how could he do as Knute suggested?

*"Believe in yourself, Steelheart,"* Knute murmured again, this time more forcefully as he tried to wake up some part of Mikel that wasn't consumed by the agony surging through his body. *"Believe in the Steelheart!"*

Mikel wanted to.

Desperately.

Yet how could he as the sliver of steel slid deeper into his chest?

About to pierce his heart.

"You cannot defeat me, girl!" Assindra shrieked.

Drin smirked. Her confidence was growing. If a scream of defiance was the best defense Assindra could offer, the combat was almost won.

Drin didn't allow her confidence to grow into arrogance, however.

Before Assindra regained her bearings, Drin was on her. Shards of the Talent blasted toward Assindra followed by glowing daggers. A constant assault as Drin refused to give Assindra the chance to recover.

And now, Assindra on her heels, a pulsing sphere of the Talent on each palm, Drin was ready to end the combat for good.

Until she heard the Dread's cackle and Mikel's accompanying groan. Glancing briefly to her side, her heart missed a beat.

"He will pay the price for loving you," Assindra cried,

enjoying the anguish that colored Drin's face. "He had his chance, girl. Live and love or fight and die. He chose the wrong option."

A bolt of the Curse swept by her, Drin ducking at the last second.

Drin had kept her anger at bay, concentrating on the combat. But now, Mikel in trouble and fading, his own mother mocking him and not caring that her son was about to die, too much for her.

Drin gave into her rage as she turned toward Assindra, Mikel's tortured expression from the pain tormenting his body burned into her memory.

She released one sphere of energy, the Talent blazing like a comet toward Assindra.

The Dark Magus ducked and slid to the side. But she didn't stop there. She kept moving. She had to as Drin tracked her, another sphere streaking toward Assindra. Then another. One more. And another.

Drin forced the Dark Magus this way and that. A constant assault driven by her rage.

Assindra shrieked in anger and fear, no longer moving of her own volition, doing whatever was required to evade the strikes that came closer and closer, until finally the assault ended.

The Queen of the Crux had cornered her. Assindra pressed up against the side of the dais.

Assindra's eyes widened in fear. She had nowhere to go. No way to defend herself. Even if she tried to form a shield from the Curse, it would be too late. The girl was too close. And she was too eager to inflict the final blow.

"If anyone is going to pay a price, it will be you!" Drin shouted. The fire within her flowed into the spheres that took shape on her palm.

Both magical weapons shot toward Assindra at the same

time, ensuring that the Dark Magus had no chance of escape through ordinary means.

Until a spinning veil of black formed right behind Assindra in barely a breath.

The Dark Magus stepped through the portal, ducking as Drin's spheres followed her and missed by no more than a hair, before she released her hold on the Curse.

The portal closed in a flash. Assindra gone, once more the Dark Magus demonstrated that her greatest skill was keeping herself alive.

Drin's fury at Assindra's escape was nothing compared to her fear for Mikel. Forcing her failure from her mind, she turned toward him, eager to help, not understanding how he could bear the pain that the Dread was inflicting upon him. Judging from the Dread's expression that the combat was almost done, Drin cursed then did the only thing she could.

She didn't have the time to fire a bolt of the Talent at the Dread.

She barely had the time to duck down next to the granite dais as a massive shape hurtled through the stained glass behind the throne.

～

THE ROAR WAS BAD ENOUGH.

Eisa's ear-splitting shriek echoed throughout the throne room. The sound of shattering glass forgotten as the ice dragon smashed through the window and skidded to a stop atop the dais, her claws digging deep furrows in the stone.

Worse was the emotion it evoked.

Terror.

Foreign to the Dread for so long until he matched wits and magic with the King of the Underworld.

Rather than try to stand his ground and fight, the Dread adopted the most sensible approach.

He ran.

Stumbling down the steps, he skidded across the floor before finding his feet again with the help of the far wall of the chamber. His attack on the King of the Underworld forgotten. His only concern defending against the beast that looked down upon him with ice-blue eyes filled not with hunger but rather rage.

Maw opening to reveal razor-sharp teeth as long as a Giant's forearm, Eisa let loose a cold blue fire. It's touch scarred the stone and tile, ice forming along the edges of the deep gouges.

The Dread protected himself just in time, understanding his fate if struck by the frigid, bone-breaking blast. Calling upon the Curse, he formed a shield that covered him from head to foot, the cold fire licking at the edges of the arced barrier.

His success didn't dissuade Eisa, however. She maintained her attack and fired blast after blast of cold fire.

Eisa needed to hold him in place and keep his focus on her. And she was. With great effect. The Dread consumed solely by his defense.

Mikel would have sighed in relief at Eisa's timely appearance if he could have.

But he couldn't.

His body not yet his own.

His nerves still fired involuntarily.

Though the pain that had been surging through him was gone thanks to Eisa's intervention, the Dread having no time for him as he fought to survive the ice dragon's onslaught.

That gave Mikel a chance with the thin sliver of metal only a hair away from sliding into his heart.

The few seconds his friend gifted him was all that he needed. Because without the pain that clouded his clarity, finally he understood.

The power that belonged to him, that was a part of him, that had been hidden from him not long after he was born, was in every cell of his body. Fused to him. He didn't know how. He didn't know why.

Although he did understand that the Light that was so much a part of him was centered in his heart.

That was the catalyst.

That was where his connection to the Light began.

Thus Knute's emphasis.

Steel*heart*.

The Bearer vague as always, though understandable in Mikel's newfound and welcome coherence.

Yet that understanding did not extend to all that he faced in that life-threatening moment.

Knowing how close he was to going to the other side, and having no good idea about what to do, Mikel did as Knute recommended.

Going against his instincts, Mikel let go.

He stopped fighting.

He surrendered to the power within him, joining with the heat that simmered within his heart and flowed out to his core and then to his extremities.

Savoring its touch.

Beginning to comprehend how he and the Light were one. How there could not be one without the other.

The heat of the Light building within him, Mikel closed his eyes.

He listened to his breathing, blocking out everything else around him. Not hearing the angry rush of Eisa's cold fire.

He felt his blood flowing through his veins. His blood boiling. Scalding him. Strengthening him. Calming the pinpricks of pain that sparked all across his body thanks to memories of the Dread's assault.

He focused on the beating of his heart. One beat then two.

Another then a fourth. The pace increasing as the Light flooded into him.

He grew warmer with every breath he took until his chest was white hot.

Then and only then did he set about his task.

He was done a heartbeat later.

The Light residing within him, nourishing him, melted the steel sliver that was so close to piercing his heart.

The most immediate threat eliminated, Mikel focused on what he needed to do next.

More and more of the Light rushed through him until he was close to bursting.

The natural magic radiated out from him, an ethereal glow gaining intensity with every breath that he took.

Until he was almost lost in the glare.

The Blade of Light brighter than the sun.

The steel transformed and replaced by pure energy.

That's when the full and terrifying knowledge of who he was struck him like a body blow. What it truly meant to be the last of his line.

Mikel wasn't just the Steelheart.

He wasn't just the Bearer of the Blade.

He was the physical embodiment of the Light.

Letting out a roar that challenged Eisa's cry and played across the scorched stone of the throne room, Mikel charged the Dread in a hobbling sprint.

Unconcerned by Eisa's stream of cold fire, certain that it couldn't harm him, Mikel swung down.

The blazing Blade of Light slashed through Eisa's fire and shattered the Dread's tainted shield. Continuing on its course, Mikel sliced into the Dread where his neck met his shoulder, cutting through muscle and bone.

Before the Dread shrieked in pain at the terrible wound, a massive blast of energy erupted.

It took Mikel several seconds to see through the glare.

When he did, he stared at where the Blade of Light had come to rest. The blazing steel, dimmer now, left a foot-deep cleft in the tile, a large crack zigzagging out from there to split the chamber in half.

There was no sign of the Dread except for a blackened imprint on the white tile that resembled the shadow of the ancient evil who sought the Blade for his own use.

Eisa hmphed. Gliding up next to Mikel, she looked over his shoulder.

He reached up and hugged the ice dragon's large head to his own, scratching absently along her jaw.

"We did win, Eisa. This time."

Mikel not yet able to pull his eyes from the sketch on the floor, he wasn't certain that he should trust what he was seeing.

The Dread was gone.

Or so he hoped.

Still, the murmuring voices of the former Bearers of the Blade in the back of his head, though impressed by his actions, suggested that the larger war was not yet complete. Only this battle won.

## 26

# A NEW UNDERSTANDING

"You look terrible." Drin's lips curled into a small smile.

Mikel walked slowly out onto the terrace of the apartment Drin had selected for her use while she stayed in the Ring. A pile of papers covered the desk behind her. All related to matters she needed to address now that she had claimed the throne of the Tor. The Splintered Empire no longer splintered after Malor Dragoran had been revealed for who he truly was.

"I feel terrible," Mikel confirmed. He was exhausted. He was still in pain. Although he was grateful that pain only radiated from his damaged knee rather than every nerve in his body.

"You know, you do look like a Broken Bear."

"Thank you?" Mikel wasn't sure if Drin had offered him a compliment.

"And a Broken Bear with quite a roar," Drin mused. "You were louder than Eisa."

Mikel shrugged, slightly embarrassed. "I was in the moment. There was a lot boiling up within me that I needed to let out."

"Clearly," Drin agreed with a raised eyebrow and a knowing smile. "When were you going to tell me that you had a pet dragon?"

Mikel smiled when he reached the railing where Drin stood, both of them looking out upon the nine levels of the Tor toward the northwest and the Barbed Path. "Eisa isn't a pet. She's a friend."

"You'll have to tell me how you became friends with an ice dragon."

"I'll think about it."

"Still trying to keep secrets from me, Mikel?" Drin chided. Teasing him, but only in part. "I thought that we had gotten past that."

"Secrets can be useful, I'll give you that," Mikel said as he leaned against the railing, knowing full well what Drin meant and ignoring her.

Drin waited. Expecting Mikel to say more. Her smile became a frown when he didn't. She looked at him out of the corner of her eye. "You're doing this on purpose. You're trying to irritate me so that I stop pushing on certain matters. I know your games, Mikel. They won't work on me now. As I said, I thought we had gotten past all that."

Mikel chuckled softly. Not missing what she was implying. Still not ready or willing to address it head on. "Sorry, a bad habit. I know."

"A habit that I will make sure you break."

"That would take a good bit of work on your part and us both assuming that we'd be spending more time together despite our many responsibilities. Now that you're Queen of the Crux and the Tor, will you still have time for me?"

"I won't have much choice but to make time," Drin said, giving him a nudge with her shoulder. "It's the only way to ensure you don't cause too much trouble for me. I don't mind dealing with the King of the Underworld so long as I can keep a sharp eye on the King of the Underworld."

Drin's real meaning wasn't lost on Mikel. Still, he didn't take the bait. "Fair enough," Mikel admitted. "Although I think that we would both agree that some of the trouble I've caused has proven useful to you in ways that you had never imagined. Perhaps even fun when looked at with an unbiased eye."

Mikel nudged her back, making Drin smile. "I'll grant you that." Not wanting to pursue the path Mikel had laid before her, at least not yet, she tilted her head toward his. "Where did Eisa go?"

"She prefers the wilder places, but she'll be back soon."

"You're leaving?" Drin's question wasn't really a question, a tinge of disappointment and concern clear in her tone.

"I don't have a choice. There's someplace I need to be, and Eisa is the best and fastest way to get there."

"But there's still more that needs to be done here," Drin protested. That was true in part. She didn't want to admit the real reason she hoped that he would stay. At least not yet. Not until he was honest with her.

"Don't worry. The Battle Lord is on the way with more soldiers. Leonardo's flying ships are proving quite useful in that regard. You'll have ten full companies on the Tor by late afternoon, though I doubt you'll have need of them. Teddy will remain here with you until everything has been settled, and based on what he, Samuel, and the rest of my crews have been digging out, you have little to fear. The Dread is already a welcome memory for those living in Graz, the Tor soldiers less than pleased at being forced to ally with the Ten Thousand. Just to be certain, however, Teddy will do what's required to ensure that any problems that arise don't last long."

"I'm afraid to ask what that means."

Mikel nodded. "That's understandable. Better that you don't."

"Still looking out for me," Drin mused.

"Just trying to offer what assistance I can."

"You don't have to do what you're doing, you know. I can take care of myself."

"You have made that abundantly clear both in word and deed," Mikel confirmed. "Still, it never hurts to have a wildcard to play when the odds are bad."

"One of the several lessons you've taught me," Drin admitted. "You know, I always wondered why you were there to help me in the Frozen Waste."

"You mean rescue you," Mikel clarified.

"Help me," Drin repeated more forcefully, unwilling to acknowledge that without Mikel's timely appearance she would have ended up in a Northern Troll's cookpot.

"Fine, help you," Mikel corrected, not having the energy or the desire to engage in an argument. "And sometimes it's better not to wonder why things happen. Sometimes it's just better to accept what happens."

Drin leaned in closer to him, her shoulder touching his. "You could have stolen my kingdom from me."

"I doubt that."

"I wouldn't have put it past you. The people of the Crux love you."

"That's something I'll need to address," Mikel said in a quiet voice, not sure what to do with Drin's praise. "I've worked hard to develop my image as the King of the Underworld. I'd hate to see all that effort go to waste."

"Maybe it's not a bad thing," Drin suggested. "Maybe it's an opportunity."

"Really?" Mikel wondered. "How so?"

"Perhaps the events that have occurred since you *helped* me in the Frozen Waste and then after that have given you the chance to exercise your power in a more direct way."

"You're suggesting ..." Mikel started, then stopped, not quite believing what he was hearing.

Drin nodded. "I am suggesting. Perhaps it's time for you to acknowledge that you don't need to exercise your power from the shadows. Not all the time. And especially not when you and I are ..." Drin hesitated, choosing her words carefully since Mikel, giving into another of his habits, was making the conversation more arduous than it needed to be, "*working together* so well and so frequently."

"I don't know." Mikel shook his head slowly from side to side. "There's a lot to be gained when exercising power from the shadows."

Drin leaned into Mikel then, her lips just a hair away from his ear. "And there's a lot more to be gained when working with me outside of the shadows."

Mikel's mind drifting in a direction better left unexplored, he realized that for the first time in quite a long time he was tongue-tied. "I will give your suggestion some thought," he murmured quietly.

"Please do," Drin breathed into his ear before finally pulling back. "You can't ignore the change that is occurring, Mikel. The people of the Crux are talking quite a lot about the Broken Bear. And I've already heard whispers on the Tor as well."

"Whispers started by whom?" Mikel asked, his tone a bit harder. He wasn't used to working in the bright light of the day, and he hadn't yet decided what he thought about the experience.

"Who can say?" Drin asked with a shrug. "You know how whispers are."

"That I do," Mikel confirmed. His gaze narrowed as he studied Drin from the side. "More often than not, I've heard that these whispers say that I'm the Queen's Broken Bear. That it's best that she not unleash me, my bite worse than my roar. Did you have something to do with that?"

"You have your way of doing things, I have mine," Drin replied, clearly having little interest in continuing along the current thread of conversation. "Now back to my original question. Why didn't you?"

"Take the Crux? I didn't want to rule the Crux."

"Why not?" Drin asked, really wanting an answer for more reasons than Mikel likely believed.

"Why would I want to be king? It's not worth the hassle. Besides, I think we can both agree that I'm more effective working from behind the scenes." He motioned with his hand. "With this face I'm more likely to scare people without the shadows to hide me."

"I'll grant you that," Drin chuckled, appreciating his self-deprecating humor, "but I think there's more to it than you're letting on."

"What makes you say that?" Mikel wondered. Caught by Drin's eyes, he picked out the specks of green in the back.

"Just a hunch."

"You're not going to stop pushing me, are you?"

"No, I'm not," Drin confirmed.

"You know I had no interest in the throne. You want to know why I helped you at the beginning and why I'm helping you now?"

"I do. I want you to tell me." Drin's smile flashed brightly, eyes sparkling, pleased that they had reached the point in the conversation she had been working toward.

"I've been helping you because I l ..." Mikel smiled, enjoying how Drin was listening with bated breath, "like you."

"You like me?" Drin growled.

"Yes, I like you. It wouldn't be right stealing from a friend."

"A friend?" Drin's tone sharpened, which only widened Mikel's smile.

"Yes, a friend," he repeated, pretending that he hadn't

noticed the spark of fire that was now dancing in the back of Drin's eyes, those flecks of green burning brightly.

"I'm just a friend?" Drin's voice increased in intensity, her displeasure obvious.

"Well, you are a friend." Mikel shrugged then gave her a look that suggested he didn't understand why she was acting as she was.

"You're saying I'm a friend," Drin murmured with a dangerous gleam in her eye, "and we are." She saw it then. In Mikel's eyes. A touch of good humor. But there was more there. A hidden truth revealed and a vulnerability that frightened him. So rather than letting loose with a tirade, she selected a more delicate approach. "However, I thought that because of the connection between us we might be ..." Drin was having a hard time completing her thought. Worried. Wondering if she had misinterpreted what she had just seen and what was happening between her and Mikel.

"More than friends," Mikel finished for her. Done with his fun, deciding that he could never gain what he truly wanted without taking a risk, Mikel reached out and wrapped a large hand around Drin's shoulders, pulling her close.

"Are you always such a pain in the arse?" Drin asked in a husky voice.

"You should know the answer to that by now." Before Drin could offer anything further, Mikel leaned down, his lips just a hair away from hers. He hesitated, believing that he was reading the expression Drin was giving him correctly. Though he was still uncertain.

Drin confirmed it for him just a heartbeat later when she lifted up on the tips of her toes. Her lips meeting his, an electricity surged through them both.

The feeling filled them with a warmth beyond compare.

Not even the Light had this effect upon Mikel.

Yet even as he surrendered to the feeling that consumed

him, relishing the touch of Drin's lips on his own, his world becoming nothing more than the woman who slipped into his arms, he couldn't get past the concerns that were playing through the back of his mind.

Because though the Tor now belonged to Drin and the Dread seemed to no longer be a threat, still a peril remained.

One of his oldest friends needed him.

For the Frozen Waste was at risk.

# BONUS MATERIAL

If you really enjoyed this story, I need you to do me a HUGE favor – please follow me on Amazon and BookBub. And if you have a few minutes, consider writing a review.

Keep reading for the first two chapters from *Rise of the Dragon Lord,* Book 4 in my series *Legend of the Dragon Lord.* Order Book 4 from my author website PeterWachtBooks.com. Also available on Amazon.

# RISE OF THE DRAGON LORD



# PETER WACHT

Rise of the Dragon Lord
By Peter Wacht

Book 4 of Legend of the Dragon Lord

ISBN: 978-1-950236-71-8

eBook ISBN: 978-1-950236-72-5

Library of Congress Control Number:  2025917431

 Formatted with Vellum

# 1. UNEXPECTED VISITOR

"Are you leaving for the Frozen Waste soon?"

"I am." Mikel stood stoically, hands pressed down onto the table. Eyes locked onto a scroll that he had been skimming for the past ten minutes. In his opinion a wasted ten minutes, because he had gleaned little of immediate use from the archaic writing. "I just need to complete a little business first."

"Such as what you're doing now?" asked the ghostly apparition that towered over Mikel.

"This is probably the most important business I have right now," Mikel countered. "What I learn, if anything, could be the difference in the Rime. Assuming, of course, that the concerns are legitimate."

"They're legitimate."

"I know," Mikel sighed. "I trust Cadmus. He's not wrong. That's why I'm reviewing all this."

"Have you found what you were looking for?" Knute Frost Lord asked, the spirit flickering and fading before snapping back into shape with greater clarity.

"Unfortunately not," Mikel muttered, shaking his head in frustration as he rolled up the scroll and placed it on the pile of tomes, books, and texts that had yielded nothing of value during his long search. That pile a great deal larger than the one with the handful of resources that had offered the tiniest bits of information that might prove useful when Mikel traveled over the Dragon's Tail Mountains to the west. "Do you believe that the Dread is destroyed? That I sent him to the other side?"

The spirit shrugged. "I can't say one way or the other," Knute stated, his deep voice a mix of sadness and disappointment. "I'm sorry."

"You saw what happened?"

"I did. As did all the former Bearers. We see what you see, Steelheart. Always."

"That's ominous," Mikel grumbled.

"Have no fear. We would never invade your privacy."

"Of course not." Mikel's agreement was half-hearted at best, not sure if he believed the spirit.

"Unless we have to," Knute admitted as if it was no more than a little thing.

"You're not making me feel better," Mikel warned, his suspicion confirmed.

"Let me speak more clearly," Knute requested.

"That would be helpful." Mikel valued Knute's knowledge and aid, but the former King of the Giants of the Rime rarely got directly to the point.

"You have the ability to block us out. What I should have said is that we see what you see when you allow us to see it."

"And based on what you've seen, you can't tell me yea or nay?"

"What I believe doesn't matter. What the other Bearers believe doesn't matter. We see what you see. That doesn't give us any insight different from yours. What matters is what you believe." The shimmering figure leaned down toward Mikel, then asked in a voice close to a whisper that still sounded like a rumble in the small shop, "What do you believe, Steelheart? What you believe will determine your actions. It has always been so. It always will be."

Mikel didn't reply for quite some time as he considered Knute's question. The scene in the Tor throne room played through his mind once more just as it had been whenever he closed his eyes for any length of time.

He wanted to believe that the Dread was gone. That he had destroyed the ancient evil with the Blade of Light.

But did he believe that just because he wanted to believe it?

From what he remembered of the combat, by all rights he shouldn't be concerned. He should be able to state with absolute confidence that the Dread had passed to the other side. That he had dispatched the evil that had played the role of Malor Dragoran and overlord of the Tor for so many centuries. The threat to the Frozen Waste and the adjoining Realms eliminated.

But Mikel listened to more than logic. He listened to his instincts. To his gut. And his gut was telling him that though he might have won that battle, the larger war had only just begun.

"I believe that with all the rumblings in the Frozen Waste, it is best to assume the worst, which is why I've spent the last few days here." Mikel shrugged, bowing down to the inevitable. "And if I'm wrong, then all the better. As Kaduna liked to say, best to prepare for the worst. Always. Because when it really matters, you rarely get more than one chance."

"Very wise," Knute agreed.

"I always thought so. Is the Blade of Light connected to the Dread?" Mikel asked, shifting the topic to a different line of inquiry that had been nagging at him ever since his combat in the Tor throne room.

"No, not to the Dread specifically," Knute answered. Next to the hazy image of the long dead Giant of the Rime who stood across the table from Mikel were the flickering figures of two other former Bearers of the Blade.

"What can you tell me *specifically*, Knute?" Mikel asked, stressing Knute's hedge and trying to keep from his voice the frustration building within him. A difficult task he would be the first to admit. Particularly since Knute seldom got to the heart of the matter with any alacrity.

"Specifically? I'm telling you ..."

"Very little," Jesai Katori interrupted, "which is a habit of yours."

"What are you talking about?" demanded Knute, turning toward the spirit on his left. The Frost Lord had spent centuries linked to the Blade of Light, his consciousness bound to the artifact and the essences of the previous eleven other Bearers. A unique way to strengthen the magic of the ancient weapon through the passing millennia. Even so, that familiarity tended to fray on occasion among the dozen strong-willed and strong-minded warriors who once wielded the Blade of Light just as Mikel did now.

"You rarely give a full answer," Maria Roucheau explained in support of Jesai. The Master Swordswoman and acknowledged savior of the Bloody Steppe shook her head more in frustration than humor. "That is why Mikel asked the question, Knute. You're qualifying your response."

"I always give the answer I mean to give," Knute stated in a clipped tone, his temper rising.

"Now you're deflecting," Jesai charged, "just as you usually do."

"Why don't you just reveal all that you know?" Maria suggested with an exasperated smile. "That would make this conversation easier for all of us. It would go a good bit faster as well. Mikel needs to make for the Frozen Waste. Soon. Because I believe he's right to be concerned. Cadmus requires his assistance."

All of the former Bearers of the Blade were Giants, either of the Rime or the Deep. And all wanted to protect the Frozen Waste from any threat, whether from without or within. The Steelheart the best means for doing that now.

"If I revealed all that I know, then how is the Steelheart supposed to learn for himself?"

Mikel snorted, unable to help himself. "You're just like the Frost Lord."

"What are you talking about?"

"It's not an insult, just an observation," Mikel explained as he sifted through the few remaining books and scrolls scattered across the large wooden table that he had not yet examined. Few of the resources he had found on the Crux were of use. Of those handful that might be, they offered little more than insinuations and possibilities with few actual details. Guesses. Myths. Whether fabrications or facts he couldn't say.

Thus, Mikel's decision to speak with the Bearers, hoping that their experiences and knowledge would provide a fuller picture of the Dread from which he could determine an accurate answer to the questions that had been plaguing him ever since his fateful clash on the Tor.

The most prominent?

What could he learn that would give him a better chance of surviving his next confrontation with that ancient evil? Because he was certain that confrontation was coming.

A confrontation that he believed that he couldn't avoid even if he wanted to.

Though in truth he didn't want to avoid it. He wanted to win it, his own survival less of a concern.

Too much was at stake. And Mikel's sense of accountability was too strong to shirk what he perceived as his responsibility.

"Explain," Knute ordered. The former Frost Lord's grim countenance confirmed that he was less than pleased at being taken to task.

"Your approach is similar to that of Cadmus," Mikel replied, referencing the current King of the Giants of the Rime and one of Knute's descendants. "He prefers to guide rather than teach."

"A time-honored approach," Knute stated solemnly. "Effective as well."

"And now a time-wasting approach," Maria countered with her usual tartness. She enjoyed breaking free from the Blade in this way and interacting with the latest Bearer called to serve. The fact that Mikel was not a Giant meant nothing to her. All that mattered was that he do what was demanded of him as a Bearer of the Blade, that he uphold their honors and traditions, and so far he had done just that. The Steelheart demonstrated a deft touch with the Light and strength of will that had served him well since he took up the Blade, and she had no doubt that he would continue to do so in the future. If, of course, Knute got to the point sometime during the current century. "Define *specifically* so we can move on."

Knute sighed heavily. Irritated. Still, he did as Maria requested. The Master Swordswoman was not someone to challenge unless there was good cause. He had learned that the hard way. "As I said, the reemergence of the Blade of Light is most likely linked directly to the Dread ... but it's not."

"Frost Lord ..." Maria warned, her voice tightening.

Knute held up his hands, asking for her patience. "It's confusing, I know. But you must understand that the Blade of Light was crafted for a specific purpose initially. To challenge an evil the likes of which the Natural World has not seen in millennia and hopefully never will again. An evil that threatened to unravel the separation between the Spirit World and the Natural World."

"The Ancient One you mean?"

"Sadly, no," Knute replied. "The Ancient One is nothing compared to the evil of which I speak. No more than the latest iteration, of which there have been several. The Ancient One is terrible in his own right, but he is no more than one image of a greater threat."

"You mean ..." Jesai began.

"Don't say it," Maria warned.

"Why not?" Mikel asked.

"It is said that speaking the name will give life and power to the evil Knute references. It will serve as a thread that the evil can follow back from where it has been banished. An evil against which we have little to defend ourselves except for the Blade of Light, and that more hope than reality."

"Are you being serious? You're not just playing with me?" Mikel asked, not quite sure what to believe. A dozen more questions popped into his mind. He held off, however, because of the deep concern visible in Knute's grave expression.

"Deadly serious," Maria explained.

"I didn't know the Giants of the Rime were so superstitious."

"Not superstitious," Jesai countered. "Cautious." He offered a deep bow. "My apologies for almost making such a terrible error."

Knute nodded, accepting his comrade's regret, before he intoned, "The dead are dead, but their sacrifice is not forgotten."

"The dead are dead, but their sacrifice is not forgotten," Jesai and Maria both repeated, bowing their heads for several seconds as they remembered those who came before them.

For a moment, Mikel didn't know whether he should ask about the significance of what had just happened. He decided against it, fearing that he would only lose more time. And, right now, time was his most precious commodity. "Getting back to the reason we're here, you think I was called to wield the Blade because of the threat presented by the Dread?"

"It makes the most sense," Knute said, Jesai and Maria nodding their agreement.

"But ..." Mikel prodded, sensing the Frost Lord's desire to equivocate.

Knute shrugged. "It could be the Dread and likely is. Or it could be something worse that is or is not associated with him."

"That's not very helpful." Mikel felt like he was back where he started when he began this conversation.

"I'm not trying to be helpful," Knute explained. "I'm trying to be honest."

It was Mikel's turn to sigh. He was afraid to ask his next question but realized that he needed to take the risk. "What could be worse?"

"Not worse necessarily," Maria said. "It just presents more of a challenge."

"Tilts the balance farther toward the darkness," Jesai added.

"So it could be the Dread or this evil that you don't even want to name or it could be something else entirely," Mikel stated, his agitation increasing. He felt like he was stuck in quicksand, head just above the surface, and no one was offering to help pull him out.

"Exactly," Knute confirmed, clapping his hands in pleasure. "In truth, however, I believe that it is the Dread and likely also what the Dread might bring back into the Natural World. Again, it makes sense. The Dread has been on the Tor for centuries. Hiding. Preparing. And now the threat he presents is greater than what was before, so the Blade has responded accordingly."

"How can you be so certain?"

"I can't, but I believe that we would have seen signs if our greater fear was justified." Knute locked eyes with the former Bearers standing with him, and they both nodded in agreement. "For now forget this greater evil that we choose not to name. Forget the Ancient One."

"Then couldn't you have just said all that when we began

this discussion?" Mikel tried to keep a serious expression on his face, but he couldn't. His crooked grin broke through.

"Must you always be so exhausting?" Knute demanded even as Jesai and Maria smiled.

"It's innate. You know how it is."

"I don't doubt it," Knute growled. "The simple truth is that the Blade of Light was first crafted in partnership between the Giants of the Rime and the Order of the Magii to deal with this evil we choose not to speak of. Since then, over the centuries, the Blade has called other Bearers, each of us charged with addressing a different threat. Thus, my response. I believe that the Dread is the reason that you, Steelheart, have been selected by the Blade. The Blade recognizes within you the qualities necessary to address this growing peril. But the Blade is not directly linked to the Dread as you ..."

"Thank you, Frost Lord, I understand now." Mikel laced a great deal of respect into his voice even as he cut off the former King of the Rime. He didn't want to get pulled down any more rabbit holes. "There is a link to the Dread but there is little that you can tell me other than the fact that the Blade of Light chose me because of the threat presented by the Dread."

"Precisely right."

"And there is no guarantee that I can defeat the Dread even with the Blade of Light." Mikel believed that he had learned that much digging through the books and tomes available to him. The history of the select company he had joined confirmed that hard truth. Several of the previous Bearers of the Blade had fought valiantly to defeat the threat they had been called to stand against though to no avail in the end.

That didn't surprise Mikel. That was the way of the world.

There was no guarantee of success.

There was no guarantee that the bards would craft and sing a tale of your victory.

There was only a guarantee that the bards would sing a tale

whether you lived or died seeking to achieve your objective. The former a triumph and perhaps even a nice surprise, the latter a tragedy.

"There is no guarantee," Jesai stated quietly, "though we the former Bearers offer all that we can to give you the best chance of success."

"Thank you for that," Mikel murmured. "And what of the Lost Carcer?"

"What of it?" Knute asked. "It was a construction of Karolingan Frost Lord in conjunction with the Magii. Cadmus was there. He is best placed to speak on that."

Mikel nodded, expecting just such a response.

"Why?" Knute asked. He recognized the glint in the back of Mikel's dark eyes. A glint that was both worrying and intriguing.

"You are thinking of what to do in case what you believe is true," Jesai said, nodding in appreciation.

"Correct."

"You fear that ..."

Mikel interrupted Knute before the Frost Lord could build up momentum again. "I simply want to understand what options are available to me. Just in case. And I want to know because that information could prove critical when I join Cadmus in the Frozen Waste. If what I believe is real, then there is little room for error."

Knute nodded, appreciating the rigor of Mikel's thinking, but before he could offer his agreement regarding Mikel's supposition Maria cut in. Her doing so earned a scowl from the Frost Lord that had no effect upon her whatsoever.

"I believe I understand why you are asking. You seek to know how the Lost Carcer functions."

"I am," Mikel stated with a hopeful smile.

"Clever, Steelheart. Clever indeed."

"Why clever?" Knute demanded, his aggravation rising. He

sensed that he had lost control over the conversation. Worse, that he was missing a key point.

Maria ignored Knute. "As the Frost Lord explained, the Lost Carcer was built jointly by the Giants of the Rime and the Order of the Magii for the sole purpose of imprisoning the rebels who failed to overthrow Karolingan. Cadmus can provide useful details that we cannot. But I believe there is one detail, the most important detail, that we can offer you."

"The Light?" Mikel asked.

Maria nodded, a smile cracking her usually grim visage. "The Light. Not the Talent. Not the Curse. Only the Light. Only you."

"So if worse comes to worst ..." Mikel prompted, several strategies already swirling through his mind.

"You have an option," Maria confirmed. "It makes sense, doesn't it?"

"It does," Mikel agreed, his thoughts traveling down several paths that led to even more possibilities. Which one to take? That might not be decided until he was in the moment. Still, better to be prepared than not. How fast he made his decision could be crucial.

"I didn't think that I would find you here."

Mikel turned toward the voice that sent a welcome burst of warmth into his chest. "Why were you looking for me?"

Celindria Dengannon strode through the doorway that led to the front of his bookshop, not stopping until she sat down on the table. One leg crossed over the other. Close enough to reach out with a finger and run it lightly over his calloused hand.

The warmth surging through him burned hotter at her touch. He glanced away from her, briefly, concerned at first that his guests were observing their interaction, then surprised that Knute, Maria, and Jesai had faded away.

Apparently Knute had spoken the truth regarding Mikel's privacy.

Mikel's focus was drawn back toward Drin's beautiful face when she reached up and cupped his chin, pulling his eyes back to hers. "You need ask?"

Mikel shrugged. The shiver running through him intensified as Drin's free hand drifted to his thigh, settling there before rubbing softly. "Just curious. Usually you don't come this way. I usually go to you so that it's not too ... obvious."

"I didn't want to wait."

"There's something you need?" Mikel asked. Usually Mikel visited Drin in the Citadel. It was safer for her to be there. And he had no trouble reaching her chambers with no one the wiser, having knowledge of all the secret tunnels leading into and out of the Crux's fortress that towered over the city of Innsbruck.

"Nothing pressing. I just wanted to see you." Drin leaned in closer, her lips close to his ear. "I was thinking about when we were last together."

A flush of heat colored Mikel's face as he grinned. He probably looked the fool, though he couldn't tell because he didn't have a mirror handy, and he really didn't care. "I've been thinking about that as well," he admitted.

"And you didn't come to see me?" Drin purred. "Such self-control." She nipped at his ear with her teeth. "You decided to make me wait? Are you teasing me, Mikel? I haven't decided if I like to be teased in this way."

Mikel snorted softly, his discomfort growing. "I've got some business that I need to deal with. You know how it is."

"You always have business," Drin pouted. Leaning back, lips pressed together tightly, she gripped his forearm then squeezed. Her other hand remained on his thigh, now rubbing higher up his leg.

Mikel didn't reply right away, frowning as a hint of warning in the back of his brain clanged loudly. This wasn't typical behavior for the Queen of the Crux.

True, she was different when they were alone, shedding her regalness, at least as much as she could. But her taking issue with his needing to deal with matters that were also important to her?

That was a first and distinctly out of character.

"It was what we discussed the other night. You said that it was essential, so I'm doing as I said I would."

"Of course you are," Drin replied with a deep and warm laugh. The hand on Mikel's forearm tightened, as did the one on his thigh. "It's just that after spending so much time with you I can't help but want to spend more."

"And me you," Mikel replied even as he tried to pull back from Drin.

He couldn't, however. Not without making a real effort and potentially embarrassing her. And he didn't want to do that despite the fact that her grip on his arm and leg was beginning to hurt, her nails pressing into his skin.

"That's all you have to say?" Drin growled seductively. "After all that we've been through, after becoming so close to one another, that's all you'll tell me?"

"I don't know what you want me to tell you." Mikel tried one more time to pull away from Drin. Carefully. Still not wanting to insult her. Still no success. Her grip was too strong. In fact, it was tightening even more. Hurting even more. "I'm not sure why ..."

"*Beware, Steelheart,*" Knute said in his deep voice, speaking to him in his mind thanks to their connection through the Blade of Light. "*All is not as it seems.*"

"Ahh," Mikel groaned softly as Drin's fingernails pierced his flesh. He looked down, Knute's warning breaking the spell Drin had been weaving over him along with blood trickling down his arm and leg.

He looked up quickly in fear, all the while knowing exactly what he was going to see.

Pitch-black eyes.

Not Drin's mesmerizing blue color that so entranced him.

"I will have you, my Broken Bear. Forever. For good."

Mikel's eyes widened as Drin's hands shifted before his eyes. Fingernails becoming razor sharp. Fingers elongating into claws.

The magical assassin born in the darker places of the world had the ability to assume the form of anyone it desired. Often the only giveaway as to its true self the pitch black of its eyes.

He wasn't speaking with Drin.

He was confronting a Nachahmen, and he couldn't free himself from the monster's hooked grip.

Mikel shuddered. He was still looking at Drin, but his mind was struggling to make sense of the disconnection between what he was seeing and what he was experiencing.

"Such an easy kill," the monster hissed.

"Not as easy as you think," Mikel growled.

"It's too late." The Nachahmen leaned in closer. "I have you. And no one will know what happened to you. Not even your pretty little Queen."

Mikel didn't try to reach for his scimitar. It was too far away, resting on the other side of the table. Nor was the mace scabbarded on his back an option. He'd never grasp it in time.

The claws, digging deeper into his arm and thigh, soon would be ripped free and punched into his gut.

Having few options, he reached out and grasped the claw that was digging into the flesh of his thigh. Gripping tightly, he refused to let go.

Mikel had learned a great many things since accepting the responsibility of serving as a Bearer of the Blade.

One of the most important?

He didn't need the Blade of Light to exercise the magic within him that the scimitar had unlocked.

As soon as his fingers touched the Nachahmen's hand, he reached for the Light.

The natural magic raced through him, heating his blood, heating his entire body.

Mikel directed that heat into the Nachahmen.

He saved himself with scarcely a thought.

The Nachahmen's face transformed into a rictus of pain, the Light burning through the monster that was made just as much of spirit as substance. The potent natural magic too much for the Nachahmen, its essence flaked away like burnt crisps of paper that curled into ash and disappeared before they hit the floor. In just a few heartbeats, nothing was left of the assassin except for the wounds on Mikel's arm and leg, and those healed seconds later when he directed the Light toward his injuries.

"Fool me once," Mikel murmured, "shame on you. Fool me twice, shame on me."

He had faced a Nachahmen once before and seen through the deception just as he had done this time. Though that previous encounter had been easier, because the assassin hadn't been impersonating Drin.

"You're angry. I understand." Knute appeared again, his form shimmering as he towered over Mikel. Jesai and Maria were with the Frost Lord once again.

"Why did you leave it for so long?"

"You know why," Maria answered.

"A lesson," Mikel sighed. He should be angry with the former Bearers of the Blade. But he couldn't be. He knew why they allowed the scene to play out. And though he didn't like it, they were right. He needed to be more wary, even around the people he believed that he could trust.

"A hard lesson," Jesai said. "Nevertheless, one that must be learned."

"I'm still not happy with you." Mikel pushed himself off the table.

"Better you angry with us than you dead," Knute stated in a casual tone, demonstrating not an ounce of regret for failing to intervene sooner.

"Now who's being exhausting," Mikel demanded, though he said it with the trace of a smile.

"I guess you're rubbing off on me," Knute replied, now smiling as well.

"And that is not a good thing," Maria grumbled. "It makes him more aggravating than he already is."

"The Savior of the Bloody Steppes speaks the truth," Jesai agreed.

Mikel allowed the three spirits to continue bickering as his mind drifted to more important matters.

A Nachahmen.

An assassin.

Deadlier than a Seeker.

And with strong ties to the Spirit World.

That required someone not only skilled in the Curse but also powerful. It was the only way to summon a Nachahmen from their home world.

So who had the skill and the power to free a Nachahmen from the Master of Spirits and set the creature to a task such as this?

Two names immediately came to mind.

One he was certain was still alive.

The other?

Mikel realized that he was asking the wrong questions.

Knute had warned him to remain wary.

Mikel needed to assume that the other name, the more powerful of the two, was still alive. Just as he feared.

And if that was the case, only two questions were worth asking.

Where was he?

And what could Mikel do to destroy him once and for all?

# 2. BAD NEWS

"How long have you been waiting?" Finn asked. Stepping out onto the terrace atop the abandoned warehouse he owned, the Magus sat down next to Mikel in the chairs placed close to the railing.

"Not long."

Finn's eyes tightened as he studied his friend. Mikel was tired. That much was clear. And not just physically. "You got past all my defenses and I wasn't even aware."

Mikel shrugged. "You know how it is."

"I do," Finn confirmed. "The Caledonii who is not a Caledonii, and because of that a Caledonii with an even greater gift than that of his kin. A gift that no one can quite understand. Untouchable by either the Curse or the Talent. My traps and tricks are useless against you."

"Not entirely useless," Mikel said with a crooked grin. "The illusion of the three spirits gripping knives and rushing toward me when I opened the door to your residence was quite entertaining."

"Glad I could offer you some amusement," Finn grunted sourly.

He shifted his focus away from Mikel. Looking out over the Churn, the Magus realized that it was the time of year when the four rivers that met at the Crux were higher, which meant more of a strain on the breakwater as the seething waves crashed over the stone with greater frequency. He'd hate to think what would happen during the floods soon to come if not for Mikel's work to ensure those living on the lower Rings were protected.

"Thank you."

"For what?" Finn demanded. He was still irritated that Mikel had slipped by his defenses so easily even though he understood that there was nothing he could do to stop him. Not with magical means at least.

"Nat is demonstrating a great deal more control with the Talent. She's not as dangerous as she was before you began to work with her."

Finn smiled, his irritation trickling away. "She's one of my best pupils. Perhaps the best if she stays on the path I've set for her."

"You think she will?" Mikel wondered. His concern was almost palpable.

"She will," Finn confirmed with a sharp nod. He understood Mikel's worry. "Of that I'm certain. She understands the lines that can't be crossed. She'll heed them."

"She knows?"

Finn nodded again, this time more in regret. "She's too sharp for me to keep something like that from her for long."

"That she is."

"We've spoken about it. She understands."

"Good. I don't want her getting herself into trouble." Mikel had taken in Nat when a deal had gone bad. She had grown on him. He had never really had a family since Kaduna died. Not until Nat had come to live with him.

"She'll get herself into trouble," Finn chuckled. His soft laugh became more of a wheeze when a brief burst of pain shot through him. He would need to rest. Soon. "You can be sure of that. But not the trouble you're worried about."

Mikel thought about that, satisfied, then looked away from Finn and stared at the boil and froth of the Churn. Hoping for a few quiet minutes and realizing that wasn't going to be possible. The Magus was staring at him. "What's on your mind, Finn?"

"You do a lot for other people, Mikel," Finn said softly. He was tired. Nat had pushed him during their training session that morning. And when he was like this it was harder for him to control the corruption that was never far from racing through his body if he let go of his self-control even if only for a second.

"What's your point, Finn?"

"I'm just saying. For Nat. For so many others here on the Crux. For me."

"Out with it, Finn." Mikel already had a sense of where the Magus was going. They had traveled down this road before. "There's no point in dancing around it."

"You can be so much more than a thief, lad," Finn sighed then grimaced, another bolt of pain shooting down his spine and into his extremities. "I see it in you. It's there if you want to let it out."

"What if I like just being a thief?"

"You weren't made to be just a thief. You know that better than anyone."

"You're sure of that?" Mikel challenged.

"Quite sure. Your actions speak for you. They say who you are."

"You're pushing me on this again?"

"If I don't, who will?"

"Cadmus for one. He's just as bad if not worse than you."

"Maybe you should listen to him."

"If I listen to him, I'll likely end up dead. Or worse."

"We all die, lad," Finn growled in his scratchy voice. "It's just a matter of choosing how that happens."

Mikel's voice had become more strident as he engaged with the Magus. He toned it down quickly. "A bad day?"

"It will be soon."

"Anything I can do for you?"

"Listen to what I have to say."

Mikel frowned. Pursing his lips, he nodded. "Tell me."

"You know that you're more than a thief even though you do everything you can to make people believe there's very little there except for the obvious." Finn reached out, grasping Mikel's forearm. His grip wasn't as strong as it once was. A fact not lost on Mikel. "You can't run from who you are. Even more, you can't run from who you are meant to be."

"What if I don't want to be who I'm supposed to be?"

"What you want doesn't necessarily matter. Not when so many people have chosen to place their faith in you. Whether you like it or not, you have responsibilities to meet. And it's not in you to ignore those responsibilities."

Not responding right away, Mikel finally exhaled heavily. He had come to see Finn for several reasons. And he realized then that this was one of them.

He was tired of taking on more. Of being asked to do more. But better that than not being asked to do anything at all. Better if he could have a say in what was to come. A reminder that only Finn could give him. "You're asking quite a lot."

"No more than you would normally ask of yourself."

"I don't know how to take that," Mikel grumbled.

"Take it as a compliment, lad. We need you. We need what only you can do. That can't be denied."

"Thanks for making me feel better about myself," Mikel stated, sarcasm dripping from his words. "As if I didn't have enough to worry about already."

Finn laughed softly. "Just telling you the truth lad."

"I'm not the hero type, Finn. You should know that by now."

"So you say and so you've said." Finn shrugged. "That doesn't mean I believe you."

"Heroes usually die when the story ends, Finn. That's why they end up heroes."

"In many of the stories, yes, they do. But not always. And you're not being asked to be a hero. I'm asking you to be who you are. Who you were meant to be. You've certainly proven more than competent when it's mattered. That's all you need to keep doing despite the additional burdens being placed upon you."

"What if I don't agree to do all that's required of me?"

"Then you know what will happen," Finn stated in a soft, sad voice. He didn't feel the need to say anything more.

Because Mikel did know what would happen. He didn't want to think about that very real possibility.

Finn leaned in close to Mikel, pulling his eyes. "I enjoy our conversations. You know that. But we've been dancing for a while and it's time to pick a partner. Why did you really want to speak with me? We've had this dialogue before, and no matter how much you fight it, in the end you'll do what you need to do. That's who you are. No matter how much you might not like it, you'll do what you need to do. So why are you really here? What can I do for you?"

"I don't believe the Dread is dead and gone. In fact, I'm fairly certain that he isn't."

"That's why you're here?" Finn asked.

"One of the reasons at least. I have little information to go on, and Cadmus could offer only so much. So I came to you hoping for more certainty before I take the next step. I need to know if my concerns are justified."

"You're worried?"

"Wouldn't you be?"

"I would be," Finn confirmed, leaning back into his chair. "Why do you think the Dread survived?"

"I just do," Mikel said. "A feeling."

"A feeling," Finn repeated, raising his hands before Mikel could protest. "I'm not taking issue with you. I know just how good your instincts are. Still, that's not much to go on. You told me what happened. I don't know how even the Dread could have kept himself from the other side."

"That's not a real answer, Finn. What do you think? Really."

"Me?" Finn asked, hesitating. He wasn't afraid to offer his opinion. Still, he wasn't sure that he wanted to. Because if he did his own fears would gain substance.

"Yes, what do you think?"

"About the Dread?"

"Yes about the Dread," Mikel growled. "Now you're being as difficult as I usually am." Mikel sighed in frustration, catching the glint in the Magus' eye before falling back into his chair. Finn was baiting him.

"Not very enjoyable when the roles are reversed, now is it?" Finn asked in a tone that suggested that he was quite pleased with himself.

"You've had your fun, Finn. Answer the question. Please."

"Do I believe the Dread is dead?"

"Yes, that's the question," Mikel confirmed through gritted teeth.

Finn sighed then shook his head as he repositioned himself in his chair, crossing his legs, the pain tolerable for the moment. No longer able to dodge the truth that had been staring him in the face. "No, I don't think he is."

"Was that so difficult?"

"Exceedingly so," Finn confirmed with the hint of a smile.

Mikel couldn't help but smile himself. With all that the Magus was dealing with, he understood that a little levity, or in this case being a pain in the ass, could go a long way. "Tell me why you believe that."

"You first."

"You really are being a pain in my ..."

"I'm not trying to be." Finn raised his hands once more to cut off Mikel's anger. "I'm in the same boat as you. Nevertheless, tell me why you believe the Dread is still with us. I need more than just a feeling or your instincts. This is too important not to get right."

"The Blade of Light."

Finn nodded toward the hilt of the scimitar currently scabbarded and set against the leg of Mikel's chair. "Why? What does the weapon have to do with your belief?"

"Just a feeling," Mikel shrugged with an innocent expression. He didn't smile even when Finn glared at him.

"Now who's being difficult?"

"It's not intentional," Mikel replied. "I just get the sense that if I had killed the Dread, I would know in my heart that the evil bastard was gone for good. And I base that on something you said."

"That I said?" Finn asked, his confusion plain.

"Yes, you had mentioned that the touch of the Blade pulled on the power of the individual."

"It drains them. Yes. You didn't feel ..." Finn didn't say anything more, tired of using the word *feel*. He wanted a more tangible word. A word with meat on it.

Mikel shook his head no. "I struck the Dread. Or at least it seemed like I did. I see it every time I close my eyes. And every time I do, I'm more and more certain that he escaped before I got past his defenses. I was a hair away from biting into him. But a hair doesn't do the deed."

Finn didn't say anything for quite some time. Lost in thought. "You would know if you succeeded, Mikel. You would know, so your doubt is enough. The Blade of Light is linked to you now. Essentially it's a part of you just as you are a part of it. If you know what you're doing, you can bleed those touched by the Curse of their ability. Because that's what the scimitar does. The Blade of Light takes the power offered to it and then uses that power against the one the power was taken from. A two-edged sword in a very literal way."

"So a good strike," Mikel murmured. "Just not good enough."

That conclusion sent Mikel's thoughts down several paths. He had been so focused on destroying the Dread that he had not considered that destroying the Dread might not be possible. That the Dark Magus who had become so much more was too powerful. Too clever. Too experienced.

Yet did that mean Mikel didn't have any options for challenging the Dread without ensuring his own death?

Or did he need to work a little harder for some solution?

"It seems so," Finn confirmed.

"Not what I wanted to hear," Mikel murmured. "Still, I needed to hear it."

"You control an immense amount of power with the Blade of Light. You control an even more immense amount of power because you are a conduit for the Light. But that does not make you all powerful. That's a key point that you need to remember."

"You have nothing to worry about in that regard. I'm just as humble now as I was before the Blade picked me."

"Of course you are." A hint of disbelief radiated from Finn's voice. "Ask it. I know you want to."

Despite the unease he felt, Mikel grinned. He always enjoyed the give and take with Finn even while he was battling the stress that was pressing down upon him. "Can I kill the Dread with the Blade of Light?"

How the Magus answered would determine the path that Mikel would need to take. The path that Mikel already had assumed he would need to take. Nonetheless, he wanted confirmation.

"Do you want the tempered response that makes you feel good or the hard truth?"

"You even need to ask?" Mikel challenged.

Finn leaned in. "No, you can't kill the Dread. But he can kill you."

End of the Bonus Material.

To keep reading *Rise of the Dragon Lord,* visit my author website at PeterWachtBooks.com or visit Amazon.

# WHAT TO READ NEXT

## THE REALMS OF THE TALENT AND THE CURSE

### LEGEND OF THE DRAGON LORD

*A Painful Truth* (short story)*

*Stealing the Light*

*Sacrificing the Queen*

*Roar of the Broken Bear*

*Rise of the Dragon Lord* (Forthcoming 2026)

### THE TALES OF CALEDONIA

(Complete 7-Book Series)

*Blood on the White Sand* (short story)*

*The Diamond Thief* (short story)*

*The Protector*

*The Protector's Quest*

*The Protector's Vengeance*

*The Protector's Sacrifice*

*The Protector's Reckoning*

*The Protector's Resolve*

*The Protector's Victory*

### THE TALES OF THE TERRITORIES

(Complete 8-Book Series)

*Stalking the Blood Ruby* (short story)*

*A Fate Worse Than Death* (short story)*

*Death on the Burnt Ocean*

*Monsters in the Mist*

*The Dance of the Daggers*

*Bloody Hunt for Freedom*

*A Spark of Rebellion*

*Shadows Made Real*

*Shadow's Reach*

*Storm in the Darkness*

THE SYLVAN CHRONICLES

(Complete 9-Book Series)

*The Legend of the Kestrel*

*The Call of the Sylvana*

*The Raptor of the Highlands*

*The Makings of a Warrior*

*The Lord of the Highlands*

*The Lost Kestrel Found*

*The Claiming of the Highlands*

*The Fight Against the Dark*

*The Defender of the Light*

THE RISE OF THE SYLVAN WARRIORS

*Through the Knife's Edge (short story)**

THE FALLEN KNIGHT SERIES

*The Death of the Dragon (short story)**

*The Dragon Awakens*

*Duel With a Dragon*

*Beware the Dragon*

*The Dragon Returns*


* Free stories can be downloaded from my author website at PeterWachtBooks.com. My books are also available on Amazon and other online retailers.

# JOIN PETER'S NEWSLETTER

This eBook is a prelude to the events in my epic fantasy series *The Tales of Caledonia* and is free to readers who receive my newsletter.

Join Peter's newsletter and get your FREE eBook.
PeterWachtBooks.com

www.ingramcontent.com/pod-product-compliance
Lightning Source LLC
Chambersburg PA
CBHW070230200726
48293CB00005B/1559